Two swings and the g
spurting from his shoul
creature fell to his knee
no support from the others, who remained at attention as
they watched the scene in horror.

"Vary your sword thrusts as I have done. Keep your opponent guessing. Keep your eyes locked onto his, and
show no mercy," Asp instructed coldly. "Above all, show
no mercy!" With that, the naga placed both hands on the
hilt of her sword and brought the weapon down with all her
strength, cleaving the gnoll's head in two. He crumpled,
and she presented the bloodied sword to the soldier from
whom she had borrowed it.

"I hope this demonstration has been of some help," Asp
stated emotionlessly.

ⓒ ⓒ ⓒ ⓒ ⓒ

THE HARPERS

A semi-secret organization for Good, the Harpers fight for
freedom and justice in a world populated by tyrants, evil
mages, and dread creatures beyond imagination.

Each novel in the Harpers Series is a complete story in
itself, detailing some of the most unusual and compelling
tales in the magical world known as the Forgotten Realms.

■ THE HARPERS ■

THE PARCHED SEA
Troy Denning

ELFSHADOW
Elaine Cunningham

FANTASY ADVENTURE

RED MAGIC

Jean Rabe

RED MAGIC

First printing: December, 1991
Printed in the United States of America.
Library of Congress Catalog Card Number: 90-71502

9 8 7 6 5 4 3 2 1

ISBN: 1-56076-118-0

TSR, Inc.
P.O. Box 756
Lake Geneva,
WI 53147 U.S.A.

TSR Ltd.
120 Church End, Cherry Hinton
Cambridge CB1 3LB
United Kingdom

To Bruce,
for his patience and encouragement.

And to the RPGA™ Network,
an organization not unlike the Harpers.

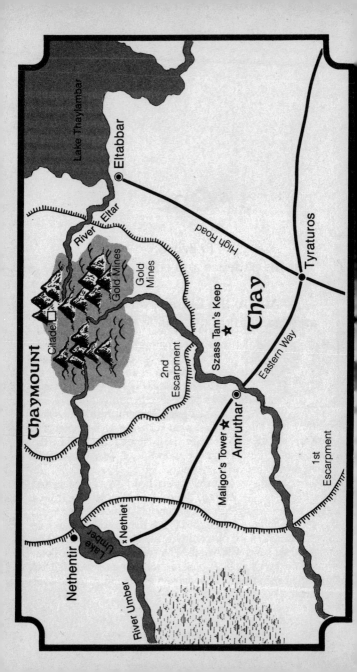

One

The crimson-draped figure paced in the damp, circular chamber, his well-rehearsed path carrying him through the darkness shrouding the smooth stone wall and to an ancient bronze incense burner. He bent over the antique from Moonshae to permit the acrid vapors to spiral upward from the basin's scented coals into the shadowed recesses of his hood. He drew the smoky gray tendrils deep into his lungs while the haze from the burner and the room's lone, fat-soaked torch danced around his flowing robes.

Maligor's garb was similar to that worn by all of the Red Wizards of Thay—dark red, the color of blood oozing from a deep, fresh wound. The robe's many folds concealed his form; the sleeves hung several inches below the tips of his thin, pale fingers, and the hood obscured his gaunt, wrinkled face. The embroidered hem, which draped on the polished mosaic floor, swirled wildly about his slippered feet as he concluded his meditation and strode to the narrow window to gaze out over Amruthar.

The dying rays of the sun stained the city's cobblestone streets a glowing vermilion. Maligor's impressive tower rose just beyond the western edge of Amruthar, its shadow pointing like a lance to the closing gate. The location offered the Red Wizard a superior view of the major business district and the two-story inn where most of his informants operated.

Amruthar conferred an impression of quiet this early evening; only a few citizens roamed the streets in the section visible to Maligor. However, appearances in Thay, he knew, were nearly always deceptive. The alleys and shadowed walkways were alive with cutpurses and burglars just starting their evil agendas. Schemers bloomed and profited when the sky grew dark, and peddlers who proffered commodities too illicit to pass off during the day even in Faerun's most wicked country.

Most of the commonfolk were huddled inside their homes, protecting their mundane existences from the city's deviate nature. Maligor could smell the coal smoke rising sluggishly from the stone chimneys as they prepared their meager dinners. For a moment, the Red Wizard wondered what lavish feast his slaves would be baking for him—a fast that would have to be discarded, as he was too busy this evening for pleasantries.

Maligor glanced past the spacious open-air market. The crude wooden stalls were being ritualistically boarded up for the evening to prevent vagrants from sleeping inside, the unsold goods packed onto wagons to be trekked home because the merchants feared to leave them here, wisely trusting no one. The morning would bring a different view, a vibrant, welcoming, bustling scene to delight the senses. The market would be crowded with retailers hawking all manner of exotic fruits, fresh vegetables, homespun and imported cloth, and shiny trinkets to catch the eyes of women with gold jingling in their bulging purses.

Likely there would be a slave dealer or two, despite the merchant guild's mandate that slaves must be sold in the stockyards so that the sellers would have to pay taxes on their illicit goods. Some of the best deals could be made purchasing flesh in the open-air market, though, because the sellers needed to move the stock quickly before the guild tried to close them down and claim its due. Maligor made a mental note to send one of his buyers there tomorrow. A Red Wizard's prestige was often measured by the size of his slave stable. And in this country, where two-thirds of the population were slaves, Maligor always strove to maintain far more than his share.

Just beyond the emptying stalls sat the fashionable alcazar of a young Red Wizard, a man who flagrantly displayed his wealth, which he had incomparably more of than common sense or magical might. The opulent abode appeared out of place in the old section of the Free City of Amruthar. Maligor smiled. Neighboring countries claimed this was the only independent city in Thay. However, Maligor and the other Red Wizards—in fact all those who lived in Thay—knew better. While the city fell under no one Red Wizard's jurisdiction and claimed decades ago to have seceded from Thay, many of the most powerful Red Wizards lived nearby and secretly directed the government by manipulating the strings of the puppet rulers. Some wizards, Maligor among them, were more obvious in their control, openly bribing and magically charming people in key positions and making Amruthar more closely influenced by the Red Wizards than perhaps any other city in Thay.

Maligor mused that the young Red Wizard ensconced in his perfect home never could be a power in the city. The newcomer likely lived here because of the closeness of the great teachers of the arcane, such as Maligor. But the young man would never climb above the rank of a simple fledgling. Maligor would see to that.

Maligor, on the other hand, had great bureaucratic and supernatural strength. He was a zulkir, the Zulkir of Alteration, one of a handful of Red Wizards who guided Thay's destiny through an all-powerful political council that directed the rulers of each city, created laws, both useful and obscure; detailed their enforcement; and described in massive volumes the punishments for lawbreakers. The zulkirs, however, only called upon Thay's courts to discipline people when it was convenient, and in fact often ordered those in their employ to commit every illegality that could be conceived. The zulkirs, who did not trust each other and did not cooperate beyond the council, could engage in whatever nefarious and heinous acts they desired. They were above the law. The council also dictated Thay's foreign policy, which at this point consisted of keeping every neighboring country unnerved and guessing.

Each zulkir personally controlled a magical discipline and oversaw all those who studied it. Maligor's specialty was transmuting objects, living and otherwise. If his current plan proved successful, he would control much more than that.

Maligor resumed watching the young sorcerer's mansion, curious about the young wizard. He closed his eyes and concentrated, visualizing in his mind being inside the elegant building, peering through the windows, glancing down corridors, searching. In a hazy vision, he witnessed servants bearing the young man steaming platters of rare delicacies. Splendid, Maligor thought. The fool will be too full and lazy to pay me any heed this evening, and he is too weak to put up the proper wards to keep prying eyes away from his home.

It was the nature of Red Wizards to second-guess their peers and ceaselessly protect their backs. The wizards frequently plotted against each other for pleasure, for personal gain, for retribution, or simply to hone their skills. This puerile behavior prevented most wizards from gaining sufficient power to rise above their brethren, and it also forestalled them from working together to expand Thay's boundaries.

Despite the magical inactivity at the young wizard's alcazar, Maligor realized that other Red Wizards in the city would be busy this night, no doubt brewing their own wicked plans to inflict pain and suffering on others for their own financial or personal reward. He fancied that none of their plots would be as devious or promising as his present scheme, for he held little respect for his colleagues. A smile gently tugged at the corner of Maligor's pale, cracked lips. None in Amruthar, none in Thay—indeed even no one else in his own tower—knew what he was up to.

He retreated from the window to the incense burner's bitter embrace. The smoke caressed his face and made his throat feel dry and his mouth taste sour. Still, Maligor enjoyed the druglike sensation, savoring it for long moments while his eyes watered from the thick vapors. Then abruptly he stiffened, detecting another familiar scent, one less pleasing—one that smelled like rotting flesh.

Stepping away from the burner, the wizard's gray, rheumy eyes peered into the shadows, probing intently until he discovered the source of the stench, then narrowing to thin slits to evidence his displeasure.

"What do you want, Asp?" Maligor's voice had a noticeable edge to it. "What catastrophe is unfolding? Surely something has gone amiss. Otherwise, you would not dare interrupt my meditation."

The wizard's tones were soft and raspy, though not by choice. Appearing elderly by human standards, perhaps sixty or seventy, Maligor was in fact more than two hundred years old. The viscous magical elixirs he concocted in his secret chambers in this tower and in his other numerous residences throughout Thay helped his frail form to stave off many of the effects of age. His voice, however, hadn't held up as well against the passage of time.

"My Lord Maligor, I'm sorry to intrude, but this truly is important." The feminine voice was sultry, caressing the stale air in the chamber like a summer breeze.

"Yes?" Maligor entreated, still peering into the darkness.

Asp's unblemished face rimmed with close-clipped sable hair edged out from the shadows. Her startling blue eyes, high cheekbones, and dainty lips the shade of ripe red yarberries, a poisonous fruit that grew abundantly in Thay, contrasted with the room's dismal atmosphere. Her long, slender neck, decorated with a delicate strand of black pearls, and her bare, white shoulders emerged from the inky blackness near the wall, but she came no closer.

"There is a spy in our midst," she whispered, studying Maligor's face for a reaction. "He's a slow-witted creature, but he could cause problems."

Maligor moved toward the woman, regarding her critically. "Go on," he rasped.

"He's a gnoll, one of the guards," she continued, her voice rising slightly in volume. "He hasn't been seen for several days now. He was sometimes stationed outside this very room. That means he could have heard us plotting, my lord. He could have knowledge of our schemes. He could be selling the information to another Red Wizard." She ran her finely manicured fingers through her short hair, pausing to compose herself before continuing.

"Perhaps he didn't think he'd be missed, Maligor. After all, you've been enlisting more and more gnolls into your service. Perhaps he doesn't really know much, but then again, maybe he does. We have to be sure. We have to do something. Our plans may not remain secret much longer if his tongue is wagging."

Maligor scowled, disheartened that Asp would bother him with such a trivial matter. He didn't care what a mere gnoll might reveal. What the venerable Red Wizard discussed with Asp, the schemes she feared could be unraveling, were only a mask for his overall goal. Still, he found solace in the fact that Asp apparently remained oblivious to his true plan.

"I have no fear of a missing gnoll," Maligor answered after what seemed an interminable pause. "But to please you, beautiful Asp, I will find him and deal with him. I will even let you help. Find something of his and bring it to me. I'll wait for you outside the tower. Quickly now."

"Yes, your omnipotence." Asp snatched her head back into the shadows and soundlessly retreated.

Maligor sniffed the air to make certain she was gone,

then vacated the chamber and ascended an iron spiral staircase that took him two levels higher, nearly to the top of the ancient tower. Muffled cries and whimpers filtered out from behind a massive pine door near the top of the stairs. The Red Wizard waved his arm, and the door slowly unlocked itself and opened to reveal a room blanketed in darkness. Maligor padded forward, unmindful of the gloom. He frequented this room so often he knew all its features by memory. Strolling toward a corner where spiderwebs were as thick as curtains, he chanted a dozen words. Suddenly flame sprang to life in a crystal oil lamp that hung from the ceiling. Smoke rose from the bowl and singed the nearest webs to illuminate the surface of a large, low table that was nearly as old as the wizard.

The worn top was covered with racks of vials filled with foul mixtures, a half-dozen ragged leather gloves, and several cages. The largest cage was brimming with rabbits of various sizes, colors, and breeds. Two had no fur. The pathetic, hairless pair stared at Maligor through frightened eyes. The Red Wizard had used them a few days ago to test a potion intended to remove wrinkles; it had proved a mild success. While the wrinkles vanished from the rabbits' skin, the concoction also caused them to lose their fur. He smiled evilly at them, deciding to try further experiments on the two later.

Another cage was crammed with squirrels and rats that cowered beyond their dead brethren, hoping to escape the wizard's notice. A third held moles and hedgehogs, most of these freshly caught by Maligor's gnoll trappers. The other cages were smaller and were filled with snakes, lizards, and other reptiles the wizard could not name. A crate under the table contained live chickens and ducklings purchased at Amruthar's open-air market.

Nearly a third of the mistreated animals were dead, and most of the others were dying, either from lack of food or from being force-fed the wizard's putrid mixtures. Maligor favored using animals for his bizarre research; they weren't as costly as humans, and their yowls and whimpers were easier on his ears than the screams of his slaves. Furthermore, he had learned years ago that animals took up less space in a laboratory and weren't expensive to feed, especially since he neglected to feed them regularly.

Maligor savored the animals' terror for long moments before pulling a scarred leather glove over his bony right hand. Opening a cage and thrusting his hand inside, he retrieved a startled hedgehog.

The wizard ignored the panicked clawing and biting of the squat creature and tightly squeezed it until he heard it squeal. Convinced it was lively enough, he carried it down the tower's staircase to the ground floor, passing bowing slaves, straight-backed guards, and magical barriers that kept intruders from disturbing his treasured privacy. Maligor gestured at the massive iron-reinforced door that served as the main entrance to his tower, and it obediently swung open on well-oiled hinges. He squeezed the hedgehog again for good measure then stepped outside into the warm night air.

Overhead, the stars shone brightly in a clear night sky. Maligor knew there would be a myriad of clouds by dawn, as many of the Red Wizards were skilled with weather control magic, and the dry ground presented a tempting challenge.

Someone would make it rain soon.

Maligor chose not to concern himself with such meaningless things, choosing instead to spend his time on spells that would improve his personal position rather than increase the yield of the crops. Dropping the trembling hedgehog on the ground, he roughly pinned it beneath his foot. The starlight, coupled with the glow spilling out from the tower windows, provided just enough light to work under and set the tone for the wizard's hellish project.

The door opened and closed behind Maligor. Turning and glaring into the darkness next to the tower's stone wall, he saw Asp. Her offensive odor was vastly diminished in the outdoors.

She grinned slyly at the wizard. "This spell is my favorite," she uttered thickly, staring hungrily at the trapped animal. "Perhaps one day you will teach it to me."

"Perhaps," he replied, turning his attention back to the hedgehog. The creature's eyes were wide with horror, a fact that pleased the wizard.

"Did you find something belonging to the gnoll?" It was more a demand than a question and sent Asp rustling through a large sack at her side. Maligor wanted to get the spell over with quickly, since he had planned to devote the evening to putting the final touches on his latest scheme.

"Yes," she answered dutifully. "Will this do?" Asp's slender, hairless arm emerged from the darkness, holding out a tattered cloak she had retrieved from the missing gnoll's barracks.

Maligor scowled at her, and she snatched the garment back into the shadows, where she savagely ripped it. A moment later, her soft hand passed the wizard a long, thin strip of dirty cloth. It fluttered in the breeze, flapping against the Red Wizard's robes.

Maligor swiftly grabbed the cloth, making certain the expensive fabric of his robe wasn't soiled by it. Satisfied, he drew the red hood back from his face so he could work more easily.

Like the majority of Red Wizards and the bulk of Thay's residents, Maligor's head was completely bald and adorned with tattoos. Wizards and wealthy, important Thayvians—and those who pretended they were—decorated their pates with elaborate designs. Only slaves had long hair. Maligor's tattoos included a bright red flame lapping on a purple field, a common symbol of the Red Wizards, and a flawless snow-white skull on an ebony triangle, a symbol of Myrkul, the god of death, decay, and corruption. Many in the civilized centers of Faerun considered Myrkul himself dead, slain in the godswar that had ripped across the world years ago. However, the Red Wizard and other loyal followers believed the dark god still lived. While Maligor cared little about deities, he supported what Myrkul stood for and believed he honored the god through various acts involving death and corruption, such as the magic he was about to cast.

The wizard tied the stained strip of cloth about the hedgehog's thick neck and began the incantation. He muttered in a monotone in an ancient, arcane language. Maligor knew that throughout the city other Red Wizards were casting spells, too. Thay reeked of magic. Spells kept troublesome slaves loyal, treasures protected, homes guarded, and enemies at bay. And among a multitude of other things, they allowed wizards to peer through walls, around corners, across the city or even farther—sometimes into the depths of a man's soul. In between phrases of his spell, Maligor wondered if other wizards were using magic to watch him.

It didn't matter, he finally decided. He kept the hand gestures required for this rite obscured; those who didn't know this particular spell weren't likely to learn it by viewing him. He knelt shakily on the rough ground. Reaching inside the deep pockets of his robe, he withdrew a crystal vial filled with a red powder so dark it seemed black. He continued the chant while measuring out a minute amount of the horrid-smelling dried wyvern's blood into his palm. Then the Red Wizard drew a circle in the powder with a jagged fingernail, and before the breeze could disturb the components, his voice rose and quickened, and he blew the dried blood into the hedgehog's face.

Maligor stood quickly and backed away, never taking his eyes from the animal as it convulsed with pain and gasped for breath. Its bristling spines moved like grass in the wind, and its eyes glazed over, changing from black to a glowing scarlet that nearly matched the color of Maligor's robes.

Asp poked her head from the shadows to get a better look, and her eyes widened in response to the macabre scene. A sly grin played across her face as she slowly ran her thin tongue over her bottom lip. The animal twitched and shuddered erratically, then began a grotesque transformation.

The hedgehog's sides heaved, billowing outward like a

puffer fish as the creature doubled its size, then doubled again. Its spines fused into its rapidly stretching skin, which flowed over its enlarging form and transformed into a mud-brown, leathery hide. Its short legs, scrambling in a vain attempt to gain purchase on the ground, elongated and spread away from its torso. At the same time, a thin membrane of flesh formed, attaching itself to the legs on each side of the shrieking beast's body and becoming webbed wings that flapped uncontrollably against the earth. The bones in the creature's head cracked and popped as they lengthened; the jaw became birdlike and filled with twin rows of sharp, jagged teeth. At the opposite end, a prehensile barbed tail sprouted and quivered.

No semblance of the hedgehog remained; there was only the darkenbeast, a sorcerous nightmare, a hideous cross between an eagle and a prehistoric lizard.

Maligor intended to create several score of these creatures to add to his monstrous army. The darkenbeasts, which could be made from most animals, even those the size of field mice, were fearsome creatures that obeyed his telepathic commands. However, they were not indestructible; they reverted to their true forms in daylight—or upon their death.

The darkenbeast wailed, and Maligor glanced at Asp. He whispered a dozen more arcane syllables, magically tugging the image of the missing gnoll from the woman's mind and transferring the picture to his transformed creature.

"Kill the spy," the wizard whispered to the darkenbeast. "Then bring me his traitorous body."

The malign beast cried out again, a horrible, mournful shriek that pierced the night sky. Then it spread its wings and gracefully lifted from the ground. The creature glided over the earth, gaining height as it distanced itself from the tower and Amruthar. Its wings beat faster and lifted it higher still.

Maligor saw his creation head west before it melted into the black sky. As the Red Wizard turned to enter his tower, he paused, gazing through the shadows at Asp. His expression softened.

"The evening has just begun," he said, deciding to postpone his schemes for a few hours.

She nodded and quietly drew him into the darkness.

*   *   *   *   *

The hawk scanned the ground, slowly circling a grove of tall trees west of the cliffs called the First Escarpment. The sheer, imposing cliffs marked Thay's main border and served as the edge of the plateau of the Priador, a large expanse of relatively flat land on which most of Thay rested.

For the past several days, the hawk had been unsuccessfully searching this territory, south of the crystal waters of Lake Umber. It would spend one more day here before giving up and returning home.

With the coming of evening the hawk selected a large oak tree, damaged by lightning, and glided toward a high, gnarled limb. The perch gave the hawk an excellent view of the waxing moon, which had just begun its journey across the surface of the pond below.

The hawk was not native to the lands around Thay. Its back was blue-gray, its belly ivory streaked with dark gray, black, and pale orange, and it had a long, square-tipped tail that was characteristic of a species normally found in Amn. Just below its throat was an unusual marking, a patch of glistening, silvery feathers in the shape of a crescent moon.

The moon had worked its way to the middle of the pond before the hawk noticed an erratic rustling in the brush. The source of the noise clumsily burst into the clearing, panting and furiously pulling burrs and leaves from its fur with big, pawlike hands. The creature was large, standing nearly eight feet tall on muscular legs and possessing a barrel chest and a form that seemed a cross between canine and man. Its dun-colored skin was covered with tufts of coarse, red-tinged gray hair. The muzzle of its hyena-shaped head was blanketed with a darker fur that matched the spine ruff that ran from the bridge of its nose, over the top of its head, and down the back of its bull-like neck.

The creature was a gnoll, attired in crude leather armor studded with bits of metal. The leather, which was too large at the shoulders and too tight around the hips, would have made the ensemble seem comical were it not for the red flame on a purple field emblazoned on the front of the hardened breastplate. The gnoll carried a circular wooden shield bearing a similar symbol that had been defaced during battle. In his left hand, he toted a spear, which was festooned with a dirty red ribbon that fluttered in the breeze.

The gnoll lumbered to the edge of the pond, where the mud oozed about his sandaled feet. He squinted with glossy black eyes to take in the surroundings and wrinkled the end of his snout, sniffing the air. Convinced he was alone, the gnoll awkwardly tossed his shield and spear to the ground and dropped to all fours to dip his muzzle for a drink. He made vulgar lapping sounds that continued for several minutes.

His thirst sated at last, the gnoll stood, brushed the mud from his hairy knees, and retrieved his spear. He glanced around the clearing again and spotted the lightning-damaged tree. His shaggy brow furrowed and he delved into a pouch at his side. The gnoll withdrew a crude, curled map and held it so the moonlight illuminated the ink markings. The tree and the pond were indicated by rough, hurried sketches.

"Right place," he stated, seeming to struggle with the human speech. He rolled the map, replaced it in the pouch, and stamped his foot impatiently. "Mudwort late, but Mudwort here." He waited a moment more, as if expecting an answer, then made a circuit of the clearing.

"Harper!" the gnoll barked anxiously. "Harper show up. Harper, not much time I be here. Mudwort be long, Mudwort be missed, Mudwort be killed. Harper? Harper!"

Unnoticed, the hawk gracefully spread its wings and

glided from the branch behind the gnoll. Its form meta-
morphosized as it descended, its talons curling, then flexing, becoming longer and growing together to form human
feet covered with soft leather boots. The beak receded,
dissolving into a smooth, male face with striking features—
high cheekbones, a strong chin, and an even, tanned complexion. The proud crest of blue-gray feathers lengthened,
fluttered in the breeze, and transformed into long blond
hair. The rest of the hawk's feathers recast themselves into clothes, the wings into a cloak that flapped gently in the
slight wind.

The man landed, and Mudwort whirled, finally catching
the scent. The gnoll stared at the man and creased his
shaggy brow, furious at himself for not noticing the human's approach.

The man stood nearly six feet tall and was thin but muscular. He was dressed in greens of various shades—
leggings, tunic, and a rich-looking, thigh-length cloak
decorated at the edges with embroidered feathers. Even
the man's eyes were green, the color of ferns after a soft,
steady rain. His wheat-colored hair hung loose below his
shoulders.

Mudwort noted that the man was barely armed; he wore
only a scimitar at his side and had no armor. The gnoll had
heard little about Harpers, but based on his limited knowledge, he assumed they were impressive and battle-
hardened. This human seemed to be neither, although he
was obviously fit.

"Harper?" the gnoll growled.

"I am a Harper," the man replied. "The one you seek."

"Harper alone?" the gnoll spat. "Harper have gold?
Harper important? Harper have friends near?" He waved
his spear for emphasis.

"I'm alone, as agreed. I'm called Galvin. You don't need
to know anything else about me."

Galvin pulled the collar of his tunic down to let Mudwort
see the silver neck chain from which dangled a miniature
crescent moon affixed to a silver harp. The charm flashed

in the moonlight and made the gnoll wonder how much it was worth.

"Harper symbol," Mudwort verified.

Galvin covered the neck chain and tossed the gnoll a black velvet bag. Mudwort's thick, hairy fingers grabbed for it but missed, and it dropped to the ground with a soft thud. Mudwort fell to examine the contents like a wolf devouring a fresh kill. Running his fingers over each gold coin he pulled from the bag, he attempted to count it. The gnoll enjoyed spying; he collected regular pay from Maligor and from other Red Wizards who paid for information about his master. This was the first time he had spied for someone other than a wizard—and had gone beyond Thay's boundaries to do so.

Giving up on getting an exact tally of the coins, the gnoll scooped the gold back into the bag and cradled it in his hand, trying to weigh it to gauge its value. After a moment, Mudwort rose, brusquely wiped a long strand of saliva away from his jaws, and growled at the Harper.

"Not enough. My talk costs more, Gal-vin!"

"That's just to get your tongue moving," the Harper answered. "There'll be more if your 'talk' is useful." The gold belonged to the Aglarond council, which had asked Galvin to contact the spy. There were rumors of Thayvian forces growing, and the council wondered if Aglarond, Thay's neighbor to the west, could be a target. The council members needed to know if they should prepare for war.

The Harper disliked wars. No matter who won, they caused a senseless loss of life. And the land, which would be soaked with blood by the end of the battle, was usually the greatest casualty.

The gnoll interrupted the Harper's thoughts. "Mudwort knows valuable things. Mudwort knows that Red Wizard Maligor wants land. Maligor is greedy and thinks he needs more land than other wizards have."

The gnoll pawed at a small cloud of gnats forming around his face. He glowered at Galvin and plopped down on a log, easing the burden from his callused feet. Balancing the spear across his lap for security, he pushed Galvin's money pouch into the dirty canvas sack that hung from his side.

"More gold now," Mudwort demanded.

"You'll have to do better than that," the Harper said evenly, planting himself in front of the gnoll and fixing his eyes on Mudwort's. "Who is Maligor?"

"A Red Wizard. I told you."

"Beyond that," the Harper persisted.

"Important," Mudwort spat. "Powerful. Maligor rich, too."

The druid sighed, quickly growing frustrated. "What does he look like?"

"Like other wizards. Maligor bald. Maligor old, wrinkled. Maligor wear red."

"Where is Maligor?" The druid moved closer.

"In Thay."

"I know that," Galvin spat. "Where in Thay?"

"In Am-roo-thar," Mudwort replied. "Am-roo-thar is a city in Thay."

Galvin began pacing in front of Mudwort, angry that the answers had to be pulled from the gnoll's feeble brain.

"What land does Maligor want?"

The gnoll pawed again at the growing cloud of gnats attracted by his saliva. "Don't know. Didn't ask."

"How is he going to get the land?"

Mudwort brightened and thumped his breast with his left fist. His smile revealed a row of yellowed, pointed teeth. "Gnolls get it for him," he answered proudly. "Maligor has many, many gnolls. Gnolls fierce warriors."

The gnoll eyed the Harper, trying to gauge the wealth the human carried while waiting for the next question. But the Harper remained quiet, rubbing his hairless chin in thought. The silence bothered the gnoll.

"Done now?" Mudwort's impatience surfaced. "Mudwort get more gold and Mudwort leave." The gnoll was worried; he had been away from Maligor's keep for several days and didn't want the wizard to discover him missing.

"No, you're not done." Galvin had a considerable amount of patience, but Mudwort was wearing it thin. Something was indeed up in Thay, at least with a particular wizard, the Harper decided. Perhaps the Aglarond council had reason to worry. He hoped there was enough gold in his belt pouch to satisfy the gnoll spy. Drawing out a large handful of coins, the Harper held them just beyond Mudwort's reach.

"Why does Maligor want more land?" The Harper's voice was even and commanding.

"Not sure," Mudwort retorted, staring at the mound of coins. "Maybe wizard needs more land for the gnolls. Many, many gnolls work for wizard. Barracks crowded." The gnoll spoke slowly, pausing between his words, trying to decide what to do about the Harper. "Maybe Maligor wants this land," he added, "This good land. Mudwort could like staying here.

"Maybe wizard Maligor need different land, tired of old land. Maybe he just wants to make Thay bigger." Mudwort growled for emphasis and swallowed a gob of spittle that had been trying to escape his mouth. "Give Mudwort more gold. Mudwort talk enough."

Frowning, Galvin brought his face mere inches from the gnoll's, ignoring its rancid breath. The Harper believed he was close to gaining some vital information.

"You want more gold?" the Harper began. "Then tell me where in Amruthar I can find Maligor."

The gnoll snorted. The information he had been passing on to the Harper was common knowledge in Amruthar. Still, it was another matter to reveal the Red Wizard's present location to an outsider. Perhaps it was a test, Mudwort considered. Maybe the Harper was Maligor's puppet, and the Red Wizard was testing the gnoll's loyalty.

"Mudwort done," the gnoll announced, deciding it was past time to return to the safety of his brother gnolls' company. "Mudwort leaving. Mudwort been gone too long anyway." He clumsily rose from the log, using the spear for support. Glancing toward the pond, he spotted his shield lying at its edge and started for it.

"No!" Galvin bellowed, his patience unraveled. "We are not done. You have a lot more information floating around inside your flea-sized brain." The Harper's arm shot out to grab the gnoll by the shoulder. His intention was to spin Mudwort around, but the gnoll was too massive, and too late the Harper realized his abrupt action might be read as an attack.

The gnoll furiously whirled, his left claw striking out at Galvin's stomach, ripping the olive-green tunic and knocking the human down. Mudwort quickly pressed his attack, making a short thrust at Galvin's chest with the spear.

Cursing himself for being careless with the slow-witted, evil creature, the Harper rolled to the side, attempting to avoid the weapon, but the shaft sank deep into his left shoulder, pinning him to the damp ground. Blood spurted from the wound and onto the grass, making the gnoll's eyes widen in morbid anticipation. Mudwort forced his advantage, threatening with his sharp claws.

Galvin cast his right arm across his chest and tried to pull the spear free, but the weapon held him painfully fast. He kicked at the gnoll to slow the creature's deadly advance, buying the Harper a few precious seconds.

In that time, Galvin's eyes sparkled in the moonlight, and his smooth, exposed skin began to sprout thick, black fur. The hair quickly raced across his prone body to obscure his clothes, while at the same time, the Harper's form expanded, becoming wider, more muscular. The tanned skin on Galvin's face also covered itself with fur, and his mouth pushed upward into a muzzle more massive than the gnoll's and filled with larger, sharper, considerably whiter teeth.

The Harper's transformation continued, his hands becoming wide, thick paws and his fingers long claws made for rending. Galvin's chest swelled as his ribs expanded outward, and his lungs voiced a deep, angry growl that reverberated throughout the clearing.

Mudwort stood transfixed as a silvery white patch of hair in the shape of a crescent moon appeared on the cave bear's throat.

"Red Wizard tricks!" the gnoll screamed as he backed away, uncertain of what to do. "Leave Mudwort be!"

Galvin's new form was stronger, although blinded by pain. This time when his right paw moved to bat at the spear, the wood splintered easily, freeing him. Blood still poured from the wound, matting the black fur and making it glisten, but the bear disregarded the injury and the part of the spear that still remained in its shoulder. It focused on the gnoll, the source of its pain, and lumbered forward.

Mudwort screamed again and ran blindly from the clearing. The gnoll's legs pounded over the earth frantically as he brushed past branches and leaped over rocks and logs in his terror-filled flight.

The cave bear pursued, effortlessly catching up to its quarry, which stank strongly of fear. Rising on its great hind legs, the bear towered above the fleeing gnoll. Slashing with its claws, it raked Mudwort's back, cutting through the leather armor and drawing blood. The gnoll shrieked in surprise and agony and swiveled to face his attacker, futilely throwing his shaggy arms across his face to fend off another blow. The bear struck again, this time shredding the front of the gnoll's uniform.

Mudwort's cries were cut off in a gurgling spasm as a third swipe bludgeoned him to the ground. Blood oozed from the gnoll's gaping mouth. The bear nudged the dying body, sniffed it, then padded to the pond's edge and sat back on its haunches to lick its left shoulder. Gradually the bear's fur vanished, and Galvin, bathed in sweat and covered with both the gnoll's blood and his own, became human again.

The Harper heard the gnoll gasp, and he rushed to the creature's side, unmindful of his own pain.

"Harper wizard," the gnoll whispered as his eyes locked onto Galvin's. Mudwort shuddered once, then died.

"I'm no wizard. I'm a druid. And I'm very sorry." Galvin stared at the dead gnoll for several long minutes. The creature's death could have been avoided, the Harper knew.

He was disgusted with himself for losing control when he transformed into the cave bear. Although his druidic skills allowed him to take the shape of various creatures while retaining his human intelligence, the pain in his shoulder had made it too difficult for him to concentrate. Galvin's animal instincts had taken over. The druid gritted his teeth and pushed the broken spear shaft through his shoulder, forcing himself not to scream. Then he ripped the hem of his cloak to make a bandage for his shoulder. The wound demanded more attention, but he wanted to put some distance between himself and this area before he stopped to tend to it.

The Harper worked hurriedly to bury Mudwort's body, spear, and shield. He didn't want to take any chances that the gnoll might be found and suspicions aroused. Galvin knew it was essential that the Red Wizards remain oblivious to a Harper presence so close to Thay.

Finished with the grim task, Galvin turned west and sprinted from the clearing; he had someone else to meet before the night ended and before the pain in his shoulder overtook him. His hair streamed behind him as he passed through the brambles and vines. The Harper threw his head back to let the breeze wash over his face and cool him. Overhead, the sky was filled with a multitude of stars and one winged creature that looked gray in the light of the moon.

* * * * *

The darkenbeast flew over the escarpment, and like a knife, it cut through the sky and sped over the trees that dotted the land beyond Thay. Its keen, unnatural eyes pierced the darkness, spying sources of heat, small animals that skittered about the ground—and something more.

The darkenbeast located Mudwort moments after the cave bear had delivered its final blow. The arcane creature circled, watching the bear transform into a human who proceeded to bury the darkenbeast's target. When the human ran from the pond's edge, the darkenbeast paused, worrying. It feared retribution for returning to Maligor without having killed the gnoll.

It must bring the Red Wizard something, the darkenbeast decided.

The beast circled the clearing again and formulated a plan; perhaps if it killed the human and brought that body to the Red Wizard, it would be rewarded rather than punished. The darkenbeast set off after its new quarry, straining its small eyes to find evidence of the human's passage through the brush.

Two

Galvin drove himself onward, trotting at an uneven pace for nearly an hour before the pain in his shoulder overwhelmed him, forcing him to pause beneath an ancient cedar. The druid intended to rest for only a few moments to inspect his bandage, but when he leaned back against the massive trunk, his knees buckled and he awkwardly slid down, snagging his cloak and catching his hair on the coarse bark before landing hard on his rump. He closed his eyes for a moment, trying to blot out the ache and straighten himself up; he was successful only on the latter account, managing to brace himself against the damp, moss-covered ground with his right hand. He felt his left shoulder and upper arm growing numb from the loss of blood.

Galvin reached for the makeshift bandage. It was too dark to see clearly, but the druid could tell the cloth was warm and wet, blood-soaked and useless. He gritted his teeth and gently tugged it loose, working to replace it by tearing off another strip from his now-ruined cloak. Propping his head against the trunk, Galvin listened to the night sounds as he tied the new dressing tight and gathered his strength. He sniffed the air, straining to catch the scent of water but finding no trace. He was thirsty and wanted to clean his wound, but he knew he couldn't afford to spend time searching for water. Already he was finding it difficult to keep his eyes open and concentrate. If he fell asleep now, he would not wake up in this world.

Pain wasn't a new experience for the Harper. Galvin had been injured several times along the path to becoming a druid, particularly when he had tried to familiarize himself with the woods and their denizens. More than one wolf had misinterpreted the immature druid's attempts at making friends, leaving Galvin with numerous scars and bruises. Eventually, however, Galvin had learned the language and mannerisms of most of the forest creatures and had been accepted by them. By studying druidic arts for nearly two decades, he had learned how to assume the animals' forms. Galvin now believed himself to be about thirty summers old, though he hadn't bothered to keep count. The animals never did, and the druid usually considered himself more animal than human. With few exceptions, he preferred the company of animals to that of people.

The druid closed his eyes again. Just for a moment, he told himself, just until some of the pain goes away. He might not be in this predicament now, he mused in his agony-tinged delirium, if his childhood had been different. He might be in a warm, soft bed somewhere, resting comfortably, oblivious to Thay and gnolls.

Galvin had been born to a pair of thieves who were members of a guild in Skuld, The City of Shadows, in Mulhorand. The druid could see his parents clearly, more distinctly now than the trees a few feet away. They had lived comfortably, providing him with toys, clothes, and nearly anything else he desired. Their illicit livelihood had been quite successful until they had robbed an ambassador in the city. Then their lives had ended at the end of a rope, and Galvin, a frightened and confused child of seven, had fled into the woods to avoid the same fate.

Surviving had been difficult; he had nearly died of starvation before he learned to watch the animals and eat the same berries, roots, and nuts they consumed. He had studied the bears hunting in the stream, and he had learned to catch fish with his hands. Occasionally he would sneak into a village to steal warm bread and pastries off window ledges and clothes that were hanging out to dry. But the more he had learned about the wilderness, the fewer trips he had made into towns. Now he avoided them altogether.

The druid struggled to open his eyes, realizing he would be joining his parents in some netherworld if he didn't get moving. He bit hard on his lower lip, drawing blood and focusing his mind on the new pain to help him stay awake. Gazing at the moon overhead, which he could barely see through the leaf-heavy branches, Galvin realized it was well past midnight.

He pushed with his legs against the trunk, trying to rise, but the pain in his shoulder kept him rooted. Despite the throbbing, which had begun to pulse down his arm, the druid knew the wound dealt by the gnoll could have been worse, perhaps resulting in his immediate death if he hadn't assumed the form of a bear. Something happened to the druid in the transition from human to animal and back again; his fatigue lessened, and minor injuries healed. This wound, however, was too deep to be erased by the transformation. This injury also was his own fault, he reasoned, as he was certain that had he handled the situation differently, the gnoll would be alive and he wouldn't be in such a sorry state.

Galvin tried to rise again, this time stretching up with his right arm to grab a low-hanging branch and arduously pulling himself to his feet.

The branches and ferns waved like wheat before him, and the ground seemed to shift. Galvin knew it was his mind that was moving, and he flung his arms backward to grab the trunk, fighting the dizziness that threatened to pull him off his feet. Drawing in a few deep breaths of the cooling night air, he held on to the cedar until his surroundings stopped swaying. Then he resumed his course through the woods, stumbling from tree to tree.

The druid moved through the foliage, bending leaves and branches, something he could have avoided were he in better condition. The forest he had grown up in was much like this, he recalled, attempting to keep his mind occupied with all manner of things to remain conscious and improve his chances of making it through the woods. His home was a temperate timberland filled with a multitude of conifers and deciduous trees. These woods were older, however, a climax forest that had two canopies, the highest being the tops of trees more than a hundred years old, while the second consisted of smaller trees and large bushes that could thrive in the diffused light. The two canopies were so dense that little starlight filtered through, making it difficult for Galvin to find his way.

Most of this forest's floor was covered with thick, soft moss, which in places grew partway up the trunks of the trees. Morels were also abundant. Galvin subconsciously noted the varieties of trees he paused to lean against—birch, cedar, oak, hemlock, pine. Temperate forests rarely had more than a handful of different species of trees. However, the wildlife was more diverse—badgers, deer, wild pigs, bears, squirrels. The predators consisted mainly of wolves, foxes, and occasional wild cats. He hoped none of the latter had picked up his trail of blood. The birds were quiet, indicating a predator was about, and he didn't have the strength to defend himself. He was a wounded animal, easy prey. He ached to turn into a sparrow and fly to his destination, but he didn't have the energy to effect another transformation.

From high above, the darkenbeast's piercing red eyes scanned the wooded area, endeavoring to follow the man's trail. The sorcerous creature glided at a steady speed just beneath the upper canopy of the forest, angling its ungainly, misshapen body to pass between the leafy branches, blotting out the moon overhead. The forest denizens scattered in the beast's wake, fearful of its powerful bearing and unnatural scent. The darkenbeast paid them little heed, intent on the man, its single purpose. It peered diligently for broken branches and listened for snapping twigs and rustling leaves to indicate the passage of something large.

At last it was rewarded. Hovering, its great wings keeping it suspended above the lower canopy, the darkenbeast noticed a trace of blood fresh enough to smell. The creature pulled its leathery wings close to its body and pointed its grotesque head downward. It plummeted toward the mossy ground below, halting inches above the earth on widespread wings. At the base of a tall cedar lay a cloth drenched with blood, and clinging to a split section of bark a few feet up the trunk was a clump of blond hair.

The darkenbeast's quarry was near.

In morbid elation, the creature rose, flying nearly parallel to the trunk of the cedar until it was high enough to gain a better vantage point. As its wings beat faster to carry it over the branches and tall bushes, the darkenbeast rolled its head back on its elongated neck and voiced a victory cry that threw the occupants of the woods into an unnerving quiet.

The creature skimmed above the lower canopy, urged on by the scent of blood and the hope of reward the man's broken body might bring.

*   *   *   *   *

Galvin ambled slowly, exhausted and thankfully near his destination. Every several feet, he stretched out his right arm to steady himself against a tree. He felt weak and apprehensive. Something bothered him even more than his wound, making the short hairs rise on the back of his neck. Insects were in abundance. Droves of flies and mosquitoes were drawn to his bleeding shoulder, their soft buzzing annoying. But there were no louder night sounds, no birds, no frogs, no snapping twigs from foxes or other night-hunting creatures. He glanced nervously about as he continued his trek, stopping frequently, the quiet nagging at him. Eventually he dismissed his worrying as silly fears brought about by his loss of blood. He glanced about once more, then pushed on.

It was shortly before dawn when the woods began to thin. Gradually the ground cover turned to ferns and large, thick-leaved waxy plants and vines, and Galvin found himself at the edge of a campsite by the great marsh. He had put almost ten miles between himself and the buried gnoll. He started toward a one-man tent at the far side of the clearing, halting halfway there and whirling shakily at the sound of hoofbeats muted in the thick grass.

"You're winded, something I thought I'd never see," a deep voice observed. "And you're late—also unusual for you, my two-legged friend. I swear by my mane that this mission might be worthwhile after all. It's just barely started, and it's already showing me a new side of you."

The speaker measured well over seven feet tall from the hooves of his front legs to the top of his head, which was crowned with a shock of curly, ink-black hair, cropped short on the sides with a hank in the back hanging braided below his shoulders. He possessed the body of a man from the waist up, boasting a tanned, muscular, hairless chest and an angular face covered with a short, well-trimmed black beard streaked with gray. The remainder of his body resembled a war-horse, big and black and powerful, the kind only the wealthiest knights in Faerun rode. The centaur, Wynter, smiled broadly at Galvin, then pursed his lips when he saw that the druid was injured.

"What happened?" Wynter's voice was unusually gentle for his size. The centaur moved closer to better assess Galvin's wound, but the druid pivoted and stumbled to the far side of the camp, where he had left his belongings. Bending to rummage in a satchel, he pulled out a wine flask, uncorked it, and took a deep draft, letting the warm, red liquid run around in his mouth before answering.

"I killed the spy, Wyn."

"Did the spy attack you? Why? How badly are you hurt?" the centaur pressed, worry etched on his handsome face.

Galvin paused to dig deeper into his satchel, keeping his back to the centaur. He valued strength and was too proud to let Wynter know his condition. Nor did he want the centaur to know he was bothered by killing the gnoll spy. Wynter was a pacifist, and the druid couldn't admit that Wynter's beliefs had affected his own through the years. At last his searching was successful, and he retrieved a handful of berries that appeared freshly picked. The druid scooped them into his mouth and swallowed, then knelt and made a show of rearranging the contents of his pack. He was growing weaker by the minute and was angry at himself for not realizing the severity of his injury. While he continued his ruse, he felt the special berries begin to work, lessening his discomfort. He didn't have the right herbs in his pouch to stop the bleeding, but he would attend to that soon.

"Talk to me, Galvin." Wynter was determined. "Tell me what happened." The centaur was patient, accustomed to slowly extracting information from his druid friend.

"It was my fault," Galvin said, glancing at the tent. He was relieved that their small band's other member, a politician from Aglarond, remained asleep. There would be time enough in the morning to discuss the situation and send the council member back to Glarondar, where Aglarond's chief officials were gathered.

"And . . . ?" Wynter coaxed, laying a large, callused hand on Galvin's head.

"The spy was a gnoll. I pushed him too hard . . . made him mad."

"And . . . ?"

"And he attacked me, but not until until I was able to get some information from him."

"Are you all right?" The centaur refused to let the issue drop.

Galvin grimaced; he never lied to the centaur, who was

the closest friend he would admit having. He usually just avoided Wynter's questions when they became too personal. However, this time he knew the centaur was going to bulldog him. He relented.

"It's a deep wound, but I'll live," Galvin finally replied, keeping his voice down so the council member wouldn't hear them. "And I'll learn not to be so careless this close to Thay." He drew his cloak over his injured shoulder, turned to face the centaur, then felt himself growing faint. He sat quickly and crossed his legs. "I'll get some rest, then I'll find some healing herbs. I'll be fine."

"Fine. At least tell me what you learned." The centaur's face still showed concern, and Galvin offered him a weak smile to put him at ease.

"It seems a Red Wizard called Maligor, who is somewhere in Amruthar, wants to expand his holdings. Red Wizards are always looking for ways to become more powerful. But there's something about this that catches my interest."

"I remember the name Maligor," Wynter interrupted. "He had just become a zulkir when I left Thay." The centaur scratched his head, then indicated the tent. "Maybe the Aglarond council member is right. If a zulkir's involved in this, maybe Aglarond is in jeopardy. Did you find out if Aglarond is Maligor's target?"

"The gnoll didn't know."

"Didn't know? Well, Galvin. Give me your best guess. What do you think is up?"

The druid leaned against his pack for support. "I'll have to go to Thay to find out."

"We, you mean." Wynter shook his head and grinned, showing a row of even, white teeth. "The Red Wizards of Thay are one of your demons, my friend. I think you're looking for an excuse to poke around inside that evil country."

The druid started to argue, but the centaur cut him off.

"I was born there, and I have no love for the country nor the wizards' malevolent politics." Wynter flicked his tail for emphasis. "You'll need me as a guide."

"I'm going, too." The tent flap parted. Despite the temperate climate, the young woman had a blanket pulled about her. Foolish civilized modesty, Galvin thought.

She was slight, little more than five feet tall, and slender and graceful like an elf. Yet Brenna Graycloak was a human, with earth-brown eyes, rounded cheekbones, and a nose that turned faintly upward at the end. In the moonlight, her skin looked pale, the complexion of a scholar who locked herself in libraries all day. Her dark red hair hung to her waist, blue ribbons intertwining with the curls and smelling altogether of lilacs. Galvin found her distracting and out of place.

"I need to know what's happening in Thay," she continued, glancing at the druid. "If there's a Red Wizard planning war, I'm going to find out about it."

For long minutes, Brenna lectured the Harpers, detailing her council's responsibility to protect the people of Aglarond and her own duty to discover Thay's current military plans. She tossed her hair back, crossed her arms beneath the blanket, and eyed them sternly.

"The council asked you to investigate all of this," Brenna stated firmly. "I'm on the council. And you're going to need my help."

Galvin sighed and changed his position, pushing his pack out of the way and lying back on the grass. He propped his head up with his right arm. He had no intention of letting Brenna Graycloak accompany him and Wynter into Thay. It would be light soon, and Wynter could escort her back to Glarondar while he healed himself. Thay was no place for a dainty politician who belonged in a city.

Galvin's thoughts drifted. He knew going into Thay might take him inside heavily populated areas, something he dreaded. He hadn't set foot in a city for more than a year, and that had been on Harper business. It was Wynter who had gone into Glarondar several days ago to meet with the Aglarond council and bring Brenna out to talk to the druid. Galvin felt uncomfortable in cities, caged in by all the walls. There were many things that caught his eye amid the buildings—well-made clothing, fine food, excellent wine—but when he had made an attempt to purchase such things during his last foray, he had felt awkward and embarrased. The few coins he had hadn't even been legal tender within the boundaries of the city, and the shopkeepers had laughed at him. So the druid remained firm in the conviction that he didn't need cities; they were dirty, crowded, and filled with unpredictable humans and demi-humans. No doubt many cities in Thay would be filled with worse. As he continued to contemplate the possibilities, a drop of rain plopped on his forehead, followed a moment later by another and another. He looked up at the dawn sky, which was dotted with bleak, dark clouds. For a moment, he thought he saw a large bird. Blinking, he realized it must have been his imagination.

Maligor's malignant creation hung undetected in the sky, concealed by the gloom and protected by the clouds from the sun's first rays. It skimmed over the thinning trees and spotted its target lying prone below. The beast hovered for a moment in the shadow of a cloud, studying the scene. It hadn't considered the possibility that the man would join others. It wanted to fight the man alone.

The darkenbeast began to circle the campsite, becoming increasingly irritated over both the situation and the rain— and oblivious to its own peril, the sun. It watched and waited and was finally rewarded when the rain became a downpour and chased the woman into the tent. The odds were improving. It would wait a few minutes longer.

Below, the creature regarded the centaur pacing in front of the prone man, the darkenbeast's quarry. The darkenbeast's unnaturally keen ears picked up their conversation.

"We'll stay here a day or two—just until you're feeling all right. Then we'll move on to Thay. I think we should take the woman along if she can keep up," Wynter said. "She seems to know her way around in cities better than you or I do."

"She stays behind," Galvin countered firmly. He would

have expounded on the matter, but he felt another wash of dizziness and decided he'd been foolish not to ask for the centaur's help.

"Wyn," he said softly. "I need those herbs now, but I'm not up to getting them. The leaves are small, fernlike. You've seen me gather them. I'll need an entire plant, maybe two. Please."

Wynter's eyes bore into Galvin's. The centaur was angry that his friend had been more concerned with the Red Wizards than with his own health. Without replying, Wynter galloped from the clearing, his hooves sending mud and water flying.

The darkenbeast circled the campsite again, its dark spirits soaring now that its quarry was at last alone. It pulled its wings close to its body, plummeting like a rock and crying loudly as it separated from a low-hanging cloud. The sound was a peculiar, irritating shriek that sent shivers racing down Galvin's back and brought him unsteadily to his feet. The druid was familiar with thousands of animals, but he had never seen the likes of this beast. It stank of sorcery.

Galvin grasped the hilt of his scimitar, but the darkenbeast was on him before he could draw the blade. With surprising strength, the creature's claws slammed into the druid's abdomen, knocking him to the ground. The darkenbeast dug its talons into the man's stomach to gain a solid purchase, then it cried again and moved to drive its sharp beak into the man's chest, straight through his heart.

Stunned, Galvin watched helplessly as the beast's glowing red eyes bore into his own and its fetid, acidic saliva dripped on his tunic. The druid shivered in fear as the beast thrust its head forward. Galvin clamped his eyelids shut in terror, then suddenly felt the pressure ease.

Before the darkenbeast could strike, its head jerked back spasmodically, engulfed in a bright blue flash that lit up the campsite like fireworks and stung the creature's eyes. The darkenbeast, still planted on the druid's chest, furiously swiveled its grotesque head to face its attacker.

Brenna stood directly in front of the tent, her arms stretched out in front of her, thumbs touching and trembling fingers spread wide. Nervously she mouthed a series of singsong phrases as her hands glowed. Azure sparks shot from her fingertips and struck the darkenbeast's hide in another brilliant blue flash. The creature cried out again in agony.

In response, the beast streaked toward Brenna, its wings beating furiously only inches above the ground.

Shocked at the creature's speed, Brenna forgot about her spell and leapt to the side. The darkenbeast crashed into the tent, which collapsed instantly. The creature thrashed about in the canvas for several moments, finally loosening itself and rising from the ground. Flapping its wings to gain speed and altitude, the darkenbeast darted into the trees and hovered in the blackness to plan a new strategy. Hidden in the darkness, it called out to Maligor.

High in his tower in Amruthar, the Red Wizard had been sleeping peacefully. But Maligor's eyes flew open, his grandiose dreams of power and wealth disturbed, when he felt the tug on his mind of the darkenbeast's summons. The wizard had no way of knowing his creation was many miles from Thay's border, but he could tell it was hurt. The wizard could feel the beast's searing pain. Maligor cast off the stupor of his sleep and concentrated, trying to form a tighter mental link between himself and the darkenbeast in order to determine what was happening. Through the creature's glowing scarlet eyes, the Red Wizard saw a campsite and a woman. There were no signs of the gnoll the darkenbeast had been sent to find. The woman was dressed in a simple cotton nightdress that was plastered against her in the rain. The darkenbeast and its creator watched as the woman rushed to the side of a man.

Galvin gasped, catching his breath after the ordeal and trying to rise. Bewildered by the creature's attack, he was equally astonished at Brenna's magical prowess. He had thought she was a helpless politician.

"Don't try to get up yet," she said, gently pushing his

shoulders down to the earth and checking his wounds. Her wet hair cascaded forward, the ringlets falling against his face.

"Did you kill the creature?" Galvin asked, again trying to prop himself up despite her admonishments.

"No, but I think I injured it. It flew off beyond the trees." She picked up Galvin's scimitar, grasped his tunic at the neckline, and used the blade to cut a V in the material. She handled the weapon awkwardly, and for an instant, the druid imagined that he had survived the perils of the evening only to perish at the hands of a clumsy enchantress attempting to perform first aid. He was relieved when she finished and sheathed his weapon.

But the councilwoman wasn't done yet. Placing her hands on either side of the V, Brenna yanked hard, and the tunic ripped in a straight line, exposing his chest and left shoulder.

"This isn't a fresh wound," she scolded. "Why didn't you say something about this when you came into camp? You've lost a lot of blood. How did this happen?"

Galvin gritted his teeth. His shoulder stung as she blotted it clean with the hem of her nightdress. "Wynter is getting some herbs. When they've had a chance to do their work, we'll be moving on."

Brenna ignored him. "This is a deep wound. You're not going anywhere for a while. Wynter and I will be making the journey to Thay. You won't." She looked thoughtful for a moment. "I'll look through my things. Maybe I have something to put on that."

Like the nine planes you'll go, Galvin thought as he watched her return to the collapsed tent. No woman is going to take my place on any Harper mission. Still, he reasoned, she was more powerful than he would have imagined, and he owed his life to her for holding off the creature. He began to wonder about the creature's whereabouts when the sky grew black above him. The beast was returning, heading straight toward the enchantress.

"Brenna!" Galvin yelled, pushing himself to a sitting position in time to see the creature swoop through the clearing toward the woman. Brenna caught sight of it at the last moment and dove into the canvas, narrowly avoiding its talons. The beast swept on to the edge of the clearing and then gracefully banked to return.

Brenna rose to her knees and pushed her rain-soaked, tangled locks away from her face in one motion. She glanced about the campsite as the creature swept back for another strike.

"Get down!" she screamed at Galvin, and then she began furiously digging through the canvas. The druid ignored her and staggered to his feet to draw the creature's attention.

But the darkenbeast, determined to finish off the woman first, paid no attention to the Harper. It reveled as it closed for the kill, extending its talons toward her throat. A moment more and it would have her. A moment more and . . .

Brenna flattened herself over the collapsed tent, her arms and legs spread wide, her left hand grasping what she had desperately sought from her belongings. She smelled the creature's rank odor and felt the air rush across her back as the thing passed inches above her. Gathering her courage, she rolled over and sat awkwardly, like a young child, amidst the jumble of rope and canvas. With the rain pelting her face, she opened her left hand, palm upward, holding her right hand above it to keep the sulfur dry. Once more she began a singsong chant, this time her voice sharp and loud.

Again the darkenbeast banked and sped toward her, anxious as it smelled her fear intermingled with the cloying scent of lilacs. Then it heard the sharp crack of a lightning bolt and smelled burning flesh—its own.

The bolt had arced from the woman's hand to the darkenbeast, striking the creature squarely in the breast and nearly splitting it asunder. The magical lightning illuminated the clearing, revealing the astonished expression on the druid's face. The darkenbeast felt its insides burn and boil, and it flapped maddeningly, not realizing it was dying.

It struck the ground and beat its wings feebly for a moment more while its body twitched.

Sheets of rain drenched the creature's smoking form as Galvin and Brenna leaned against each other for support. Then they stepped forward cautiously to get a closer look at it.

The beast twitched once more, then began to shrivel.

*   *   *   *   *

Ensconced in his tower in Amruthar, Malignor screamed.

The Red Wizard felt the lightning surging through the darkenbeast's body, experienced its death throes. When it was over, he threw back the red silk covers from his bed, breathed deeply to clear his mind, and rose to pace about his bedchamber. Maligor was puzzled. He had sent the creature after a gnoll, but he in his mind, he had seen it fight a woman. He had seen the woman conjure a magical blast of lightning. The woman could be a Red Wizard, Maligor thought, despite her long hair. Had she already killed the gnoll? Was she protecting it? Or had the darkenbeast crossed paths with her merely by accident?

Maligor was so caught up in the mystery, working the puzzle through his mind again and again, that he unknowingly relaxed his personal wards, the magical guards that kept prying eyes from him.

A pair of eyes watched him now, deep-socketed, ancient orbs that stared at a crystal ball and through it watched Maligor pace. The observer, a lich and rival Red Wizard, sensed that Maligor was up to something. A creature of the living dead, the lich had all the time in Faerun to discover his adversary's plan. He had no need for sleep or food, but he did have a need to keep the other Red Wizards in check. He was perhaps the most powerful Red Wizard in all of Thay, and he had no intention of allowing another wizard to challenge his standing.

The lich smiled evilly and continued to spy on Maligor.

I will find what you are plotting, and I will crush you utterly, the lich thought as he leaned back in his fine, leather-padded chair and listened to the rain outside his window. It was a large storm, the lich knew, covering an immense area, from Amruthar well into Aglarond. It had been one of his better weather enchantments, and the downpour matched his mood.

*   *   *   *   *

The rain continued to beat down in the clearing.

"What's this?" Wynter's deep voice boomed. The centaur galloped into the campsite, his hand pushing the wet curls out of his face. "I'm gone a few minutes and disaster strikes." He looked sharply at Brenna and arched an eyebrow, then glanced down at the transforming darkenbeast.

Before the trio's eyes, the shrinking darkenbeast's skin began to bubble like boiling oil, producing a noxious stench that made Brenna back up several paces. Then the thing began to melt, leaving behind only the tiny, withered, winged husk of something that looked long dead.

Wynter prodded the thing with an extended hoof and gasped as the creature continued to transform. Its dried-out neck and legs shook visibly, then slowly began to retract into its decomposing torso. The lifeless wings beat the ground, as if the dead creature was trying to fly again, then were washed away by the pounding rain. What was left of the darkenbeast was a lump of dried flesh with bristling spines, the smoldering corpse of a hedgehog.

Galvin knelt and gently turned over the hedgehog's body. Tied about its neck was a dirt-stained piece of tattered cloth.

"Sorcery," Brenna muttered, shivering. "I don't know of any wizards in Aglarond who would have the power to do something like this. It could be the work of a Red Wizard. I wonder why the thing attacked us."

"It probably followed me," Galvin volunteered, looking up at the enchantress. Brenna's nightdress was soaked and soiled with dirt and blood, and her hair lay slick and straight from the rain.

Wynter moved between the pair and dropped a small sack in front of Galvin. "Your herbs, my friend. I suggest you use them quickly in case that creature has a friend or two." The centaur's right front hoof pawed at the ground nervously as he looked at the hedgehog. "You know how I feel about magic, Galvin."

Brenna glanced at Wynter. "There's no shortage of magic within the borders of Thay."

"That doesn't mean I have to like it." The centaur's tone was solemn.

"Second thoughts?" she queried, a concerned expression on her face.

"No." The centaur turned suddenly and trotted toward her tent. "I'll help you repair this. Maybe you can still get a few hours rest. Then I'll take you back to Glarondar."

"I'm going to Thay with you!" she declared as she sloshed after Wynter.

"No, you're not," Galvin said as he watched the pair begin to struggle with the canvas. The tent seemed to put up a fight of its own against the centaur and the enchantress, then finally yielded as the centaur anchored the center pole. The drenched councilwoman quickly slipped inside. Cursing the foul weather, Wynter trotted back to Galvin.

The druid was preparing a poultice from the herbs, but he was having difficulty keeping it dry. Galvin was usually unmindful of the rain, seeking cover from it only in the fiercest storms. Usually he reveled in it, enjoying the sensation as the water splashed over his skin. Now, however, he simply tolerated it.

Wynter began to dig a hole to bury the hedgehog. "We're not taking one step toward Thay until you're well," he stated firmly.

"I'll be fine by tomorrow," Galvin grunted. He considered himself in charge of this expedition, and he wasn't about to take orders from a centaur. He watched Wynter place the charred hedgehog into the earth and build a small mound over it. Satisfied the creature was at rest, the druid returned to his soaked backpack and lay down beside it. He quickly fell into a deep, troubled sleep.

It was dark when Galvin awoke. The moon and stars shone overhead, and the druid cursed himself for sleeping most of the day away. He felt the ground around his hands; the grass was dry, the earth only slightly damp. He ran his hands over his clothes—they, too, were dry. He cursed himself again, realizing his first guess was wrong—he had slept for more than a day and a half. His shoulder felt sore, but not nearly as bad as before. The herb poultice had healed it considerably. He flexed his fingers and rotated his shoulder. The numbness was gone.

Reasonably healed, the druid knew he would be able to travel. He stretched on the ground and was debating taking Brenna back to Glarondar tonight when he heard her voice—and Wynter's. He listened to pick up their conversation.

"It won't help my political career any to go jaunting off into Thay as a spy," he heard Brenna say. "My rivals will surely use it against me, claiming I have more interest in what goes on outside my country than in Aglarond."

"But if we uncover some plot against Aglarond, you'll be a hero," Wynter commented.

"Perhaps, but I think the negatives will outweigh it. Do you have any interest in politics?"

"I don't, and I don't care to," Wynter countered. "But I do know something about people. And—" there was a lengthy pause as Galvin strained to hear what came next— "you're going to have to find some other way to gain fame. Galvin says you're staying behind, and I trust his judgment. Thay's a harsh place—no place for you. I know. I was born there."

Galvin sat up to watch the pair. Brenna sat cross-legged on a straw mat outside her tent, her arms crossed defiantly. Wynter stood above her, looking amused.

"Can you keep up with us?" Galvin asked.

She looked through the centaur's legs at the druid and nodded emphatically.

The druid glanced up at Wynter. "We leave at dawn."

The centaur grinned broadly and joined Galvin. "I'm not sure about her motives, but she just might be an asset. At least she knows her way around cities."

Galvin frowned, hoping desperately that he hadn't made a mistake by allowing Brenna Graycloak to come along.

Three

Maligor reclined on a crimson-dyed leather divan in the center of his immense bath chamber, his head resting on a green silk pillow recently imported from Shou Lung. Although he was thin and stood only about five and a half feet tall, he looked large on the couch; he chose his furniture to make himself appear imposing. A half-dozen of his favorite pleasure slaves attended him. Two, who had been born on Maligor's slave plantation and were hardly more than children, massaged his feet, applying expensive, musky oils. The scent was sweet and heavy and permeated the air. Another pair, blond twin sisters kidnapped by pirates from their sea captain father in Orlumbor, worked diligently to manicure and polish his hard yellow nails. The fifth, the eldest of the human slave women, a buxom twenty-year-old from Ravens Bluff, sat on a stack of pillows near his right shoulder. Slowly rubbing a damp cloth across his forehead with one hand, she used the other to gently run a sharp blade over his temples and across the top of his head, shaving the fine stubble growing there. She took ex-

41

treme care not to cut him; her predecessor had died horribly in the laboratory several days ago for just such an offense.

The women wore sheer, colorful fabrics that left nothing to Maligor's imagination. He dressed all of his female slaves thus to prevent them from hiding weapons that could be turned against him. The women's hair extended to the middle of their backs, while the children's hung about their shoulders. It was an indication they had been slaves for many years. However, the sixth slave, an elven woman in a short, rose-hued gauze tunic, had silvery-white hair that reached barely below the lobes of her pointed ears. Maligor had owned this prize only a few months. She sat apart from the group near a black iron cage filled with finches. Strumming an ebonwood lyre, she sang a mournful old elvish tune that Maligor could not understand. The Red Wizard usually enjoyed her music. Tonight, however, he found the tune annoying. It prevented him from concentrating.

The wizard owned more than eight hundred slaves, a considerable stable. Most were male laborers who worked at various tasks around his properties. Several dozen were warriors and sailors who had been captured in nearby countries. Fewer still were slave women who attended to his needs. He continually added to his stable, as the Red Wizard needed a steady supply of slaves to replace those who died of overwork, old age, or, more likely, because of his malicious magical experiments.

There were few Red Wizards who owned more slaves than Maligor. Slaves made up about two-thirds of the country's population and were considered one of Thay's major imports. Maligor prided himself on having some of the most exquisite slaves.

This evening, however, his pleasure slaves were doing little to please him. The Red Wizard's mind was elsewhere, concentrating on another woman—the one he had seen before his darkenbeast died. Maligor still puzzled over her. He had sent the darkenbeast after an errant gnoll guard, yet through his telepathic link with the darkenbeast, he had picked up no trace of the gnoll—only the red-tressed beauty.

The woman was confounding. If she was in Thay, she might be a slave because of her long hair. But she was not one of Maligor's. Perhaps she was the slave of another Red Wizard, the same one who had solicited the services of the missing gnoll. Perhaps she herself was a Red Wizard—but if she was, why had the darkenbeast attacked her? And what had happened to the gnoll?

Maligor pursed his lips, causing the slave shaving him to tremble. Continuing to puzzle over the matter will do little good, he thought. The gnoll, wherever he is, knows nothing of my real plans. But the woman . . . who is she? *Where* is she?

"Finished, my lord," the buxom slave announced timidly, interrupting his thoughts. Looking frightened yet expectant, she wiped the damp cloth across the top of his head with a shaky hand and replaced the shaving blade in its case.

Maligor eyed her sternly and ran his hand over his head to inspect her handiwork. He watched her bottom lip quiver and her face grow pale in fear that her performance was less than satisfactory. For a moment, he was tempted to find fault with her, then decided to be uncommonly kind.

"It is barely adequate, but it will do for tonight. Tomorrow make sure you do better."

Visibly relieved, she rose and joined the elven woman. The other slaves continued their tasks. Maligor stared past them to the blackness beyond the room's small windows. It was late, and from his position all he could see was a small section of sky and a few tiny stars, the bottom claw of the Malar constellation. He pulled his thoughts away from the dead darkenbeast, pondering instead what was transpiring under the stars in Amruthar at this moment. At least he would know about that within a few hours, as he had informers stationed in several taverns and on select street corners to pick up gossip. Maligor enjoyed the ability to keep track of most of the city's seedy activities without leaving the safety of his fortified tower.

Maligor felt comfortable and secure here. His tower stretched sixty feet above the rich Thayvian soil. It boasted a crenellated top, where seasoned fighters were always stationed within easy reach of massive mounted crossbows and jugs of oil that could quickly be set aflame. The outer walls were made of solid granite, eighteen inches thick in most places. All the windows in his keep were of the same size—eight inches wide by two feet high. This small size made for better defense. Each was barred or covered with protective spells to keep unwanted things from entering or the wrong eyes from looking inside. To complete his defenses, the wizard had magical guards and wards scattered throughout his premises and skilled guards and loyal slaves on every level.

"My Lord Maligor," a soft voice came from just beyond the chamber. "You summoned me?"

"Yes, Asp," Maligor replied thickly as he continued to stare at the sky. "You're late."

"I was drilling the gnolls."

Maligor sneered, hating to be kept waiting. "Enter. We have much to discuss."

The bath chamber was lit by dozens of thick red candles on curved iron stands that were placed around the walls and near Maligor's divan. They kept away the shadows, except those in the darkened doorway where Asp now stood. She poked her head out from the gray entrance, glancing around the room and at the nervous slaves. Sliding her shoulders and arms out of the shadows, she maneuvered herself entirely into the chamber, revealing her serpentine body.

One of the twins gasped. Throwing both hands over her mouth, she dropped the manicure tools, sending them clinking in several directions across the polished white marble floor. She scooted away from the divan, unmindful of Maligor's burning gaze. The other slaves also appeared startled, but they were wiser. They remained rooted to their posts.

Perturbed, Maligor silently marked the twin for stringent punishment, then turned back to Asp.

His lieutenant noiselessly slithered toward the divan, the candlelight playing over her glittering crimson and charcoal scales and causing the scales to reflect eerily on the marble. From the waist down, Asp resembled a colorful sand boa with a ridge of armored, triangular-shaped scales down her back and a tail that tapered to a black point. From the waist up, she was a lovely young woman, more beautiful than even the slaves in the room. She was a spirit naga, a member of a race of unhuman women, and Maligor knew she could shape-change into any human or demi-human form. He wondered whether this was her true appearance or merely a magical fabrication. It really didn't matter, he reasoned. He was dishonest enough with his own body, cloaking his years with his potion bottles.

Her true appearance did not matter; he found her easy on his old eyes. Still, his other senses found her unsettling. Like all spirit nagas, or "snake women of the underground" as many men preferred to call them, Asp smelled of rotting flesh. And that scent, coupled with the musky oil on his feet, made Maligor wince.

Her tail undulated back and forth over the smooth floor, then acted as a brace as Asp rose like a spitting cobra to address him. From the tip of her tail to the top of her head, Asp measured almost twenty feet long.

"My Lord Maligor, may I speak freely here?" She glowered at the slaves and hissed at the elf for emphasis. Abruptly the music stopped.

"A moment," he answered, his eyes reluctantly leaving the human part of Asp's form and turning to his slaves. He clapped his wrinkled hands once, and guards stationed beyond the entrance moved in to escort the slave women to their chamber. With a bony finger, he indicated the twin who had shown improper behavior, and a guard nodded and smiled knowingly as the slaves were ushered from the room.

Asp was pleased to see the women's alarmed expressions and felt amused that one would be whipped—or worse—because of her. She enjoyed terrifying Maligor's female slaves and often went out of her way to do so. The snake-woman claimed she did it to put them in their place, while adding to her own sense of superiority over humans.

Maligor chose to believe she was jealous.

For nearly three summers, the naga had been the Red Wizard's companion, initially studying under him as an apprentice, then gaining a trusted position as leader of his guard force and chief instructor of his army. They shared an unusual relationship that couldn't quite be considered affection. Maligor believed himself incapable of love.

Still, the Red Wizard enjoyed her company and respected her abilities and cunning, using her to his best advantage. In turn, the keenly intelligent Asp used Maligor to help her gain stature in Thay and more wealth than she could have stolen from the drow and other races who dwelt in the underground. In those three years, the Red Wizard hadn't noticed the snake-woman age one bit. Not one wrinkle had formed on her delicate face; not one silver hair shone on her head. He knew a naga's life spanned many human generations, and in that respect, he considered her a fitting confidante. Maligor intended to live a very long time.

She glided to his side, wrapped her tail around the base of a stack of pastel satin pillows next to the divan, and eased herself onto them. She rarely used furniture, finding most of it awkward for her body, a human folly. But if she remained upright, she would tower above Maligor, something she knew the wizard would not tolerate.

"My army . . . ?" Maligor began.

"Their training is progressing satisfactorily," she replied. "I drill the gnolls to the point of exhaustion."

"Good," he said simply, peering into her lidless eyes. "My beautiful general has a fist of iron."

"My lord?"

Maligor reached up and gently brushed her cheek with

the back of his hand.

She smiled coyly, then her face took on an intense expression. "My lord, I'm curious about the gnoll guard—the missing one you sent the darkenbeast after."

The Red Wizard sighed and dropped his hand from her face. "Your concern is the army, Asp. That's what I called you here for. I want a detailed report."

"But my lord . . ." the naga began.

"The matter of the errant gnoll has been taken care of," Maligor lied. "Now to other things. We have much work to do, my lovely."

The wizard propped himself up on an elbow and gazed harshly at Asp while she detailed the army's numbers, capabilities, and state of readiness. In the candlelight, the naga's eyes appeared nearly luminescent. With those eyes, she could charm lesser men and often did, forcing them to do her bidding. That ability helped her to deal with Maligor's soldiers.

"Then the army is ready," the Red Wizard concluded. "It is time to take action, Asp. I have been content for too many years with my holdings and position as Zulkir of Alteration. None of the wizards in my school have the power to challenge me. But the other Red Wizards, the other zulkirs . . ." He paused, thinking primarily of Szass Tam, his arch rival. "It is time to show them I am an unstoppable force. It is time I became the most powerful Red Wizard in Thay."

Asp extended a smooth, slender hand and gently laid it on Maligor's shoulder. Her thin lips smiled and her eyes sparkled.

"It is your rightful place, my lord, to reign supreme among the Red Wizards. With my help, you will become all-powerful. None will be able to challenge you." She brought her face so close to his that he could smell the fragrance she had dabbed on to mask her own odor. The fragrance reminded him of lilies.

"You have a plan?" she posed.

"Yes," he replied simply. Maligor stretched his limbs on

the divan, then pushed himself off it. The marble floor felt
uncomfortably cool to his oiled, bare feet. Raising the hem
of his red robes, he stepped into his red satin slippers and
glanced over his shoulder at Asp.

Her eyes were wide in anticipation of learning his new
scheme, but Maligor did not delude himself. He knew the
snake-woman would support him only because she stood to
gain something as well.

Striding across the room, past a large, gray marble tub
set into the floor, Maligor reached a waist-high walnut cabinet filled with bottles of rare wines and liqueurs. He
stooped and paused, intently studying the labels through
the beveled glass, then opened the cabinet and grasped
what he considered an unusual delight. The bottle was
round like a melon at the bottom, but its neck was thin and
twisted in a spiral. Although decades old, the bottle was
spotless; the glass was thick, tinted blue, and filled with the
Moonshaes' finest peach liqueur. Reaching farther into the
cabinet, he retrieved two pear-shaped, clear crystal gob-
lets. Slaves usually handled menial tasks such as this, but
the wizard didn't want other ears present just now. Returning to the divan, he sat and passed the bottle to Asp.
He held a goblet in each hand, waiting. The naga's eyes
narrowed, and a corner of her lips turned slightly downward. Maligor knew she preferred thick noxious mixtures
that would make most men wretch. But to please him, she
would drink the liqueur.

She thrust the painted nail of her left index finger into the
cork, twisted once, and popped it open, discarding the remains on the floor for the slaves to clean up. The spirit
naga poured one glass nearly full of the sweet-smelling,
amber-colored liquid, but the second she filled only halfway. Asp knew the ritual. She took the glass with the
lesser amount and raised it to her lips. Taking a full swallow, she nodded to Maligor and licked the sweet-tasting
liqueur off her bottom lip with her thin tongue. Maligor, ever fearful of poisons or other contaminants, never drank
first.

"For many long months, we've been adding to our army of gnolls and men—and taking other measures to boost the guard force." Maligor stated the obvious to Asp, who knew the strength of his forces better than the Red Wizard did. "We will march our army southeast of Eltabar where a certain young Red Wizard is just starting to rise in power. His manor is almost directly east of Amruthar."

"But that's days from here!" the spirit naga interjected, nearly spilling her drink. "Won't he and the other wizards become suspicious? An army of gnolls can hardly be ignored."

Maligor chuckled. "You do well in training the soldiers, sweet Asp. However, you lack my knowledge of military strategy."

The spirit naga hissed at the insult, but Maligor continued.

"We will first gather the army here, then march it south. This will cause all manner of speculation, as there are several likely targets south of Amruthar. Some may even think I want land directly to the south of this city to increase my local holdings. Others may think I'm after Amruthar itself." He smiled at his plan.

"While the suppositions are bandied about, the force will head east under the cover of darkness, then north to our target. If any Red Wizards in the south decide to meet my army, they will meet nothing, and the young Red Wizard southeast of Eltabar will be undone."

Asp thought a moment. The plan was too simple for her devious mind.

"But what if wizards join forces to attack the gnolls? They certainly have the power," she speculated. Asp prided herself on knowing the military strengths of most of the ranking Red Wizards in Thay and was certain that if three or more wizards joined forces, the gnolls and men wouldn't last long.

"You know that won't happen," Maligor countered. "Red Wizards are a suspicious lot and rarely act in concert. We forever scheme against each other. It seems to be in our makeup, dearest Asp, a prerequisite to becoming a zulkir or to achieving any significant power. No, I think the wizards to the south will worry over my army—some are probably worrying now. Doubtless one or two have been watching you through crystal balls while you drill the gnolls."

He took a large mouthful of the peach liqueur and tilted his head back to let it run slowly down his throat. Making a mental note to acquire several more cases of the vintage, he took another drink. Then he stood and glanced down at Asp through the glass. Tilting the crystal goblet between his palms and watching the liquid run around the sides gave her complexion an exotic look.

Asp drained the rest of her liqueur in one gulp, grimacing at its sweet taste and hoping Maligor would not think to pour her another. "The young wizard southeast of Eltabar—who is he? How good are his defenses?"

Maligor raised an eyebrow and lied once more. "His name is for another day—tomorrow perhaps, after I have cast a spell to prevent him from hearing his name uttered. As for his defenses, he is young. He has yet to establish an army of any consequence."

Asp smiled openly. "Then we are doing him a favor, my lord. If we do not attack him, another wizard will. Better for him to be defeated by you, who will be the most powerful Red Wizard in Thay."

Maligor enjoyed Asp's flattery, even though he knew it wasn't sincere. He wondered if she realized when he was not being honest with her. He reached out and stroked her smooth, soft cheek, then finished his drink.

"The success of this campaign is in your hands, my lovely," Maligor uttered in barely more than a whisper, staring unblinkingly into her eyes. "The army will move under your direction. Are the soldiers prepared for such a grand plan?"

Asp rose from the pillow, careful to rest lower so she was no taller than Maligor.

"They are ready, my lord." She twitched her tail back

and forth like a contented cat, pleased that she was being given responsibility for the march. "Your men nearby number three hundred; your gnolls number four times that. They are anxious to cleave the skulls of your enemies."

Maligor began to pace, rubbing his chin with his right hand to appear pensive and concerned. He assumed his act was convincing. "Are they in the best shape possible, able to handle a march of several days followed by a brief siege? The wizard, though young, will have magic at his disposal, and possibly a few apprentices. With a handful of spells, they could cut an army by a fifth or more."

Asp took affront at his doubts. "My lord! Your soldiers know fighting styles from faraway lands, and I've given them a cunning and ruthlessness that will push them to success. If a fifth fall to spells and arrows, the remainder will sweep over the young wizard instantly. We will crush him, and I will bring you his head."

Asp's eyes had lost their sparkle, replaced by a dark gleam that showed a mixture of excitement and anger. Maligor knew from her expression that she supported his plan and would work to implement it without too many questions.

The spirit naga was so caught up in the prospect of taking another wizard's land, likely assuring herself a share in the wealth, that she failed to notice Maligor's amused glance.

"Your force is divided now," she said, continuing her report. "Some are camped near your slave plantation twenty miles north of here; more are stationed slightly north of that in the woods. A third are to the south, drilling, and the remainder are in barracks near this tower. They must be brought together."

Asp looked as if she would continue her explanations, but Maligor interrupted, not wanting to waste time listening to military strategies about which he had no concern. "Dearest Asp," he said softly, "I have every confidence in you. Your approach has merit, and I trust your instincts. You are the warrior, not I. Tomorrow, make sure you visit each unit of men and gnolls. One of my flying carpets will be placed at your disposal. The army must be at its peak."

"Of course," she said, her tail still twitching. "And after we defeat the young wizard?"

"We divide the spoils."

"And then?"

Maligor winked at her and poured himself another glass of liqueur. "We won't stop there, of course. Growth is good for the soul and necessary for surviving in Thay."

He strode to the divan and eased himself back on the supple leather cushions, balancing his glass on his chest. "I need to relax," he said, yawning for effect. "Attend to your forces, and we will talk more tomorrow night."

She bent to kiss his forehead, carefully placed her glass on the floor near the stack of pillows, and slithered from the room.

When Maligor heard the door close behind her, he laughed, a soft maniacal chortle that made the guards stationed at the entrance shiver.

Beautiful fool, he thought as he sipped the liqueur. *Fortunate for me that she is so blind. My true plans lie elsewhere, Asp, and are grander then you could ever imagine. My true plans would make even you pale.*

Maligor's scheme included the naga and dictated she have a significant role, but it would not be a role she would fashion for herself. *She would not direct an army, or even a single gnoll,* he mused. *I will pull her strings, and she will help me achieve wealth beyond her own imagining and power to put me beyond the other wizards' grasps.* He finished the liqueur and let the glass fall to the floor, shattering.

Although the drink was having some effect on him, Maligor was actually becoming drunk on dreams of power. The Red Wizard's plans had taken him far in his life, through the ranks of the School of Alteration and eventually to its head as zulkir, where he had a hand in Thayvian politics and therefore a say in the very direction of the evil country. His forces were many and challenged that of the lich Szass Tam, whose legions of undead were legend. But he was certain his ambition surpassed the lich's.

Maligor could accomplish his goals without the aid of the snake-woman, he knew, but her presence would make certain things easier. His mind once again focused on the red-haired sorceress encountered by his darkenbeast.

Maligor stood, avoiding the slivers of glass, and steadied himself. He padded toward a sunken marble tub filled to the brim with water now grown tepid. Crouching unsteadily at its edge, the Red Wizard reached into a pocket of his robe and groped with his bony fingers. Rewarded, he withdrew a small clump of dried flower petals. Crushing them between his fingers, he dropped them into the water and concentrated, trying to remember every detail of the woman's face, every curl that cascaded over her forehead.

Ripples formed on the surface of the water, pushing the flower petals toward the edges of the tub. Then the water calmed, and in the center of the water's surface, the woman's visage appeared. Maligor strained his senses to hear her.

* * * * *

"Wynter," Brenna intoned in a musical voice that nearly mesmerized the listening Maligor. "It's nearly dawn. Shouldn't we be leaving now?"

"We'll eat first, then start toward Thay," replied a deep voice. The Red Wizard could not identify the speaker. "Don't worry. We'll be inside that evil country soon enough."

Thay. Maligor's mind raced. Then the woman really could be a Red Wizard, an ambassador, perhaps, stationed in a neighboring land. Red Wizards were known to let their hair grow long when they mingled with others outside of Thay. It helped them fit in with many cultures and disguised their true heritage.

"I could use something to eat, too," the woman replied.

Maligor watched her slender hand rub her stomach through the cloth of an expensive dress. The woman's hand was bedecked with rings, marking her as a person of some wealth. The Red Wizard strained to see past her to get a hint of her surroundings, but the grayness of the day kept him from seeing very far. All Maligor could make out were the legs of a massive black war-horse behind her and tall grass everywhere. At least he knew the woman was outdoors, sitting on the ground probably, and not likely within the confines of a city. But he couldn't determine any real hint of her location.

"I'll help you pack up the tent," the deep voice continued.

"Thanks, Wynter," she replied in her melodic voice. Then her lips pursed and her delicate brows furrowed. The sorceress scratched at the back of her neck and then glanced about.

High in his tower, Maligor wondered what had caught the woman's attention. In another moment, he knew. The woman's eyes snapped open and she stared straight ahead. The Red Wizard saw her face plainly in the surface of the water. Her lips flew apart in a warning.

"Wynter, we're being watched! Someone's scrying on us!"

"Scrying?" the deep voice queried, obviously unaware of what the sorceress was talking about.

"I'll explain later," she said, her melodic voice becoming harsh and commanding.

Maligor watched as her intense eyes squeezed shut and she threw her hands over her ears. The Red Wizard heard her mumble something—magical words, he knew, but he was unfamiliar with them. An instant later, the water in the tub began to bubble, wiping out the image of the unnamed sorceress. Maligor bent closer to the surface of the water but saw nothing except the bottom of the tub and the crushed petals swirling about.

"Damn!" he swore, rising shakily to his feet. Maligor paced about the tub, still intent on the woman. "I must find her," he whispered. "I must know what she's up to."

* * * * *

"What is scrying?" Wynter persisted. "I don't understand."

"It's a form of magic," Brenna replied. Gazing up at the centaur's angular face, she frowned. "It's a way to watch people through crystal balls and other devices."

Wynter still looked puzzled.

"You can't see who's watching you, but sometimes you can tell you're being watched." Brenna scratched at the back of her neck. "But only sometimes. More often than not, you'd never have a clue that someone was spying on you."

"How did you know just now?" the centaur asked uncertainly.

Brenna could tell he only half believed her. "Goosebumps," she answered simply. "I felt an odd sensation, and I had the definite feeling someone was watching us."

"And now?"

"The presence is gone," Brenna stated.

"Good," Wynter said, feeling more relaxed.

"Only good to a point," the sorceress countered. "Whoever or whatever was watching us probably knows we're going to Thay."

The centaur scowled and trotted toward Galvin.

* * * * *

The Red Wizard continued his circuit of the tub, convinced now that the woman was a power to be reckoned with. Maligor was furious; he had little time to devote to the mysterious enchantress. He had his own goals—and his own personal army—to contend with.

Maligor knew he couldn't attempt to scry on her again, at least not for a while. He'd have to wait several hours until he regained enough magical energies. Needing to take his mind off the red-haired woman, he decided to check on his forces—forces that only he knew about.

Even Asp remained oblivious to Maligor's secret army. Although the spirit naga was the only being in whom he placed any semblance of trust, he nevertheless limited her knowledge. He would tell her of this other army only when the timing was right.

It is time to check on my soldiers, he reflected, pleased with himself about what awaited in the basement. He sauntered from the chamber as erect as his aged back and the liqueur allowed and motioned the guards not to follow.

"Instruct the slaves to put out the candles and clean the room," he ordered as he passed. "I am finished here for the evening." The guards moved immediately to comply.

Satisfied with their promptness, the Red Wizard descended the spiral staircase that led to the bowels of his tower. Passing guards on every level, he nodded to them and noted that all of them seemed alert tonight. Maligor's security was stronger in the evening than in the daytime; he knew many wizards preferred to act at night. Tonight Maligor had placed several special guards and had cast powerful wards to keep even the most powerful of sorcerers from scrying into his domain. He planned to add to his army this evening and wanted no one else, not even Asp, to watch. He would have to keep her very busy with the gnoll troops for the next several days or she was bound to become curious about his work.

As Maligor proceeded past the ground level, the stairway widened. He had had it constructed this way to better accommodate the large creatures he often kept below. He passed through several doorways that appeared, when closed, to be sections of the wall, but which pivoted or slid back to open. Only skilled thieves or special spells could reveal the stonework as doors.

It took the old wizard several minutes to reach the deepest underground level. It was quite damp here, and slime and mosses coated the walls. The guards at this level had never been human. They were vague, misshapen forms that, except for the rise and fall of their massive chests, stood unmoving against the foundation. He passed them

all, taking note to construct a few more such guardians tomorrow as an added precaution.

Eventually he reached a large chamber where the stonework along the walls appeared older than the rest of the
tower. The oval chamber, lit only by a dozen guttering,
tallow-soaked torches, was more than two hundred and fifty feet long and nearly half that in width. At first the room
appeared empty, wrapped in shadows that writhed and
breathed in the meager torchlight. Then, as Maligor's eyes
became accustomed to the darkness, he made out the
shapes he was searching for. Darkenbeasts. Nearly a thousand of them.

The creatures huddled on the filth-encrusted floor, clung
to the walls, and hung from the high ceiling rafters like
bats. Some hovered in the air, waiting for others to move
so they could gain a choice place to rest. An unusually large
darkenbeast, much bigger than a man, claimed a crumbling
altar in the center of the room. Whatever dark purposes
the altar had served centuries ago, Maligor was uncon-
cerned about them now. He was certain his own foul plans
dwarfed those of the chamber's earlier owner, and his plans
didn't call for altars or ritualistic sacrifices. They relied on
the wizard's own magical abilities and wits.

The room smelled foul and acidic, burning the Red Wizard's eyes and making it uncomfortable for him to breathe.
If the chamber weren't so deep below the ground, the odor
would soon alert Asp and the tower's other occupants that
something grotesque was living here. He gagged from the
stench of the darkenbeasts and continued to survey his
grand army.

It had taken the Red Wizard months to accumulate this
force, working through the night turning bats, lizards,
snakes, rats, and other animals into the evil darkenbeasts.
The intense magic had exhausted him, leaving him feeling
his advanced years. But the incantations had kept his mind
sharp for his plans for power. Many of his gnolls had gone
hungry so the wizard could use their livestock and transform the docile beasts into his loathsome creatures. He

wanted at least a few hundred more beasts before he would be satisfied with the force. That wouldn't be difficult, as he had slaves purchasing reptiles and other small creatures from the open-air market in Amruthar. Bought in small quantities, the tiny creatures would not evoke suspicion, but would still add needed numbers to his growing army.

Maligor did not concern himself about feeding the creatures; they were products of sorcery and could go without sustenance for weeks. They received enough nourishment from the bodies of ill-behaved slaves, unfortunate soldiers, and animals that had failed to make the transition to darkenbeasts successfully. He knew he would have to use his darkenbeasts carefully, since without the darkness, they would perish. But there were enough caves, abandoned buildings, and underground complexes in Thay to enable him to move his forces under the cover of darkness when the time came.

The Red Wizard reached out with his mind, contacting the large darkenbeast on the altar. It took him a moment to adjust to the creature's weak brain, but soon he was able to see through its eyes and perceive with its senses. He could feel the oppressiveness of the room, could feel the breath of the creatures who stared balefully up at the altar at the large creature who rested there. And he could feel the strength that coursed through the powerful creature's limbs. The scent of the chamber was overpowering and caused his mind to reel. Still he maintained contact through the beast and directed it to fly above the others, circling the oval room.

Maligor experienced the sense of soaring, flexing wings that were his, and yet were not. He cried with the beast's voice, a loud shriek that quieted the other creatures. Flying faster and higher, Maligor manipulated the beast to glide just below the ceiling, upsetting the perches of the darkenbeasts hanging there and causing them to join the larger creature in flight. Faster and faster Maligor felt himself go, and he felt himself desiring the open sky, where his flight would have no limit. A flurry of leather wings appeared before him as more darkenbeasts rose from the walls of the chamber, threatening to snuff out the torches with the breeze created by their wings.

Controlling the largest of the beasts, Maligor caused the others to move out of his way, in much the same manner that he ordered his guards and slaves. He continued to shriek at them, demanding a response.

The darkenbeasts' mournful cries rose to an obscene cacophony in an evil chorus. He savored the terrible noise. The offensive smell no longer bothered him, for he was a part of it. He had become one with the beast. He flexed the darkenbeast's talons as he would his own fingers and turned its head as he would his own. He continued to circle until nearly all the chamber's inhabitants had joined his exuberant flight.

Then his mind reached out once more, touching the nearest darkenbeasts, then those farther away. Within moments, he controlled a dozen, then two, three dozen, and more. The nature of his sorcery enabled him to link telepathically to one, several, or all of his dark creatures, directing their actions and receiving uncompromising cooperation.

Maligor felt himself flying in many different directions at once. At first the sensation was glorious, but then it became disconcerting. He concentrated harder and drew the darkenbeasts' thoughts together, making them fly according to his will. The scene in the room altered. What a moment before had been chaos now was orchestrated movement. A ring of black circled the room, with the darkenbeasts flying in graceful patterns, performing a lurid ballet. Their cries rose as one, hideous and deafening, threatening to rise above the layers of stone and earth and warn those in the tower above of their presence.

Maligor, realizing the potential for problems, urged his force to land, then began to release their simple minds. Immediately the stench of the place overpowered him again and he retched, nearly doubling over. Gasping, he focused his attention on the large darkenbeast that had returned to the altar.

Soon, he telepathically communicated to the creature. *We will fly again soon.*

The Red Wizard staggered from the chamber and began the long ascent to his tower.

Four

In the clearing, Galvin waited for dawn to break and watched Wynter help Brenna pack her tent. The druid was disturbed at overhearing the sorceress's revelation that someone had been magically watching them—"scrying on them," she had called it. A Red Wizard possibly, Galvin thought. No . . . if someone had been spying on them, it was definitely a Red Wizard.

No matter, the druid decided. The mission would continue even if someone in Thay was aware of them.

A soft breeze blew across Galvin's face, refreshing him and causing him to get a good whiff of himself. Caked blood and sweat made him stink worse than a dirty, wet wolf. He was certain his companions would make a worse analogy, and he resolved to take care of his odiferous condition—and get breakfast—while they finished packing. The sky was still dark and devoid of clouds, but it was tinged with gray and deep blue, indicating the sun would be up in less than an hour. He scanned the horizon for several minutes, fearing another transformed beast might be nearby, but he saw nothing.

He was certain a Red Wizard was behind the obscene creature that had attacked them; Galvin wanted to believe that. If the creature was sent in retaliation for his killing the gnoll spy, he speculated, why weren't more of the beasts dispatched? Perhaps whoever or whatever had sent the beast had only meant it to be a warning. If that was the case, it was a warning the druid didn't intend to heed.

His fever was gone, and his shoulder felt considerably better, although it was still stiff. It would serve as a physical reminder, at least for a few more days, of his folly with the gnoll. He listened to a bullfrog croaking in the distance. It was searching for a mate; the druid could tell by its prolonged, deep, throaty song. Closer, he heard the buzzing of insects. There were plenty of them in this area, particularly mosquitoes, because of the recent rain and the nearness of the marsh. Fortunately, Galvin mused, insects never bothered him.

"Gnats!" the centaur reached back and swatted his rump with his hand. "You always find the nicest places to camp, Galvin. Plenty of water. Shade in abundance. And more insects than blades of grass."

The druid ignored his friend's complaints and rubbed his hand over his chin, feeling the scratchy stubble growing there. He grabbed his dirty canvas satchel and started to jog toward the trees and the welcome gurgling of a nearby creek, but he slowed almost immediately when a knifing pain cut through his shoulder and into his chest. I'm not entirely well yet, he decided.

Glancing back over his shoulder, he saw the centaur watching him closely and looking concerned. Galvin forced a smile and turned and headed into the trees.

By the time Galvin returned with an armload of fruit, the sun was beginning to edge above the horizon. Brenna was reclining on her rolled-up tent. Two satchels sat just beyond her. She wisely had packed lightly, the druid surmised, unlike other city people he knew. She wore her hair twisted in tight braids about her head. That, too, was practical, since they would be traveling among trees and bushes that would hopelessly tangle it. But her garb was far from functional. Today she wore a long blue gown of heavy cotton that was full along the bottom and edged with lace; its only saving grace was the tight sleeves. Galvin resigned himself to the thought that apparently all wizards dressed in billowy, expensive drapery. Maybe they felt that made them appear more important than people who dressed practically. Still, she looked pretty in it, he thought.

Galvin had taken time to bathe, shave two days' growth of beard off his face, and wash his hair. Still wet, it lay flat against the sides of his head and dripped on the back and shoulders of his cloak. He had changed into the only other set of clothes he had brought, which consisted of a forest green tunic, darker green leggings, and a plain knee-length cloak—also green. He regretted ruining the cloak he had worn yesterday. It had been a gift from a female Harper associate in Tsurlagol who had had designs on the druid. That had been a few years ago, and Galvin hadn't been interested in romance. But he liked the cloak and had worn it often. Wynter frequently chided him because he dressed only in green, but the druid considered it a functional color in the forest, since it helped him blend in with the foliage.

Wynter eyed him and winked. "A special occasion? Or are you just trying to impress the lady?"

The centaur's longbow was slung over his right shoulder, and an embossed leather quiver full of arrows rested between his broad shoulder blades. His staff, a thick piece of black-stained oak nearly eight feet long, rested against a tree. Beyond that, Wynter carried only a small leather sack strapped to his waist. It contained several silver and gold coins and a silver pin—a harp inside a crescent moon. Galvin often envied the centaur because he didn't need to pack clothes and other human essentials.

"No meat this morning?" Wynter continued, eyeing the druid's selection. The centaur knew Galvin refused to eat animal flesh, choosing instead to live on fruits, nuts, and vegetables he recovered in the wild and on bread and cheese he traded for with traveling merchants. Wynter, however, had a fondness for roast pig, despite the fact it didn't sit well in his equine stomach, and was glad his friend never objected when he ate it or grew angry when he repeatedly offered to share the flesh with the druid.

Galvin handed the centaur a large piece of citrus fruit. "This is better for you," he said.

Brenna eagerly selected a few pieces of fruit for herself. Galvin wondered what she and Wynter had eaten while he slept. Probably little, he thought. The centaur wasn't a very good hunter; he was a farmer by trade, when he wasn't gallivanting off with the druid on Harper assignments, a profession that kept him fit and well fed. Galvin noted that Wynter devoured the fruit eagerly, and Brenna was eating hers ravenously.

The councilwoman finished first, glanced at her bags, and then looked to Galvin for assistance.

"I won't be able to carry all this," she said, adding a weak smile.

The druid returned her smile, strapped on his scimitar, slung his satchel over his shoulder, and eyed her thin, shapely frame. "Then you'd better decide what to leave behind."

The sorceress puffed out her chest and readied a verbal assault, but the centaur stepped between her and the druid.

"I'll help you, Brenna," Wynter offered.

Galvin looked at the centaur quizzically. The druid had never known him to make such an offer to anyone. Wynter didn't want anyone to consider him a packhorse.

Openly smiling at the druid, Wynter balanced the rolled canvas tent across his long horse's back and secured it so it wouldn't slide off. The maneuver wasn't easy, but the centaur made it seem effortless. Next he looped the larger of her two bags over his left shoulder.

Galvin was mollified to see that Wynter was at least making her carry one bundle. The druid had learned at a very early age to carry only the bare necessities into the wilderness, as the extra weight only slowed him down. Brenna would have learned that lesson fast if the centaur hadn't agreed to help. Now she might never learn.

The druid shrugged and set off on the journey toward the First Escarpment. Wynter and Brenna fell in behind him. The druid knew it would take the trio most of the day to reach the imposing cliffs that placed Thay at a higher elevation than the surrounding countryside. Galvin decided to lead Wynter and Brenna north and east, following the River Umber, which would take them straight into Thay. It would be easier to travel along the river because water would be plentiful and the centaur was familiar with the territory. It was the route Wynter had taken when he had fled the country years ago.

As they traveled, the sun climbed and the trees thinned, giving way to a flat plain. Waist-high wild grain waved in the morning breeze and stretched invitingly to a thick stand of pines on the horizon. Galvin listened to the rhythmic swishing noise the grain made against Brenna's dress as the enchantress made her way through the field behind him. She was lagging behind, and the druid feared if she couldn't pick up the pace, it could take them twice as long to reach Thay.

The centaur moved effortlessly over the flat ground. He stretched his arms away from his body, nearly parallel to the earth, and threw his head back. Wynter relished the sun and the long hours he spent under its rays on his farm. The warmth felt invigorating on his tanned skin.

Wynter reached down and pulled loose a handful of the crop, examining the grain carefully. He decided it was a variety of wild wheat. He grew something similar to this, although it didn't grow this well. The centaur wondered why Aglarond hadn't built farms on this ground. The soil beneath his feet was certainly fertile; the wild grain seemed to thrive on it. Likely the nearness of Thay kept the farmers from settling it, he thought. The threat of the Red Wizards kept a lot of people from doing what they would like.

The River Umber rolled lazily through the plain, cutting a broad course into Aglarond. The Umber regularly overflowed its banks because of the Red Wizard's rain spells, helping to keep the area fertile. The centaur considered this the only good done by the Red Wizards. Before their interference, sages described this area as a savanna, windswept and subject to frequent droughts.

The trio followed a course nearly parallel to the river, staying well back from its muddy banks. Wynter could tell that the Umber was an old river, since it meandered like a boa constrictor, comfortable in its course. He knew when they came closer to Thay, its path would straighten. The waterfall that fell from the First Escarpment breathed new life into the aging river, giving it a quick, even current—at least for a number of miles.

Near midmorning, the fields ended at the edge of a pine grove. The tall branches provided enough shade to keep out the hottest of the sun's rays. Farther into the woods, the pines gave way to deciduous trees, mainly walnuts, hickories, and oaks. The travelers paused in the grove for more than an hour. The druid told Wynter the break was needed because Brenna was tiring. While that was true, his real reason was to rest his shoulder. He collected more herbs for another healing poultice and applied it while Wynter gathered a bag of nuts. Feeling much better, Galvin called an end to the break and resumed their trek.

The druid followed a path closer to the riverbank now, where the trees thinned and the land could be navigated more easily. For the next four hours, the councilwoman kept up surprisingly well, negotiating through tall weeds, wrestling with bushes that seemed to clutch at her dress, and slogging her way through wide patches of mud where the river had overflowed its bank and then receded. However, about midafternoon, when she was concentrating on the tricky footing in some muddy ground, she neglected to see a low-hanging branch. Wynter and Galvin had sidestepped it, but she walked right into it blindly, giving her head a good banging and somehow managing to fasten her braids securely to the thick foliage.

"Damn!" she cursed, dropping her satchel in a puddle and pulling with both hands to try to free her hair. "I hate this horrible, gods-forsaken place!" The Harpers turned to see one of her braids uncoil from around her head. It was still obstinately attached to the branch, and it looked like she was playing tug-o-war with the tree, using her hair for the rope. Galvin watched with amusement. She would eventually succeed, but the tree was putting up a good fight.

Wynter trotted to Brenna's side, holding the branch steady so she could tug the braid loose. Her fingers worked furiously, pulling and fraying the braid and angering her even more. Finally it came loose, and she stood red-faced next to her muddy bag, eyeing her mud-soaked hem.

"Damn!" she swore again, forgetting her cultivated manners and firmly swatting the tree branch.

"That's enough," the druid stated, walking toward Brenna and Wynter. "No need to take out your frustration on the tree."

"Oh, no?" she said sarcastically, batting at the branch again. "I'm tired, I'm wet, I'm dirty, and I look horrible." She struggled with the braid, trying to twine it back about her head, but the gold clasp used to fasten it was missing. "Damn!"

She moved to strike the branch a third time, but the druid's arm shot out and his hand closed firmly about her wrist.

"I said that's enough."

Brenna fumed and glared at Galvin. Wrenching her arm free, she fell to her knees and began feeling about among the ferns for the clasp.

"Let's move on," Galvin urged as he scanned the ground and spotted the glint of something metal—her hair clasp—in a puddle. "There it is. Grab it and let's get going."

The sorceress, still on her hands and knees, looked up at him haughtily, then glanced back down at the puddle. "You're so kind to help me find it," she said sarcastically.

"So uncommonly kind." She stretched forward and plunged her fingers into the puddle, retrieving the clasp, which was partly covered with mud. She tried to clean the clasp in the murky water, but the mud was lodged in the intricate filigree work and wouldn't wash out.

Wynter bent forward and offered her a hand to help her up. Ignoring it, she rose, then looked about for her satchel, which was sitting in another puddle. Picking up the bag, she swung it clumsily over her shoulder, causing mud to drip down her back and spray over Wynter's chest. Angry and puffing, she started to follow the bank to catch up to the druid.

Quickly reaching his side, she thrust out an arm and grabbed his shoulder. "We're stopping right here until I clean up," she said firmly. When he shook his head from side to side, she added, "You'll just have to wait for me. That's that."

Her ultimatum delivered, the councilwoman dropped her bag, stuffed her hair clasp in a pocket, and started toward the river.

The druid turned toward the centaur and grimaced. Galvin noticed that Wynter was keeping his distance from the woman. Safe, the druid observed, but the safe approach wasn't always the best—especially when he was in a hurry.

"We're not waiting," the druid said simply, expecting Brenna to accede to his decision. Instead, she ignored him and bent to unlace her boots. Determined, the druid strode purposely toward her.

"Galvin, don't . . ." the centaur began.

But the druid was not about to be slowed down by a pacifist centaur and a politician who was overly concerned about her appearance. In a handful of steps, Galvin reached Brenna before she could step out of her boots, grabbed her about the waist, and threw her over his good shoulder. She kicked and struggled, her fists beating futilely against his chest and her knees bludgeoning his back. She reminded the druid of a deer he had pulled out of a mud bog last month.

Galvin held her fast and resumed his trek along the bank of the river, wishing he would have grabbed her the other way so her face was behind him.

Wynter, slack-jawed at the performance, fell in behind them.

The sorceress continued to kick and squirm, even though she realized his strength would prevail. Furious, she tried another tactic. "Wynter, help me!" she gasped as she continued to pummel the druid's chest.

"Galvin," the centaur admonished. "Put her down."

The druid tarried only long enough to scowl at the centaur. Then he lengthened his stride. Wynter came alongside them on the side toward the stream, watching the river and avoiding Brenna's angry gaze.

"She's out of her element, Galvin," Wynter said softly, watching a large leaf swirl in the current, "but at least she's trying." He brushed the mud specks off his chest, then finally turned to glance at the sorceress. She groaned as one of her boots fell free and hit the ground behind her.

"I hate you!" she sputtered at Galvin.

Galvin ignored her and looked up at the centaur. "She's very trying. But at least this way we'll make better time."

An hour later they stopped to rest. Galvin dumped Brenna unceremoniously amidst a patch of tall grass. Wynter watched the sorceress right herself and sit cross-legged on the ground, fuming. She tried to pick the caked mud from her skirt hem. Her face was red from anger. She was exhausted from struggling with the pigheaded druid.

Brenna's limbs ached. Most of her exercise back in Aglarond had consisted of strolling from her home through the city streets to the council chambers or the wizards guild's library. She took a rented carriage to market and to various civic functions, and she was silently cursing herself now for being so out of shape physically. Being one of the youngest members of a council dominated by elves and half-elves, she had argued that she was the natural choice to travel cross-country with the Harper duo. She hadn't thought it would be so physically demanding. From her perspective, Galvin and Wynter looked the same as they had before the trip started, and that frustrated her all the more. No, Galvin looked even better, as his shoulder was healing.

The sorceress said nothing to them for quite a while, and although the druid usually enjoyed the quiet, he found this silence uncomfortable. He determined he had made a mistake in letting her come along in the first place and would rectify the situation now.

Trying to act civilized, he broke the silence. "Brenna," he began, "we can't turn back now, but if you don't think you can make it, I can leave you along the bank a few miles up the river." The druid knew where a stream branched off from the river there; merchants regularly traveled downstream to reach the villages to the south. He was certain the enchantress could arrange transportation with a passing merchant. The area was relatively free of large predators and should be safe. He guessed she wouldn't be on her own for more than a few hours.

"You're not leaving me behind!" she snapped. "I have to go to Thay. Thay is a threat to Aglarond. Not that you'd really care about that."

"I understand."

"I bet you do," she spat. "You spend your life in the woods trying to understand animals, not people."

"I understand Thay," Galvin answered, avoiding her eyes and leaning back on the grass to stare into the sky. The druid knew about the evil country because he had studied it, had questioned merchants journeying from the major Thayvian cities, and had spent long evenings with Wynter discussing the country's ills.

"I might as well be talking to a parrot. The conversation would be better." She stuck out her bottom lip and glared at the druid.

"The Harpers are interested in Thay, too," Wynter offered. "This mission is important to both our organization and Aglarond." The centaur looked at Galvin. "We should

let her in on the plan," Wynter advised. The druid continued to watch the sky, and the centaur took his lack of objec-
tion as agreement.

"We'll pose as Thayvians," Wynter began, noting that
Brenna seemed to be calming down a little. "Centaurs
walk freely in the streets of Thay, and humans are the dom-
inant race. We'll have no trouble."

"And?" Brenna was curious.

"Then we listen for rumors, study the current political
situation, and gather as much information as we can about
this Red Wizard Maligor or any other Red Wizard who
might make trouble against Aglarond. The more we learn,
the better the Harpers can deal with any threat."

"That's it? Just gather information?" The sorceress's ire
was rising again. "I thought we were going to *do* something."

"Getting information is doing something," Wynter countered. "The Harpers can't act in force unless we know
what we're up against."

"And you think posing as Thayvians will get us that information?" Brenna returned.

"Yes," the centaur stated. "We haven't been able to
learn much from outside Thay. Inside the country, posing
as Thayvians, it should be another matter. Of course," he
added softly, "spying is dangerous. If we're found out,
we'll likely be put to death."

The sorceress dug into her pocket to retrieve her gold
hair clasp and began picking the dirt out of it with her long
fingernails. "I know it's dangerous, but I'm doing it for my
home country." She glanced at the druid. "Look, Galvin,
you don't really have a home. I mean, you live in the
woods. It's not like feeling you're a part of a country. When
it comes right down to it, you're only responsible for yourself. But when you live around people, as I do, you feel
responsibility toward them."

"I have a home," Galvin said tersely. He propped himself
up on his elbows and frowned at Brenna. Standing up, he
brushed the dirt from his tunic. His home was the wilder-

ness of Faerun, and he considered himself the protector of the animals who lived in it.

"Fine. You have a home." Brenna ignored the centaur's gentle nudge, not sensing when to quit. "It's just that my home has lots of people—people who may be in grave danger." She paused to blow her hair away from her eyes. Several stubborn strands stuck to her sweat-stained forehead and she had to move them aside with her hand.

"Our country's history is wrapped up with the Red Wizards. We've battled them on and off for decades." She paused again, this time to untwine a braid and take another deep breath. Galvin had her started, and she wasn't going to stop until she finished her say or passed out from exhaustion.

"In the past when we've fought the wizards' forces, like in the battles of Singing Sands or Brokenheads, we were able to defeat them, but our casualties were high. Our ruler, the Simbul, doesn't want another war. Or if we must fight, she wants to know it's coming so we can be prepared."

The druid turned his back to Brenna and resumed his course along the riverbank. The centaur bent at the waist and extended a hand to help the councilwoman up. This time she took it.

"We're not making good enough time to reach the First Escarpment today," Wynter said. "We'll probably travel another couple of hours, then camp for the evening."

"We can make it. I'll walk faster," she volunteered, although she knew she had pushed herself hard already and would have trouble keeping up with only one boot.

The trio, with Brenna in the rear, continued along the bank. Close to the river, ancient willows, one with a trunk nearly as thick as Galvin was tall, dug their roots into the earth to drink thirstily from the river. Their long, whiplike branches danced in the breeze and swept the ground. Galvin carefully moved a few branches aside and disappeared under the largest willow's umbrellalike canopy.

Dozens of small yellow parrots perched in the giant tree

chittered excitedly. When Wynter and Brenna passed through the willow branches and emerged on the other side of the tree, they saw two of the birds sitting on the druid's shoulder. Galvin was several yards ahead, and he appeared to be talking to them. Wynter moved quietly toward the druid, but Brenna kept her distance.

She stared at Galvin as he chittered back at the birds. Finally curiosity got the better of her, and she took a step forward, her bare foot landing on a sharp rock. "Ouch!" she gasped, balancing herself on her booted foot. Standing on one leg, she pulled the other up in front of her, turning the bottom of her foot up so she could inspect it. Dirt clung to her heel and the ball of her foot, and blood flowed from a gash just behind her toes.

Some distance ahead, out of hearing distance, the centaur and druid conversed, oblivious to Brenna's discomfort.

"I don't want to get too close to Thay's border tonight anyway. We should camp a ways back from it," Wynter said. "At least one of the wizards uses patrols of undead."

Galvin shivered at the thought. "I prefer to deal with living creatures." He nodded in Brenna's direction and added, "But I'm not sure about that one."

"Good thing she's too far away to hear you," the centaur replied. "She's spunky, though. She'll make it. I just don't think she's used to this much walking. Maybe I should keep an eye on her."

"Are you coming?" Galvin yelled back to Brenna as the birds flew from his shoulder.

Brenna wiped the blood from the bottom of her foot with the hem of her dress and limped to catch up. The centaur fell back and matched Brenna's stride. He noticed she paused every few steps. She had pulled up the hem of her skirt and held it in her right hand, leaving her legs exposed from the knees down. It made for faster hiking, but her legs and one bare foot were getting scratched by the weeds and bushes.

"He's mad at me," she sputtered. "And he's just walking

fast to humiliate me." Brenna watched Galvin, noticing that he took long steps and didn't look down at the ground. Chipmunks, rabbits, and other small creatures accepted his presence, not bothering to run at his approach. But when she and the centaur came near the animals, they scattered into the dense foliage. The land reminded her of rain forests she had read about in Aglarond's libraries, and she suspected she would have enjoyed the scenery under different circumstances.

"If he likes animals so much, why does he have anything to do with the Harpers or anybody else?" She winced as a branch of a thorn bush grazed her calf, leaving a pink welt. Hiking with one booted foot and one bare foot was decidedly awkward. Bending over, she pulled her other boot free and hurried to keep pace with Wynter.

"The Harpers needed someone with his talents. He's been with them for quite a number of years, helping them with various problems in and around Thesk, Aglarond, Yuirwood, and the coast. He was even involved with the godswar a while ago."

Brenna lowered her voice so the druid couldn't hear. "What's so special about Galvin that the Harpers wanted him?"

The centaur frowned. "Remember, he's a druid, what some people call a nature priest. He has talents neither you nor I could fathom. And with the Harpers, he puts those talents to good use. Listen, it's simple. The Harpers are a diverse group of people. The organization's strength lies in its diversity. I didn't hear you asking me why I'm with them. I would think that to you I'd be more out of place in the Harpers than Galvin."

"No . . . you're different. You're . . ." For once, she was at an impasse for words.

"I'm Galvin's friend," Wynter finished. "He brought me into the Harpers." The centaur explained that several years ago a group of bandits were raiding farms. It was just after the farmers had taken their crops to market and had been paid in gold coins. The centaur's farm was among those hit, and he helped Galvin catch the thieves. After that, Wynter joined the Harpers. "I've no regrets," he concluded. "I still find time to tend my farm between Harper missions. And when I'm away, well, at least it gives the weeds an opportunity to grow."

"But what about your families?" Brenna brushed against the centaur to avoid another thorn bush. There seemed to be a growing number of the annoying plants. She noticed that while the trees remained thick, blotting out some of the sun, the ground cover seemed to be increasing.

Wynter smiled ruefully. "Galvin and I have no families. My relatives are in Thay. I haven't seen them since I was a child. As for Galvin, his parents were killed when he was young. He's been on his own—and alone—since then."

"How did his parents die?" she persisted, puffing to keep up and hopping to avoid rocks and thorns.

"It was . . . an accident," he said, continuing to plod forward, staring at the horizon. Through an opening in the vine-covered trees, he thought he caught a glimpse of the First Escarpment. Galvin had told Wynter about his parents stealing something from an ambassador—a Thayvian ambassador. Even though the stolen items were returned, the ambassador demanded their deaths and their property. The ambassador's wishes were fulfilled, and Galvin grew up hating Thay and civilization in general.

"So he's not married," Brenna mused. "But he's got the Harpers."

"He has some friends in the Harpers," Wynter admitted, "But few of them are really close. Basically he's a loner."

"What if I wanted to join the Harpers?" Brenna asked. Her voice was somewhat muffled, since her head was directed at the ground to avoid obstacles.

"That depends on you," Wynter replied, speeding up his pace. "It depends on how much time and effort you're willing to sacrifice. It depends on whether you're willing to put your life on hold and on the line for whatever cause might come up."

"Are there any politicians in the Harpers?"

"Sure."

"Who? Name some," she encouraged.

"I can't do that," Wynter stated flatly. "We're a secret organization, remember. Part of our strength lies in our anonymity."

For the next hour, the pair fell into silence, and the gap widened between Brenna and Wynter and Galvin, who was several hundred yards ahead of them. At times they lost sight of Galvin in the trees, and the sorceress struggled to close the distance, knowing the centaur was lagging behind with her out of courtesy. Her feet burned, and it took considerable effort to keep going. She yearned to stop to rest and tend to the blisters on her feet.

Eventually she and Wynter lost sight of Galvin altogether, and she was worried they had become lost. However, the centaur concentrated on the ground, spotting signs of the druid's passage here and there and assuring her they were on course. The centaur tried to increase the pace, but Brenna could move no faster.

"He won't let himself get too far ahead of us," Wynter offered.

"Shhh! Listen," Brenna whispered.

"I don't hear anything."

"That's just it," she said, her voice barely audible. "No birds . . . nothing."

The flora had remained as lush as when they first entered the woods many hours ago, but now there were no parrots, chipmunks, or other signs of life. Only a few miles ago there had been so many colorful birds that they looked like flowers on the trees. Straining her eyes, she couldn't spot even one.

Ahead, she and Wynter saw Galvin step out from behind a tree and motion them to stop. The druid placed his palms against the trunk of a willow and closed his eyes. He laid the side of his head against the bark.

"What's he doing?" Brenna asked, puzzled.

"He's talking to the tree," Wynter explained.

"Yeah, sure he is," the enchantress retorted sarcastically. But she was glad for the opportunity to stay put. Her side was aching from hiking so long, her feet felt as if they were on fire, and she welcomed the rest.

After several minutes, the druid stepped back from the tree, opened his eyes, and started back toward the centaur and Brenna. He appeared drained, Brenna noted, while a short time ago he had seemed reasonably fresh and energetic.

"We'll camp over there," he said, pointing at a patch of ground near the willow. Thorn bushes were still plentiful, but there was enough space between them to accommodate the three travelers.

A rush of relief washed over Brenna. She prayed the trip tomorrow wouldn't be as long; if it was, she'd never be able to make it. She didn't believe she could take another step without shoes. As she looked for a spot relatively free of thorn bushes, she listened to Galvin and Wynter.

"Mushrooms and nuts—for dinner?" the centaur complained.

"There aren't many animals around here."

Wynter grumbled. "Even the animals know it's not safe this near Thay, eh?"

Wynter glanced at Brenna and dropped her rolled-up tent and bag at her feet. She considered the tent, and for a moment she thought about unrolling it, setting it up, and crawling inside. But only for a moment. Instead, she dropped to all fours, slumped to her stomach, placed her head on the canvas, and immediately fell fast asleep.

Brenna woke shortly after dawn to the smell of something cooking. The land was bathed in a thick fog, and through it, she saw Wynter standing before a small fire turning on a makeshift spit what looked like the leg of a deer. Nearby, Galvin was rubbing something into a piece of hide. The young councilwoman struggled to a sitting position. Her legs ached and felt like lead, and her neck was stiff from sleeping at such an awkward angle.

However, she refused to appear beaten. Standing and smiling weakly, she greeted her companions good morning, grabbed the smaller of her bags, and looked around. It was so foggy she had to ask the druid directions to the river, which she was surprised to hear was only a few yards away. She returned about half an hour later, feeling her way through the fog and wearing a new dress, which was beige and decorated with tiny pink flowers. It was no more practical than the ruined blue one she tossed on top of her tent.

"Well, shall we be moving on?" she inquired, feigning being chipper, rested, and ready to go. It was a good performance, she decided. Actually she felt like curling up in a ball and sleeping for a month. Still carrying her bag, she cocked her head in the direction of the First Escarpment.

"Put these on first," Galvin instructed, tossing a pair of hide moccasins in her direction—the hide he had been working on. "Antelope skin. It's thick enough to be comfortable and provide some protection."

The sorceress dropped to the ground and gratefully pulled on the moccasins. She cast a glance in the druid's direction, wondering if he had killed the antelope in order to make the moccasins.

The druid kicked dirt over the flames to douse them while the centaur packed a large chunk of roast antelope into his bag. Then Galvin started toward the escarpment, and Wynter bent to pick up Brenna's tent and larger bag.

"Just the bag," she said, not wanting to bother the centaur with something she wouldn't have the energy to unwrap. "Leave the tent behind. Sleeping under the stars is just fine."

The morning fog hung low to the ground and extended upward about fifteen feet. The thick haze looked ghostlike, giving the woods a haunted appearance. Even Galvin had difficulty moving through it, since it cut visibility to only a few feet. The druid wended his way slowly through the trees with one arm extended in front of him and the other off to the side. He looked like a blind man feeling for obstacles. The thorn bushes tore at his leggings, and he tried to push the treacherous branches aside so they wouldn't prick Wynter and Brenna.

As the sun rose higher in the sky, it burned off most of the fog, revealing the brilliant jade and emerald hues of the large-leafed trees that dominated this section of the woods.

Pressing closer toward the escarpment, they heard the pounding rush of water. Emerging from the edge of the woods shortly after noon, they saw the magnificent falls that cascaded nearly three hundred feet down the First Escarpment and roared into the river. The moisture at the base of the falls looked iridescent, creating a miniature rainbow.

"It's—it's beautiful," Brenna gasped, trying to take everything in.

"I've never seen anying more spectacular," Wynter admitted. "But it's sad to think such loveliness marks the boundary of Thay."

"How do we get up?" Brenna asked, still not taking her eyes from the falls. The escarpment looked imposing. Its rocky face ran nearly perpendicular to the ground, and the sorceress couldn't help herself from looking at the steep cliff in awe.

Layer upon layer of limestone and granite formed the escarpment, the varying bands of rocks looking like orange, tan, and white ribbons. In places, rocks jutted out at odd angles like daggers pointed toward Aglarond. At intervals, lone, stunted trees struggled to survive on thin, rocky ledges. The escarpment stretched from one horizon to the other. Brenna saw no way up or around the rocky barrier.

"There's a main road that cuts through the cliffs south of the river, but we can't take that route. It's guarded closely. But don't worry, we'll find a way." Wynter knew there were other roads and trails that led up the First Escarpment; they were used by slavers, merchants, and other travelers moving in and out of Thay for various reasons. But there were patrols stationed along every one, and only those travelers with the right reasons for coming into or leaving the country were allowed to pass.

Galvin kept just inside the tree line, safe from prying

eyes, and started searching to the north. Wynter and Brenna plodded along behind him. The trio scrutinized the base of the escarpment as they moved but saw only sheer, jagged rocks.

"When I was young, my father would take me to the top of the cliffs," Wynter reminisced. "He'd tell me how grand Thay was, how it sat above the rest of the world because all other countries were beneath it."

"Your father?" Brenna asked, pleased to at last hear something about the centaur's past.

Wynter's eyes looked sad and distant. "My father worked on one of the largest slave plantations in Thay. His dream was to run the plantation. He certainly had the temperament for it. He had no qualms about beating slaves or killing those too ill or old to work. I couldn't stomach watching my father flay the skin off some poor soul's back. I tried to change things, but my family was set in their ways. They believed in slavery, and they weren't going to listen to a child. I left when I was twelve. That was more than a decade ago."

Wynter clenched his fists and stared at the cliffs. He had promised himself he would never return to his homeland. He was wishing now that he had kept that promise.

"Let's try farther north," Wynter suggested. "I remember some places where the cliff isn't quite as steep. Slaves used to try to escape down the escarpment there."

"Did any of them ever make it?" Brenna queried.

"A few, probably, though I doubt many did. At least when I lived with my father, I don't remember any being so lucky. They usually killed the slaves they caught trying to escape." Wynter's tone was solemn, and his expression was troubled from talking about the slaves. His hands shook visibly. "But they didn't kill the strongest slaves. Instead, they beat them into submission. Strong slaves are treasured."

Finally they reached a place where the escarpment was not so imposing, although it still stretched more than a hundred feet into the sky. The sun had already begun to set, blazing an orange haze across the top of the cliff so it looked like burnished gold.

"This will have to do, eh?" Wynter said, inspecting the rocky surface.

Galvin examined the slope carefully. Though it was less steep than it was farther to the south, he knew it would still give the centaur difficulty. For a moment, he pondered searching for a better place to enter Thay. After several minutes, he decided on a different alternative.

"Give me a moment, Wyn," he directed as he started up the cliff. The druid was as agile as a monkey, yet displayed more grace. He easily found handholds and footholds and hauled himself up the cliff until he reached a steep section where he doubted the centaur could pass. Then he reached out with his hands and touched the steep rock face.

Below, Brenna watched in amazement as Galvin seemed to work the rock like clay, shaping it into natural, low steps. It was druidic magic Galvin channeled to shape the stone, sculpting it to fit his mental picture. Finished, he scrambled up the remainder of the cliff, his long blond hair flying behind him, turning gold in the rays of the setting sun. Finally he crouched at the top like a mountain lion, surveying his companions below and then glancing around behind him to make sure he was alone. Satisfied, he motioned Wynter up.

The centaur pushed upward with his muscular rear legs and angled the human half of his body forward as he propelled himself up the cliff. Bits of rock flew away from his hooves and rolled down the cliff face in his wake. Brenna had to step back to avoid being pelted. Near the top, the centaur's momentum slowed, but his four legs continued to pump to keep him from rolling down to the ground below. Brenna feared he would slip and come hurtling to his death in front of her, but at last he made it, breathless, sweating, and showering dirt over the edge of the cliff as he cleared the top.

A minute later the druid threw a long rope over the side. The sorceress assumed he had been carrying it in his satchel. It wasn't long enough to reach the bottom of the cliff, however. Its end flapped about twenty feet from the ground. But the climbing was easier toward the base of the cliff, and Brenna had little difficulty scaling the rocks on the lower part of the slope. When she reached the rope, Galvin indicated with his hands how she should tie it about her, then motioned for her to use her feet against the rock, as if she was climbing it.

The sorceress followed his instructions, although she considered using her own kind of magic, such as casting a spell to levitate to reach the top of the cliff. It would have been easier, and it likely would have kept her dress in better shape.

At the top of the First Escarpment, the trio turned to gaze into Thay's interior. They stood near a wooded area, but the trees were cultivated, planted in evenly spaced rows, and each one was shaped by careful pruning. The trees were laden with citrus, yellow and orange fruits that looked ripe and inviting in the sun's dying rays. Thay was known for its fabulous fruits, born of the wizards' weather control spells and tended laboriously by slaves.

"I don't remember the orchards being heavily guarded at night," Wynter said. "Of course, as a child I never paid a lot of attention to the guards. Beyond the orchard, we'll likely find a road. We'll have to get our bearings to determine our route to Amruthar."

The centaur took a last glance at Aglarond below. Then he said softly, "Let's get away from the cliff edge. Patrols march along the escarpment all through the night."

"Agreed," the druid said, staring into the setting sun. He thought that perhaps Wynter was right—the wizards liked their foul country because it rose above the surrounding land, placing them on a sort of earthen pedestal. Galvin knew they considered themselves superior to all other occupants of Faerun.

Galvin shook his head to whip his long hair away from his face and began to trot toward the trees. Wynter and Brenna followed close behind. The sorceress shivered. It was one thing to talk about coming into Thay on some grand spying mission for the good of her country, but it was quite another thing to actually be here.

What little she had seen of the land so far didn't look particularly hostile. Indeed, the grove before her was more beautiful than any orchard in Aglarond or Mulhorand, which she had occasion to visit on council business. But she knew this country had no natural right to be so verdant. From its location and prevailing weather patterns, it should be dry and plagued by frequent droughts. She also knew it was perhaps the most evil place in all this part of Faerun, and it was drenched in magic. Suddenly her own magic seemed insignificant.

It felt cool in the orchard. The shadows from the trees were lengthening as the sun continued to slip below the horizon. Galvin estimated they would have another half-hour of twilight, and they would have to make their way through the orchard in that time. Wynter explained that the bulk of the slave crews started work at dawn, sometimes earlier, and it wouldn't be wise to be caught here then. Most slaves had no compunction about turning in trespassers or Thayvians discovered in the wrong territory. Such discoveries often resulted in the slaves being rewarded.

They were nearly through the orchard when the sun disappeared on the horizon and the sky turned a darker blue. In another half-hour, perhaps not even that long, the sky would be totally black. Brenna began to worry that they might become lost in the hostile country.

Just then a sharp cry cut through her thoughts and rooted the Harpers in place.

"You! Intruders! Stop and surrender!" a disheveled figure stepped out from the shadow of a large citrus tree, surprising the trio.

Brenna and Wynter had difficulty noticing any details, but Galvin's acute eyes picked out a half-dozen more shapes behind the first figure. Their discoverer was human and was evidently in charge of the group; those in the shadows

were orcs, pig-faced sentries who were more monster
than man.

Galvin smelled their offensive odors and noted that they
wore crude uniforms similar to the one worn by the gnoll
he had killed, yet different enough to indicate they served
another master.

"There are seven of them," Galvin whispered.

"What did you say? Speak up, trespasser!" the human
called.

Quick to realize that they faced an orchard patrol, Wynter trotted forward, roughly pushing Galvin out of the way
and knocking the druid to the ground. Galvin's rump stung,
and he started to get up.

"We're no intruders," the centaur said sternly, planting
the tip of his thick staff on Galvin's chest to keep the druid
from moving. "I work at the slave plantation near Thaymount, and I'm returning these runaways." He curled his
lip when he glanced at Brenna and waved his arm indicating
she should move near Galvin. She complied, cowering visibly.

The man came closer, motioning his orc charges to join
him. "You're a long way from Thaymount, centaur. Your
plantation workers were lax to let a pair of slaves get this
far."

"They're a tricky pair, these two," Wynter said. Then he
thumped Galvin with the end of his staff and ordered him to
get up. The druid stood next to Brenna and cast his eyes at
the ground sullenly. Brenna copied him.

"These two escaped many days ago," Wynter continued.
"I was sent to retrieve them, and if I didn't find them, I
was told not to come back. It wasn't hard to follow them.
The clumsy fools don't know how to cover their tracks."
He smiled at the sentry.

Wynter reached out with his free hand and yanked Brenna's hair to pull her closer to him. She yelped in surprise
and pain. "I would've killed them, but the boss wouldn't
have stood for it. No. Not at all." He yanked on Brenna's
hair again until she cried out. "She's been around awhile.

Him, too. Look at the hair. It would have been my mane if they'd gotten killed."

The patrol leader grinned, showing a row of dirty broken teeth; the front two were missing. Despite his poor appearance, Wynter guessed he was probably an able fighter. He was muscular, the sleeves of his uniform fitting snugly over the large biceps beneath. A longsword hung in a tooled leather scabbard on his right side, while a broadsword hung on his left. Half a dozen daggers were strapped to his chest. The orcs behind him each carried two weapons.

"So . . . they're special slaves," the sentry observed, his attention obviously directed at Brenna. "Why don't you let me see just how special the female is. Then I'll let you pass through the orchard. No problems."

"I couldn't do that," Wynter retorted, pulling Brenna closer to him. "This pair is prime breeding stock. You'd better let us pass. I'm not looking for any trouble."

The man motioned his orcs to remain still. "Breeding stock? A wizard's stock?"

"Yeah," Wynter replied. "They belong to a zulkir. Do you want me to say his name nice and loud, just in case he might be listening?"

"No," the man growled morosely. "You can go."

He waved a thick arm forward, and Wynter proceeded. Brenna stuck close to his side, and Galvin walked a few paces in front, prodded along by the centaur's staff. The three were relieved that the ruse had worked, but their optimism was crushed when one of the orcs shouted, "Weapon, boss! Slave weapon!"

The speech was crude, but the trio knew the meaning. The patrol had spotted Galvin's scimitar. All eyes had been on Brenna before, which is likely why they had gotten this far.

"Run!" Galvin ordered, but Wynter and Brenna were already in full stride.

The sorceress was lagging behind, however. The day's journey and the climb up the cliff had already taxed her to her limits. Wynter doubled back to get her.

"Help her up on my back!" Wynter yelled to Galvin.

"No time," Galvin replied, positioning himself between the centaur, Brenna, and the oncoming orcs. "They're on us." The druid drew his scimitar and squinted his eyes, reaching out with his mind to the citrus trees.

The screaming orcs, led by their angry leader, closed fast, and the druid could smell the dried sweat on their grotesque bodies. Their lips curled back in a hyenalike snarl as they chanted for the trespassers' blood.

Galvin continued to concentrate on the trees, and in response, the branches snaked forward like striking snakes to entangle the orcs. The limbs whipped around the orcs' flailing arms and legs, holding them fast and hoisting them several feet above the ground.

The lead sentry struggled and barked a few orders in the orcish tongue, but his charges were slow to respond, looking astonished at the branches that were like ropes about their limbs.

Brenna took advantage of the situation to begin a spell. Her singsong chant was uneven because she was out of breath. Still she persevered, padding through the grass toward the entangled guards as she continued to murmur the arcane words. When she stood in front of the sentry, she finished the incantation. His struggles stopped, and he stared at her with wide, attentive eyes.

"I've bewitched him," she announced over her shoulder to the Harpers. "He'll be mine for several days, but now that I have him, I'm not so sure what to do with him."

"He can be our guide," Wynter answered. "Can you make him lead us?"

"Sure," Brenna said. "I could even make him cook for us and polish your hooves if you want. What about the orcs?"

"The entanglement won't last much longer," Galvin said, a touch of concern in his voice. The orcs had begun to strain against the branches. "Do you have something else—some spell to keep them quiet about all of this?"

The enchantress smiled broadly, pleased to have Galvin

ask her for help. She searched through a small pouch at her side, gathering more spell components.

"I can try to make them forget about us, but I'm not sure it will work. They seem rather dense. But I'll do what I can." She breathed deeply and began another enchantment. Between phrases, she thought she heard the druid say, "Thanks."

When she finished, she returned to the Harpers and her charmed friend. "We'd better get out of here," she suggested, "just in case it didn't work."

Wynter fell in behind Galvin, Brenna, and their newfound guide. The centaur's legs felt weak; he suspected it was nerves. He continued to remind himself how much he hated this country as they proceeded to move deeper into Thay.

Five

Two levels above his sorcerous army, Maligor paced in front of a cell door. The Red Wizard was tired, having just completed a series of spells that added a hundred more darkenbeasts to his forces. His exhaustion left him with little stomach for this place. The corridor stank of urine and sweat. The eight cells in this area were rarely cleaned, and they were almost always occupied. The wizard was constantly displeased with enough slaves, soldiers, and townspeople to keep them full. The horrible conditions kept the prisoners dispirited and easy to handle, and diseaseS usually kept the place from becoming too overcrowded.

Sometimes Maligor elected not to feed the occupants for a week or longer, leaving the corpses of those who starved to rot in the cells with the survivors. And when prisoners were tortured, it was prolonged and in full presence of the others. Maligor enjoyed watching the contorted faces of the captives as one of their kind was whipped and gutted in their full view.

But the prisoner beyond this cell door was different. He had been brought here only a few hours ago, not to be punished, but to reveal information Maligor considered crucial to his plans.

Maligor continued to pace in front of the cell until he heard through the door the clinking of chains and the scratching noise a key makes as it turns in a lock. Confident the two gnoll guards had secured the "guest," he raised his robe to his ankles and extended one slippered foot to prod the cell door open. He entered cautiously to make sure his expensive clothes didn't brush against the filth on the door, then stepped down carefully into the cell chamber. When his eyes adjusted to the gloom within—the room was lit with a small, oil-burning lantern—he saw his guest chained to the far wall.

The man was squat, but he had a broad, sturdy frame and a barrel-like chest. Maligor saw the cuts and bruises on the man's body and imagined he must have put up a substantial struggle to avoid being captured. His head hung limply forward against his chest; the gnolls had probably pummeled him into unconsciousness, the wizard mused. At least the guest didn't seem to be seriously injured.

The man was bald, and his head sported a design—a pale orange, four-taloned hand, indicating that he was a worshiper of Malar, the Beastlord, one of the commonly worshiped deities in Thay. Maligor himself favored Myrkul, whom the Red Wizard considered a far superior power and whom he honored with the permanent tattoo of Myrkul's symbol on the center of his forehead.

Maligor doubted his visitor's loyalty to Malar, since the man's symbol was painted rather than permanent. It had begun to fade from the rivulets of sweat that ran down his brow. The other symbols on the man's head were already obscured. The Red Wizard scowled in frustration; much could be learned about a Thayvian's beliefs and politics from studying the symbols on his head. The man's clothes were well made and in good repair, but they were dirty, covered with dust and powdered rock. In the soft glow of the lantern light, the powder gleamed, making the Red

Wizard's eyes widen and twinkle in response.

"Rouse him," the Red Wizard ordered.

The gnolls were quick to comply, shaking the man and splashing water on his face from the leather flask that hung at the man's side. The guards were among the largest gnolls Maligor had at his disposal, each a little more than eight feet tall. Looking like the offspring of a canine and a human, the gnolls' dark fur blended in with the cell's shadowy decor. Their small, shiny eyes glared out from above their hyena-shaped muzzles, and they lolled out their tongues, waiting for their master's next command.

Gradually the man's eyes came open, and he raised his head to stare at the gnolls' evil visages. Tilting his head to avoid their foul breath, he glared straight into the wizard's face.

"Zulkir Maligor!" the man gasped. "I am not under your personal command! I have done nothing to offend you. By what right did you bring me here? The Council of Zulkirs will be furious when they learn what you have done!"

Maligor's lips produced a thin, evil grin that quickly silenced the frightened man.

"The council isn't going to know," the Red Wizard replied menacingly. "I'm no fool. This dungeon is fully protected from the prying eyes of other wizards." He leveled his gaze on the man, who had begun to sweat even more profusely.

"Willeth Lionson," Maligor stated, finally addressing the man by his name. "Tharchion Willeth Lionson." The Red Wizard didn't know the man personally, but he knew much about him. Being on the Council of Zulkirs, Maligor had helped select Willeth to oversee Thay's gold mines. The Tharchion was accountable to the council and had allegiances to no individual Red Wizard.

"Tharchions do not just disappear!" Willeth sputtered. "The other wizards on the council will miss me. You can't get away with this, Maligor! Release me at once!"

"No one is going to miss you," Maligor countered. "You were expected to be away from the mines, remember, Willeth? You told the council you were leaving today for Tantras to look at some new mining equipment. Your dedication to improving the productivity of the mines has left me the opening I have been waiting for. And I have been waiting for a very long time."

"No! I have friends, guards. They will wonder where I am."

"It's unfortunate—for you—that you were lax today, leaving the mine without being accompanied by extra guards. The few guards you took were easily overcome by my gnolls."

Willeth strained against his chains, but they were anchored solidly to the wall. "I have other guards!" he screeched. "The guards who were to take me to Tantras."

"The guards who were to accompany you to Tantras have been killed," Maligor said calmly. "You have many guards, Willeth. The few I ordered dispatched will not be missed. Nor will you, Willeth."

The tharchion pulled at the chains again to show his defiance, and the gnoll guards snarled. "You can't win, Maligor! If you return me to the mines, you know I'll tell the council about this. And if you keep me from returning, they'll find out. I'm in charge of the mines! You may be one of the most powerful Red Wizards, but the rest of the council is strong enough to challenge you. Szass Tam—"

"The Zulkir Szass Tam will never know," Maligor interrupted. "Willeth Lionson will return from Tantras in less than two weeks, reporting to the council that the equipment should not be purchased, since it is inferior. Then Willeth Lionson will go about his business directing operations at the mine. Unfortunately, that Willeth Lionson won't be you. You'll have to stay here."

Maligor flicked his wrist and a gnoll guard slammed his fist into Willeth's stomach. The tharchion let out a rush of air and doubled over as much as the chains allowed.

"I advise you to cooperate," Maligor instructed. "Otherwise, your dying could take a seriously long while and be excruciatingly painful."

The tharchion raised his head and glared at the zulkir. "The foul ones take you to the scum-filled belly of the underworld!" he cursed. "You'll gain nothing from me. Nothing!"

"Dear Willeth, I do admire your resolve. The council chose well when they selected you. But I am low on patience today." He nodded to the gnoll guards, and in unison their large, hairy fists smashed into Willeth's chest. They repeated their blows until Maligor heard the soft crunch of ribs. Then the wizard motioned for the gnolls to stop.

"I want to know about the gold mines, Willeth. How many slaves work there? How strong is the guard force? How many foremen? Where and what are the magical defenses?"

The Red Wizard knew all the information he wanted was spread out among the members of the Council of Zulkirs. That was so no one wizard would know too much and become tempted to take over the mines. But Willeth was the one single person who harbored most of that information, and Maligor intended to extract it from him.

"Talk to me!" Maligor persisted.

Willeth coughed, and saliva and blood trickled from his mouth. "I don't know all of the magical defenses. I intentionally kept myself ignorant of such things to prevent something like this from happening. And even if I told you what I know, the Council of Zulkirs would stop you. They'd see you gathering your gnolls to march on the mine. They'd join forces if they had to—just to stop you!" He coughed again and Maligor beamed.

"You are indeed a simpleton, Willeth. Yes, I am gathering my gnolls. I have been for weeks—three garrisons, one in the city and two nearby. But they won't be attacking the mines." Maligor paced in front of the man.

"My sweet associate Asp—you wouldn't know her, but she will soon know your mines intimately—is in charge of drilling my gnolls. That is no doubt drawing the attention of nearby wizards, including the council. The gnolls are practicing long and hard, thinking they will be marching against another Red Wizard. Asp thinks so, too." Maligor laughed, a throaty chuckle that echoed off the cell walls.

"Maybe I actually will have to select a Red Wizard some-where to attack, or perhaps some stuffy baron who offend-ed me years ago. After all, I shouldn't waste my gnolls' training. Nor should I disappoint the Red Wizards who will be looking for me to do something. Do you have any sug-gestions? Anyone in Thay you particularly dislike?"

"You—you wretched, evil dog!" Willeth was trying to goad Maligor. The tharchion, who was in agony, considered himself a dead man now, and he hoped the wizard would get angry enough to kill him before gaining any information about the mines. "You are . . . not fit to . . . walk on Thay-vian soil! You are—"

"Tsk, tsk, Willeth," Maligor said. His tone was conde-scending, like a teacher lecturing a misbehaving child. "I'm no more evil than the rest of the wizards . . . just a little smarter, perhaps. And insulting me won't help your condi-tion."

Willeth's chest heaved. It was getting difficult for the tharchion to breathe. He wondered if his shattered ribs were poking into his insides. He decided to get the wizard to keep talking, hoping he would be dead by the time Mali-gor finished his crazed discourse. "If you . . . take your gnolls . . . to attack someone else . . . how will you . . . get the mines?"

"I have power and forces you could only dream of," the Red Wizard said evenly. "My gnolls are numerous, one of the grandest armies in Thay. It is probably only because of their great numbers that Szass Tam or another Red Wizard hasn't already attacked me. But my gnolls are nothing. My true army is much stronger, and it is that army that will seize the mines for me."

"And if you . . . do take the mines?" Willeth posed, his breathing becoming shallower still.

"*When* I take them," Maligor corrected.

"When you . . . take the mines . . . the other Red Wiz-ards will band together . . . and seize them back from you.

No one Red Wizard . . . has the power to hold the mines."

"Willeth, you do count me for a fool. My plan is so intricate and sublime that no one will even know I control the mines." Maligor looked at the puzzled expression on the tharchion's face. "The precious flow of gold to the country won't stop, at least not for a few years. You still don't understand, do you? And I can see that I don't have the time to explain it to you. My gnolls struck you too severely. I fear you haven't long to live."

The Red Wizard stopped his pacing and moved closer to his captive, just far enough away so the man's chained arms couldn't reach him. "So you'll have to talk now—quickly. Tell me about the mine's defenses."

"Go to . . . the underworld!" Willeth spat.

The gnolls moved to strike the tharchion, but Maligor held them back with a glance. The Red Wizard mumbled something Willeth could not understand. It was magic, the tharchion knew, as Maligor's hands began to glow, radiating a soft, pink haze that stretched in rays from his fingers to Willeth's eyes.

"You will beat me to the underworld, tharchion," Maligor said, his voice a singsong chant that mesmerized Willeth. "But before you go, you will be my friend. My closest, dearest friend. Friends share secrets, Willeth. I am your very best friend, and you will share all of your secrets with me. Tell me about the mine, friend Willeth. I want to visit the mine. And since I'm your friend, you wouldn't want me to get hurt there, would you? Tell me about the defenses—where the magical traps and spells are placed. I mustn't get hurt, friend Willeth."

The tharchion's eyes glazed over, and the pupils became small and fixed. "My friend," he croaked. "Can't let . . . my friend be hurt . . . when he comes to visit me in the mines. Be careful, friend, the mines . . . are very dangerous if you do not know where to walk."

Then the words began to pour from Willeth's bleeding lips, detailed summaries of the spells and creatures that protected the mine, facts about the number of guards and their weapons, and descriptions of the foremen who directed the slaves and other workers. Deep in his mind the tharchion screamed, rebelling against what he was helpless to stop. But still the words continued to pour forth, and part of Willeth was happy. It was such a good thing to help a dear comrade.

"I need to know more, friend," Maligor purred. "You know so much about the mines, and I'm so very proud of you for that. No one knows more about the mines than you do. Tell me how much gold is mined each day. Where are the strongest veins? Only you can tell me these things, my friend. Only you know so much."

Willeth babbled on, reciting production figures, quality of the veins, the expected life of various tunnels, and the names of the foremen who shared some of that information. Maligor memorized everything the tharchion said, filing the statistics away for later use.

Then Willeth divulged something unexpected. The tharchion wanted to please his friend, and he hoped this tidbit would make Maligor particularly happy.

"Today," Willeth began, his voice showing as much enthusiasm as his dying body would permit, "a foreman took a slave force . . . to the deepest part of a tunnel that we thought was mined out. The force . . . was to close the tunnel, but then the strangest . . . and most wonderful thing happened. A portion of the mines collapsed. A dozen slaves were . . . killed in the process, but we had used . . . the most expendable slaves for the task. And when the dust cleared . . . a cavern was revealed. It was an underground cave, and the walls glistened. See the gold powder on my clothes? It came from there. We found a new vein . . . bigger than any previously discovered. I was saving the information, friend. I was . . . going to tell the council about it when I returned from Tantras . . . with a request to buy equipment. I thought . . . the wizards . . . would let me buy new mining equipment then."

Willeth sobbed and more blood rushed from his mouth before he continued. "I'm not . . . going to be able to tell them now. I know I'm dying. Could you . . . tell them, friend?"

"Of course," Maligor lied. "Friends always help each other. But I have one other thing to ask you, my very best friend." He motioned for the gnolls to unchain Willeth and ease him to the floor. Maligor reached into a deep pocket of his robe and drew out a rolled-up piece of beige parchment and a hunk of charcoal.

"Please, friend, draw a map of your mine. Only you could draw such a thing. Don't forget to include that new cave. And please hurry."

Willeth fell to the task. The Red Wizard moved the lantern closer to provide better light. The map was crude, as the tharchion's hand shook terribly, and the parchment became spotted with blood. It took Willeth several minutes to complete the rough drawing. Then, before Maligor could take it away from him, Willeth added X's to indicate traps and magical defenses.

"You've done very well, my friend," Maligor said in soothing tones that relaxed Willeth. "This is a fine map. It will help me to find my way about in your wonderful mines."

Willeth coughed, and Maligor noted a flowering splotch of blood on the tharchion's chest. The man looked up at the wizard with a pained expression on his face.

"The pain . . . Help me . . . please."

"Of course, friend," Maligor said. He reached down and grabbed the map and the lantern, then stepped to the doorway. He turned to address the two gnolls.

"Are you hungry? Eat him."

Moments later, Maligor paced in the hallway, waiting for his gnolls to finish. The Red Wizard was satisfied. If other zulkirs tried to contact Willeth while he was supposedly in Tantras or became suspicious of the Willeth Lionson who would address the council in two weeks, nothing would be learned. It was possible to contact the dead or locate bodies through special enchantments. Szass Tam knew such spells and likely would try to employ them if the new Willeth Lionson did not meet with his acceptance and the lich guessed the true Willeth was dead.

But it will soon be impossible for those necromantic enchantments to yield any valuable information, Maligor mused. The Red Wizard knew the necessary spells required a body—or at least a significant portion of one—and he had no intention of leaving behind enough remains to fuel such spells.

The council will have no choice but to accept the new Willeth, Maligor concluded. And the new Willeth will be cloaked with enough protective spells to pass any cursory inspections.

The crude stomping of the gnolls leaving the cell disturbed Maligor's musings. The sated guards grinned at him.

The Red Wizard ordered the gnolls to gather Willeth's bones, clothes, and boots into a canvas sack. These were seasoned guards and knew enough to comply with Maligor's orders with alacrity. But they were not without curiosity.

"Gnoll troops," one of them began, addressing the Red Wizard but showing enough respect not to meet Maligor's gaze. "Gnoll troops practice but not fight? Not fight for mines?"

Maligor's eyes narrowed. He had erred in keeping two of his best guards in this cell. Slaves were easy to replace, and he had plenty of gnolls, but gnolls weren't easy to educate for special tasks such as guard work. Now he would have to order at least two more trained; these two had just become expendable.

"Gnolls not good enough?" the curious guard pressed, shaking the bag containing Willeth's remains. "Gnolls good warriors. Gnolls could fight for mines. Gnolls brave fighters."

"Of course they are," Maligor said unctuously, "and you are the bravest among them. That is why I selected you as my personal tower guards."

"Then why do gnolls train?" The gnoll was too inquisitive and obviously wouldn't stop the questions until Maligor supplied some answers. This gnoll had been with the wizard several years and did not fear retribution for a few simple and direct questions.

"The gnoll forces will fight," Maligor replied. "I just haven't decided what. You see, the other Red Wizards will be watching the gnoll army. And they'll keep their eyes on the gnolls wherever they march. That army is very important, and may well have to fight armies the other wizards send against it. But while that army is marching, another army, a very different army, will go to the mines. The Red Wizards won't be expecting that and probably won't notice. They must not notice. So you see, my dear friends, my very best friends, the gnoll army is very important indeed."

The two gnolls looked up at Maligor, their eyes filled with a pink haze, identical to the haze around the wizard's hands.

"Friend Maligor," the curious gnoll stated. "Friend Maligor knows gnolls important."

"Slaves tonight?" the other gnoll asked. "We get girl slaves tonight? We helped friend Maligor with the mining man."

"Of course," the Red Wizard lied, his voice soothing and melodic. "You will have your pick of the female slaves, my dear friends. But first wouldn't you like to see my other army? You will be the only friends I have ever taken there."

"Yes," they barked, nearly in unison. Their yellow-tinged teeth showed as they grinned widely.

"Friend Maligor show us now?" one begged. "I want to see now."

"Then I mustn't keep my cherished friends waiting," the wizard stated, placing one hand on the inquisitive gnoll's shoulder. "Come with me. But leave your weapons and the sack of bones here. We mustn't scare the army."

The gnolls dropped their staves, daggers, and other items to the floor, then carefully set down the sack containing what was left of Willeth Lionson. They followed Maligor down the corridor, fighting for the position closest to their friend.

Maligor spoke to the gnolls along the way, continually reminding them of their good friendship and all the wonderful times they would share. The gnolls bantered back as they proceeded through the dark corridors and down the stairs to the lowest level of Maligor's complex, where he kept the growing force of darkenbeasts.

"My friends should walk in the chamber so they can see the army up close," the Red Wizard encouraged. "Only my best friends get to pet the darkenbeasts."

The two guards moved forward excitedly, like small boys in a room full of toys. While they marveled at the disgusting, rancid-smelling creatures, Maligor reached out with his mind, contacting the darkenbeasts and dropping his mental control of the gnolls.

Kill them! his mind cried. And in an instant, the chamber was filled with the flurry of shadowy, webbed wings. Unlike the tharchion, Willeth, the gnolls did not have time to scream.

* * * * *

The charmed orchard guard led Brenna, Wynter, and Galvin deeper into the citrus grove.

"Do you know where we are?" Brenna asked the centaur.

Wynter didn't reply. His attention was fixed on something moving in a nearby tree.

Brenna followed his gaze, squinting through the darkness. Then she recoiled when a pair of yellow-orange eyes peered back. The sorceress clung to Wynter's side and noticed that Galvin was watching the creature, too.

"What is it?" she whispered.

The charmed guide overheard her and strode obligingly toward the tree. "I think it's an imp," he offered, moving close enough to touch the branch the thing sat on. "See the wings?" The man waved his arm, tracing the outline of a wing, then turned to grin at Brenna. "It ain't gonna hurt you. If it was gonna attack, it would have snuck up behind you. You wouldn't have seen it just sitting here."

The thing in the tree glared at the man, growled like a cornered dog, and flapped its wings, causing the branches to rustle and a few pieces of fruit to fall to the ground. Pushing off from its perch, the thing's misshapen body hovered above the treetop.

The fiery-red-skinned creature had a manlike form, with short arms and legs. In the moonlight, its claws glistened. Its wings were small and batlike, and they beat furiously as the small creature began to gain altitude, its thin, barbed tail uncurling. Its face was a grotesque mockery, with grossly exaggerated features—a thin, pointed chin, a long bulbous nose, and pointed ears that stuck several inches above its bald, wrinkled head, from which sprouted grotesquely twisted horns. The creature growled again, then flew north.

"Yup," the guide said, "it was an imp, all right. Too bad it's so dark. A little more light and you could've gotten a better look at it."

Galvin had never seen such a creature and wondered if it was related to the beast that had turned into a hedgehog when it died.

Brenna trembled and reached up to touch the centaur's arm. "An imp is an evil little creature. I've heard that evil priests and wizards use them as familiars—extensions of themselves."

"Yeah," the guide said nonchalantly. "Lots of wizards in Thay use them. They help the owners keep tabs on their property. That one probably belonged to the wizard who owns this land."

Their curiosity satisfied, the Harpers and Brenna urged their guide to adopt a faster pace, and they continued their trek through the orchard.

*   *   *   *   *

Several hours after the demise of his guards and several stories higher in his windowless study, Maligor met with a young apprentice, a stocky girl whose clean-shaven head and pudgy face looked like an overripe cantaloupe. She knelt near the wizard, who sat in his favorite high-backed red leather chair, and bowed. As she did, the symbol of Myrkul tattooed on the top of her head pointed up at the Red Wizard. Today she wore a perfume that smelled like roses; Maligor noted that she used it too liberally, but he decided that it was a refreshing change from the air in the chambers below. She was one of the wizard's most adept pupils, possessing a ruthlessness and intelligence that surpassed even Asp's. The wizard had grand plans for her— someday—when he grew tired of the spirit naga and when the girl grew older and gained enough magical abilities to be of significant use.

For now, he was content to use her for errands. Maligor trusted her; he had guaranteed her loyalty when she came to study under him a year ago. The wizard had abducted her parents and put them to work on his slave plantation. If she displeased him, they would die horribly. That threat, coupled with the girl's voracious appetite for magical knowledge, kept her faithful and eager to please him.

"Master Maligor, I came in answer to your urgent summons." The girl raised her head, and her large brown eyes met his. "What may I do to aid the Zulkir of Alteration?"

"It is a most important task I entrust to you, Jutta." He ran his wrinkled hand across the top of her head. "There is a large canvas sack near an empty cell in the dungeon. Inside are the remains of a prisoner. Others may be looking for him. He was a merchant who dealt in slaves and spices," Maligor lied convincingly. "His remains must be scattered."

He slowly rose to tower above the girl and indicated she should stand. Jutta stood awkwardly on her short, fleshy legs and smiled expectantly, pleased to be assigned something important to do. The Red Wizard removed a ring from his right middle finger; it was a platinum band edged with brass and covered with tiny runes. Placing it on the smallest of her thick fingers, he grasped both of her hands and looked into her cherubic face.

"This ring will enable you to fly. All you need do is concentrate. The magic is simple. Take the canvas sack and scatter the bones over the cliff, down the length of the First Escarpment. Make sure each of the bones is miles apart . . . the remains of the clothing, too. Do you understand?"

Jutta was delighted; this sounded like a most important mission. "I understand, master, but even flying, it could take many hours to traverse the entire escarpment," she said. She dropped her gaze to look at the magic ring. She was awed that the Red Wizard would entrust her with one of his own valuable items.

"I can do this thing," she said, pushing her shoulders back to stand proudly. "No one will see me."

"Very good, Jutta," Maligor praised. "I have chosen my apprentice well. When you return, you will be rewarded. I will teach you new spells."

Jutta rushed excitedly from the study, her right hand out in front of her as she went, her eyes on the ring.

Maligor returned to his chair, eased himself down on the soft cushion, and waited for his next visitor. He did not have to wait long.

A shushing sound filtered in from the doorway, becoming louder as Asp slithered closer. She stopped just beyond the door, where the wizard could see her. The spirit naga made no effort to move silently today, her tail undulating back and forth, keeping the guards a respectful distance away. She sniffed the air, and her lidless, serpentine eyes narrowed to imperceptible slits. Asp pointed her chin up, opened her eyes, and glared at Maligor.

"Roses," she hissed. "I smell the perfume of roses."

When the Red Wizard provided no explanation, she glided to his chair. Rocking back on her snake's lower half so her face was lower than the wizard's, she grimaced.

"Maligor, what do you need of a lowly, fat apprentice? I am here to carry out your plans," she hissed.

"Jealousy does not become you, beautiful Asp," he retorted silkily. "Especially in one who has no need to be jealous. Apprentices were made for insignificant tasks . . . things that are too far beneath you. Apprentices do not share in my greatest plans, nor will they share in the fruits of the conquests."

Slightly appeased, Asp smiled and allowed her face to take on a radiant sheen. "My apologies, zulkir. I will not be jealous again. Now, on to things of greater significance. I have come to report on the gnolls' training."

Maligor leaned back, kicked off his slippers, and extended his feet so Asp could massage them. "I have waited anxiously all day to hear your report," he fabricated.

"I visited each garrison today, and I took them through a variety of fighting maneuvers. Some have difficulty mastering defensive tactics, but the sergeants have been working with them hour after hour."

"Good," Maligor said. "How long will it take to join the three garrisons?"

She gently massaged his rough heels as she continued. "That depends on where they are to be joined. If they are united outside this tower, about a day. But this location poses some problems. There are several Red Wizards in the city, and the presence of so many soldiers will concern the wizards and frighten the officials and people of Amruthar. I suspect the wizards will do something about it.

"I recommend instead that we join them south of the tower, well outside the city boundaries. Uniting the garrisons there could take two days, three if we move them at night and keep them a good distance from the tower. That would give us the best chance for success. No doubt the local wizards would know what is happening, but they are not likely to interfere, thinking your target is south of the city and out of their domain." She finished the massage, kissed his feet, and tenderly guided his toes into the slippers.

"Your military mind is becoming sharper, Asp. That is what we will do, then—march them south of this tower and Amruthar. Start them moving tonight. Then, three days from now, the garrisons will be joined, and we can put our plans into motion."

The spirit naga sensuously licked her lips. "It will be glorious, My Lord Maligor."

"Glorious," he echoed, thinking instead of the Thayvian gold mines. In three or four days, his darkenbeasts would be released—those in his tower and those he was storing elsewhere. "Soon it will begin," he said aloud. "The other wizards will never be able to stop me, beloved Asp. In just a few days."

Maligor looked into his unhuman associate's exquisite face. For a brief moment, he imagined that her eyes sparkled like gold.

Six

Brenna's charmed guide continued to lead the trio through the well-maintained orchard, pointing out imps and other less predictable creatures as they journeyed. Traveling was easy, since the ground was level and the grass short and well tended. The strong, cool breeze rustled the branches of the citrus trees and refreshed the Harpers and the sorceress, whipping the hair away from their faces and catching the enchantress's dress so it swirled madly about her ankles.

The bald guide eyed the woman. Even in the starlight, he could watch her curves as the wind tugged her dress back and forth. Trying to gain her attention, he paused to point at a dozen soft yellow lights in the trees to the north. The lights resembled giant hovering fireflies.

"Pretty, huh?" he whispered into Brenna's ear. "I like to sit and look at 'em."

"Beautiful. What are they, uh . . . I'm sorry. I don't know your name."

"Elwin. My name's Elwin. C'mon. I'll take you closer so

you can see 'em. But be quiet. We don't want to bother 'em."

Brenna cautiously urged Elwin forward, keeping an arm's length from him. The Harpers followed close behind. The fireflies' glow became lanterns hanging from branches, illuminating the trees so the forty or more slaves working there under the watchful eye of armed orcs could see to pick the fruit. Suddenly Wynter stopped, and for a moment, Galvin worried that the centaur would try to free the obviously mistreated group.

"If we start leaving a trail of dead guards and missing slaves, they'll be onto us," Galvin whispered.

"I know," Wynter said in as soft a voice as he could manage. "I was just watching. It brought back some old memories."

It was late when Elwin directed them to a small but thickly wooded area behind an abandoned barn. It stood a few miles from the orchard, and he claimed there was a clearing inside. Traveling in the darkness had slowed their progress. They weren't as deep into Thay as they had expected to be.

Brenna suggested staying in the barn; she envisioned sleeping on a pile of soft hay. But Elwin insisted that patrols watched empty buildings carefully, because runaway slaves were drawn to them. She sighed and reluctantly agreed to accept the patch of trees. The vegetation was overgrown, and Elwin had difficulty climbing through it, but he seemed to know what he was doing. The leaves of the trees and bushes were wet; the drops of water shone in the starlight. It had rained here recently, perhaps only an hour or two before.

The centaur followed the guide, making a thrashing sound as his massive form disappeared into the foliage. Following him was relatively easy, Brenna discovered, since he had made a small path through the brush. By the time she reached the center of the clearing, she discovered that Galvin was already there. She had assumed he was behind her. Irritated at his speed and quietness, she muttered something under her breath, not caring at the moment if he heard her.

Patches of tall grass were scattered in the clearing. Elwin made a show of stomping them down for Brenna. He gallantly waved his arms, indicating she should sit.

"This place should be safe," Elwin announced. "I've used this spot before when I skipped out on patrol duty. We're not too near a road. The orcs'll stay away because of all the bugs and 'cause it's so wet. It rains a lot here 'cause of the orchard."

Brenna scowled and fell to her knees, reaching out with her hands to find some place that was dry. "You mean it rains because of the Red Wizards."

The enchantress was frustrated that she couldn't find a dry spot to sit on, but she was too tired and proud to complain about it aloud. Rummaging in her smaller bag, she pulled out a heavy linen cloak and laid it on the ground under an elm. She sat unceremoniously on it, no longer caring if she wrinkled or ruined her clothes. Letting out a low moan, Brenna gingerly removed her antelope-skin slippers, leaning forward to accomplish the task. Her legs hurt too much to move them closer to her torso.

"Gods, I'm tired," she said, and she began to rub her feet. They were blistered and sore, and for a moment she wished there was enough moonlight filtering through the trees so she could look at them.

"Want me to do that for you?" Elwin offered.

Wynter tapped the guide on top of his bald head. "Why don't you get some sleep now?" The centaur was surprised when Elwin complied without argument. The guide leaned back on the ground, stretched, made himself comfortable, and began to snore softly.

Galvin sat spread-eagled in the center of the clearing, watching Elwin. Satisfied the guide wouldn't pester Brenna, the druid began to search through his satchel. He had difficulty finding the correct root in the darkness, but eventually his efforts were successful.

"Here," he said to Brenna, tossing her an object that

looked like a misshapen carrot. "Rub that on your feet. It'll help get rid of the blisters. Crack it first so the juice oozes out."

Wynter glanced at the druid, about to comment on his friend's compassion, but Galvin glared at him. Don't say anything, the druid warned with his look.

Wynter smiled. "I just wanted to point out we should stay here in the grove tonight. We'd be wise to wait until the morning slave crews start before we move on."

Galvin nodded then turned his attention back to Brenna. "Wrap your feet. Amruthar's not going to be a short hike."

"Thank you for being so concerned," she snapped.

"I am concerned," the druid said simply. "I can't let you slow us down. I don't intend for this mission to take weeks."

"Slow you down?" she fumed, rising to her knees. "With a spell, I could fly to Amruthar!"

"Provided you knew where the city was."

"I know where it is."

"And you think that would be a good idea?" Galvin posed. "A great accomplishment, flying off on your own. More like a great liability."

"Don't talk to me about liabilities. At least I know how to talk to people. I know how to be civil. But you—" she sputtered, waking Elwin and drawing his attention. "You've got less manners than an orc!"

"I'm honest with people. And at least I don't shout at them," Galvin returned evenly, wishing he had never offered her the root.

"No, you don't have to shout," she taunted. "You can insult them just fine without even raising your voice. Ever try to be nice to someone?"

"I was trying to be nice to you." Galvin grimaced.

She propped herself into a sitting position and picked up the root. "Oh, go talk to a bullfrog or something," she groused.

"Hey, pipe down, willya?" Elwin broke in. "I had a long shift before the trip here, and I'm trying to sleep. I can't

guide you anywhere tomorrow if you keep me up all night."
The man dropped his head back into the grass. "Sheesh!
Do they always fight like that?"

"No," the centaur replied, watching Galvin and Brenna
glare at each other. He was relieved to see that the sorceress was using the root on her feet. "In fact, I thought they
were just starting to get along."

"If that's getting along, I wish they'd get along somewhere else," Elwin grumbled.

"Elwin, you've got me curious," the centaur said softly.
"Your name means 'friend to the elves' doesn't it? There
aren't many elves in Thay, so that must mean you're not a
native Thayvian."

"You're pretty smart, centaur," Elwin mumbled, sitting
up and brushing the grass and dirt from his side. He
yawned, displaying his broken teeth. "I'm originally from
the Sword Coast . . . worked on a pirate ship. A few years
ago, our ship started hauling slaves to Thay. I got to like
this place, so I stayed." He winked at Wynter. "The orchard patrol pays well, and I do a little slaving on the side—
children."

Wynter was losing his patience with the evil man.
"Elwin," he said evenly, "does your slaving operation ever
take you into Amruthar?"

"It takes me a lot of places," Elwin answered, sounding
businesslike. "Amruthar's only one of 'em. Largest city
around here. Two or three times a week, slaves are
shipped in and put up for sale. They're cheaper than cattle."

"Amruthar," Wynter pressed angrily, not wanting to hear
another word about Elwin's slave practices. "What is the
city like now? Are the streets patrolled? Can slaves on missions for their masters walk freely? Who rules the city?"

Elwin sighed. "I've never been hassled much in the city.
If you haven't done anything to offend a wizard or tharchion, you should be all right."

"Are there many centaurs?"

"Like you? Not many are as big as you," Elwin said, "but

there are plenty of your type walking around."

The man sickened Wynter. The centaur believed every being had a right to choose his or her own course in life. Elwin had chosen his course long ago, but the slaves he and others in Thay dealt in could not choose. And Elwin seemed to think of them as nothing but a commodity.

"We're looking for a Red Wizard who's supposed to be in Amruthar," Wynter continued.

"A Red Wizard? There's plenty of 'em in Amruthar. Plenty all over Thay, for that matter," Elwin said with a snicker.

"His name's Maligor," Galvin interjected. "The gnoll said the Red Wizard Maligor was staying in Amruthar."

There was silence in the clearing. The charmed man nervously rubbed his scarred chin and looked at each of his companions.

"You're in over your heads," Elwin said. "Maligor's a zulkir. I ain't taking you to no zulkir. But I'll take you to the outskirts of Amruthar."

Wynter's right front hoof pawed at the ground. "Go to sleep, Elwin," the centaur stated.

In a few moments, the man was snoring again. Exhaustion also overcame Brenna, and a few minutes later her head fell to the damp, mossy floor in uneasy slumber.

Galvin and Wynter talked quietly for a while, discussing the best route to the city. They were hopeful they could move into Amruthar, get the information the Aglarond council and the Harper organization wanted, and then move out within a day or two.

In a short time, the Harpers decided it was time for them to rest, too. They discussed who should take first watch; neither Harper felt comfortable about leaving the small group unprotected. In the end, Galvin decided he would stay awake. But as the centaur chose a spot to sleep, his keen nostrils picked up a disturbing, almost imperceptible smell, reminiscent of something from his childhood. The breeze was carrying the scent of rotting flesh into the clearing. Finally, with a jolt, he recognized the smell.

"Galvin! Undead!" Wynter called, alerting the druid and waking Brenna and Elwin.

The druid's eyes peered into the darkness, searching. He smelled them first, then saw their decaying bodies coming ever nearer. At first glance, the figures appeared human, and in life they might have been. But now their flesh was gray and decomposing, and it clung to their bones like tattered sails on a mast. Their hair appeared wirey, tangled, and bug-ridden, and their deep-socketed eyes, seemingly devoid of intelligence, bore straight ahead into the clearing. They were moving in through the trees, slowly making their way past the tangled branches.

"They've surrounded us!" the druid called. He cursed himself for not hearing their approach. How could he have been so careless? The undead were halfway through the brambles and would be on the group in moments. In the darkness, Galvin couldn't be certain how many there were, but he guessed there were at least a dozen. Grimly he drew his scimitar.

Out of the corner of his eye, Galvin saw the centaur move toward the shambling corpses on the other side of the clearing, his staff thrust out in front of him as if to keep them at bay. Brenna was rising and reaching into her small bag, no doubt planning to use some magic on them. He hoped it would work.

"Elwin, wake up!" the sorceress ordered as she continued searching through her bag. Her hands shook terribly. Brenna had heard and read about the undead, but she had never expected to meet any of them. She glanced over her trembling shoulder. The petrified slaver was awake and was pulling two daggers from the strap around his chest, crouching to meet the charge of the undead.

The creatures stumbled through the trees and bushes, the pale, rotting flesh on their bones catching and clinging to the branches. The stench from the walking cadavers was overpowering and made the Harpers and Brenna dizzy.

Most of the corpses' hands were intact; their fingers

were bony and ended in long, filthy nails that curved in toward their palms like claws. Their eyes glowed a hellish, dull yellow-orange.

The first undead broke into the clearing and lunged at Wynter, its long arms flailing to scratch the centaur's body. Its mouth opened and a thin, snakelike tongue darted out and uncoiled in the air. The centaur cringed. Ghouls! he thought, staring at the tongue used for sucking marrow out of bones. To be killed by a ghoul meant to become one of their kind—provided the ghoul pack wasn't hungry and didn't eat you first.

Wynter shouted out to his companions what they were facing and thrust forward with his staff to keep the loathsome creature from touching him. The long, carved staff lodged itself in the caved-in chest of the corpse, making a sickening crunching sound as it splintered brittle ribs. Already dead, the ghoul wasn't to be stopped this easily. With both hands, it grasped the wood and began to pull itself up the staff, hand over hand, unmindful of the wood that pierced through its body and emerged out its back.

In response, Wynter heaved with his great strength, lifting the staff and the ghoul along with it. He swung the staff to the right, slamming the suspended ghoul into another of its foul companions just emerging from the trees. Their bodies collided with a horrifying thud that left both creatures lying stunned on the ground. Continuing his attack, the centaur pulled the staff closer to him, stepped on the attached ghoul, and wrested his weapon free. Then he proceeded to trample the two on the ground, turning them into a mass of broken, splintered bones and tattered flesh.

Ghouls had broken into the clearing all around them now, presenting Elwin, Brenna, and Galvin with their own battles.

The druid reacted quickly, slicing forward with his scimitar and cutting one creature nearly in half at the waist. The vile corpse continued to press onward despite the difficulty of staying on its feet while trying to keep its torso from toppling off to the side. As it lurched forward awkwardly,

Galvin swung again, this time cleaving off an arm and further unbalancing the thing. It fell forward, squirming on the ground, but another quickly stepped in to take its place.

"Don't let them touch you!" Galvin called to Brenna. "Their touch can paralyze you!"

Although the sorceress didn't have any idea how powerful the undead creatures were, she had no intention of letting these walking corpses get anywhere near her. She backed herself into the center of the small clearing, almost bumping into the druid, who was now fighting two of the things. Placing a pinch of powder in her sweaty palm, she slapped her other hand on top of it, rubbed furiously, and waited for a trio of ghouls to come closer.

When they were so near the odor almost caused her to vomit, she extended her arms, her hands outstretched and fingers spread wide, her thumbs touching. In the next instant, her hands burst into fire. The blazing flare lapped across her fingers and reached out several feet, causing the ghouls' flesh and raggedy strips of cloth to burst into flames. She watched with revulsion as three ghouls flapped their arms in an attempt to put out the fire. For once, she was glad of the dampness in the clearing; there was little danger of the trees catching fire and placing the travelers in further danger. The magical flame burned hot and quickly, leaving behind a trio of charred, unmoving skeletons.

Elwin wasn't faring as well as the others. The self-made slaver was frightened so badly that the jabs he was making with his daggers were shaky and clumsy. Eventually, after repeated attempts, one of his twin daggers sunk into the chest of one of the cadavers, but the blade did little harm. He pulled it free and leapt to the side to choose another target.

Elwin crouched again, bringing one dagger upward and forward into the abdomen of a large ghoul that was missing its right arm from the elbow down. One more thrust and it would fall, he thought, holding his breath to cut the stench.

A second ghoul moved in silently from the slaver's side, catching Elwin's head in both hands. The ghoul raked its

nails across Elwin's scalp, ripping a piece of skin loose from
the man's bald skull. The slaver screamed and dropped his
daggers as he tried to push his new attacker away, but the
ghoul only ambled closer. Pressing up against Elwin and
lifting him by his head, the undead creature snapped his
thick neck. The ghoul took a bite out of Elwin's cheek, cast
him to the ground, then fell upon his body, tearing off
chunks of flesh with its filthy nails. Anchoring its feet
against Elwin's chest and grasping the slaver's right leg, it
pulled until the leg came free. Another ghoul stopped to
feast on Elwin, but the two behind it continued to move
forward, bent on the living targets.

Wynter had lost count of the number of ghouls he had
killed by the time he was able to pull back and help Galvin
and Brenna. The druid appeared to be faced with the most
desperate struggle. He was standing on one ghoul, which
appeared to be finally dead, while holding off another three
with his scimitar. The two that had passed by Elwin were
eyeing Brenna but keeping their distance, obviously concerned about her magic. Wynter started toward the druid.

Galvin kicked at a ghoul in the middle, sending it sprawling, then swung his scimitar in a vicious downward stroke
at the one to his right. The weapon cut through the
corpse's shoulder blades and lodged halfway down in its
chest. The ghoul seemed to grin as it reached forward and
clawed the druid's exposed arm. Galvin immediately felt
sluggish, his arms and legs heavy. He felt the talons of his
other attacker rake his left arm as he became rooted to the
spot.

"No!" the centaur screamed, bringing his staff down on
the ghoul that had Galvin's scimitar in its chest. Wynter
smashed its head like an overripe watermelon, ending its
unlife. Continuing his assault, the centaur trampled the remaining ghoul into oblivion, then swung to see Brenna
wrestling a tall corpse.

The sorceress obviously had taken out one of the pair.
As the centaur dashed forward, he saw a decaying body
lying at an odd angle across her bags. Part of its chest was

missing.

"Back up, Brenna!" he called, rearing on his hind legs.

Brenna fell back on the ground, unmoving, her clawed cheek exposed. The ghoul turned to meet Wynter's front hooves, which fell on it hard. In a berserk rage, the centaur pounded the undead into the soft ground, continuing to rear and stomp on it well after it had ceased to move.

The centaur's chest heaved from fear and exertion. He was the only one standing in the clearing. It was too dark to make out all the details, but he could see Galvin's frozen outline and Brenna lying on the ground, motionless. Elwin's corpse lay in pieces, but the ghouls who had dined on him were nowhere to be seen. Although Wynter was relieved he didn't have to fight any more of the creatures, he was worried about the surviving ghouls' absence. Ghouls were intelligent undead, and he feared they would report the incident to their dark master or gather more of their kind for another assault.

Determined not to wait for any undead reinforcements or to take time to assess his friends' conditions, Wynter picked up the paralyzed Galvin and slung him across his back. He cradled Brenna in his arms and carried the pair of them and their belongings out of the defiled area and into the abandoned barn. If guards looking for escaped slaves chanced upon the trio, Wynter thought, the Aglarond council would have to contact more Harpers to continue the spying mission.

Inside the dilapidated barn, the centaur placed the sorceress near a large mound of straw, laying her down gently near the barn wall and placing her head on some hay. Watching her closely, Wynter saw her chest rise and fall shallowly. Tears fell from his angular face, and his hands trembled. Wynter didn't want Brenna and Galvin to die. Aside from losing his friends, their deaths would leave him alone in a country he considered one step removed from hell.

The centaur laid Galvin near her and cringed when he saw how irregularly the druid was breathing. Wynter pulled off the druid's tunic so he could clean the gashes left by the undead. Galvin's arms had been raked by the claws of the creature, and the area around the red welts was swelling. Rummaging through the druid's satchel, the centaur found some of the herbs Galvin had used on his shoulder earlier. The centaur was uncertain how to apply them, so he crumbled them in his fingers and laid them across the gashes.

Next he tended to Brenna. Wynter tore off a strip from the hem of her dress and soaked it with water from his waterskin. Kneeling awkwardly, he cleaned the blood from her cheek where the ghoul had clawed her. The scratch marks weren't deep, but they marred her pretty face.

The centaur wore a circular path in the dirt as he trotted around the unmoving forms of Galvin and Brenna. Through a gaping hole in the barn's roof, the stars shone brightly, illuminating the sheen of sweat on the centaur's back. Wynter feared the undead would return, or perhaps a patrol of a worse kind would find them. His friends' long hair would make them look like escaped slaves, so if they were caught here they would be killed or put on a slave plantation, never to see Aglarond again.

Wynter shivered and glanced about the barn. There were too many shadows to make out everything, but he noted a few piles of moldy straw, damp because the roof provided little shelter from the rain. One toward the back of the barn was large enough to hide Brenna and Galvin behind it in the event he heard someone approaching the barn. He didn't want to move them unless he felt he had to. It looked like the barn had had a loft at one time. Now it was completely hollow inside, and rotted boards lay along the walls and near the center of the floor to outline where a second story used to be.

The entire structure tilted a little to the east, and Wynter suspected it wouldn't survive a heavy windstorm. The dirty hay inside smelled musty and was coated with little bits of fur. It probably served as a haven for mice and other rodents. A few rusted farm implements were scattered along the western wall—rakes, a hoe, bits of tack. He took note of those that might serve as weapons.

The centaur continued to guard his friends until daylight filtered in through the roof and he could no longer stay awake. Standing between the barn doors and the prone druid and sorceress, Wynter slept on his feet. He awoke late in the afternoon to find Galvin and Brenna still unmoving. Wynter peered out one of the larger cracks at the front of the barn. In the distance, he saw the orchards and spied a few slaves moving among the trees, picking fruit. The centaur was careful not to touch the wood of the barn. The structure appeared so old and rotted that he feared it could easily fall over.

Wynter kept his vigil, dosing on and off until well after midnight, when Galvin finally shook his paralysis. The gashes on his arms smarted, but they were slightly healed by Wynter's efforts.

"How . . . how long has it been?" Galvin asked, sitting up and glancing about the barn. "I remember . . . Brenna! Was she killed?" The druid panicked and brought himself quickly to his feet.

"She's still alive—barely, I think," Wynter replied. "She was clawed, too. She's paralyzed."

Galvin rushed to the enchantress's side and moved the fingertips of his right hand over her scratched face. He closed his eyes and hummed softly, an old druidic prayer taught to him as a youth. He rarely used healing magic, which took a great deal of concentration—something he usually lacked when he himself was injured. The druid preferred to rely on herbs and natural mixtures. But he had none of the latter handy, so he continued the prayer. After several minutes, Brenna's breathing began to deepen, although she still remained unconscious. The scratches on her face began to heal, and Galvin rose.

"She'll be all right," he stated simply, his voice showing his relief. He began to examine his surroundings and noticed that Wynter looked different somehow. Then he realized why—the hair on the centaur's head was short, not more than an inch long. His long curls and braid lay in a pile on the barn floor.

"What did you do?" Galvin pointed at the centaur's head.

"We need to look like Thayvians, remember?"

Brenna finally came to several hours later. Sunlight streamed in where planks of wood had rotted away in the walls and through the hole in the center of the roof. The rays warmed her face. She slowly sat up, then pulled herself to her knees.

"I've come to the conclusion that it's decidedly unlucky sharing a camp with the two of you," Wynter said dryly. Despite the tone, he was thankful his companions were for the most part uninjured. He tossed the enchantress her satchels.

"I left Elwin behind in the clearing," the centaur added hesitantly. "There wasn't much left of him."

"Why did the undead attack us?" Brenna didn't understand. "They were horrid. Gods, but I feel for the people who live in this country."

"The ghouls must have heard us talking. That attracted them," Wynter said flatly, eyeing her and Galvin. "We were none too quiet."

"They were quiet, though," Galvin added.

"You could never have heard them approaching anyway," the centaur offered. "Undead only make noise when they want to." He smiled at Brenna, then reached a hand up to tug on his own short locks. "You've got too much hair, young lady, but the sheep shears I found should remedy that."

A look of horror crossed her face. "What—what do you mean?"

"I mean you should cut it, shave it off," the centaur instructed. "You need to look like a native Thayvian, a wealthy one if you've got another pretty dress." He extended the shears to her. "These'll take off most your hair. Galvin's scimitar can take care of the rest."

When the sorceress didn't take the shears, Wynter dropped them in front of her.

The druid unsheathed his scimitar and ran his thumb

along the curved blade. He stared meaningfully at Brenna's curls.

"Oh, no, you don't!" she cried, finally realizing what the Harpers meant for her to do. She glanced in alarm at the centaur's cropped hair. "Shave off my hair? Do you have any idea how much time it takes to get hair to grow this long? I haven't cut my hair in ten years."

The druid smiled. "I'll pose as your slave."

"You mean you're not cutting your hair?" she said angrily.

"Slaves have long hair."

"Listen," Wynter said, trying to console Brenna. "You'd make a better Thayvian than Galvin. You've got the bearing, the social graces."

The sorceress puffed out her chest, angry at herself for not realizing when the Harpers had discussed this plan in Aglarond that it would come to this. She fingered the shears, crossed her legs, and sat them in her lap.

"I can make myself look bald without shaving my head," she announced. Concentrating and chanting, the sorceress sat stock still as her face took on a magical radiance. The glow covered her hair, then disappeared, leaving her appearing bald.

Wynter sighed. "Nice try, Brenna, but it won't work." He stepped toward her, bent over, and reached forward to feel around her shoulders until he grabbed a handful of hair.

"I can't see it, but it's there," he stated. "Amruthar's filled with wizards. Some of them are bound to see through your illusion. We can't risk it. You'll have to shave it off."

Brenna's shoulders sagged. "I know," she said. "I'm sorry. I should have known I was going to have to do this if I entered Thay." She gritted her teeth, picked up the shears, and tossed her head forward. Grabbing a handful of hair with one hand and wielding the shears with the other, she began cutting.

"Look at it this way," Wynter teased. "You'll be right in style in Amruthar. And if we live through this and you get back to Aglarond, maybe you can start a fashion trend there." He grimaced as he watched the shears slip in her hand and nearly nick her head.

When Brenna was finished, about a half an inch of hair remained on her head. It was uneven and looked comical, but the Harpers remained straight-faced.

The druid padded forward, knelt in front of her, and held up his scimitar. Here, let me help."

Brenna bent her head forward, and Galvin began to scrape the sharp blade across the back of her scalp. The druid was careful, not wanting to cut her. Wynter had told him most Thayvians prided themselves on their appearance, and he doubted that scars were in fashion. When he was finished with the back half of her head, he tilted her neck upward and started to run the knife across the front half of her scalp.

"I don't know why Thayvians have an aversion to hair," Wynter said. He wanted to make conversation because the silence in the barn felt uncomfortable. "They've been shaving their heads for more than two hundred years. It all started with a few wizards, I understand. Now only slaves have long hair. The longer the hair, the longer someone's been a slave."

"You mean everyone but slaves is bald?" she asked softly, looking slightly sick.

"All the wizards, everyone considered wealthy or middle-class tharchions, merchants, and even most of the peasants—they don't want to be mistaken for slaves. Most centaurs cut their hair as short as mine. Everyone in my family had short hair," he concluded.

"Was it hard for you to leave your family?" Brenna asked. Galvin winced at that question as he finished shaving the last of her locks. He began to run the blade across her now bald head to smooth it. He was surprised when Wynter answered.

"Yes," he said slowly. "My family was my life, and the slave plantation was the only home I knew. I had three brothers. They took to the life there. I just never fit in. When I was old enough to make it on my own, I left. I don't even know if my father ever went looking for me."

The centaur stood still in the center of the barn. "I cut my ties with my family when I left Thay. I'm only here because of Harper business. When we're done in Amruthar, I'll leave again." The centaur paused and looked at the councilwoman. She was rubbing her head, obviously uncomfortable with the feel of it.

Brenna stared at the pile of red curls in her lap. Ten years' worth of hair, she thought. No use regretting it. Shrugging her shoulders, she stood up, shaking the curls off her dress.

"Beautiful," Wynter observed.

Brenna tittered and twirled to brush the last of the hair from her dress. "At least it won't take me long to wash it," she said, finally smiling.

The skin on her head was an even, creamy peach tone, free of blemishes. She had a high forehead that glistened in the light that filtered through the barn. The absence of hair drew more attention to her eyes, which Galvin found himself staring into. They were large and round and ringed by long lashes.

Brenna blushed and bent to pick up an armload of hay and deposit it on top of her hair. "A pretty dress, right? That's all I need to look like a wealthy Thayvian."

"Almost," Wynter said. "We'll have to paint your head first. When you were . . . sleeping, I gathered some berries and crushed them. They should do fine as long as it doesn't rain. The important people in Thay—or at least those who think they are—always paint designs on their heads."

The centaur explained that many men permanently tattooed their heads so they wouldn't have to bother about changing designs. But many of the women went to shops to have their heads painted, preferring to have different symbols from time to time as fashions changed.

The centaur trotted over to Brenna, carrying a shovelful of smashed blue and red berries. Brenna's lower lip quivered, but she stood still.

"We'll give you a dainty little barbed whip cascading over your forehead like a spray of flowers," Wynter said as he smeared his fingers into the mixture and applied it to her head. "The whip's the symbol of Loviatar, the Maiden of Pain, one of the regularly worshiped deities here." Before the centaur finished, he added a lightning bolt with a ball on one end above her right ear. "That's the Harpers' symbol for 'dangerous magic here,' " he explained.

Brenna changed into a dark orchid dress with voluminous sleeves and a rounded, lace-edged neckline. She looked striking in it, even with her bald head, and added a crystal and gold necklace to make herself fit the image of a wealthy Thayvian.

"Well, this is it for my wardrobe," she said with a touch of disappointment in her voice. "I've ruined everything else."

Wynter pushed open the barn door, which teetered precariously on one rusted hinge. The countryside appeared different by daylight. The orchards in the distance yielded the faintest fragrance of citrus blossoms. The sky was as blue as the Sea of Fallen Stars, and it stretched, cloudless, from horizon to horizon. A dirt road that had been sprinkled liberally with white gravel cut through the grass and pointed toward the east. Weeping birch and crimson maples lined the road.

Galvin had expected the countryside to look bleak and the trees twisted like Thay's evil rulers. Instead, he found it quite pleasant. He glanced at the small clump of trees behind the barn and shuddered, remembering the attack of the undead. Deciding to put some distance between this place and himself, the druid padded toward the road, with Brenna and Wynter following.

The druid could tell that the road was well traveled. Most of the gravel had been washed to the sides by the rain, and carriage and wagon tracks made deep impressions in places.

"Are you certain this leads into Amruthar?" Galvin asked Wynter.

The centaur pursed his lips. "I hope so. Elwin talked

about a road before he fell asleep last night. It's the only one I see."

Galvin turned to Brenna. "If we're stopped, Wynter's the chief foreman on a slave plantation your father owns, and he's going to Amruthar to buy slaves. You're traveling with him so you can shop. I'm your slave—on hand to carry any packages."

"If I'm wealthy, why am I walking?" she challenged.

"You were on horseback," Wynter stated, "but the horses were stolen by thieves."

Brenna beamed. "Fine. I'm just looking forward to being in a city again, even if it is in Thay."

Wynter glanced at the druid. "You'll enjoy this, too, won't you, Galvin?"

The druid rolled his eyes, drew his lips tightly together, and continued ambling down the road.

Seven

The lich sat hunched over a centuries-old rosewood desk cluttered with bones of fingers, vials half-filled with assorted dark-colored powders, and yellowed scrolls curling at the corners and covered with runes and scratchings. He peered at the markings with his deep-socketed, ancient eyes and slowly scanned them.

The lich was very old. His pale, paper-thin skin was stretched across his face and limbs, making him appear gaunt, almost skeletal. Fine wisps of white hair were scattered atop his age-spotted head, and his lower lip hung loose, as if it had no muscles to control it. Despite his appearance, the lich was not infirm.

The lich was Szass Tam, the most formidable Red Wizard in Thay.

Across the far edge of the desk, almost beyond the reach of his bony hands, stood five thin candles that had burned down to various heights, none taller than three inches. The wax had dripped into knobby white piles that nearly obscured the candles' small pewter holders, indicating that the lich had been at his desk for some time. The flickering candles were the only source of light in the immense room, which was a combination library-laboratory, and they illuminated little more than the desktop. The walls were lined with shadow-draped bookcases that stretched to the ceiling, interrupted only by two windows that were shuttered and curtained with heavy black velvet. The thousands of books gave the room its overwhelming smell of old, musty paper; if Szass Tam were alive, the odor might have bothered him.

Although it was midmorning, the lich kept the room bathed in dimness. He preferred the candles to sunlight. Even though the undead Zulkir of Necromancy could walk about in daylight, unlike many other types of undead, he preferred the sepulcher-like comfort of the gloom.

On the center of the desk, where a spot had been cleared atop the gleaming wood, a crystal ball, little bigger than a man's fist, rested on the wings of a platinum-edged bronze dragon figurine. Szass Tam had many crystal balls, and he used them frequently to spy on various wizards, tharchions, and other forces in Thay. However, this particular ball was his favorite, and perhaps his most powerful. The polished, enchanted crystal was several hundred years old and had originally belonged to the lich's mentor. Szass Tam had acquired it a long time ago when his magical power increased after he killed his teacher, wresting from the dead man all sorts of arcane devices, elixirs, and books. Dozens of the latter rested on the shelves behind him, their pages now so brittle that the lich avoided handling them unless absolutely necessary. Szass Tam still kept his mentor with him as one of the undead skeletons that patrolled the zulkir's property. It was not out of a perverse sense of superiority, Szass Tam knew. The lich just hated to let dead bodies rot when they could be animated and made to serve him.

Szass Tam drew his arms about the crystal in a protective and covetous gesture and ran his fingers over the cool, perfect surface. With the lich's mental coaxing, the sphere began to pulse with light, appearing a thing alive, and colors—azure, rose, gold, and pale green—danced inside it. The ball glowed more brightly, and the lich moved his face closer. His eyes, appearing as hot, intense pinpoints of red light, peered through the crystal and beyond the confines of his keep, past two villages and to harvested farmland. He concentrated, and the colors parted, revealing a puzzling scene being acted out many, many miles away amid dried, broken cornstalks—a spirit naga castigating a unit of gnolls.

The naga, whom Szass Tam had been observing in Zulkir Maligor's company for the past few years, slithered back and forth in front of a dozen nervous gnolls, gesturing grandly with her arms as her tail swished wildly, obviously berating them for something. Beads of sweat stood out on the creatures' shaggy brows, causing the lich to wonder what they had done wrong.

"Again!" Szass Tam heard the naga yell, her voice as clear through the crystal ball as if she were standing in the same room with him. "You will try it again!"

The twelve gnolls paired off so that each had an opponent. Half assumed a classic defensive stance that the lich remembered seeing several years ago in one of the military books in his library. The others were clearly on the offensive and moved forward, howling and swinging with the flat of their blades. Szass Tam smiled. The naga was not using the gnoll force well.

Overall, gnolls, which were reasonably numerous in Thay, were savage, and their shaggy, wild-dog visages made them fearsome foes. But they were inclined to fight awkwardly with swords, finding it difficult to wrap their pawlike hands about the hilts of the weapons. Their swings rarely varied, making them too predictable. Szass Tam decided the spirit naga would have been better off leaving them to fight with their claws and long, sharp teeth. It would be more natural for them and probably would have better results. "Civilized" fighting was not always the best approach.

Szass Tam believed his own army to be the strongest in Thay. Skeletons, zombies, ghouls, ghasts, wights, and worse made up the bulk of his forces. The undead required no food, except for the ghouls, which usually ate their opponents. The undead did not sleep, and they were fierce because they were bound to the lich and did not fear death. Like any army, the undead had generals; these were the vampires, who possessed a horrible cunning and cruelty, and they did a superb job of ordering about the undead troops. The lich's generals didn't waste time instructing skeletons in the art of swordplay or teaching zombies how to defend themselves. They simply pointed their charges at a target and demanded they move in. The only drawback was that not all in his army were able to move about during the day. Because of this, Szass Tam also relied upon living soldiers.

Szass Tam continued to observe the naga, whose face took on a rosy tint, the blush of anger. He concentrated again, listening through the crystal to capture her words.

"Clowns!" Asp screamed. "I lead an army of clowns and fools! You are sluggish, clumsy oafs! You're far too predictable. You'll never stand long against a well-organized foe. Listen to me! I can turn you into warriors the likes of which Thay has never seen. And if you pay attention to me now, you just might live through the upcoming battle." Her eyes narrowed and her tongue snaked out over her red lips as she reviewed the assembly. In the background, more than three hundred gnolls stood at attention, intently watching their dozen brothers who were the current object of the naga's wrath.

Asp slithered among the twelve, who awkwardly jumped to attention. With amazing speed, her arm shot forward and grabbed a broadsword from a startled gnoll.

"Watch me!" she hissed, motioning for one of the soldiers to step forward. The disconcerted target complied quickly, and she began to circle him, rising and falling on her snake body, making him feel ill at ease.

"Defend yourself, clown!"

The naga waited for the gnoll to draw his weapon, then smiled when she noted that it wavered in his trembling hand. She circled him as more sweat gathered on his face, then moved closer and nodded for him to assume the defensive stance he had been practicing. His brothers backed away to give the pair room, and she lunged out at him, striking like a cobra and swinging her sword so it clanged loudly against his. The gnoll fought to retain hold of the weapon and bent his knees for a better defensive position. He seemed afraid to return her swing, a fatal mistake in Asp's eyes.

"Good," she said as she ran her finger along the edge of her blade. "You've mastered the right defensive stance. Now, everyone observe this, and we'll see just how well your fellow can preserve his mottled hide."

Asp continued to slash at the gnoll, and each time he brought his sword up to parry hers. She was toying with him, having picked a soldier less competent than most for her morbid demonstration. She made three more swings, each stopped by the soldier. Then the naga tired of the game and changed her rhythm, catching the gnoll off guard and slicing through his shaggy hide and into his rib cage. The gnoll howled in pain, dropped his sword, and held his hands over the wound in an attempt to keep the blood from spilling out. He backed away from Asp, thinking the demonstration over, but the naga pressed her attack, swinging at his right arm.

Two swings and the gnoll's arm fell to the ground, blood spurting from his shoulder and jetting onto the naga. The creature fell to his knees, pleading for his life but receiving no support from the others, who remained at attention as they watched the scene in horror.

"Vary your sword thrusts as I have shown you. Keep your opponent guessing. Keep your eyes locked onto his, and show no mercy," Asp instructed coldly. "Above all, show no mercy!" With that, the naga placed both hands on the hilt of her sword and brought the weapon down with all her strength, cleaving the gnoll's head in two. He crumpled, and she presented the bloodied sword to the soldier from whom she had borrowed it.

"I hope this demonstration has been of some help," Asp stated without emotion as once again she began to slither back and forth in front of the gnolls. "Soon you will be joined by two other forces, both larger than yours, and you will march on a mission of great importance, a mission in the name of Zulkir Maligor. You must be at your best. Anything less will bring quick death upon you and disgrace to the zulkir."

Asp wiped an index finger across her arm to collect her victim's blood, then licked it off with her thin tongue while the gnolls watched.

"Your sergeants will work with you the rest of the day. See to it that you pay attention. For Maligor!"

"For Maligor!" they chanted.

Szass Tam stared at Asp's exquisite face and wondered idly how a creature of such beauty could be so malicious. For a moment, he almost envied Maligor. Then the lich muddled over the gnoll force.

The Zulkir of Necromancy had held his position for nearly two centuries, and during that time, he had watched wizards and other zulkirs build forces, march against each other, or march against the armies at the borders of Aglarond and Mulhorand. Few of the attacks had been successful, as the wizards never worked together. When they fought each other, they simply managed to perpetuate mistrust and suspicion between the wizards; this led to political treachery and double crosses.

The lich doubted that whatever Maligor was planning would work either, but nevertheless it gnawed at him.

Szass Tam knew that Zulkir Maligor, in charge of Thay's School of Alteration Magic, had contented himself the past few decades to false dealings with lesser wizards and power plays that netted him shares of wealthy merchants' profits and goods. Maligor didn't strike the lich as the type of wizard who favored physical assaults or large-scale battles, and because of that, the lich had not viewed Maligor as a threat. He thought Maligor had been keeping the gnolls as more of a deterrent to other Red Wizards than as an offensive force.

Szass Tam, on the other hand, frequently went on the offensive. Typical of all liches, he desired nothing more than to enhance his own power at any cost. And Szass Tam's idea of power was nothing less than complete control of Thay. However, unlike the other zulkirs, Szass Tam had centuries in which to work his evil plan. Szass Tam was not of this world anymore, having progressed beyond mere human existence to an undead state. Like his undead army, he no longer required sleep or food, which allowed him all the time he needed to lavish over magical tomes and build his supernatural might. Furthermore, he possessed an unearthly patience that would let him wait a dozen decades or more before he moved against all of Thay to swallow his fellow zulkirs and proclaim himself king of the evil land. During that waiting time, he would research spells the other wizards only dreamed of and increase his army of undead.

And also during that time, he would continue to work with the Council of Zulkirs, watching each zulkir closely and keeping abreast of all their schemes and dealings. Szass Tam would continue to note their weaknesses and strengths in order to decide how best to overcome them when the time was right to strike. That time would come far in the future, when some of the current zulkirs would be rotting in their graves, waiting for the lich to enlist them into his army. For now, the lich enjoyed toying with the other wizards; he would not move against them until he was certain he could crush all of them—and preferably all at once. He would not work with them individually in the meantime. He did not trust any of the other Red Wizards, and he regarded joining forces with them as a show of his own weakness.

Gazing at the crystal ball, Szass Tam saw the naga instructing a smaller group of gnolls who wore leather breastplates and were more heavily armed. Perhaps these are Maligor's generals, the lich mused. Asp was demanding better performance. The clang of swords covered up most of the conversation; the gnolls were working hard to improve.

Tiring of the display, the lich ran his hand over the crystal, and the colors reappeared, obscuring the scene. The glow from the ball faded, and Szass Tam pushed himself away from his desk, taking up the scarlet robe he had laid across the back of his chair and putting it on over his simple, long linen tunic. The robe hung loosely on the lich's cadaverous form. The folds draped to the floor and made the costly garment appear several sizes too large.

Szass Tam did nothing to mask his appearance when he was alone or with his undead minions. Only in public did he put on a truly human face—one of a tall, scholarly man with jet-black eyes and fleshy cheeks. To walk around looking like an undead creature would unnerve too many important Thayvians. He also knew that appearances were frequently deceiving in his country and that other zulkirs and their underlings also masked their true likenesses.

His frail-looking arms were nearly lost in the sleeves of the silken robe. The edges of the garment and the trim around the hood were embroidered with gold thread seeded with garnets. The lich enjoyed the fineries of human manufacture, like his expensive clothes and jewels. Others of his foul kind preferred to remain in the clothes they died in, looking like ill-preserved mummies and smelling like the grave. Szass Tam believed clothes presented an image, and thus he always decorated himself in the latest and most costly fashions.

He glided to the bookcase nearest the door and made a slight gesture with his left hand. Immediately he seemed to grow taller. The folds of the robe, which lay about his feet like a pool of blood, vanished, and in an instant, the hem barely touched the floor. The lich was floating, his slippered, skeletal feet dangling in the air. Pointing a bony finger toward the ceiling, he rose higher, ascending slowly, like a marionette pulled by invisible strings. He levitated up several feet, moving as a ghost, until his eyes were level with the topmost shelf. For several moments, he hovered in the air, studying the bindings of the books, which were worn and unreadable because of the passage of time. He grasped a thick red book from the center of the shelf and opened it to the first page to make sure it was the work he sought. Satisfied, he descended like a feather to the floor and padded from the room, reading the book as he went.

The volume was one of military strategies, a subject that the lich usually only had a passing interest in. He was curious about it now primarily because of Maligor's gnoll forces. Szass Tam glided through the halls of his fortified keep, passing skeletons, wights, mummies, and other creatures. He had four keeps in Thay; this was the largest, situated between Amruthar and Eltabar. It was ringed with graveyards, where more of his minions slept, waiting to be called to his defense if need be. The lands around this and his other keeps were patrolled by undead—in the evening with all manner of creatures, including several vampires and ghosts under his control, in the day by living men and by skeletons and zombies cloaked in heavy robes to help hide their appearance.

Szass Tam was more of a force to be feared after dark because his most powerful undead could only walk under the cover of darkness. Still, he knew the other zulkirs considered him too powerful a force to threaten even in bright daylight.

The lich continued to pace in his keep, lost in the writings of some long-dead general. It amused him that humans sought to gain land, influence, wealth, and glory through wars, only to lose all those things because of their mortality. He knew that Maligor had lived beyond a normal human lifespan. Most of the other zulkirs had also prolonged their lives by magical means. But Maligor was the oldest on the council other than Szass Tam, and the lich knew that the Zulkir of Alteration intended to live forever. However, Szass Tam was confident that Maligor didn't have the arcane ability to turn himself into a lich at the onset of his

death. Drinking potions to extend his life would not work
eternally. At some point, the magic would burn him up.

Why then does he vex me? Szass Tam wondered. Why
do I bother to concern myself with Maligor's petty doings?
Why do I waste my time watching him, watching his spirit
naga? The lich persisted in questioning his own motives as
he continued to scan the book.

It is my stance in Thay, he concluded, knowing the answer all along. If Maligor grows in power, that diminishes
my power—even if nothing about me or my land is affected.
I can't have that. No, I must do something about it, and I
must do something without the other wizards learning I am
taking action. But first I must discover what my living
brother is up to.

Szass Tam hated mysteries.

The lich continued to peruse the book for several more
hours, then returned to his library-laboratory to find the
room plunged in darkness. The candles had burned themselves out and dripped wax onto the desktop. Cursing,
Szass Tam pulled back a velvet curtain, letting moonlight
pour into the room. He closed his eyes and thought of
someone, and several minutes later she appeared with a
cleaning rag in one hand and a bundle of new candles in the
other.

The thin, pleasant-looking, middle-aged woman glanced
at the zulkir, who now appeared as a tall, scholarly man
with jet-black eyes and fleshy cheeks. She bowed to him,
smiled, and moved to the desk.

"Sorry, master," she said quietly. "I should have known
to check on you, but I thought the candles would burn longer, and I really didn't want to interrupt you. Forgive me.
These should last a good while." The woman, one of three
dozen living servants he harbored in his keep, busied herself removing each drop of wax from the desk and from
around the pewter holders with a thin-bladed knife. Then
she carefully put the new candles in place and lit them. The
woman knew the desk was important to Szass Tam, being a
very old "gift" from his mentor.

"Do you require anything else, master?"

Szass Tam smiled and shook his head. "That will be all, Charmaine," he said. The lich favored the woman, who had served him well for three decades. He provided her only with food; instead of gold, she sought immortality. The lich had promised to have one of his vampires give her eternal life when he was finished with her employment—probably in a few more years. Then she would continue to serve him faithfully forever.

Charmaine closed the door behind her. Szass Tam pulled the curtain shut, walked to his desk, and sat to gaze into the crystal ball again. It would be the last time he used it today—prolonged use was mentally taxing, even for him. It could also be dangerous. The longer the lich's mind remained linked to a scene in the ball, the more his consciousness wanted to stay there. He ran his now fleshy hand over the ball, felt its cool smoothness, and concentrated on Zulkir Maligor.

The colors danced, coalesced, and parted to reveal Maligor's face. The crystal ball appeared cloudy because of the wards Maligor had in place. The lich was furious and concentrated harder. Still the colors swirled.

At the same instant, Maligor felt something, a tugging at his mind, a tickling sensation that made it difficult for him to concentrate and made him edgy. He tried to keep at bay the persistent presence that was trying to contact him. The force was strong—definitely another zulkir, Maligor determined. He was angry at himself for so focusing his attention on his work that he had let his guard down. Still the mind reached out to his, and still Maligor resisted. Like a child caught doing something wrong, the wizard fluttered about to cover his work, then strolled to the window.

Maligor had the power to keep the probing zulkir from disturbing his endeavors, but he was curious, and he wanted to know who wished to contact him and why. Opening the barred window and inhaling the fresh air, he dropped his guard more and let the presence come.

Maligor's eyes narrowed. It was Szass Tam.

"Zulkir Maligor," the lich intoned in a rich, even voice. "We must talk."

Maligor glanced out over the open-air market, which was crowded at midday. He caught the faint smell of chickens and other livestock and vegetables drying in the sun. He surveyed the scene for several minutes, making the lich wait.

In his library, Szass Tam merely smiled. Maligor's show of preeminence was lost on the lich. Szass Tam was content to wait and peer through the crystal ball at Maligor, studying the darkened circles beneath his adversary's old eyes. Maligor hadn't slept much, the lich knew. His fingers were stained with ink, he was tired and unkempt, and he was most certainly up to something. Still, he was not so weary that he was careless. Szass Tam strained to see past him into the room beyond to catch a glimpse of what he had been doing. All he saw was a plate of food and a half-empty glass of wine. Even that picture was hazy because of the magical wards.

What was he up to? the lich continued to wonder. Maligor's puppet, the spirit naga, wasn't with him. Perhaps she was still in the field drilling the gnolls, where the lich had viewed her hours earlier. It was unusual for the evil beauty to be far from her mentor's side, where it was easier to gather up the crumbs he left behind.

"Talk, then," Maligor said, satisfied he had made his rival wait long enough. "You have my attention for a few moments. Is this something about the next meeting of the Council of Zulkirs? That is two weeks away. And you already know my stance on strengthening the First Escarpment forces."

"I don't care about your position on the escarpment," Szass Tam replied, allowing a wavering vision of himself to appear in the air before Maligor. He knew the form would hold Maligor's attention. "I care about your gnoll forces. I want to know what you plan to do with them."

"Surely you don't think I'd be foolish enough to take them against you," Maligor said, feigning surprise. "I'm no fool, Szass Tam. My forces are not meant for you."

The scholarly vision of Szass Tam solidified, but only to Maligor. Others would have seen only air. "I respect your intelligence," the lich lied. "You are among the most powerful zulkirs in Thay, and I know your wisdom would not allow you to challenge me. But I still want to know who your gnolls will challenge."

Maligor smiled. If Szass Tam was bothered by his gnolls, other wizards and tharchions would be concerned also. The lich's interest also made Maligor aware that he would have to set his plan into motion very soon to prevent other wizards from moving against the gnolls. He remained quiet, mulling over the situation and waiting for Szass Tam to continue. He didn't wait long.

"I want to know your scheme, friend zulkir." The lich's voice dripped with sarcasm. "I want to know what you are about. I may even want a piece of your plan."

Maligor thrust his hands in his pockets and rotated his neck to work out the stiffness. There was no hiding from the lich that he had been working on something.

"Very well," Maligor said, pretending defeat. "I should have known you would take an interest in my dealings. And I am certain that if you've been watching my gnolls, others have as well. I just want to be able to move them without interference, Szass Tam. If you desire a 'piece' of my plan, I will undoubtedly have to give it to you. With your undead army, you'd wrest it from me anyway. But if you are to take your 'piece' at least give me some aid in this endeavor." Maligor fingered a lump of gold in his pocket as he considered how to phrase his false plan.

"I plan to march against a young Red Wizard from the magical School of Illusion, who is likely beneath your notice. His name is Rembert Wellford, a distant cousin to a tharchion in Eltabar, and he has recently completed his apprenticeship and has gone off on his own.

"The young man has only begun to build his forces and attempt to make a name for himself in Thay. If I don't march against him, another wizard will. He isn't a major power, and I will keep him from becoming one. It isn't that I expect him to grow to any significant stature. I don't think he has the mettle or guile. Besides, if his position was my concern, I would let him be and concentrate on something else. It is his land that interests me."

Maligor watched Szass Tam's image, content that he had intrigued the lich's prying nature, although he remained skeptical whether the lich believed him or not. The lich would be a fool to, he knew.

"The land is rich, some of the richest earth in Thay," Maligor said truthfully. "In my lifetime, I have never been concerned with crops and weather spells, but I have come to realize that those things also equate to power. The land isn't far from another expanse of property I own, so conquering it would serve to increase my territory."

"Nor is it far from some of my land," Szass Tam said.

"Hence, your 'piece,' as you call it," Maligor continued. "I will divide this land with you. Of course, I will take the larger portion, since it will be my gnolls fighting for it. Still, you will have a significant section of land. All I ask is that you use your skeletons and zombies as a deterrent. I don't want them to join my gnolls. This is my undertaking, and my force is more than up to it. I just want you to gather a group of your undead to make some other wizards nervous. It will split their attention so not all eyes are on me."

Maligor was becoming increasingly pleased with himself, certain that his plan sounded plausible.

"You wouldn't oppose me in this, would you?" Maligor queried, seeking some response from the lich.

"No," Szass Tam said simply. "Although I am curious why you have just now developed an interest in fertile land. Still, your plan is interesting. Does Rembert Wellford suspect anything? And his neighbors . . . are they powerful? Where precisely is this land?"

"The land is south of Eltabar, nearly directly east of Amruthar," Maligor said as he continued to finger the gold in his pocket. "His neighbors are inconsequential farmers under the jurisdiction of other wizards. While the wizards are a concern, the farmers are not—they can't possibly stand up to my gnolls. And I don't think Rembert has a clue. Even if he did, he could do nothing to stop me. If he has associates, they aren't likely to step in to aid him. Helping Rembert would only leave them open to my wrath. His former mentor, the Zulkir of Illusion, wouldn't help him either."

"You've planned well," Szass Tam said. "But Rembert's land has importance beyond its agricultural value, although you haven't mentioned that. The land isn't far from the sanctuary of the Zulkir of Illusion. It is within striking distance, a good military perch if you are considering positioning yourself against the zulkir."

Maligor didn't respond at first, letting the silence linger. He feigned looking disconcerted and cast his eyes downward at his slippered feet.

"Well, there is that about the land," Maligor admitted, allowing himself an evil grin. "I suppose the property's position is just as important as the richness of its soil."

"I want half the land," Szass Tam demanded quietly. "That will keep you from becoming too strong. And I will not help you," he added in a tone that brooked no dissension. "I will not muster any undead to draw attention away from you—and to me. I will not give you a portion of my army to aid in your plan. However, I will not oppose you, and that is of consequence. Nor will I spread word of your scheme."

"I could indeed expect no more from you," Maligor said graciously, accepting the lich's part in his ruse, "and when I am successful, half the land will be yours. We are agreed, then?"

The image of the lich wavered, became ghostlike, then melted away.

"We are agreed," the air replied.

Maligor felt the presence depart. Then he concentrated to shield his mind from any further interruptions and closed the barred windows. His plans couldn't be progressing better, he thought, delighted that the lich seemed certain of his target. But Maligor knew the Zulkir of Necromancy, knew that he was capable of backstabbing and twisting promises. No doubt the lich planned to take all of Rembert Wellford's land once it was in the hands of Maligor's gnolls. The lich wouldn't settle for a mere half, and taking all of it would be a likely double cross. Or, far less likely, perhaps Szass Tam would try to take the land before Maligor's gnolls could get there.

Perhaps the gnolls truly will have to move against Rembert to keep the lich satisfied and unsuspecting, Maligor thought. And if a young, power-hungry Rembert had to fall to mask the real plan, it would be an added benefit. Then there was Asp, the zulkir added to himself. He would no longer be lying to the naga if he really did go after an important piece of land.

Maligor padded to his marble-topped table, pushed aside his cold plate of boiled fish, and placed a page of parchment before him. Dipping a quill in honey-scented ink, he began to pen a spell. Four completed scrolls, neatly tied with cord, lay on the right-hand corner of his table. Next to them lay a half-dozen blank scrolls waiting for Maligor's attention. He sipped a glass of spiced blackberry wine between passages.

The Zulkir of Alteration was obsessed with increasing his darkenbeast army. Under cover of last night's darkness, he had moved half his force, along with their inhuman guardians, to the basement of an abandoned grain mill north of Amruthar. That left room in the tower's lower level for more darkenbeasts.

Maligor recognized his limitations. A human mind could hold only so many spells within it, only enough to let him create four or five dozen darkenbeasts a day. However, by transferring those spells onto paper instead—the scrolls in front of him—he would be able to create far more of the beasts tomorrow. He had been adding to his magical scroll collection, having nearly two dozen now. Tomorrow, or perhaps the next day, he would read them all, transforming every loose rodent and caged animal in his tower into a deadly creature.

That many darkenbeasts should be enough, he thought. Maligor paused, then decided to take stock of his other magical constructs and servants. It wouldn't do to take all of his forces out of the tower and leave it unprotected. He took mental inventory of his golems, magical creatures that were manlike in form but were made of stone and clay. They moved slowly, but they were relentless and powerful, and some were ensorcelled with special powers that allowed them to breathe flame. He also had a dozen apprentices here, only half of which he would take with him to the gold mines. The remainder should have enough defensive spells to keep anyone who might make it past his magical guards and wards and golems at bay. There were also the gnoll tower guards and slaves, should anyone be so foolish to attack his holdings.

All of that should be more than enough, if for some reason another Red Wizard decided to attack his keep while he was gone. However, he remained confident that all energies would be directed against his gnolls and their false battle plans.

Reveling in the intricacies of his scheme, the Red Wizard went to the cabinet and retrieved more blank scrolls. More darkenbeasts, he thought—many, many more darkenbeasts. He resumed penning the enchanted scrolls.

* * * * *

In his library, Szass Tam leaned back in his chair, staring at the clear crystal ball that sparkled in the light of the thick tapers. It was undeniable that Maligor had lied to him; the Zulkir of Alteration would have no reason to tell the lich what he really intended to do with the gnolls.

Szass Tam reverently pushed the crystal ball to the side of his desk and cleared a larger space in the center. He rose, paced to a map holder, and ran a slender, bony finger over the unmarked tubular map cases. The lich selected the center tube, which contained a map showing an over-

view of the central portion of Thay. He returned to his desk
and pulled the map from its container. Spreading the
clothlike parchment out on the desk, he placed a candle on
each corner to weigh it down and prevent it from curling.
Amruthar showed several inches from the western edge of
the map.

Running his left index finger from Amruthar to the land
now held by Rembert Wellford, the lich imagined Maligor's
gnolls marching on the young illusionist.

One thing was certain, Szass Tam decided. Maligor
wasn't interested in Wellford's holdings. The lich studied
maps of Thay until well in the evening, formulating possible
uses for the gnolls and probable targets. He was frustrated, however, finding nothing that stood out as Maligor's likely goal. He resigned himself to continuing his
postulations and to keeping his "agreement" with the
Zulkir of Alteration.

It was well after midnight when a weary Charmaine
rapped on the door. "So sorry to disturb you, master," she
said, her voice muffled behind the wood, "but one of your
minions insists on speaking with you."

Szass Tam put on his fleshly form and gestured toward
the door. It creaked open, revealing Charmaine, in her
bedclothes, holding a candle. A ghoul stood next to her,
attempting to keep its distance from the flame. The undead
man shuffled forward, bits of its rotting flesh clinging to the
doorframe as it passed through. The ghoul at one time had
been a jeweler in Eltabar; gold glinted from around his
wrists and neck where his neck chain and bracelets had imbedded themselves in rotting flesh. Pieces of expensive
clothing still hung on his unnaturally thin frame.

"Will there be anything else, master?" Charmaine queried softly.

"No. You may go."

Charmaine gracefully retreated down the hall, the candlelight marking her passage.

The lich turned to face the undead creature as it ambled
toward him. The ghoul had difficulty speaking, since half of

its lower jaw was missing. Szass Tam opted to pull the information from its undead mind rather than translate its guttural words into understandable conversation.

The ghoul told Szass Tam of the patrol he was a part of, how they had spotted movement and heard voices in a small grove of trees and how the ghouls had hungrily moved in to investigate. In the center of the trees were three humans, one of them likely Thayvian because of his bald head, and a centaur. The bald man died quickly, but the others were unusually strong and resourceful, killing most of the ghoul patrol. It told its master how it escaped to relay this information directly, since somehow in its decomposing brain, it believed the information was important.

Szass Tam mentally pressed the ghoul for more, and it complied, telling him in detail what the surviving humans, a blond-haired man and a fire-haired woman, looked like. To the ghoul, the centaur appeared much like those who worked on the slave plantations and elsewhere in Thay. The lich didn't find the information especially interesting, assuming that the ghoul described a pair of slaves and their centaur keeper.

But then the ghoul mentioned a shiny chain it saw dangling from the blond man's neck. It was adorned with a polished silver moon affixed to a harp. The jewelry had come loose from under the man's clothing during the fight, and the ghoul noticed it because it disliked silver.

Szass Tam's abandoned his fleshly form as the ghoul continued to describe the unsuccessful battle to the half-listening lich. The lich's eyes, now pinpoints of hot light, stared into the dark corners of the library.

"Harpers," he whispered.

Eight

"Don't!" Galvin admonished, grabbing Brenna's hand roughly before she could scratch her bald head. He held it for a moment, feeling how soft and smooth it was, how thin and small her fingers were, then released it when he caught her looking at him.

"But it itches!" she moaned. "It feels like ants are crawling on my scalp."

Wynter, who led the procession down the road toward Amruthar, paused to watch the scene between the druid and Brenna Graycloak, who had stopped several yards behind him. He decided not to involve himself in the conversation and continued on down the road. They'd catch up when they were finished, he thought, and he'd trot slowly, just in case.

This was the trio's second day on their journey to Amruthar. Today the sky was filled with cottony white clouds. The centaur was certain a wizard would manage to coax rain out of them sometime before dark, and he was tired of getting wet. He wanted to be in Amruthar by nightfall. In the city, he knew that with only one or two of his gold coins, he could get a

143

steaming feast and a sturdy roof over his head. Wynter was hungry. He was tired of the fruit and nuts Galvin provided. The centaur's cavernous stomach rumbled in response to his thoughts, and he cast his view about the countryside, searching for something else to occupy his mind.

The road narrowed as it wound between young birches, some of them recently planted. Wynter noted that many of the lower branches of the trees had been trimmed to shape them. Ahead, the land changed from flat meadows and landscaped orchards to low rolling hills. Cattle grazed on a rise to the left. Wynter stared at the slow-moving cows and imagined himself eating a thick steak.

His stomach rumbled again, and he turned and concentrated on Galvin and Brenna to keep his thoughts from food.

"It really itches!" Brenna complained.

"That's from shaving your head with a sword," Galvin explained.

"*You* shaved my head," she said tersely. "I only cut my hair off."

"Just don't scratch it," the druid scolded. "If you scratch it, it's going to itch all the more, and you'll leave welts."

"You're enjoying this," she fumed.

"Yes," Galvin answered simply, immediately regretting his response. He started shuffling down the road, hoping the argument had ended.

"Oaf!"

"At least I'm honest." Galvin sighed, wishing fervently he hadn't started the conversation. He picked up the pace, and Brenna kept at his shoulder.

"Try being a little more polite and a little less honest."

"I don't want you to stand out. We have to fit in, remember?"

"I know, I know. You needn't talk to me as if I were stupid," she huffed.

"Sorry." Galvin was a little surprised to find himself apologizing for something so trivial. "Besides, if you scratch, you might ruin the barbed whip Wynter painted."

Brenna smiled ruefully. "I want to find a mirror," she remarked. "Then I'm going to buy a hat, a broad-brimmed one that will cover up my bald head."

"We've more important things to do than go shopping," the druid interjected, stopping again and staring into her eyes. He was dreading entering the city, especially a Thayvian one, but he didn't want Brenna to know just how apprehensive he was. "We've got to find out where this Red Wizard Maligor is and what he's up to."

"And to do that," Brenna interrupted, "we'll have to poke around in Amruthar. You're going to draw too much attention if you parade around like that. Hence, we shop."

Galvin gave her a puzzled glance.

"Your clothes," she explained. "They're filthy and nearly worn out. I'll pass for a wealthy Thayvian easily enough, but no slave of mine is going to look like a herd of pigs trampled him. We'll get you into some better clothes, but nothing too fancy. And I could use another dress or two. If we have to spend more than one day in Amruthar, we're going to need more than one thing to wear."

Galvin frowned, then brightened. "It's a nice thought, but we haven't enough gold to buy clothes."

"Of course we do. You've got the gold you were going to pay the gnoll spy, and I have more than enough with me." Brenna jingled the coin purse at her side to emphasize her point. "And if we're really pressed, I can always sell my necklace. I have lots of others at home."

Defeated, Galvin nodded. She was enjoying this too much, he realized. Once again he envied the centaur; Wynter never had to bother about clothes.

"We have to get to Amruthar before we can do anything," he said, a bit sulkily. "We can't be too far now, can we, Wynter? Wynter?" Galvin glanced up the road, surprised to see the centaur several dozen yards ahead. The druid was amazed that he could become so engrossed in a discussion with the sorceress that he would lose track of what was going on around him.

Turning to face Brenna, Galvin saw her grinning broadly.

She started off at a brisk pace to catch up with Wynter, and
the druid fell in behind her. Her stamina had increased no-
ticeably during the past few days. Galvin knew her muscles
must ache, being unaccustomed to so much traveling, but
she wasn't complaining, and she was keeping up. Grudg-
ingly he had to admire her for that.

As the trio crested the first low rise, they saw the walls
of Amruthar in the distance. The city sat at the base of
three squat hills. Their slopes were covered with small
farms and were a brilliant green from the riot of well-
watered crops growing there.

Ahead of them on the road, perhaps a mile distant,
Galvin noticed a small wagon pulled by a pair of work-
horses. The wagon, which must have been from a local
farm, was filled with some type of crop.

"We're too far away to see them clearly," Galvin began,
"but the walls look massive."

"And it's patrolled by lots of guards," the centaur surmised, continuing to lead the procession closer to the city.
He explained that the larger cities in Thay, such as Amruthar, had high, thick stone walls held together with mortar.
Smaller cities usually had wooden walls, although some had
stone walls if the residents were wealthy and influential.
Even the smallest of Thayvian communities had at least a
spike-filled ditch surrounding it, and all of them had a guard
force. The resident wizards wanted their homes well protected.

"A few walls have spells on them. Eltabar's did when I
visited it," the centaur continued. He reminisced about that
dark city's invisible, domelike shield. "I was with my father. He said he wanted me to see the city. He had other
reasons for going, of course, most notably slave-trading. I
had heard about the dome, and I just had to test it out. I
picked up a rock and tried to throw it over the brick wall. It
bounced right back at me, and I knew the stories were
true. My father was angry and never took me there again."

"Fortunate for you," Galvin observed as he sidestepped
a deep rut in the road.

"Why are all the cities walled?" Brenna asked, looking ahead at Amruthar. "They can't possibly be afraid of Aglarond or Mulhorand this far into Thay, and Rashemen, the land of the witches, won't bother them."

"The wizards are afraid of each other, so they build walls," Wynter said. "Funny. I doubt any wall could stand up to a Red Wizard. But at least they keep out the undead." His pace was faster now.

The trio grew silent as they neared an august tower on the western side of Amruthar. It sat a few hundred yards south of the road they traveled on, and they gave it a wide berth because of the numerous guards milling around outside it. Several slaves tended herb gardens outside the tower's front doors. One looked up and stared at the Harpers and Brenna as they passed by and entered Amruthar through the main gates.

The gates were guarded by a quintet of heavily armed and armored men on top of the barbicon. Wynter surmised there were additional unseen guards and other defenses. The men watched the centaur and humans enter but said nothing. The Harpers tried not to look back and were pleased that their appearances had gotten them through without question.

It was late afternoon, and the city teemed with activity. The road led to a merchants' district, where the sites and sounds overwhelmed the druid. Stalls—some looking like permanent parts of the city and others appearing to have been carried in today—lined the street.

The nearest stall had rows of dried peppers hanging from strings, so many that little of the stall's wood showed through. On the ledge, peppers were piled high—long, thin green ones, pear-shaped yellow varieties, red peppers of many shapes and sizes, and purple ones that were large and bulbous and inviting. The vendor was a bald, hawk-nosed man with a ruddy complexion. He noticed the Harpers watching him and beckoned them closer.

"Hot chili peppers! Sweet bells! Mild wax peppers!" he barked. "The best in Amruthar!" His voice was scratchy and deep and had an irritating quality that cut through the noise of the crowd. Galvin and Wynter ignored him and moved deeper into the marketplace.

Brenna had become distracted by a booth off to the right. An elderly, heavyset woman with a sprinkling of age spots on her bald head was selling bolts of colorful cloth. In another time and place, the sorceress would have been tempted to buy some cloth from her and have the fabric made into dresses. The cloth looked rich—most of it, anyway. One bolt had metallic threads running through it and was no doubt expensive. Spotting Galvin and Wynter moving away from her, she hurried to catch up, elbowing her way through a group of gossiping women.

Brenna noted the market was just as busy, perhaps even busier, than the ones she frequented in Mesring, Dlusk, and Furthinghome back in Aglarond. The goods were similar—at least those she had been eyeing appeared to be. And the people wore the same expressions: the merchants seemed friendly, the shoppers looked stern-faced and ready to bargain, and the children eyed everything in wonder. The only difference was that nearly everyone she saw was bald. Those who had hair were few, and their hair was cut so short that parts of their scalps peeked through. She noticed only humans in this crowd. In Aglarond, the marketplaces in the largest cities would also attract dwarves, halflings, gnomes, and elves.

The sorceress was familiar enough with the social structures of cities to notice that most of those shopping were from the middle class. Their clothes were neat and reasonable, but they were made of simple material and lacked the embroidery and trim preferred by the wealthy. There were also some peasants, who seemed most interested in the stalls that sold second-hand wares. She spied a few people who were obviously affluent, judging by their clothes and bearing. One stood apart from the stalls and watched someone purchase oils. Brenna smiled. The person doing the buying was probably her servant, maybe a slave, as his hair fell to the lobes of his ears. Just as in any other city, she thought, the rich couldn't be bothered to soil their hands by purchasing something from a commoner on the street.

"Pretty lady? Pretty, pretty lady? Want to buy my fruit?" A peddler was calling to her. "Special price for you, pretty lady." He held up a bright pink, banana-shaped fruit.

Galvin took her by the arm and steered her to the center of the street, where there was less traffic and they were farther from the merchants. His hand felt clammy.

"Stop it," she whispered. "Let go of me. You're my slave, remember? Act the part."

The druid dropped her arm and glared at her. Falling in step behind her, he cast his head toward the ground, as he had observed other slaves doing. Peering out the corners of his eyes, he scanned the marketplace. It had been several years since he was in a district like this, and he found it threatening and close. It reminded him too much of his early life, when his parents would take him to a marketplace where the shoppers were ripe for pickpocketing. The victims would be distracted watching the cute young Galvin, so it was easy for his parents to cut their purses. The druid put his hand on his money pouch and continued through the market.

To his right, peddlers were selling candles, oil lamps, knitted blankets, brass trinkets, and citrus fruit. To his left, they bartered for chickens, tack, costume jewelry, pots, pans, and other household items. He noted a few were selling clothes, and he nudged Wynter.

"Not here," the centaur whispered. "The wealthy—and most of the middle class—don't buy their clothes and fineries in an open-air market. They go to shops where the prices are higher, but the goods are usually better."

The centaur reached forward and tapped Brenna on the shoulder. "We want to move through the market and into an established business district. One can't be far away. I'm going ahead. Follow me at a short distance and pretend you know where you're going."

"You're in charge here," Galvin said. "I'm out of my element." He studied the buildings as he walked behind Brenna. They were nearly through the open-air market. He felt relieved; ahead, the crowds thinned considerably.

Unlike other cities Galvin had visited, Amruthar had few wooden buildings. The stalls were wood, and the overhangs and posts supporting some of the balconies were wood. The wood looked old and weathered, showing that the city was far from new. But the majority of the buildings were made of clay bricks and mortar. A few had been added on to recently; the clay bricks on the second story were of a darker color, indicating they were newer than the ones on the ground floor.

A few blocks later, the street changed from hard-packed dirt to cobblestones, and the facades of the buildings looked fancier, evidence that people of wealth lived here.

The druid felt caged in by the buildings, which stretched three stories tall in this neighborhood. There was no way out but to follow street after street like a rat running through a maze. He couldn't see a sign of trees or open spaces; the only green things were the sod roofs that covered nearly every structure. To him, the sod was the city's only redeeming feature. Too bad he couldn't walk on it. The cobblestones were uncomfortable.

Galvin knew he should adapt. Nearly all of the Harpers lived in cities, and the majority of missions were in well-populated areas. He had never declined an assignment from Harper leaders that would take him into a city, but he had frequently made himself scarce when he knew one was going to come up. He couldn't dodge all of them; he certainly didn't want his peers to realize his weakness. And this mission was one he welcomed because of his hatred of the Red Wizards.

For most of his life, he had considered city people weak, dependent on the city for food, shelter, clothing, and protection. Few could properly defend themselves, and fewer still would be able to survive in the wilderness. They feared being alone, Galvin thought, so they congregated in their stone buildings inside stone walls.

Ahead, Wynter came to a stop. Galvin and Brenna could see he was talking to someone, but the figure stood in front of the centaur and was mostly obscured. The centaur's tail swished back and forth lazily, then he bent forward to shake the figure's hand.

The centaur continued on for several more blocks, turning down one street, then going up another, his hooves clopping rhythmically on the cobblestones. Brenna noticed that the city was built like a wheel; the major streets were like spokes emanating out from a central hub, probably the government district. Wynter was heading down one of the spokes, toward what looked like the city's stable district. Here the cobblestones ended and the dirt road began again.

Brenna strolled closer, then suddenly stopped. Galvin looked up at her and noticed she had turned pale. Beyond her, in Wynter's direction, was a series of pens. All of them contained people. The druid stared openmouthed at the sight. Like cattle, the people milled about slowly as workers directed them away from the corners so the pens could be cleaned.

Wynter paused several yards from the pens and glanced over his shoulder, nodding for Brenna and Galvin to join him. Still shocked at the tableau, they padded forward.

"I'll look over the slave pens for an hour or two, inspecting the merchandise and talking to other buyers." The centaur's eyes were sad as he stared at the pens. "Since Maligor's a zulkir, he's bound to have plenty of slaves. Maybe I can find out a little bit about our wizard friend here."

Brenna took the initiative now, happy for an opportunity to get away from the pens. "Galvin and I will go shopping."

Wynter had heard the location of a respected business district only a few blocks away and pointed the sorceress and Galvin in that direction.

"Meet me back here in two hours," Wynter advised. "I won't be able to stomach the pens any longer than that. If you're not here by then, I'll know you've found trouble and

I'll come looking for you." Wynter pawed at the ground and lowered his voice. "One of the slavers is watching us, so let's be about our tasks."

Brenna tugged on Galvin's sleeve, guiding him toward the shop district Wynter had described. She knew they had followed his directions correctly when the cobblestone street began again.

There were sidewalks in the small but fashionable business district—planks raised above the cobblestone streets and covered with awnings to keep the shoppers dry during showers and cool during the heat of midday. There were plenty of Thayvians about, but not nearly the number as in the open-air market.

Galvin saw that these people acted differently, more refined and courteous. They didn't shove each other to get a better position near a store window. Most were dressed well, and aside from the slaves they had in tow to carry their packages, they didn't strike him as objectionable. Obviously not everyone in Thay was bad. The druid wondered what kept the good people in such an evil land.

"We don't have much time," Brenna said, summoning his mind back to the business at hand. "The sun's starting to set, and if this is like other cities, that means businesses will be closing soon."

"How about this one?" he suggested, pointing at a women's dress shop, the exterior of which was made of rose-colored stone rather than clay bricks. The large front window was trimmed with light blue paint, and bright red flowers were arranged in a planter in front of it. A deep green dress with sequin trim hung in the window.

"Good choice," she said, thinking Galvin was looking at the dress; in fact, he was staring at the flowers. "But that particular dress is a bit flashy for me. I want to look rich, not gaudy. I'll go inside and see what I can find. There's a men's shop next door. Make use of it."

Galvin waited until Brenna was swallowed by the women's shop, then he shuffled toward the men's clothing store and fumbled with the door latch with his sweaty hand. At last it creaked inward, and the smell of cedar rushed out to meet him. He padded slowly inside, forgetting to close the door behind him.

"High class for a slave."

The man behind the counter startled Galvin, and the druid whirled around to face the speaker, his eyes at the same time taking in row upon row of folded clothes and brass lanterns that cast a soft, even glow throughout the shop's interior.

"Sure you're in the right shop?" the proprietor persisted, eyeing Galvin intently, as if memorizing every detail about him. The man was thin and bald, and the riot of tattoos on his head made it look as if he was wearing a cap. His skin was nearly white from lack of sun and it had the appearance of parchment, frail and brittle.

"Are you in the right place?" the man asked, his voice rising. He emphasized each word.

"My mistress . . ." the druid stammered, uncertain of what to say and debating whether to flee back out into the street.

A glimmer caught in the man's dark blue eyes. "Hmmm . . . I see," he said, rubbing his manicured hands together. "She wants you to look presentable, huh?"

"Yes," Galvin said nervously, glancing about and spying a rack of cloaks, several of them green. The druid hadn't been in a clothing store since his youth. The memory was uncomfortable, as were the outfits his mother had ordered him to try on.

He quickly attempted to take everything in, realizing he must look foolish. Focusing on the glass counter in front of the proprietor, he tried to relax and failed miserably.

"Haven't been in a place like this before, huh? It's rare that we get one of your kind here."

The druid cast his eyes on the polished floor that smelled faintly of lemons and clenched his fist. He understood why Wynter was so opposed to slavery.

"I need clothes," Galvin said simply.

The proprietor laughed and waved his hand at the racks

and neatly stacked piles of clothes. "Go ahead. Just don't get anything dirty."

The druid lost himself in a long aisle of cedar shelves, grateful to be out of view of the shop owner. He scanned the shelves until he spied a stack of green tunics. Quickly grabbing the one on top, he trotted back to the counter.

"Right size?"

The druid shrugged.

The proprietor shook his head at Galvin. "Turn around. Here." The bald man strode from behind the counter and held the tunic up to Galvin's back, snickering when he discovered the shoulders were far too small. "You need something bigger. C'mon, I'll help you. Your mistress better appreciate this."

"Do Red Wizards ever shop here?" Galvin asked as the man ushered him back down the aisle.

"Sometimes," the man replied, muttering softly about the stupidity of slaves.

"Any zulkirs?"

"Why does a slave care where Red Wizards shop?"

"Just interested," Galvin replied glumly.

Replacing the tunic Galvin had selected, the man ignored the druid and thumbed through a stack, pulling out an olive-green shirt. He handed it to Galvin and strolled deeper into the store.

"Need some leggings?"

Galvin nodded. The druid realized there were enough articles in this store to clothe an entire village.

"What color?"

The druid flushed. "Umm, green. Or brown. It really doesn't matter."

The bald man shook his head and pulled a tan pair of breeches from another stack. Holding them in front of the druid, he smiled, pleased he had guessed the size correctly.

"And a cloak. Green or gray, I suppose," Galvin added, remembering the green ones he had spotted when he came in. "I guess the color isn't important."

The proprietor shuffled to the racks and scanned the garments. Galvin watched the proprietor pull out a plain gray cloak the color of hearth ashes. Satisfied, the man returned to the counter and began scratching on a sheet of curled parchment, figuring out the cost.

Galvin shifted back and forth on his feet. "I should have another set," he decided. "Just in case."

"In case of what?" the proprietor quipped.

In case I'm stuck in Amruthar for awhile, Galvin thought. But he kept the thought to himself.

"All right," the man sighed, dropping the parchment with a flourish and escorting Galvin down another aisle of clothes.

The druid emerged from the shop wearing his second purchase, consisting of light brown pants with a voluminous-sleeved ivory shirt over the top and a cloak. The cloak was rather elaborate—green trimmed with a lighter green embroidery. Its suede collar was dyed green and pinned together by a simple iron clasp in the shape of an owl's head. Galvin actually liked the outfit, even though the two changes of clothes had cost him all of his coins. He suspected that the proprietor had charged him too much, but he knew better than to argue.

He waited outside the women's shop for several minutes, catching admiring glances from several Thayvian women who passed by and feeling increasingly ill at ease. One woman stopped to demand directions. She had a pleasant voice and obviously seemed to know where she was going, but Galvin avoided her attempt at conversation and began pacing nervously in front of the shop window. Eventually Brenna came out in a midnight blue dress trimmed with light blue lace that fit her tightly from neck to hips, then flared out to hang a few inches above the ground. Like Galvin, she carried a package under her arm. The druid eyed the bundle and guessed there were two or three dresses in it.

"Nice," she said, giving Galvin the once-over. "Good taste. Find out anything while you were in there?"

The druid shook his head.

"Well, I found out that Maligor has an army in the woods. A bunch of gnolls." Brenna seemed pleased with herself and noted Galvin's surprised expression. "Women gossip," she explained. "But the women in the shop didn't know what the army's for."

Smugly nodding across the street, the sorceress added, "Want a bath?" Just then the bald shopkeeper closed and locked the door of the men's store behind them and put up a "closed" sign. The shops were starting to shut down for the day, and that meant they would have to meet Wynter soon.

They scampered across the street, sidestepping the patrons emerging from the bathhouse cleaned and perfumed. The bathhouse windows were fogged, and the scent of soap greeted them as they hurried inside.

After Brenna vouched for the behavior of her slave, they were led into a large room. Steam drifted upward from a dozen large, waist-high wooden tubs, two of which were occupied. The room was divided, one side for women, the other for men.

Brenna waltzed away from Galvin, and an attendant herded the druid to a tub in the back of the room. Galvin noted there were no other slaves here.

The attendant held out his arm for Galvin's clothes, and the druid quickly turned around. Carefully removing his Harper neck chain and stuffing it discreetly into a pocket, he discarded his clothes and climbed several steps. Settling into the tub, he gasped at the unaccustomed heat. Slowly he eased himself into the water, watching his flesh turn pink from the hot liquid. He glanced over the side of the tub, determined to discover what made the water so warm.

"Problem?" the attendant asked, as he handed Galvin a cake of yellow-tinged soap.

The druid shook his head and grabbed the soap, noting it smelled earthy and rather pleasant. Watching a pudgy bald man in a nearby tub, Galvin imitated him, rubbing the cake up and down his arms, then submerging himself to rinse off the lather. The druid found he was getting used to the warm water, and he enjoyed the sensation.

Across the room, he caught a glimpse of Brenna slipping into a smaller tub. Her pale skin shone through the steam, and the druid found himself staring at her. He knew that some city residents cloaked themselves in modesty, but in this bathhouse, people didn't seem to worry.

The sorceress dipped her face into the water, scrubbing at her forehead. Holding her breath, she sank into the recesses of the tub and emerged to spot the druid staring at her.

They left the bathhouse a half-hour later, cleaned and perfumed. Brenna had new designs painted on her head—a curved-bladed dagger and the symbol of Malar, the Beast Lord. Refreshed, they sauntered toward the slave pens.

"That wasn't too bad," Galvin admitted, angry at himself for not thinking of their spying mission while delighting in his bath.

Brenna tittered and Galvin reddened, then glanced down the street to hide his embarrassment. The slave market was only a few more blocks away.

She tugged at his sleeve.

Galvin turned and looked at her. The last rays of the sun glinted off her polished scalp and reflected warmly in her eyes. He found himself staring again.

"You're supposed to walk behind me, remember?" she said. The folds of her dress swished softly as she passed by the druid, chin tilted toward the rooftops.

* * * * *

Wynter's childhood rushed at him as the centaur toured the slave pens. Nearly four dozen slaves milled about the largest pen; these were not prime stock and could be bartered for. There were four other pens. One contained women who were too fat, too old, or too ugly to be used for pleasure slaves, but could work well as domestic servants.

Another, the closest, was filled with young men, obviously laborers. The third was crowded with families—at least the slavers were trying to sell them as units. The fourth held dwarves, halflings, and children. There were no elves for sale today.

Wynter eyed the stock, remembering how his father had examined slaves. The conditions in the pens looked as deplorable as when he had visited the markets in his youth. The slaves were allowed no privacy, could not talk long to each other without the guards fearing they were plotting to escape. They wore very little clothing. Potential buyers didn't want the merchandise concealed. Wynter saw that about a dozen of the young laborers had fresh whip marks on their backs, the blood glistening in the fading sunlight.

"Can I help you today?" a tall, young man called as he came toward the centaur. The man wore a leather tunic that was much too large for his lanky frame, and he carried a whip at his side. His bald head bore an unusual tattoo made to look like a beholder. His skull served as the monster's body, with many eye stalks painted in a ring around his head. The creature's central eye was painted on the man's forehead.

"Just looking. A poor selection, it seems to me."

"That's because you're shopping late," the man replied matter-of-factly, fingering the whip. When he smiled, the beholder's central eye rode up on his forehead. "We had a big auction this morning, and a few of the wizards bought the best of the lot. There're still some good ones left. Depends what you're interested in. You can have the dwarves cheap."

The man gestured, and the slaves moved closer so the centaur could get a better look. One scarred young man glared at the slaver. The slaver returned the stare and flicked his wrist, the whip snaking out from his hand and striking the man in the cheek, drawing blood.

"I was interested in quantity—a few dozen to work the fields near Thaymount," Wynter interjected, hoping to keep the slaver occupied so he wouldn't whip any more slaves. "I'm the chief buyer for a slave plantation there."

The man whipped the slave again, harder this time, then grinned at Wynter. "You've traveled a long way." His expression caused the beholder's central eye to rest about an inch above the bridge of his nose. "The best of the lot are gone. Sorry to disappoint you. You must be from the Agri Plantation. You work for Blackland Ironhoof?"

Wynter's dark eyes narrowed. "He's my father."

"Long time since someone from that plantation's been here. Heard you're doing all your buying from Eltabar lately. Heard you have a good breeding program, too." The slaver kept up the conversation, not noticing the centaur's unease. "Yep, biggest plantation in northern Thay. Eltabar running low on slaves?"

"No." The centaur pawed at the ground. "So which wizards beat me out of your best stock?"

"The Zulkir of Alteration, Maligor, got the best of them, or rather his woman did. A young Red Wizard near the market bought quite a few, too. He's still here. I can introduce you."

The centaur looked across the pens and spotted a scarlet-robed man eyeing the group of slave families. "No. But I am curious about Maligor. Where can I find him?"

The slaver laughed hard enough to make all the painted eyes on his head wiggle animatedly. He slapped his hand against a bony hip and stared up at Wynter.

"Now, I don't know anyone who wants to find a wizard as powerful as Maligor, at least anyone who works on a slave plantation—especially when the wizard seems to be up to something." The eyes eventually stopped quivering, and the slaver scratched a spot on his head above one of the eyestalks. The design remained unaltered; it was a permanent tattoo.

"Maybe I have some pleasure slaves to sell him," Wynter said, deepening his voice and making the conversation instantly somber. "Where can I find this woman or one of his other agents? And do you know what he's up to?"

"Don't know. Don't care. I mind my own business. Too

bad your daddy hasn't taught you to mind yours. If you want to find one of his agents, look in the Gold Dragon Inn. You'll have to wait outside. They don't let centaurs in no matter how much gold they have. Maligor's people usually have a thorny vine tattooed around their necks. Looks like a collar, and I promise you that Maligor keeps them on a tight leash."

The slaver glanced over his shoulder at the wizard scrutinizing the slaves in the pen. "Now, if you're not going to buy anything . . ." He smiled broadly, grabbed the centaur's hand and shook it firmly, then moved toward the young Red Wizard.

Wynter peered across the slave pens at all the doleful expressions of the occupants. He knew that slavery existed in other pockets of Faerun, but nowhere was it more blatant than in Thay, and in no other country were there more slaves than free men. He reached inside his money pouch and felt the coins, then trotted determinedly toward the slaver.

* * * * *

Galvin and Brenna neared the place where they had left Wynter. The number of people on the streets was dwindling, and the druid was feeling more at ease—until they turned a corner and he saw the centaur leading five dwarves by ropes.

"Damn!" Galvin cursed softly, running toward Wynter. Brenna hurried to catch up, but her new dress made running awkward.

"What are you doing?" the druid fumed, glaring up into the centaur's face. "Don't tell me you bought these slaves!"

"I had to," Wynter replied.

"No. No, you didn't. This is just great, Wyn."

Brenna caught up with the Harpers and tugged on Galvin's arm. "Take it easy, Galvin. It's done now."

Galvin glanced down at the dwarves. They were dirty

and haggard-looking, and the ends of their snarled beards were tucked under the ropes tied about their waists. The clothes they wore were too big—discarded human outfits, no doubt. Healthy dwarves would have had too much girth for the clothes, but these were obviously malnourished.

The five stared up at the druid with hatred etched in their eyes. One strained against the rope Wynter held.

"Listen, I'm sorry," Galvin began, apologizing to the slaves for his outburst.

"They don't understand you," Wynter interrupted. "They only speak Dwarvish."

"Wonderful," Galvin replied, fingering the clasp of his cloak nervously. "Well, bring them along. We'll let them go when we're outside the city."

Brenna smiled weakly at Wynter. "Find anything out?"

"Yeah," he said softly. "Our next stop is the Gold Dragon Inn. Maligor's agents, and likely those of other wizards, frequent the place. A slaver told me Maligor is up to something, but he didn't know what. He wouldn't say what, anyway."

"After that we'll need to find a place to stay," Brenna said, jumping backward to avoid a shower of dirt the smallest dwarf kicked in her direction as he mumbled something she couldn't understand.

Wynter pulled on the dwarf's rope and was greeted with a solid kick to his leg. "That's enough!" he snapped, snarling at the dwarves. His angry expression subdued them into a disgruntled quiet.

The centaur looked at Brenna and shook his head. "I don't want to stay inside the city tonight. There's a stable for centaurs, and there are several inns for you, but I don't think we should separate again."

"I know we shouldn't separate." Galvin's tone was commanding. "We camp outside town."

"Well, okay," Brenna interjected. "Let's get moving, then. The Gold Dragon Inn must certainly have food. I still have a handful of coins, and I am definitely hungry. Shall we?"

Several minutes later, Brenna and Galvin were seated at a table in a crowded candlelit room and had ordered their meal. Galvin brushed at the dust on his breeches, acquired when one of the dwarves had tripped him in the street.

The Gold Dragon Inn was obviously a popular place. Most of the clientele appeared to be from the middle and upper classes, although there were a few slaves in the company of their masters. A well-dressed woman with a raven painted on her head glared down her nose at Galvin.

"How do we find anything out here? Talk to people?" Brenna asked.

"Shh!" Galvin shushed softly. "We listen. See those four over there?" The druid nodded in the direction of a foppish-looking group. "They're talking about the Council of Zulkirs. The pair to our right is planning to magically charm someone. And the man behind me talking to the plump, elderly woman is chatting about Maligor."

Brenna leaned back in the padded mahogany chair. The inn was warm, the atmosphere acceptable, and her companion handsome. She wondered how he could pick out the bits of conversation floating around the room. She could only make out a few words here and there, perceiving everything else as an irritating, indecipherable murmur. Galvin continued to cock his head from one side to the other, his eyes darting in the direction where he was listening. Brenna assumed he had acquired his acute hearing in the woods; people in cities learned to shut out sounds.

The waiter was short and stocky. As he bent over the table to serve their food, Brenna noted his head bore a symbol of Malar, similar to the one on her own head. She didn't hear him ask if she wanted anything else; she was already stuffing forkfuls of beef into her mouth. Galvin's dinner of potatoes and vegetables didn't look as savory to her. He motioned for the waiter when he was finished and asked for a large, steaming plate of beef. Brenna looked at him quizzically.

"For Wynter," he said, then resumed listening to the diners' chatter.

When the beef arrived, Brenna paid the man extra for the plate, and Galvin, carrying the meal, followed her outside.

Outside, the street was coated in thick, gray shadows; there were fewer people about now, and they walked near the buildings and congregated under the corner lamplights. A small throng was gathered about Wynter, laughing.

Brenna and Galvin hurried over to see the centaur struggling to remain on his feet. The dwarves had encircled him, their ropes twisted about his legs. One of the stocky little men was beating on the centaur's flank. The druid was angry that the onlookers had done nothing to help Wynter.

Forgetting how a slave should act, Galvin thrust the plate of beef into Brenna's hands and rushed forward, elbowing his way through to the centaur. Grasping the closest dwarf, Galvin picked him up and shook him, then carried him around Wynter until the rope was untangled. Setting the stocky man down on the street, the druid picked up a second and did the same thing, then a third.

The small crowd began to laugh again, and the druid glanced up to see that the first dwarf he had tended to was wrapping the rope about the centaur's legs again. Wynter looked at Galvin forlornly and tried to sidestep the rope. This action only resulted in his becoming entangled with another rope leash.

The beef was cold by the time Galvin had untangled all the dwarves and warned them to behave. Grabbing their leashes from the centaur, he began herding the uncooperative slaves down the street like untrained dogs. Wynter ate hungrily as he followed, Brenna at his side.

As they neared the north gate, the druid related what he had learned.

"It looks like Maligor is preparing for some kind of war. His target appears to be another wizard."

"Then he's not after Aglarond?" Brenna asked, sounding relieved.

"Or any other neighboring country," Wynter added. "Still, we're here. Let's poke around a little more tomorrow to be certain. Rumors aren't facts, and any information will be valuable to the Harpers.

"From what I gathered," Wynter continued, "Maligor is one of the most powerful wizards in Thay. He's got to be close to two hundred years old, and no one is expecting him to die anytime soon."

"The man I listened to said Maligor has been amassing an army of gnolls. Rumor has it that he has several hundred camped northwest of Amruthar." Galvin lowered his voice. "By the way, his tower is at the west edge of the city. I suspect it's that massive building we passed just before the gates."

The druid began to walk faster, tugging the dwarves behind him. When he was within fifty feet of the gate, the dwarves began to mumble among themselves and suddenly sat down on the ground, almost in unison. Galvin yanked and pulled on their rope leashes, but he couldn't budge them.

"Damn, Wynter," the druid cursed. "Why did you saddle us with these dwarves? We really don't need this problem right now." He tugged again, and the dwarves glowered at him.

As Brenna padded up quickly to help, the largest of the dwarves reached out an arm, caught her by an ankle, and pulled until she fell to the dirt road.

Fuming, Brenna scooted away from the slaves and began to brush the dirt from her dress furiously.

"Wynter!" she shouted.

The centaur wisely kept his distance from the dwarves, noting that the incident had drawn the attention of the guards at the gate. He glanced at Galvin and Brenna and shrugged.

"The slaver said I might have a few problems with them," he said softly. "They weren't very expensive."

Galvin grabbed the ends of the rope, turned, faced the gate, and pumped his legs, pulling like a draft horse. Huffing with the effort, he eventually found himself moving forward slowly, pulling the struggling dwarves.

On the barbicon above, the guards laughed and opened the gate. Galvin and the dwarves, followed by Brenna and Wynter, emerged through the gate into a tent town. The ragtag community consisted of about six dozen tents of various construction; some were large and made of stout canvas, others were merely large blankets thrown over a cord tied between two posts. Some people, lacking any tent, slept on blankets on the ground. There were a number of large dogs about the area, guarding merchants' goods and families.

The tent town was almost a permanent fixture, a fringe district of Amruthar, judging by the packed, grassless earth beneath the tents. Most of the residents were here only to sell their goods, then move on to another town to acquire more inventory. However, the place also served as a more or less permanent home to some of the city's poorer residents who couldn't afford lodging inside the walls.

Galvin, Wynter, and Brenna picked their way among the inhabitants, watching the evening activities as they went.

"Okay," Wynter stared as he helped Galvin drag the dwarves. "So Maligor has an army of gnolls. I don't think a thousand gnolls could take this place. There are too many wizards here to fight back. His target has to be outside the city. Besides, if you could find out about the gnolls by simply going to dinner, you can be sure all the wizards around here know about them."

"It's puzzling," Galvin admitted. "In any event, we need to get a close look at Maligor's place."

"Get those slaves outta here!" an old woman barked as one of the dwarves lobbed a clod of dirt in her direction. Her companions cackled and encouraged the dwarf to try again.

Galvin and Wynter pulled harder. They passed by a large group of campers who obviously knew each other. The men had circled around a fire for a game of chance. Near them, two women in brightly colored scarfs danced about a campfire. The conversation was abundant and covered the weather, the day's business, and the city's tax policies.

One group was even discussing Maligor's gnolls.

The travelers and their slaves selected a spot on the edge of the tent town where they could talk freely and weren't likely to be invited by their neighbors to share in any festivities. Wynter used crude hand signals, indicating the dwarves should sit. They refused, of course.

When he merely shrugged and ignored them, the dwarves finally sat, looking defiant. Brenna edged forward cautiously and began working the knots loose from about their waists. She held her breath; the slaves hadn't bathed in a long while. When she had finished untying them, she backed away, put her hands on her hips, and inspected them.

"If we take them to Aglarond, I can get them cleaned up and give them a few gold pieces," she said.

"*If* we make it back to Aglarond," Wynter added, surprised the dwarves weren't bolting.

"We've more things to worry about than the dwarves," Galvin said as he stretched out on the ground. Brenna lay down a few feet away from the druid and watched him.

"I'm just glad I was able to buy a few slaves their freedom," Wynter said softly, not wanting any nearby campers to hear. He vividly described the condition of the pens to Galvin, then waited for a response, but the druid had had enough conversation for the day and pretended to sleep.

Nine

Asp clung to the shadows outside Maligor's tower. The nearby gnoll guards paid her little attention, knowing it was healthier not to question the spirit naga about her business.

She rested back on her snake's lower body, leaning her shoulders against the cool, smooth stone wall and twitching the end of her tail through the dewy grass. In her pale, slender hands, she cradled a large weasel. Asp ran her fingers through its silky fur and hissed softly to the creature. The weasel seemed to enjoy the attention and lay still for the naga's caresses.

"Maligor will be proud of me," she hissed in a barely audible tone. "I've watched him closely. I, too, can create darkenbeasts."

The naga slithered farther along the wall, away from the guards and toward the rear of the tower. Setting the weasel down amid a thick clump of grass, she scratched its neck and lay on her belly to watch it sniff a patch of clover. Then, reaching in her pouch for the powders she had "borrowed" from

167

Maligor, the snake-woman sprinkled them on the weasel's back and began mumbling the words she had heard Maligor recite.

She kept her voice soft, not wanting to draw the attention of the guards or any slaves who might be milling about. The weasel's nose began to quiver, finally sensing danger. The moment it started to bolt, Asp's tail shot through the grass like a striking cobra and fastened itself about the animal's back legs to hold it in place.

The frightened weasel tried to squirm free, but the naga persisted with the spell. By the time Asp had finished with the words, the creature had begun the horrid metamorphosis.

The weasel shed its hair as its skin bubbled and oozed. Asp quickly drew her tail away and slithered back a few feet. The thing cried out, almost like a human infant, as its bones stretched, making loud popping and cracking sounds. Talons formed at the ends of its front feet, yet its back feet remained those of a weasel. Then its jaw elongated; rows of long, jagged teeth filled its misshapen mouth. The thing continued to grow until it was as big as a bull and appeared a cross between a weasel and a lizard.

The naga gasped and covered her mouth in surprise. Even though she had used the same words, the spell wasn't working as it had when Maligor cast it. This darkenbeast was too big and was retaining many of its weasel features—its hind legs, ears, stubby tail, and round, frightened eyes. Its skin was covered with festering boils, as if the thing were diseased. For a moment, the naga considered calling for the Red Wizard, hoping he could correct her miscast magic. Then she realized he would be angry because she had cast a spell he had not yet taught her.

Nervously she eyed the creature as it continued its transformation. Webbed wings covered with short gray hair grew from its sides. The darkenbeast, whimpering loudly in pain from its transfiguration, turned its hideous head toward Asp, its crimson eyes glowing with hatred. The thing hopped toward her, flapping its deformed wings and nearly succeeding in rising from the ground. The naga gathered herself to her full height and prepared to defend herself with magic.

But the darkenbeast stopped inches from her. Its stench was overpowering and kept her from concentrating to cast any enchantments. The naga held her breath and looked into the monster's face. Suddenly she realized that the thing was waiting.

"Attack the peasants," she hissed, mentally picturing the camp outside Amruthar's northern gate.

The darkenbeast turned and lumbered away, then awkwardly took off into the night sky toward the city's northern edge. The creature was hardly graceful, as Maligor's creation had been. Instead, it was clumsy and unbalanced, and the naga hoped someone would kill it quickly so it wouldn't return to her and cause problems.

She slithered into the tower, casting a last glance at the diminishing form of her misbegotten darkenbeast.

* * * * *

In the tent town, Wynter listened to the dwarven slaves talk among themselves. Their deep voices sounded pleasant enough, and he wished he knew what they were saying. They had been hungry, devouring an entire sack of fruit that Wynter had purchased for them. Brenna had tried speaking to them in several languages, hoping the dwarves would understand something. She told Wynter she wasn't sure if the slaves spoke only Dwarvish or if they were playing ignorant.

"It doesn't matter," Wynter said. "They'll be free soon . . . as soon as it seems safe to let them go. I just wish I could tell them that."

Brenna smiled and decided the least she could do was help clean up the dwarves. She uncorked her waterskin and padded toward them. Suddenly she heard a commotion coming from the direction of the gate. Turning, she saw the guards on the gate lining up across the barbicon, drawing their longbows.

Screams from the merchants nearby filled the air, and in the gathering darkness, the enchantress saw a grotesque flying creature diving toward the center of the tent town.

"Galvin!" she shouted as Wynter galloped past her toward the attacking beast. The centaur had his staff held out before him like a lance, and merchants jumped out of his way as he charged through.

The druid sprang to his feet in time to see a dozen guards on the barbicon loose arrows at the winged creature. The beast screamed terribly and plummeted into the mass of tent town residents. Galvin and Brenna rushed toward where they had seen the thing fall, elbowing their way through the growing crowd.

The druid soon found himself at the forefront of the assembled merchants, and like the other onlookers, he stared slack-jawed at the creature. Four arrows were lodged deeply in the grotesque beast's underside. Obviously dying, it flapped its monstrous wings weakly, raising a small cloud of dust.

A child screamed as the creature's skin began to bubble and pop, boiling away like water. The wings quivered and beat faster as they shriveled and were drawn into the rapidly diminishing form of the beast. The crowd backed up, yet none turned away, engrossed with the vile tableau.

Finally the creature's leathery skin began to recede, revealing the silky, blood-soaked fur of a large weasel. The animal lifted its head, a stream of blood trickling out of its mouth, then it twitched once more and died. The crowd lingered, each lost in his own thoughts, wondering precisely what it was he had seen. At last the guards from the barbicon made their way into the tent town to disperse the throng.

One guard stooped over, picked up the body of the weasel, and turned to carry it inside the city. The guards ignored the shouted questions from the crowd. Disgruntled that they would get no information from the guards, the crowd began to break up and return to their tents.

Galvin found Wynter and Brenna near the gate. "I—I saw it, Galvin," the sorceress said evenly. "Before it hit the ground, I saw it. It was like the thing that attacked us in Aglarond. Do you think someone knows we're here?" Brenna glanced about nervously.

"I don't think so," Galvin whispered, noting that a few of the merchants who had returned to their camps next to the gate were staring at the trio. The druid strolled toward their own makeshift camp. Brenna and Wynter followed. "I think it would have gone straight after us if it was meant for us."

"That makes sense," Wynter agreed. "We were on the edge of the tent town and would have made easy targets."

"I hope you're right," Brenna said. She shivered, more from fear than the cool night air, and continued to glance behind her occasionally toward the gate.

The druid paused to wrap his cloak around her shoulders. As he did, he noticed that the tent town had resumed its former appearance, just as if nothing had happened. He shrugged and continued striding toward their camp. Galvin wondered if attacks such as this were commonplace here. It could explain the merchants' nonchalant bearing in the aftermath of the attack.

"The dwarves!" Wynter shouted suddenly, trotting to the edge of the tent town. "They're gone!"

The former slaves had left their ropes behind and left the Harpers' possessions untouched. The druid knelt on the ground beside a footprint left by one of the dwarves, then glanced to the north.

"They went toward those trees," the druid observed.

"Thay's not a safe place to be at night," Wynter said nervously.

"Nothing's safe from those dwarves," Galvin concluded. "We were going to free them anyway." The druid rose and brushed the dirt off his knees. Before he had taken a handful of steps toward his belongings, a cry pierced the night air.

"Jujus!" a woman screamed. "Juju zombies! Szass

Tam's undead will kill us all!"

Once again the tent town leapt to life as the cry of "stiff-walkers" passed like a crashing wave from the outer rim of tents to the city gates. The Harpers determined from the people's cries that Szass Tam was behind the attack and that the "stiff-walkers," or undead, were the shadowy creatures they could make out shuffling toward the tent town.

The people on the outer edge of the tent town, including Brenna, Wynter, and Galvin, were the first to react. The night-cloaked figures had already come upon some of the campers there, silently lifting their blankets and awkwardly prodding through their tents and lean-tos. It was obvious the undead were looking for something—or someone.

The merchants grabbed their torches and lanterns, hoping the light would keep the undead creatures at bay. The women gathered their children and ran toward the gates. As the campers pushed closer to Amruthar's walls, the ragged-clothed corpses shambled through the canvas and discarded belongings, the stench of their decaying bodies wafting across the tent town. There were ten of the things that had long ago been living creatures. They had hollow eye sockets and skeletal frames, and despite their degree of decomposition, they still had vaguely human shapes. The undead regrouped at the edge of the tent town, then, as one, they glanced up with their empty sockets straight toward Brenna and the Harpers.

The trio hadn't moved far in this time, waiting to see what the zombies would do. After several long moments, the undead began to advance, with their broken, yellowed teeth bared and claws outstretched.

Brenna screamed in terror. "They're here for us!"

"Get your back to mine and Wynter's," Galvin commanded. "We'll stand our ground till the peddlers are safe inside the gate." Galvin motioned for Wynter to form a small ring. In the back of his mind, he wished they had decided to stay inside Amruthar's walls.

The druid was genuinely frightened that the sorceress

might have hit the mark—the zombies did seem to be after them. Glancing around, he saw no fatalities among the peddlers, just toppled tents and disturbed bedrolls, so the undead weren't mindlessly killing everything that lay in their path. If they truly were after the three heroes, they would continue on like thoughtless automatons until they had captured their victims or until their intended victims had dispatched them. The zombies had the advantage, Galvin knew, even though there were only ten of them. Undead beings didn't tire, and they never had to sleep.

Brenna dug about in her satchel for her spell components while she desperately called for the retreating merchants to band together to fight the creatures. She knew that the sheer number of Thayvian peddlers could overwhelm the undead attackers, and she was unnerved that Galvin seemed to want the campers to run. Her pleas for their help brought a scowl from Galvin and fell on deaf ears. Already screams of terror were filling the night sky as the merchants continued to flee, blotting out all other sounds. The enchantress wondered if Amruthar's guards would open the gates and let the tent people inside or leave them to be slaughtered.

Galvin's eyes flashed in the starlight, and he began to transform, not caring if anyone saw him. He needed a body that would catch the zombies off guard, yet could fight viciously. He fell to all fours as thick, coarse orange and black hair sprouted from his face and hands and spread like melting butter to obscure his clothing. Sharp white teeth emerged from his swelling feline snout, and long white whiskers pushed outward through the fur around his nose. His ears stretched until they became pointed. At the same time, the druid's body grew, its torso elongating, its frame becoming heavier and more powerful, its legs more muscular. His hands and feet became wider, grew thick pads, and sprouted razor-edged claws where human nails had been. From his rump, an orange tail striped with black sprang forth and grew until it was nearly four feet long.

The tiger twitched its tail back and forth as it bared its

fangs and growled deeply at the approaching zombies. The great cat, its saucerlike, emerald green eyes sparkling in the moonlight, leapt forward, displaying a patch of white fur on its chest in the shape of a crescent moon. The tiger's claws raked the abdomen of the nearest zombie and knocked it to the ground.

Wynter brought his staff down hard on the shoulder of another. The centaur saw more shapes moving in from the darkness, a second wave of undead.

"Run, Brenna!" the centaur barked, striking his staff solidly against the head of a gray-skinned shambler that had once been a hobgoblin. With a sickening thump, it struck the zombie's face, caving it in, but still the thing continued to advance.

At the same time, the tiger tore through a pair of zombies in front of him. Rearing up on his hind legs, he slashed the face of one zombie and sunk his teeth into the chest of another. The two zombies fell to the ground, and the tiger continued the assault, ripping chunks of dead flesh from them until they ceased to move. The attack left a terrible, fetid taste in the druid's mouth, but he persisted, trying to slay as many of the undead creatures as possible. Still, he knew physical efforts would not be enough. He glanced around quickly, then looked up at the sky.

There were now about four dozen of the creatures. Wynter had already dispatched several, ramming his staff through their grotesque bodies and pounding other shamblers into the ground with his hooves.

Brenna had ignored Wynter's order to flee. She was holding her own, keeping the monstrous cadavers at bay with shardlike magical missiles that repeatedly sprang from her fingers. She reveled in her small victories, but she knew that she and the Harpers were tiring, while for each juju that fell, there were several more to take its place.

Galvin growled fiercely as his mind touched a thick rain cloud overhead. He was calling on his most powerful nature magic, a spell he had used only a few other times in his life because he didn't like to interfere with nature. Gently he coaxed the cloud, mentally tugging at it, all the while keeping two jujus away from his companions with his tiger body. Then he felt the energy and force inside the cloud. The electricity pulsated and sparked, and he begged it to plummet earthward.

The lightning bolt streaked from the cloud, forking again and again, skewering more than two dozen of the foul creatures and burning them to blackened husks. The sky thundered, then fell silent again, and a soft rain began to fall.

For a moment, Galvin believed the thunder was continuing, and he wondered if his efforts had started a storm. But then he realized that the noise was the shouts and cheers of the onlooking crowd. The merchants had sensed that the trio had magic on their side and were overcoming the tremendous odds against them. Many peddlers stopped in midflight and turned to watch. A few yelled for the guards to open the gates, but most continued to shout their praises and applaud the heroes, ecstatic that someone was standing up to a Red Wizard. Then a number of them grabbed swords and dashed to join the fray.

Wynter felt a rush of excitement, as he realized the Thayvians were going to stand up to the undead and risk the wrath of a Red Wizard. In his heart, he believed there must still be some hope for the country. The evil couldn't overcome everyone's spirit. He stared at the undead. The zombies had paused, confused.

These were unlike any zombies the centaur had seen in his younger days in Thay, and they bore no resemblance to the ghouls they had battled yesterday. These juju zombies had never been human. They were the remains of orcs, goblins, gnolls, and perhaps worse, magically animated after their deaths. Each was repulsively distinct, and each had a thick, leathery hide, rotting clothes, and a stench that made Wynter's eyes water. They were far more terrifying than animated human corpses. Some were only recently dead, their bodies largely intact. Others had apparently moldered in their graves for some time. One had no chin, while another was missing an ear. Yet another had only one arm.

Not waiting for the zombies to decide on a course of action, Galvin charged the closest ones, raking them with outstretched claws and biting at their legs. Sensing the surge of emotion from the crowd, he cast his large head over a tawny, black-striped shoulder to see Brenna calling the merchants forward. His tail switched in anticipation of the battle being over soon.

A small wave of merchants reached the jujus, which had begun to shamble forward again. The peddlers beat upon them with swords, clubs, shovels, and pans. For a moment, the zombies looked perplexed and began to back away, clawing at the air in front of them to keep back their attackers. The peddlers who had stayed behind by the gates cheered loudly.

Galvin turned for an instant toward Amruthar to see the city's wall crowded with guards and onlookers. Wondering if the city would open its gates to him as a hero, he returned to the grisly task of slaying the remaining undead. Then his optimism quickly vanished.

The druid's vision was superior even to his usual keen sight in this animal form and allowed him to see beyond the jujus to the next wave of zombies. And to a pair of men. Although Galvin couldn't see them clearly, there was something about them, some palpable evil perhaps, a quality he could not identify. But it was something that made him shiver.

The two who stood at the rear of the zombie reinforcements were pasty-faced and gaunt, draped in black-as-night cloaks that hung nearly to the grass. Unlike most free people in this country, these two had hair. One's blond tresses fell nearly to his shoulders, yet neither of them had the bearing or appearance of a slave. They stood like statues. Galvin couldn't tell if they breathed, and he wondered if they were Red Wizards wearing something other than their traditional garb.

With a simple gesture, one of the mysterious men directed the jujus to lumber toward the city.

Galvin sprang forward, pushing over the largest of the

oncoming jujus. His massive paws planted firmly on the zombie's chest, he ripped out its throat with his sharp teeth. As he finished slaying the thing, he felt something brush up against him. It was cold, but his keen feline eyes saw nothing. He ignored it and proceeded to attack another target.

The merchants continued to cheer as Brenna and Wynter fought their own undead opponents. They realized they were finally winning the struggle, and they pushed the undead farther away from the city—until the centaur felt the cold touch of something he could not see.

Wynter cringed at the rake of cold, black hands. His legs buckled as he felt his strength drain away, and he watched helplessly as deep gashes appeared on his equine body. The centaur's human torso swiveled back and forth as he cast about, looking for the source of his pain, but all he saw was blackness. Shadowy hands clawed him repeatedly, while zombies moved in to bludgeon him. The centaur fell to the ground under the weight of a swarm of undead.

Galvin whirled and raced to his friend's side, only to find himself stopped inches from the fallen Wynter by a cold, black force. The druid charged against it, finding something solid yet unseeable in the darkness. He batted out with a paw, then gored the air futilely until his back legs crumpled from the force of an invisible aggressor. It was as if the very night was fighting him.

Galvin jerked his head back and forth, catching glimpses of fleeing and falling merchants and Wynter being pummeled by the zombies and something he could not see. The centaur's side heaved, and his legs kicked out spasmodically.

Then, out of the corner of Galvin's eye, he saw the two white-faced men moving closer and recognized them for what they really were—vampires. One had Brenna cradled in his arms; the druid couldn't tell if she was alive. The other stared at Galvin in his tiger form, his red eyes knifing through the darkness and mesmerizing him.

The druid flinched. In all his travels, he had never met

one of the lords of darkness, but he had heard enough about vampires to know that the power they commanded was unearthly. Eyes that he would never forget dug into his brain, commanding him to stop fighting, to surrender. Galvin felt helpless, powerless, and was compelled to follow the vampire's mental instructions. The eyes became his world and moved closer, commanding him again. And the druid responded, shedding his tiger skin and transforming back to his human shape. He became oblivious to his surroundings, to Wynter's condition, to the mass of peddlers streaming toward Amruthar's gate. He knew only the eyes.

Then he felt himself being lifted by tangible, man-shaped shadows, the same shadows that had brought about the Harpers' defeat, and passed to the blond-haired vampire. The lord of darkness casually tossed the druid over a bony shoulder. The vampire's body, even through the heavy black cloak, felt as cold as ice. The druid prayed to the forest gods that the thing would kill him now rather than drink his blood. Galvin could think of no worse fate than to become an undead creature living on the blood of others and serving in some Red Wizard's hellish troops.

Galvin succumbed to a forced and unnatural sleep. Behind him, under the explicit orders of the vampires, the shadows and jujus constructed a litter to drag Wynter. The city gates opened, letting the peddlers and their families inside, then closed tight. The guards knew better than to confront the forces of a Red Wizard. They stayed at their posts, and from the barbicon, they watched as the litter was completed and the undead moved off into the night.

The master of the undead wanted all three heroes, and the zombies and shadows knew that to disappoint Szass Tam meant unending torment or worse.

As if in a dream, Galvin saw himself moving across the countryside, through a meadow enveloped by soothing, cool darkness and devoid of natural creatures. Then he moved through a small wooded area where the trees had been long dead and their branches twisted into grotesque positions. He imagined the limbs were outstretched arms trying to grab him and pull him inside their hollow trunks. But he was safe, too far away for them to reach him, yet not far enough away from whatever was making him shiver. Just past the trees lay a defiled and overgrown graveyard. Half the graves had been opened and their tombstones knocked to the ground. He assumed the occupants were serving a Red Wizard and that the remainder of the graveyard's occupants would eventually do the same.

He continued his hours-long journey, only now realizing in his dream state that his legs were not transporting him. He felt as if he were floating. It was an uncomfortable sensation, and he struggled to wake up. Then he thought of Brenna and was saddened she wasn't in his dream; he couldn't see her, and that made him feel alone.

Eventually the druid realized the dream was real; he was watching a twisted Thayvian countryside from the shoulder of his captor. The ground was barren here, and he was being carried toward an imposing stone structure, a small castle surrounded by a low stone wall on top of which were positioned, at even intervals, barbed iron spears pointing slightly outward. The macabre fence looked like long black talons against the sky's grayness. Galvin knew the journey had been a long one. It would be dawn soon.

The druid was carried through an opening in the wall. To his right and left stood tall men in tattered cloaks, their faces hidden by cavernous hoods. There were more men behind him—skeletons, he knew, because their bony hands clasped spears and swords and the bones of their ribs showed through their worn garments—but he paid little attention to them. He was thinking about the building in front of him and of Brenna Graycloak.

Then the nightmare began. The second vampire came into the druid's view; the lord of darkness held Brenna in his pale white arms. Galvin feared she was dead, that Wynter was dead. Then he prayed they were alive so they wouldn't become zombies in an undead Thayvian army.

Galvin struggled, then felt himself falling, experiencing a

sharp jolt of pain as his shoulder, then the rest of his body, met the cold stone floor of a room. Gradually he opened his eyes to see Wynter barely breathing only a few feet from him; the centaur's body was riddled with clawlike gashes, and he lay on a crude, blood-soaked litter. Brenna was lying on a couch, her face bruised and her eyes closed. Her chest rose and fell regularly, giving the druid some relief.

The room was furnished simply but elegantly with carved, polished furniture; rich tapestries; and heavy black velvet curtains that covered the windows and kept the druid from knowing the time of day. The floor was smooth and immaculate. It gleamed in the light of thick candles held high by sconces. Galvin wondered how the centaur had been brought into the room, then answered the question himself when he saw the large, ornate double doors.

The two vampires glided past the druid. They seemed eerily graceful and elegant, their expensive cloaks swirling behind them. In back of them shuffled a handful of juju zombies, their tattered clothes dragging across the floor and their stench filling the air. With considerable effort, Galvin leaned forward, propping himself up on his elbows. He wanted to see where the undead were going.

His spirit was crushed when he saw them assembled before a red-robed figure.

"Harpers," Szass Tam intoned almost emotionlessly as he moved from in front of the vampires directly into Galvin's line of sight. The lich was in his fleshly form, giving no hint to the druid that he was himself an undead. He was adorned in a scarlet satin robe embroidered with red-gold threads that shimmered in the light of the myriad candles placed about the room. The sleeves were voluminous, and as the zulkir moved, the folds looked like flames licking up his arms. Szass Tam slipped toward the couch and placed a cold hand on Brenna's forehead; she moved in fitful slumber, and he smiled evilly.

Galvin pulled himself to his knees.

"What do the Harpers want in Thay?" the lich asked Galvin silkily, all the while keeping his eyes on the enchantress.

"She's not a Harper!" Galvin shouted, his voice waking Brenna and causing the lich to raise one eyebrow. "Who are you? What do you want with us?"

"I am Szass Tam," he said softly as he rubbed his hand across the top of Brenna's bald head, tracing with his index finger the designs painted there. "I am the Zulkir of Necromancy, the most powerful Red Wizard in Thay . . . and your master."

It all came crashing down on Galvin then, and it made sickening sense. While undoubtedly other Red Wizards in Thay had undead at their command, only the Zulkir of Necromancy controlled a large force of unliving, and it was likely that only he could command vampires.

"You killed nearly every ghoul in one of my patrols the other night. That brought you to my attention and piqued my curiosity. One of them who managed to get away spotted your silver charm. Undead dislike silver, so he remembered it."

Brenna recoiled from the zulkir's touch and pushed herself into a sitting position, then shrank back from the wizard. She still felt weak from the attack by the shadows, and the room was spinning. She felt even more faint when she saw the unmoving form of Wynter.

The lich smiled at her, then moved to the center of the room and regarded the trio.

"Harper spies," Szass Tam said evenly. "I don't like the Harper organization and its politics. Harpers are nothing more than meddlers in other people's affairs.

"I remember many decades ago when I crossed paths with some meddling Harpers. I defeated them with ease and needed no potent sorcery to do it. Your organization is unruly and ineffectual, poking into everything and commanding nothing. Your membership is secret, so you have no single strong leader. You are fools."

The lich turned his back on the heroes and glided to his desk. Slowly he opened the lower right-hand drawer. It was filled with all manner of souvenirs—daggers, totems, odd bits of jewelry. He rummaged through it until he pulled out a tarnished chain made of heavy links. It bore a charm—a silver moon affixed to a harp. The lich had a half dozen similar chains and pins taken from spies his minions had killed over the past dozen decades. Those Harpers, whose charms the lich kept, were now part of his undead army.

The lich paused, remembering. It had been probably thirty or forty years since Szass Tam's forces had last discovered a Harper. He had given the organization little thought. Until now. Until these three had virtually dispatched one of his patrols.

Szass Tam dropped the heavy chain on the desktop and leveled his gaze at Galvin. Leaving the desk drawer open, he moved from behind it to face the druid. The Harper wisely remained quiet and didn't protest as the lich reached for the neck of Galvin's tunic and pulled it down until he saw the Harper charm. The cold fingers grabbed it and yanked, breaking the chain and pulling it away from Galvin.

The lich voiced a throaty laugh and held the chain before his eyes, letting it sway back and forth as he examined it. "Fine silver, probably mined by dwarves north of Tantras. I prefer gold, since it is worth more and is far more malleable. I hope this trinket doesn't mean much to you."

Szass Tam returned to the desk with the prize, rubbing his thumb in a circular motion over the silver moon charm, then depositing the charm and broken chain unceremoniously in the drawer.

"I'm collecting them," he announced. "Maybe I should start collecting Harpers instead."

Brenna slid from the couch and joined Galvin on the floor. "What are you going to do with us?" she asked weakly.

"Harpers," Szass Tam repeated, spitting out the word like it left a bad taste in his mouth. "Harpers, I will keep you alive, but you will work for me. You will begin by telling me what you are doing in my country."

Galvin and Brenna remained silent. Neither had any intention of giving the zulkir any information or satisfaction. The pair looked defiant, and their obstinacy amused the lich.

Szass Tam motioned to one of the vampires, who stepped in front of Galvin. The lord of darkness turned his white face downward, catching the druid's gaze. His red eyes bore hypnotically into the druid's.

Galvin tried to fight the vampire's control but found he couldn't look away. The piercing red eyes were all the druid saw.

"Why are you here?" the lord of darkness whispered.

Galvin's mind screamed in rebellion, but his voice cooperated in fluent tones. "We entered Thay at the request of the Aglarond council," the druid began.

"No! Stop!" Brenna tried to interrupt him, shaking his shoulders in an endeavor to bring him to his senses. When that proved useless, she turned her attention to the vampire. "Release him! I'll tell you what you want to know."

"Silence!" the lich demanded, crossing the room and slapping Brenna hard enough to send her sliding several feet across the floor.

The vampire continued to probe Galvin's mind and force an explanation from him.

"The Aglarond council heard rumors that a Red Wizard was building a large army. The council feared the wizard planned to march against Aglarond. Wynter and I were the nearest Harpers, and we agreed to help."

"And the woman?" the vampire pressed. His voice was dry and hollow. "Who is she? Was she the one who called the lightning outside Amruthar's gates?"

The color drained from Brenna's face as Galvin continued to answer.

"She is an Aglarond council member, a young politician who decided to accompany Wynter and me. She commands magic, but it was I who called the lightning. I am a druid."

The vampire plied the druid for more information, under the direction of Szass Tam. "What did you hope to accomplish in Thay?"

"We wanted to pose as Thayvians so we could find out what the Red Wizard Maligor was up to. If he was planning to march against Aglarond, the country would have to prepare for war."

"Maligor!" Szass Tam screeched. "What made you think the Zulkir of Alteration was plotting war?"

The vampire who held control of Galvin had to repeat the question.

"I found a gnoll informer who worked for Maligor. He was willing to sell his loyalty to whoever had the most gold." The words poured like honey from the druid's mouth. "The gnoll told me that Maligor was planning to march against someone, perhaps another Red Wizard."

"Perhaps," Szass Tam echoed slowly. "I find it most unusual that the Harpers, the Aglarond Council, and I should all be interested in Maligor. Coincidences should not be taken lightly."

The vampire's face tilted to meet Szass Tam's eyes.

Brenna realized that, just as the vampire had charmed Galvin, the Zulkir of Necromancy held the same power over the vampire. It was a horrible chain of command, with Szass Tam at the top. The lich whispered to the vampire in tones so soft she couldn't make out what was being said. Turning to Galvin, she noted that a sheen of perspiration had broken out over his forehead.

"I'm sorry," the druid began, not looking in her eyes. "I had to tell him everything he wanted to know. I had to. I felt like a puppet."

"It's not your fault." She tried to console him, edging to his side again. "Their power is far greater than ours. It's just our dumb luck to have drawn the attention of Szass Tam." The sorceress draped her arms about Galvin's shoulders, then stiffened when she noticed the Red Wizard looking at her.

"How feminine and sickeningly touching," Szass Tam purred. "You'll have time enough to enjoy each others' company later, after you've finished working for me."

"Never!" Galvin roared, shrugging off Brenna's arms

and rising to his feet. He kept his eyes focused on Szass
Tam's, not wanting to fall victim again to the vampire's control. "I'm a Harper, zulkir. I've dedicated my life to fighting
for good. I'm not going to help you. I'll die first!"

"And if you die, you'll help me anyway," the lich replied.
The vampires backed away from the zulkir as he laughed, a
rich deep, throaty chuckle that sent goose bumps racing up
and down Galvin's and Brenna's spines. Szass Tam leveled
his gaze on the pair and willed his fleshly illusion to melt,
the pink skin flowing from him to reveal his gaunt, corpse-
like body. The lich's robes hung about him, and his arms
and face appeared as bones covered by incredibly old, thin
flesh. He threw back his skeletal head and laughed once
more, then focused on the pair, the red pinpoints of his
eyes staring out at them through deep sockets.

Brenna screamed again and again at Szass Tam's true
visage. She threw her trembling hands over face, and her
shoulders shuddered terribly. She shook her head back and
forth, trying to deny the creature before her. She had
heard that one of Thay's zulkir's was a lich, the most powerful form of undead to walk the realms. On trembling legs,
she rose to stand behind Galvin, finding little comfort in the
druid's closeness.

Szass Tam glared at her. "The dead are under my command, just as death is my domain. I'm beyond the living,
Harpers, and I'm beyond your feeble protests. You will
help me—living or dead. You will do exactly as I say.

"And if your performance is satisfactory," the lich continued, "I will let you go. My plans do not call for meddling in
Harper affairs or evoking the wrath of Aglarond dignitaries
and statesmen. I have no desire to involve myself in such
trivial things right now. So if you perform well, we will both
be satisfied. You will learn what Maligor is up to, and I will
have ended his miserable little plot."

Galvin's resolve appeared firm. "What makes you think
we'll help you willingly?" he protested, though deep down
he knew that if the lich wanted their aid, the Harpers would
be forced to comply. He was curious, however, to learn just

how the lich would force them and if they truly would be freed afterward.

"Since you wish to continue this, very well," Szass Tam sighed, moving slowly in front of his desk. He leaned backward against it, placing his bony hands flat on the polished surface and resting his slight weight on them. The zulkir's red eyes vanished, leaving the sockets black like pits. He drew his thin lips tight and languidly rocked his head back and forth.

Galvin and Brenna saw their surroundings waver, then turn to mist, then change. They were on the edge of a city at dusk; the sorceress recognized it as her hometown.

Looking down the main street, they saw a legion of undead—skeletons and zombies, led by a pair of vampires—ripping people from their homes, tearing soldiers' limbs off, and tramping over the dead and dying. The spectacle worsened as they spotted Wynter, his flesh hanging from his ribs and arms, his eyes hollow sockets like Szass Tam's. The centaur was leading a pack of ghouls that were headed straight toward the government buildings. Like a ghastly play, the scene continued to unfold until it seemed no one remained alive in the city.

Then Szass Tam appeared on the capitol steps, waving his arms and commanding the dead Aglarond citizens to rise and join his forces. The lich waved his arms again, and the scene shifted once more.

Brenna and Galvin were back in the zulkir's room, and Wynter remained wounded nearby.

"That is one possible future," Szass Tam uttered, his voice lowering for impact. "Councilwoman, you will tell me that Aglarond's forces can stand up to mine. And for a time, perhaps they could. But if I move at night, I am much more powerful, for the night is frightening and hides much, and my army would be in its element. Your soldiers would stop some of my troops, but not before many in Aglarond died. And with each death, I would become even more powerful, for death is my domain. And in the end, I would win."

Brenna shuddered, wondering if the lich really was powerful enough to accomplish a raid on Aglarond. If he were so strong, she thought, why wasn't he trying to take the country now?

He caught her doubts and offered the pair another illusion.

The room dissipated around them, the walls becoming mist and parting to reveal an ancient graveyard overgrown with weeds and sprinkled with small, stark trees. Galvin and Brenna shivered in the shadow of a massive marker, so weathered the pair couldn't make out the inscription or date on it. The sun was setting, casting an orange haze over the desolate landscape and causing the shadows to lengthen from the gravestones that stretched off toward the horizon. The graves went to the edge of Galvin's vision, and he and Brenna began to stroll down a row of waist-high markers. Two stones came into focus. They bore the names of Galvin and Brenna.

The ground shifted before the two stones, and the dirt began to be pushed away from underneath. Thin hands, covered in places by white flesh, clawed upward and grasped for a solid hold against the ground. Then arms emerged, skeletal pale in the waning light. Finding purchase, one pair of arms straightened and pulled, and the decaying form of the druid tugged itself from the grave. A tattered green cloak hung loosely from its form, and a silver neck chain with a harp and moon clung to the flesh about its frail neck.

The corpse stooped awkwardly and extended its hands to a pair of arms still struggling in the ground. The dead druid extricated the body of Brenna Graycloak from its resting place.

Together the corpses stumbled deeper into the graveyard, where more zombies were emerging. Brenna and Galvin fell in line with the others and marched toward the horizon.

The room returned.

Szass Tam had moved away from his desk and now stood only a few feet from the druid and Brenna.

"What—what do you want us to do?" Galvin asked quietly.

"I want Maligor stopped," the lich replied simply. "The threat he poses to me is not from his gnoll army. If he is planning to march his gnolls against another Red Wizard, it will be a weak one. I know Maligor, and I know he won't go up against something that might offer too much resistance. If he wants to march his gnolls against Aglarond, he would not be able to take much of the land. But I don't want him succeeding in any attempt. A victory for him diminishes me. Do you understand?"

Galvin nodded. "You understand that Brenna and I do not have the power to stop him. Despite the magic at our command, his magic is superior. And he has an army."

Brenna couldn't stay silent any longer. "Why don't you go after him yourself?" she said to the lich. "If you think you have the power to take Aglarond on your own, why don't you take him instead?"

The lich snarled at her. "Fool. I cannot yet afford to overtly take on another wizard. I prefer to exercise power from a distance."

"Galvin's right, though," she argued. "He and I can't take Maligor."

"Not alone," Szass Tam said. "But I will supply you with enough aid."

For a third time, the room dissolved, and Galvin and Brenna found themselves on a wide plain. There were orchards in the distance, and to their far right stood the walls of Amruthar. All around them were undead beings—skeletons, zombies, and other creatures that could walk about in the light of day but should have remained buried. There were also a few dozen living men, trained fighters, from the look of their muscles. The men wore nondescript armor and carried featureless shields. The undead were wrapped in cloaks and robes to help hide their true nature.

Szass Tam stood in front of Brenna and Galvin, once again wearing his fleshly visage.

"You will lead my army of undead," he commanded, "and

no one will know from whence they come. Oh, the wizards who care will be able to guess who is behind this force, but the great masses of people will not know."

Galvin swallowed hard and surveyed the illusionary force. He imagined the real one would look little different.

"You will lead this force to Maligor's tower. It stands outside Amruthar, so you will not have to contend with the city's guards. You will only have to deal with the gnolls assembled there. The fight could be difficult, but if you wish to live, you will win it."

"I want Wynter at my side," Galvin demanded, daring to interrupt the lich's instructions. "The centaur is my friend and a good fighter."

"I watched him," Szass Tam countered. "He fights only when pressed."

"I'll fight better with him nearby," Galvin said honestly.

"Very well," the Zulkir of Necromancy relented as the room re-formed for the last time. "I will grant you this one concession, since I have no major use for a zombie centaur."

Szass Tam padded toward Wynter, who was breathing more shallowly than before. The centaur's skin appeared ashen, but it glowed suddenly as the lich extended his hands over him. Szass Tam knelt and touched his palm to Wynter's human chest.

Galvin was amazed that a man who was so tied to death should have the ability to renew life. The gashes healed before the druid's eyes, the centaur's breathing became even and deep, and the color returned to his skin. The blood Wynter had lost was magically restored somehow, and he was renewed with vigor.

"Galvin!" Wynter gasped, untangling himself from the litter and rising and backing away from Szass Tam. "The Zulkir of Necromancy! We are his?"

"Only for a time," the druid answered his friend. "We've an errand to perform for him."

Wynter looked puzzled, since he was not privy to anything that had passed before, but Galvin kept him silent with a narrow glance.

"Now, my Harpers," Szass Tam said, motioning for a pair of jujus to open the double doors. "Follow your escorts to your chambers. You look tired. You should sleep. It wouldn't do for you to go up against Maligor when you're not feeling your best."

Galvin followed the jujus from the room, the vampires falling in line behind Brenna and Wynter. The double doors closed behind them, and Szass Tam's laughter echoed through the thick wood. The sound trailed the heroes down the hall and into their dark chambers.

Ten

Maligor sat alone in his vast library, staring out the window at the tops of the city's buildings silhouetted in the early morning sky and at a cloud formation that reminded him of a dragon he had slain in his younger days, a hundred and fifty years ago or so. The cloud wavered like a moving creature, then slowly floated out of his view. The Red Wizard wondered what the landscape and the clouds would look like from his gold mines.

Undoubtedly better.

The Red Wizard felt that his life would be better there, also. He would have more power, more wealth, more of everything that every Red Wizard in Thay wanted. And he would have it all to himself.

"Soon," he said to the air. "But first, to my health." Maligor eyed a thin crystal vial he had been holding in his right hand, inspecting it in much the same way a jeweler would examine a fine brooch. He ran his stiff, wrinkled thumb up and down the side of the vial, feeling the cool smoothness and dwelling on the power within it. The liquid inside was a pale, pearly green that moved sluggishly as he tilted the vial back and forth, evidencce of its thick viscosity. He pondered the contents for a time, long enough for another cloud to move across his window and reduce the light spilling into the room.

The Red Wizard had mixed the concoction late last night, feeling especially tired, morose, and old. He had waited until this morning to drink it, however, not wanting to fritter away any regained youth in sleep.

Maligor detested age. He considered it his only weakness and the one thing that could possibly stand in his way of eventually becoming ruler of all of Thay. So he fought it the only way he knew how—with his elixirs, powders, and arcane scrolls that hinted his soul was no longer his own. But Maligor never feared the repercussions of his magic or the well-being of his immortal spirit. He fully intended to live forever, and let the dark forces that hungered for him be damned.

To a renewed decade, he thought as he uncorked the vial, threw his head back, and downed the contents in a single, long draft. The mixture slowly oozed down his throat, burning as it went, bringing tears to the wizard's eyes.

For a moment, Maligor stood motionless. Then he jerked to his feet like a marionette being pulled by a vicious puppeteer, and the vial dropped from his hand, shattering into fine fragments on the marble floor. Gasping in pain, he doubled over, trying to clutch at his stomach through the thick red robes. His insides seethed and churned, seeming as if they were trying to fight their way out. He crumpled to his knees and clawed furiously at the marble, struggling to keep quiet so the guards outside wouldn't run in to defend him from an unseen menace and ruin his experience. He imagined piles of gold, trying to focus on something pleasant to lessen the pain. Still the pain in his gut persisted, but through it all, Maligor smiled, satisfied that the elixir was working properly.

For several minutes, he rode out the agony, then gathered himself up from the floor and wiped the sweat from his face with the sleeve of his robe.

Breathing deeply and inhaling more air into his lungs than he had been able to for the past several years, he collected his thoughts, then anxiously and purposefully strode from the room. The guards at the library door fell in behind him in military precision. Maligor didn't speak to them or to the other guards and servants moving about the hallways who stopped and stared hard at him, some with open mouths. He dismissed them with an indignant scowl and moved hurriedly to his bedchambers, leaving his escort outside and rushing to a long mirror on his closet door.

The imported beveled glass proved to Maligor that the pain was worth it. The wrinkles around his eyes were few and shallow; his skin felt softer, tighter, and the ache of age in his fingers and hands was lessened considerably. He flexed his fingers again and again and grinned sheepishly. Then he dwelled on his hair and beard and the face of a man in his early forties.

The same potion that rejuvenated his body, causing him to shed decades, also caused his hair to grow. It was long now, hanging several inches below his shoulders, and as black as a cave. It ringed his head, leaving him a small bald spot on top where the symbol of Myrkul stood out. In places, the black hair was streaked with a few strands of gray. He felt it with both hands, running his fingers through it. It felt silky, and he shook his head to watch it whip about his face, then fall in wild disarray around his neck and shoulders. Finally his right hand moved to his beard. It was full, coarse, and not as dark as the hair on his head, peppered with iron gray and white. It hung nearly to his waist and felt odd and heavy, making the skin on his chin and around his mouth itch terribly.

The Red Wizard marveled at his appearance; never before had drinking one of his life-extending potions restored this many years. Maligor mused that perhaps his body was becoming used to the potions, and in accepting them, the mixtures were having better effects. Conversely, he considered with a scowl, it could mean that the next potion would present an even more drastic change on his body. He didn't like unpredictable magic, but he certainly liked this.

"Another lifetime," he said to himself, insufferably pleased, running his hand over his bald spot, tracing the outline of the white skull there and posing before the glass. Basking in his own company, the wizard stared at his image for nearly half an hour.

Changing into a new scarlet robe, he waltzed to his wine cabinet, his gait lively. He selected a bottle, the label of which was yellowed with age and unreadable, snatched two glasses, and padded to his couch. Maligor considered wine the only thing that improved with age.

"Asp!" he shouted to the guards beyond his chamber. "Bring Asp here at once!" He wanted to share the excitement of his new form with her.

Maligor had finished his fourth glass of wine by the time the spirit naga arrived. She slithered into the room and moved in front of him, coiling her snake half into a tight spiral and resting backward on it, not visibly reacting to his new appearance. She was not her usual prim self this morning. Her hair was disheveled and her face and arms were smudged with dirt. She had the faint odor of sweat about her, which Maligor considered at once repulsive and alluring.

"You're drinking rather early," she stated, dispensing with the formalities he demanded and snapping him out of his good mood. The naga was furious he had risked his life by drinking the longevity potion; she wanted him alive until he gained enough power so she would have a sizable share of wealth and influence for herself. If he died before their plans were realized, she would have to leave Thay. None of the other Red Wizards would stand for the presence of a power-hungry spirit naga who served a wizard that had schemed against them.

Asp let her anger surface. "So you're younger," she hissed. "And you're celebrating by drowning yourself in wine."

"Beautiful Asp, won't you join me in a drink?" The wizard's manner was drunkenly gracious as he extended a half-filled glass of dark red liquid.

"No," she spat.

Maligor raised a shaggy eyebrow; never before had the naga refused him.

Asp rose on her snake's lower body to tower above the Red Wizard. "Those elixirs could kill you," she fumed, "yet you risk it to regain your youth."

"Enough!" Maligor snarled. His pleasant disposition had turned increasingly sour. "I won't tolerate your insolence. Watch yourself, my pretty Asp. I could kill you with a word and replace you before your body grew cold!"

Maligor's anger had sobered him. He slammed down the empty glass, breaking it. Reaching forward, he grabbed the naga's shoulders, digging his nails deep into her tender skin with a new strength that made her wince.

"You will treat me with respect," he ordered, his face inches from hers. "You will obey me. You will lick the soles of my slippers if I desire. And you will never talk to me in such a manner ever again."

The naga trembled but sat pale and silent until he released her. She rubbed her shoulders where the white marks from his nails stood out. She fumed with contempt and hatred, but she held her thin tongue, believing the wizard really would kill her if she angered him further.

"I beg your forgiveness, my lord. I'm tired, and I've been drilling the gnolls steadily for the past three days. The task has made me thoughtless and foolish."

"Eloquent to the last, Asp," Maligor said, stepping away from her and to his mirror, where he could look at himself again. He fancied that he looked more handsome with hair.

The Red Wizard caught the naga's image in the reflection of the mirror and stood there, enjoying watching her squirm. He imagined that soon other wizards would find themselves in her position, under his thumb and bowing to his mandates.

After a while, Asp broke the uneasy silence.

"Why did you summon me, Lord Maligor?" She remained face forward, not looking at him, and continued her courteous but strained dialogue. "I thought you wanted me to stay with the gnolls."

Maligor paused before answering, giving her more time to feel uncomfortable. Finally he took his eyes away from his younger form. He pivoted to face her, twirling his left index finger in his beard. He still needed her—for a few more months, anyway.

"And you shall return to them," he said, the edge gone from his voice and his expression almost emotionless. "It is time to bring them all together and begin our reign of terror."

He padded back toward the couch, eased himself onto the soft leather, and met her uncertain gaze. "We will bring them here—all of them. As they camp outside my tower, you can instruct them a final time. Then you will lead them to glory."

Asp blanched but somehow found the courage to softly rebuke him. "My lord, if we bring them here, it will unnerve the wizards in Amruthar and draw the attention of Szass Tam."

Maligor touched Asp again, this time stroking her chin and gently wiping away a smudge of dirt. "Let them think what they will. Their fear makes us stronger, and no one in Amruthar would dare go on the offensive against my army. They'll simply wait. And watch. And worry."

Asp rose with Maligor. In an uncharacteristic gesture, he escorted her to the door.

"I have your loyalty in this?" he posed, hoping she would agree; he couldn't afford to eliminate her yet.

"You have my loyalty, my being, and my love," she replied huskily, once again guardedly comfortable in his presence.

The Red Wizard kissed her deeply, as if to cement her fidelity, then shooed her from the room.

Once again alone, Maligor returned to his mirror. What to do with his appearance, he thought. Red Wizards in

Thay had no hair. Those outside of Thay, such as ambassadors and spies, wore hair to conform with the styles of whatever society they were in at the moment. He should shave it, he knew, to fit in. He should summon a slave and have her deal with it. Or, he thought, he could let it be. For a time, at least.

Maligor stared at the tresses that now set him apart from his peers. He would leave them alone, he decided. Shaving one's head wasn't a required act, just fashionable, and he believed he looked better this way—and more sinister.

He chose to look in on Asp, to make sure the spirit naga was carrying out his orders. He didn't doubt that she would gather the gnolls; he just wanted to make sure she attended to it right away.

The Red Wizard retrieved a large crystal ball from a shelf in his closet. It felt heavy in his hands, although Maligor was pleased to note that it didn't take any effort to carry it. The crystal was smooth, flawless, and only a few weeks old. He had acquired it from a merchant who dealt in the arcane.

Maligor had used the crystal only a few times and had been pleased with its effectiveness. He realized nearly all of the Red Wizards possessed such devices, and some—like himself—had several. However, Maligor used only his newest acquisitions, those he determined were enchanted within the past year. Even though magic kept its potency, he preferred using things with little age to them.

He sat on the couch, holding the crystal in his lap and staring into its center. Concentrating, he caused a soft yellow glow to flow from his eyes, down his arm, and into his hand. The light pulsated and glowed, then arced to the crystal. When the glow faded, he saw Asp; she had used her innate enchantments to shift form and give herself legs. Fully clothed, she rode a heavy black war-horse away from the tower heading north.

Maligor wondered if other wizards were watching her as well.

He hoped so.

For the next several hours, he watched as the naga reached one unit of gnolls and ordered them to march to Maligor's tower. The Red Wizard checked with his guards to make certain the naga had sent word to the other gnoll units to gather in Amruthar.

It was late in the evening by the time the first group of gnolls reached Maligor's tower. The three hundred soldiers camped on the sculpted lawn and jeered at the growing number of guards along the walls of the city.

Wearing a chain mail vest that glinted in the torchlight, Asp moved among the gnolls, demanding their attention and best behavior. The naga, who had resumed her natural form, was forced to kill two of them to set an example before the assemblage came to order.

"Listen to me," she hissed. "Tomorrow you will be joined by more of your brothers, and the day after that still more. You will dress in armor, and you will fight for Maligor."

Asp continued to parade herself in front of the gnolls, some of which still seemed preoccupied by the guards on the walls. The chain mail fit her tightly, showing off every human curve and looking like a metallic extension of the scales on her snake body. She enjoyed the rough feeling of it over her skin.

"When we are all together, when we are one army, we will march to victory!" she exclaimed. "We will suck the marrow from our enemy's bones!"

A cheer went up from the gathered gnolls, and Asp did nothing to quiet them; she was pleased she had captured their spirit and devotion. She also enjoyed the show of power and hoped the watching Amruthar guards saw her as a threat.

The second group arrived at Maligor's tower late the next afternoon. They were fatigued from the forced march from the woods, but their mood soared when they saw the other gnolls and the city guards on Amruthar's walls.

Asp let her troops revel throughout the evening, feeding them dozens of roast pigs that slaves had purchased that day in the open-air market. The gnolls sang deep into the night, their canine voices sounding more like the howling of sad dogs than music. She joined in the merriment, wanting to keep her distance from Maligor for a while.

Here Asp was in charge, looked up to and respected. Although she was still the Red Wizard's puppet, the strings were looser here, and she could bask in her superiority.

The city guards remained on Amruthar's wall. Maligor observed them from the window of his study and pondered what defensive actions the wizards and tharchions in the city might be taking. He had been watching less powerful wizards on and off through his crystal ball and knew they were nervous. Some had been casting protective spells throughout their homes and along the city walls to strengthen them. A few had left the city for places elsewhere in Thay, such as Eltabar—a place no Red Wizard was powerful enough to attack. Fewer still did nothing out of the ordinary, simply going about their evil business. Maligor considered these wiser; he knew that they realized he would not attack the city.

The Red Wizard also scried on the young illusionist, the one he had told Szass Tam he would send his gnolls against. That wizard had no hint that he was in danger as Maligor worked against him to cover his real goal of the Thayvian gold mines. He would fall easily during Maligor's ruse.

When the remaining third of Maligor's army reached the tower the next day, the city streets of Amruthar nearest Maligor's property were deserted. Maligor looked at the vacant open-air market, where stray dogs sniffed at the empty food stalls. An occasional guard or peasant could be seen standing against a building. Using his crystal ball, he looked farther into the city; there were few people about. However, on the far eastern edge of the city, life went on as usual. He thought about sending a dozen or so gnolls to the other side of Amruthar to see if he could frighten the residents there as well.

Maligor took his own precautions, warning his tower guards to stay especially alert and increasing the magical defenses within and on the exterior of the tower. He was too far along in his plans to risk getting careless.

The Red Wizard wanted to make sure he was protected against the unlikely possibility that a rival wizard decided to launch an attack against him in the hope of forestalling whatever action the Zulkir of Alteration planned.

He refused to meet with Asp on this day, instructing his servants and guards to inform the naga that he was too busy with his research to be interrupted. This irritated the naga, but she continued to follow his orders, drilling the assembled throng of gnolls and keeping a careful eye on Amruthar.

Some of the gnolls dared to ask her if the city was the target or if a wealthy baron's land just outside the city walls was their goal. The gnolls hoped the latter possibility was correct; most were tired of marching and didn't want to go much farther before they attacked something.

"No," she told them simply. "Striking near Amruthar, despite your numbers and fierceness, is foolish. Too many people command too much magic here. Our target is elsewhere."

The gnolls weren't satisfied with her answer, but they were too afraid of the naga to push her on the matter, just as she was too frightened to push Maligor. The naga wanted to move the troops now, before the city did something and before the gnolls became restless and difficult to manage.

Still Maligor would not grant her an audience. Asp's only contact with the tower came from guards who, toward evening, carted out large wooden boxes filled with the finest weapons the gnolls had ever seen. Asp bullied one of the guards into revealing where the weapons came from. The supplier proved to be a merchant's caravan headed toward Mulhorand.

There were far from enough weapons for all of the gnolls; only about a third of them would be able to discard their nicked blades and spears for shiny new ones. Asp and her sergeants selected the best warriors and presented them with the new weapons.

Those she intended to put up front were equipped with runkas, thick staffs with long central blades and two smaller ones at their base. The largest of the gnolls she also provided with renntartsches, large wood and leather shields that were reinforced with iron and attached to the breastplate of their armor. They made the unit look especially formidable and freed up both of the gnolls' hands for battle.

The best fighters were presented with glaives, halberds, long swords, and estocs, swords with stiff blades. A hundred suits of new armor also were distributed—coats of plate, hornskull helmets, kettle hats, chain vests, lamellar armor, and hardened leather breastplates that were slit at the sides to accommodate the gnolls' large bodies.

Asp was pleased, certain the arms would give her force the advantage against their foe. She let the gnolls work with the new weapons to grow accustomed to the improved armor, explaining to the remainder of the gnolls that they must be content with their leather, scale, and padded armor until after the battle. With the spoils of victory, more armor would be purchased, she promised.

Near midnight, Maligor agreed to see her. Slithering into his lantern-lit study, Asp started to complain about not knowing in advance about the new weapons, then held back her remarks, remembering his anger at her only two days ago.

The Red Wizard appeared rested and at ease, yet his mood suggested he was eager to put their scheme into motion. Asp was eager, too, but the strenuous activities of the past few days were taking their toll. She looked haggard, her complexion showing a hint of ruddiness. Her scant hair was unkempt and oily, and she smelled worse than usual. Maligor noted that she was too tired and preoccupied to use her magic to put up even an illusion of beauty.

Although disgusted, he said nothing to her. If he needed to gaze on loveliness, he would summon his pleasure slaves later.

"The gnolls are ready," she said, drawing his attention. "But they grow impatient and fitful, and I am tired of watching Amruthar's guards."

Maligor forced himself to tolerate her appearance and embraced her, smoothing her short hair.

"At dawn, sweet Asp," he whispered. "They will march at dawn. You must rest, however, or you will be in no condition to lead them. I want you at your peak. Tomorrow everything will be set into motion."

He felt the naga relax, glad that the moment to fight had come. A pity, he thought, that she would not be leading the gnolls anywhere. She would not be involved in any battle, and that might crush her spirit. He had been lying to her to keep her loyalty; he intended to use her in the mines.

"I want to talk to your sergeants," he continued. "I want to personally commend them for their diligence. Don't you think that would be a good idea?"

She straightened, slowly pulling herself away from his embrace and trying to appear as the general she considered herself.

"That will mean a great deal to them, Maligor," she said evenly.

"Good," he replied. "Send them to me. Then get yourself to bed."

Asp smiled and her eyes sparkled. She nodded and slithered from the room, returning to the tower many minutes later with eight armored gnolls. Maligor met them in the entry chamber, not wanting the gnolls' mud-encrusted boots to track dirt into the tower. The naga retired to her own room, leaving Maligor to deliver his message.

However, when the Red Wizard was positive the naga was out of hearing distance, he delivered a quite different speech—one that did indeed inspire the gnolls, but one that left Asp out of the picture.

"You are the backbone of the army," he began in a commanding tone, letting his eyes bore into theirs. "You do not need the naga to lead you. You are the leaders, the generals, and victory will be assured with the units under your guidance."

The gnolls grinned, their canine teeth reflecting yellow in the chamber's light.

"At dawn, you will lead the army south. I will tell you the target then. I do not fear that you will leak this information," Maligor said, his words now soft like velvet, "but I know that other Red Wizards have the power to pull things from minds. We don't want to give them an opportunity to learn our target."

He noticed that the smallest of the gnolls was glancing at the staircase Asp had crawled up minutes ago, and he suspected this one was loyal to the naga.

"Don't concern yourself with Asp," Maligor said, guessing the gnoll's thoughts. "I will inform her of the change of command in the army. I will deal with her wrath. Now go. We all need to rest before the morning."

But the Red Wizard still had work to do. It was fortunate he was younger now; lack of sleep would have taken its toll on his older body. Thrusting his hands in his deep pockets, he strode down the tower's main corridor and started the long descent to the darkenbeasts below. Along the way, he visualized how the creatures would fly from the bowels of his home, up the stairs, and through the corridors like a wave of death. It would be a splendid sight. Tomorrow.

Beneath his tower, the number of darkenbeasts had swelled. They were crowded into the large chamber; no space was vacant, and the Red Wizard had to concentrate to keep from retching from the smell. His mind snaked out, contacting the creatures, quieting and comforting his children and telling them that tomorrow they would have a new home with plenty of room and plenty of food for rending. Then he contacted one of the oldest darkenbeasts, one of his firstborn, whose mind was very familiar to him.

Maligor concentrated again and began a series of orders.

Fly north, my child, he began, picturing caves and abandoned buildings. *Fly to the places you see in my mind. Others of your kind are waiting there.*

The creature's mind was linked firmly with his, and Maligor sensed the wanton joy it was feeling, the anticipation of flying.

When you are there, we will tell the other darkenbeasts about our plan, Maligor continued. *We will tell them about tomorrow when all of us will fly to our new home. Now go.*

The favored darkenbeast shrieked with delight and used Maligor's mind to learn the way out of the tower. It flew up the stairs, through the long corridor, and hovered before the large doors. It shrieked again, and the frightened guards opened the doors.

Then it was out into the night air, flying low until it passed far from the city, then soaring to a higher elevation, relishing the feel of the wind rushing past its wings. Maligor felt the sensation, too; his mind soared as he climbed the stairs to his bedchamber.

Eleven

A legion of fifty skeletons marched behind Brenna, Galvin, and Wynter. The fleshless skeletons were armed with spears, broadswords, hand axes, and other weapons; some were mounted on skeletal horses, their bones clinking together and sounding like wind chimes. In a grotesque way, their appearance was almost humorous. Some were dressed as men would—in pants, tunics, and hats. Others wore robes and cloaks. But the majority sported bits of outfits or fragments of blankets. Szass Tam felt that dressing them in some sort of clothing would help hide their appearance, especially during the day, until they were close to the walls of Amruthar.

Following the skeletons shuffled a division of zombies, also about fifty in number, some of which were so recently dead that Brenna thought they could pass as human. At first she wondered why Szass Tam didn't put these up front. However, on closer examination, she discovered that their stench gave them away and made them more repulsive than the animated bones. All of the zombies were clad, some in armor. They

205

shuffled forward with their eyes cast on the ground in front of them, since they were unaccustomed to the sunlight. None of these carried weapons, intending to fight with their claws, which were filthy and carried diseases.

The remainder of the undead numbered about forty— jujus; zombie monsters, including a quartet of decomposing hill giants; yellow musk zombies, which were part man, part plant; and a few things with manlike shapes that the heroes couldn't identify.

Even though they preferred the comforting darkness of night, all of these undead were able to move about freely in the light of day. The Harpers and Brenna worried what might join their legion after the sun set a dozen hours from now.

The centaur wore barding, horse armor that made him feel as if he were being treated like an animal rather than a man. But from a distance, he thought he would appear to be a knight on horseback, and he rather fancied that idea. His rump was covered with a crupper—segmented, padded metal plates riveted together that extended to just below the tops of his back legs. A hole allowed his tail to poke through.

On his back was a flanchard, another piece of smooth and polished plate. It looked as if it had been molded to his body but possessed none of the flexibility of his natural hide; it connected to the crupper and extended to the start of his human torso. The flanchard chaffed a little and felt heavy and uncomfortable; Wynter had never worn armor before. However, he knew it would protect his flanks, and that was where the bulk of his injuries had been sustained earlier. The peytral portion—the section that would normally protect a horse's neck—had been discarded. Instead, Wynter wore part of a human's plate—a cuirass, a backplate and breastplate over a heavy quilted shirt. Oddly, that part of the ensemble fit him almost perfectly and was surprisingly easy to move in. His head was protected by a close helmet, the visor of which was up so he could see more easily. Of Mulhorandish make, it didn't match the cuirass, being newer, more ornate, and covered with stamped designs.

In metal gauntleted hands, Wynter carried an enchanted bardiche, a formidable pole-arm that consisted of a stout wooden staff with a long, slightly curved blade at one end. It had been ensorcelled to strike more easily and was weighted so that when it struck opponents, it could slice off limbs. It was sharpened until it glinted keenly in the sunlight.

Although Wynter hadn't been specifically trained in the use of such a weapon, the centaur was confident his mastery of the quarterstaff and experience with a pike would suffice to allow him to use this weapon if he truly had to. He switched the bardiche back and forth between his left and right hands, getting accustomed to the feel of it. It seemed finely balanced and could no doubt cleave a skull in two with little effort. The centaur disliked killing, fighting, and even carrying such weapons, yet his appearance gave the impression he was spoiling for a fight.

Szass Tam had forced Wynter to dress like this, reasoning that his large size might cause opponents to select him as their first target, but the armor should give him enough protection. Conversely, the centaur knew his stern countenance would cause at least some opponents to reconsider facing him, perhaps giving the Harpers a psychological edge.

His companions were not armored as formidably as the centaur, but they were also protected, equipped, and looked impressive.

Galvin had declined Szass Tam's offer to be outfitted in the finest full plate mail. The druid was adamant that all the metal would hamper his movements, and thus would be more of a hindrance than a benefit. He settled on wearing a mail shirt, the links of which were small, tight, and afforded adequate defense, while being flexible enough to satisfy him. Over it, and against his strong objections, he wore a sleeveless black tabard that bore the lich's symbol, a skeletal hand crushing a fleshy one. Galvin took it to mean Szass Tam believed the undead would one day conquer the living.

The druid's kite-shaped shield was painted black and had a
large, open skeletal hand in the center of it. He rode a
heavy war-horse, also black. It had chain barding and a
flowing ebon cloth decorated with embroidered skulls that
hung on both sides of the saddle. The druid was an accom-
plished equestrian, having often ridden the wild horses of
Faerun, but this mount unsettled him. It was trained for
war, it walked with practiced, measured steps, and it
lacked the spirit of the wild horses. When he was finished
being Szass Tam's pawn, he intended to leave it behind.

Galvin had left his scimitar with the lich, but not by
choice. The Zulkir of Necromancy insisted the druid carry
an enchanted blade, a long sword that would make him a
more stalwart opponent against Maligor's minions. Further, he worried the druid by explaining that there may be
some forces under Maligor's control that could only be
harmed by magical spells or weapons. Galvin preferred the
feel of his own weapon, which seemed an extension of his
own hand, but he wasn't in a position to argue with Szass
Tam.

Brenna was the least affected by the lich's demands. Her
attire was simpler. Being a wizard and unable to wear armor because it could interfere with her spell-casting, she
had been provided with an arcane defense—silver etched
golden bracers that fit high on her forearms and felt as light
as parchment. The lich claimed they afforded almost as
much protection as the plate Wynter wore. Brenna was
skeptical, but she accepted them sullenly, finding some
consolation in the fact she didn't have to leave any of her
possessions behind with Szass Tam.

She had a harder time stomaching the charcoal-black
robe he gave her. It was too large, falling in folds about her
feet, and the shoulder seams extended several inches
down her upper arms. The neckline, cuffs, and hem were
trimmed with bits of bone. From the cut and the lingering
scent of perfume in the fabric, she knew it was a woman's
robe, and she wondered what the previous owner had been
like. She must have been six feet tall and twice Brenna's

girth. The enchantress got goosebumps thinking about the garment and considered shedding it and putting on something different. However, she suspected Szass Tam was watching them somehow, and for some reason, he seemed insistent the trio dress in a grim fashion and display his markings.

Her mount was slight but muscular, a young gray riding horse with a long, jet-black mane and an ebon saddle. She hoped she would be able to release it outside of Thay once they had fulfilled their agreement with the lich. She didn't want something so spirited to be trapped inside this country.

Brenna thought a moment, watching Wynter lead the cortege. She doubted her horse really would have a chance at freedom, uncertain as she was whether Wynter, Galvin, or she would either. She was convinced that her fate would be grim—death at the hands of Maligor's forces or eternal servitude to the lich. If they survived their encounter with Maligor, she didn't believe Szass Tam would let them go. Success would make them too valuable as puppets and too knowledgable as free men.

Wynter and Galvin had remained silent since they left Szass Tam's keep a half-hour ago. To keep her mind from dwelling on the glum possibilities, Brenna studied the terrain. Even by daylight, the land near Szass Tam's keep looked dead. The ground was flat, the trees that dotted it were twisted and black. Only weeds grew, and they were the thorny kind.

As the miles floated by and they moved farther from the lich's property, the land changed dramatically. Tall grasses grew on the plain, and there was an abundance of trees and bushes. In the distance to the west, north, and south, the enchantress saw precise rows of citrus trees, looking like dark green stripes on the land. She tried to imagine what this land would look like without the Red Wizards' influence. It would probably be barren, she decided, like the ground near Szass Tam's keep.

Brenna wondered what Galvin was thinking about—the

lich, perhaps, or Maligor. The Harpers were likely to be taking this worse than she was, she thought, knowing that Wynter and Galvin claimed allegiance only to themselves and to the Harpers, and they were not bound by civil responsibilities beyond what they decided to accept—such as this mission into Thay. Their forced loyalty to Szass Tam, even though supposedly temporary, must be causing them great inner turmoil. Brenna had found herself in situations before in which she had to follow the majority dictates of the Aglarond council, even though she didn't agree with them. Although those dictates were never evil, she tried to tell herself this current dilemma was similar to those experiences. She tried to believe that.

Brenna wished the Harpers hadn't agreed to investigate the evil country and cursed herself for not staying back in Aglarond. But if she hadn't kept herself entrenched in political events at home, she wouldn't have cared what the Red Wizards were up to, and she'd never have known the two Harpers. She wished she had shown Galvin more understanding earlier. Melancholy reflections continued to flood her mind until she noticed Galvin was talking.

"At least you could talk about it." The druid was speaking to Wynter.

"Talk about what?" Wynter's voice was hard to catch, as he spoke straight ahead and was a half-dozen yards in front of Brenna. "Talk about this country? The lich? I remember my father fearing Szass Tam, yet all the while hoping the slave plantation would come under his influence. My father wanted to work for Szass Tam. The Red Wizard who controlled my father's plantation wasn't as powerful as the lich. I'm not sure any Red Wizard in Thay, or any wizard anywhere else in Faerun, for that matter, is that powerful. And now here we are working for Szass Tam. I can imagine quite a few people in this gods-forsaken country actually envy us."

"The lich isn't all-powerful," Galvin interjected. The druid rode up even with the centaur to make the conversation easier. "If he was, he would have taken over Thay years ago. Besides, he's dead. I would think that limits him."

"Don't kid yourself, Galvin. Szass Tam is more powerful dead than he ever was alive. Humans—and centaurs—are mortal. And any mortal, unless he has enough magic behind him, isn't a part of the world long enough to have any lasting power." The centaur swiveled his human torso to face the druid. "Some of the Red Wizards are very old, my friend. Centuries old. Time has given them power, and Szass Tam has existed longer than any of them."

"If he's so powerful," Galvin pressed, "why doesn't he deal with Maligor himself, and why hasn't he taken over this whole stinking country? If he's so powerful, he doesn't need us."

Wynter paused a moment, as if trying to get the wording right. "Because he can keep his hands clean by using puppets like us to do his work."

Brenna had ridden up near the Harpers and had been listening intently. "Maybe he's just waiting a few centuries until the time is right to strike," she offered.

The three became silent and continued to move across the Thayvian countryside toward Amruthar. They paused for an hour at the edge of a small citrus orchard after they had marched half the day. Galvin wanted to rest the horses. The undead needed no rest, food, or water, but the Harpers and Brenna needed all of those. They cooled themselves in the shade of the citrus trees and talked little during their rest, watching the undead, who stood unmoving like statues, waiting for the order to continue on.

Perhaps Szass Tam's symbol of a skeletal hand crushing a living one bears truth, Galvin thought as he used his black tabard to wipe the sweat from his face. Maybe the tireless undead would someday rule Faerun. An army of soldiers who had no human needs and could move as silently as a snake could easily defeat living soldiers.

The druid reached up to pluck a piece of fruit. The ripe fruit was sweet, and the juice ran down his chin when he bit into it. Gazing over their army, he compared it to the number of undead he had seen around and inside Szass Tam's fortress. He assumed that if the Red Wizard Maligor was making a bid for something, he would have to throw all of his army at it, and it was evident Szass Tam was providing the heroes with only a fraction of his forces to deal with the threat from Maligor. Galvin considered discussing the situation with the centaur, then saw him eyeing the undead.

"We should reach Amruthar near midnight. We might as well take the undead against the gnolls right away," the centaur observed. "I want to get this over with as soon as possible. I want . . ." Wynter stopped and stared into the orchard. His nose twitched. "I'll be right back."

The centaur trotted off and disappeared behind a row of large citrus trees. Galvin shrugged and turned to Brenna; she was grimacing at a nearby hill giant. The decomposing creature appeared to leer at her. However, the druid realized, the creature's expression was caused by its missing upper lip. Galvin sat down beside her.

"We'll make it through this," he said reassuringly, placing a hand on her shoulder.

Before she could reply, a scream sliced through the air.

"Wynter!" Galvin shouted, jumping up and racing into the orchard where he had last seen the centaur. Brenna was on his heels, waving her arm frantically behind her, trying to keep the skeletons from following.

As Galvin cut through the trees, he saw Wynter standing motionless beneath a large citrus tree. Wrapped around the centaur's legs and the base of the tree was a thick length of light green vine. Dark green buds and ivylike leaves covered much of the plant, and bright yellow flowers splashed with purple dotted the vines. The heavy scent of musk filled the air.

The druid drew his blade and dashed forward, slashing at the nearest vine. The weapon sunk halfway into the pulpy tendril, releasing a dark red sap, and he tugged to pull the blade loose. Before he could remove it, however, Brenna pushed him and fell to the ground on top of him. Over their heads, the druid saw one of the yellow flowers spray a purple mist of pollen at the spot where he had been standing. The fragrance was overpowering, an inviting musk that seemed to encourage him to come closer to the blooms.

The sorceress rolled off Galvin and tugged on his arm, breaking the enchantment. "Move away, Galvin!" she cried. She pulled again, and the druid crawled away from the plant, backing up so he could keep his eyes on the blossoms.

Wynter had remained still, a silly smile spread across his face and his eyes half-closed. Galvin and Brenna noticed that the vines had released the centaur's legs and had inched forward, away from the trunk of the tree, pointing all its blossoms toward the druid and the sorceress.

"What *is* that thing?" Brenna gasped, rising to her feet. The druid stood beside her, scanning the grove for more of the plants.

"I—I don't know," he answered. "I've never seen anything like it before." The druid kept his eyes on the blossoms. "Wynter! Wynter, come here."

"He's not moving. It's like he's in a daze," Brenna said nervously. "Galvin, look! There's a skeleton near the tree."

The druid took a step closer and peered over the thickest vine. He saw a human jawbone and a broken rib cage. "We've got to get Wynter out of there!" Galvin closed his eyes and spread his arms out to the sides, palms toward the plant. He began humming softly, then he swayed gently back and forth. After several moments, he opened his eyes and stretched his right hand out toward the plant while continuing to sway. A tendril slowly snaked toward him.

Brenna cringed and considered pulling him back. Then she noticed the vine begin to sway back and forth in time to the druid's movement. She edged forward and motioned to Wynter, hoping fervently he would move while the druid had the plant distracted.

"Arrh!" Galvin bellowed, dropping to his knees and throwing his hands to his temples. He would have fallen forward to the ground, but the enchantress grabbed him about the waist and hauled him backward, out of the way of another blast of pollen. Brenna dragged him several feet back, until she was certain the plant couldn't reach them.

The druid gasped, shook his head back and forth as if to clear it, then looked up at her. "It . . . it was human." Galvin was almost breathless. "I spoke with it. I told it to release Wynter."

"And . . . ?" Brenna coaxed, glancing back toward the still entranced centaur. The vines were slowly winding themselves around his legs; one was wrapping itself about Wynter's waist, edging its way under his armor.

"The plant was a yellow musk zombie, like some of those creatures we have with us," Galvin went on. "Somehow when the zombie died, it turned into this. Brenna, we've got to get Wynter out before the plant turns him into a zombie!"

"I'll get help," Brenna called as she rushed down an aisle between the citrus trees.

Weaponless, the druid advanced once more on the plant, this time intent on wrestling with it. A large vine slithered forward, and he pounced on it like a cat. Thrusting his booted heel against the vine, he pulled, breaking off a piece of the thing, only to find his chest coated with the reddish sap that spurted from the severed vine.

He glanced up just in time to see another vine—this one covered with the yellow flowers—arc toward him. The druid rolled to the side, avoiding multiple blasts of the pollen, and neared the vine where his sword was lodged. With one strong pull, his blade came free, and he leaped backward just in time to avoid a whiplike tentacle.

The air in the grove smelled strongly of musk, sweet and heavy. Galvin was finding it hard to concentrate and the blossoms were increasingly inviting. In a daze, he stepped forward.

When Brenna returned with a dozen skeletons in tow, she saw Galvin standing motionless a few feet from the trunk of the plant, one of the tendrils inching up his leg. Another vine was creeping up the centaur's chest, over his armor. Still another had wrapped itself around Wynter's head and was poking a tendril into the centaur's helmet, where the visor stood open.

"Kill it!" the enchantress ordered, pointing at the plant. The skeletons plodded forward, unmindful of the pollen bursts that quickly spurted out toward them.

The bony fingers of the undead skeletons tore into the vines, tugging at the pulpy tissue and pulling the tendrils free from the centaur and the druid. Brenna watched as the plant fought the skeletons, extricating its own roots and using them as whips against the undead creatures.

The plant's attacks were futile. While it could knock one or two of the skeletons down with a flailing vine, the undead creatures quickly rose again and began to beat upon the plant once more.

Galvin blinked his eyes, roused from the plant's power by the sound of clinking bones. For a second, he stared at the scene, then dashed forward with his blade.

It took nearly half an hour for the skeletons and Galvin to kill the plant. Even after it was dead, the undead creatures persisted in pulling it apart and pummeling it until Brenna called them off. Wynter had remained like a statue throughout the battle, oblivious to the plant and his rescuers.

Galvin picked his way through the pulpy mass to the centaur's side. The druid reached up and pushed the centaur's helmet from his head, revealing a bloody circular patch on Wynter's temple. Green ooze was mixed with the blood, indicating that the plant had made the wound.

"Wynter. Wynter!" Galvin urged. The druid ran his hand along his friend's long back, then nudged the centaur's arm.

The centaur slowly blinked and cast his face down sluggishly at the druid. "Who—who are you?" his deep voice queried.

"Wynter, don't you recognize us?" Brenna hurried to the centaur's side. "I'm Brenna, remember? This is your friend, Galvin. Are you all right?"

The centaur reached his hand up to his wounded head,

his fingers feeling the blood. "Galvin? Brenna?" he repeated in a childish tone.

"Yes," the druid coaxed. "Don't you remember us?"

"Are we going to play? I'd like to play now."

"Wynter!" Galvin barked. "Snap out of this!"

"Don't yell. I'm sorry," the centaur apologized sheepishly. "Can we play later?"

"Yes, later," Brenna cut in. "But you have to come with us first. We have work to do. We'll play later."

The centaur seemed satisfied and reached his hand down to take Brenna's. The enchantress led him from the orchard, with Galvin and the skeletons falling in behind.

When they had rejoined the undead army, Brenna mounted her horse and looked back uncertainly at Galvin. The centaur stood behind the druid, a silly grin spreading across his face as he scrutinized one of his gauntlets.

"Let's get moving," the druid said in a businesslike manner, his concerned expression contrasting with his tone. "We'll have to watch Wynter closely; he's like a child. Gods, what made him wander off into that orchard?"

"The plant," the sorceress said simply. "He must have caught a whiff of that pollen."

"Then we need to be doubly careful. Maybe there are more of the things nearby." The druid glanced forlornly at his Harper friend.

"I've seen spells do things like this," Brenna offered as she scrutinized Wynter's face. "They make people feeble-minded, cause them to loose their sanity, become useless. The spells are usually only temporary."

"And this . . . ?"

"I don't know," she said uncertainly. "If he doesn't come to his senses, maybe we can find someone in Amruthar to help him."

"And if not?"

Brenna frowned and shifted position in her saddle.

The procession resumed its march toward Maligor's tower.

* * * * *

High in a tower room, Maligor was too preoccupied to magically cast his vision about looking for the reactions of others to his gnoll troops. Had he not been so preoccupied, he might have received a hint that Szass Tam was sending an undead army to Amruthar. He was taking for granted that the gnolls' presence was causing the city's wizards to add to their own defenses. He hoped all the nearby Red Wizards were paying attention to his gnolls.

Delirious with himself, excited about this night's activities and his impending control of the Thayvian gold mines, Maligor was unable to stand still. He paced in his library, twirling a long strand of black hair around and around his right index finger until it hung alongside his face in a limp spiral. He wanted to relax . . . needed to relax. But he also needed his wits about him, so he kept away from the wine cabinet—a most difficult task.

He continued to pace, mentally rehearsing his impending sermon to the gnolls. He had decided last night that he would address them all prior to their upcoming battle. Asp was out of the picture as far as his gnolls were concerned. The spirit naga had served her function in the army, training the gnolls well. The army was to her credit, Maligor forced himself to admit. She was so power-hungry that she saw disciplined troops as a way to improve her own image and increase her standing. And the Red Wizard was certain she believed that taking another wizard's land for Maligor meant she would be tossed some juicy scraps.

"Simpleton," he said, thinking of the beautiful naga, who was oblivious to what was transpiring around her. He would enjoy putting Asp in her place while using her to complete the greatest scheme in Thay's recent history. Nagas were usually creatures who dwelled in ruins, caverns, and other such desolate places. The mines would fit her well and remind her of her place in the workings of the country.

"What is going on?" Asp hissed, slithering through the

doors she had forcefully thrown open, leaving two startled guards shaking behind her. "The gnolls aren't following my orders! They refuse to march! The army was to move this morning!"

Maligor glared at the guards for allowing his meditations to be interrupted. Then he turned his anger on Asp.

"What is going on is none of your concern, naga!" the Red Wizard barked. "I don't take into my confidence snake-women who have no respect for me, who burst into my room uninvited. I warned you before about your audacity. Now you will suffer for it. Because of your recent tantrums, I have decided to take the army away from you. You won't be leading them anywhere."

"Nooooo!" Asp's scream cut through the air like the cries of one of the wizard's tortured prisoners. "Maligor, no! You can't mean this! Look at everything I've done for you!"

Her shrill voice drew the attention of the guards, who entered the room prepared to defend Maligor. A stern glance from the wizard kept them at the ready, yet they did not move. In the hall beyond, the Red Wizard heard the pounding of footsteps. More guards were coming to his aid.

"The gnolls! They're battle-ready! I'm responsible for that! I've taught them how to fight, how to defend themselves, how to wage war with something besides their filthy claws! You have one of the best-trained armies in all of Thay! And it's my doing. My doing, Maligor!"

Maligor smiled thinly at her tirade and let her rant on until she was nearly out of breath. Her once porcelain-pale face was red with rage.

"You know nothing about war!" she ranted, spitting out the words, her reeking saliva spattering on Maligor's robes. "You can't take away the glory that is rightfully mine!"

More guards streamed into the room, a dozen of them with their longswords drawn. They held their position and watched Maligor and Asp, waiting for the naga to attack him.

"I've earned the right to lead them! You can't take that away from me! Maligor, please!" Asp had difficulty forcing the last word out from her throat; it made her appear weak in front of the Red Wizard's guards. "Don't do this to me."

"Don't worry, Asp," Maligor said in soothing tones that coaxed some of the pink away from her cheeks. "Don't think that I would take all of that away from you.

"I've already done it."

"Nooo!" she screamed again, rising on her snake's tail to her full height.

In response, half the guards rushed forward, grabbing her hands and tail. She struggled, sending two of them flying across the polished marble floor, then stopped, knowing that even if she defeated the guards, Maligor could kill her.

"Leave us," the Red Wizard ordered the guards. "But stay close at hand in the event the snake-woman presents a problem."

Asp's chest rose and fell quickly, and her eyes narrowed in hatred to paper-thin slits. She eased back on her tail so she would be shorter than the wizard. It was the only token of respect she was willing to afford him at the moment.

The wizard paced in front of her in slow, measured steps, then turned abruptly and his hands shot forth from his robe. A green bolt of light ran from the middle finger on his left hand to the chamber's door. The door frame glowed softly.

"These words are not for the guards. The spell will keep them from hearing anything," Maligor explained. "My plans are for your ears only. It is time to let you in on my true goal."

Asp blanched, and her eyes widened with a dawning of comprehension. "But the gnolls . . . ?" she began.

"Are just a ruse," he finished. "Although I actually am quite pleased you trained them so well. They definitely are a convincing deception."

The spirit naga gritted her teeth. "You used me! How

could you have let me put everything into training the army, to let me think I would lead them in battle? How could you do this to me? I'm loyal to you, and not without power. I thought you cared about me."

"My dearest Asp, it's true that I care about you—as much as I am capable of caring. And I certainly care about your abilities."

He padded to the room's largest window; it afforded an exquisite view of the land on which the gnolls were encamped.

"They do look magnificent." He spoke to her as he continued to watch his soldiers mill about. "And . . . perhaps they will be successful fighting a lesser Red Wizard, and I will win all the way around. Although if they win, I have promised Szass Tam a share of the spoils."

"Szass Tam is involved in this?"

"No, not really. He's just interested. He's been watching the gnolls, and I led him to believe the gnolls were going after someone's land. I think I recall offering him half if he didn't interfere."

"Then if I am not to lead the gnolls, what do you intend for me?" she hissed softly.

"You will play a role," he stated evenly, still watching his troops.

"And if I choose not to?" she posed nervously.

"You have no choice—at least not if you wish to live and have any power in Thay. I need you, Asp, and I don't want to kill you, because in a way I am fond of you. But if you won't help me willingly, I can find a magical way to force your cooperation. Then when my plan is finished, I will have to eliminate you."

"Of course," she agreed. The spirit naga knew Maligor couldn't afford to release someone who had been in his confidence for several years. "It seems I have no choice. I will help you. But I do not have to like it. Or you."

The Red Wizard moved away from the windows, drew the curtains closed, and strode to a stiff-backed, carved wooden chair. He unceremoniously sat in it; his younger body didn't require being pampered by soft cushions. Asp slinked to his side like a petulant child.

"It will be glorious, beautiful Asp. My plan is golden." He straightened himself, placing his shoulders squarely against the chair back. "Do you know much about the tharchions in Thay? Their influence, positions, appearances?"

"I know about some of them, Maligor—from reputation and pictures only. I am more knowledgeable about the other Red Wizards and their forces."

Maligor noticed that the naga had dropped the "my lord" when she addressed him. The lack of respect bothered him, and he would correct her attitude later. For the time being, he would let her be, knowing she had lost enough pride and dignity for one day.

"There is one tharchion in particular to concern ourselves with. He is nearly forty and squat, but he has a broad and sturdy frame. His body fits his place of work. The tharchion has a husky, barrel-like chest. Although he is clean-shaven on his head and face, wisps of black hair can be seen under his arms and just above his breastbone." Maligor's description was detailed and precise.

"Despite the tharchion's high position in Thay, he chooses to paint his head, like many of the women in Amruthar and Eltabar, rather than suffer permanent tattoos. The principal design on his head is a pale orange, four-taloned hand."

"The symbol of Malar, the Beastlord," Asp interjected.

"He wears other symbols, too," Maligor added, "but I'm afraid he was sweating rather profusely, afraid of my gnolls and of being in my dungeon. Unfortunately the paint ran and I couldn't make them out."

"You have a tharchion in your dungeon?" The naga was astonished. She was keen on Thayvian politics and goings-on, far more knowledgeable than she would admit to Maligor. But she hadn't heard of any tharchion disappearing.

"Had. When I was finished with him, the gnolls ate him. His bones are scattered along the escarpment. So, no, I don't have a tharchion in my dungeons. Now, to continue with my description.

"His clothes were well made and in good repair, but they were dirty, covered with dust and powdered rock from walking about in the mines."

"The tharchion the Council of Zulkirs assigned to oversee Thay's gold mines! You killed him?"

"I need you to look like him." Maligor waited a moment to let Asp absorb everything. "In fact, I need you to look *just* like him—close enough that you could fool his wife, the slaves under his charge, and the mine workers. I know you have the ability to do that."

Asp glared at him. "There's been no news of the tharchion's disappearance. Someone has to know."

"I don't think so," Maligor continued, pleased with himself. "You see, the council thinks he's outside of Thay. Well, his bones are, at least. Let's see what you can do."

The spirit naga backed away from his chair and concentrated. It was difficult for her because her mind was filled with questions. The transformation took longer than usual. All spirit nagas possessed the innate ability to change their appearance to human or demi-human bodies, although Asp only did so on Maligor's orders. She found the forms distasteful and at a disadvantage because they had legs instead of a tail.

Her beautiful features dissipated, running from her body like melting wax. She stood before Maligor a faceless, limbless column of flesh that began to take on new features. A head emerged from the column, bald and with pudgy cheeks. Eyelashes sprouted from the flesh over emerging, round eyes. Bulges appeared on the face and molded themselves into ears, a nose, and pale, bulbous lips. An age spot materialized below her left cheek—Asp remembered seeing that on a painting of the tharchion.

The transformation continued down the length of her body. A chest formed and became broader. Flab appeared along her midsection, and patches of black hair sprouted just above the breastbone and beneath the figure's flabby arms. The column of flesh separated below the man's groin, becoming stocky legs ending in short, wide feet.

The physical changes made, the naga created clothes—plain but functional, trappings she imagined someone like the tharchion would wear in the mines. The clothes looked like cloth and would feel like material to the touch, but because they were part of her body, they could not be removed. If necessary, she could polymorph them to appear different—sweat-stained perhaps, or of fine quality if the tharchion had to meet important guests.

"Excellent!" Maligor crowed with delight. "That's very close. You'll have to make a few adjustments here and there. His earlobes hung lower, I recall, and his fingers were shorter and thicker. I'll give you a mental image of the man in a little while, and you can make the necessary changes before we leave."

The naga had recovered a fraction of her pride and enough courage to pursue answers to her questions. "Tell me what this is about, Maligor. I know now it has something to do with the mines, but if you take the gnolls up there, they won't have a chance. Every wizard in the area will put his forces against you, especially the other zulkirs. The mines have been set up so no one wizard can control them. Your gnolls won't have a chance."

"You don't listen well, do you, dearest Asp? I told you the gnolls are after a wizard's land. There are enough gnolls to attract the attention of the nearby wizards. The gnolls will keep everyone occupied while we make our bid for the mine. No one will even notice."

Then Maligor told her of the multitude of darkenbeasts that would leave at dark when all eyes were on the gnolls.

"We'll leave with them, you and I. It will be truly glorious."

"A wonderful plan," Asp admitted with a hint of sarcasm. "But you will eventually be found out. If you take control of the mines—and even if you set me up as the tharchion—someone will notice when the gold goes into your pockets and the country gets nothing. Then you'll be undone."

Maligor beamed. He had been waiting to unravel the

meat of his scheme.

"The country will be undone. But it will take time. Dear Asp, if everything goes well—and I am certain it will—no one in Thay will be the wiser that there has been any change in the operation of the mine. You see, with you in place, business will go on as usual, and the country will continue to have a steady stream of gold filling its coffers. However, during the next several years, we will skim the mined gold—in increasing amounts as the next decade draws to a close. You will claim that the veins are beginning to thin out, and all the slaves and workers who will be in my control will agree with you. And if any zulkirs care to investigate, we will use magic to hide certain rich tunnels. They will believe you, and we will become rich.

"Nor do I intend to stop there. You see, the wizard Maligor will not have made any bids for power during those years, possibly crushed from the defeat of his gnoll troops in their attempt to wrestle land from a young illusionist. Of course, I will have to fabricate another story if they really do take the land. Perhaps the wizard Maligor was satisfied with that expansion and has no plans for any other."

Asp continued to listen, fascinated by the scheme that was sounding more and more plausible.

"However, the wizard Maligor will have been researching magic—alchemical spells that will turn lead into gold. The research will be successful, using our pocketed gold as proof. And my alchemical achievement will be a boon to Thay's economy. The country will have gold once more. Of course, to get the gold, other Red Wizards will have to come under my influence. In the end, I will be the most powerful Red Wizard in Thay. Nothing will stand in my way."

"And what of me? What will happen to me?"

The Red Wizard's face softened slightly and he leaned close to Asp.

"Your domain will be the mines, dark and dismal as they may seem to you. But it will not be forever. You will have a share in all of this, I promise. Every great man needs his queen."

Maligor was relieved that Asp appeared to be accepting that story. He would keep her with him as long as she proved useful. If she became too hotheaded and belligerent, however, he would have to find another naga.

"The plan is wonderful," she hissed. "I had wanted glory at the head of an army, but the subtlety of this intrigues and excites me. When do we move?"

Maligor grasped her pudgy male hands as he rose from the chair. He couldn't bring himself to embrace her while she was in the guise of the tharchion.

"The gnolls will move out tonight, about an hour after the sun sets. Since it will be dark, it will take a substantial amount of effort on the parts of the wizards to follow them and guess their intended target. Then, with all eyes on them, I will loose the darkenbeasts, creating a low-lying fog to cover their exodus and casting spells of silence to hide their cries. I have more darkenbeasts, too, not far from here. There are more than enough to capture the mines."

Asp appeared puzzled. "And how will we reach the mines?"

"Magic," Maligor replied. "We will fly, too. Then we will sit back and watch my creatures do their work."

"You are brilliant, Maligor," Asp said, her tharchion eyes shining.

The Red Wizard left her several hours later to meet with the gnoll army. As the sun set, he stood before the dog-men, resplendent in his youthful appearance and scarlet robe. Maligor paced grandly in front of them until he was satisfied all eyes were on him.

"We will move soon!" the Red Wizard began. "The night is our ally. You can see in the blackness, but your adversary cannot."

Asp, in her tharchion guise, watched Maligor from the shadowed recesses beyond the tower window. She couldn't help envying the admiration he was receiving from her gnolls.

"We are unstoppable!" she heard Maligor cry. She stared at the growing enthusiasm in the gnoll army. "With your strength, your sword arms, and your courage, you shall tread over the opponent's forces, grinding them beneath your hairy heels."

The wizard's voice quickened and rose. The words carried to even the gnoll soldiers gathered at the back of the throng. "The ground will turn red from your victims' blood. The sky will turn black from the flock of ravens drawn to feast upon the corpses of our enemies. Victory is ours!" he screamed.

"For Maligor!" the gnolls replied as one.

The Red Wizard cast his arm to the northeast. "There, near Eltabar. Take the lands of the young Red Wizard. Crush him utterly!"

The gnolls beat their weapons upon their shields, creating a din of clanging metal that drowned out the rest of the Red Wizard's victory speech.

The dog soldiers marched, and all eyes from Amruthar were on them.

Maligor ran into his tower as he mumbled the words of an incantation. He continued mouthing the spell as he raced down the stone steps to join his darkenbeasts below. By the time the spell was completed, a thick fog had blanketed the land around his tower and the western edge of Amruthar.

The darkenbeasts felt the wizard's excitement and began to soar about their subterranean chamber, faster and faster, on their leathery wings. Maligor's mind reached out, contacting one, then another, then a dozen, then still more until his thoughts were intertwined with all of his macabre creatures.

The darkenbeasts' cries spiraled upward from the chamber, unnerving everyone in the Red Wizard's tower. Louder and louder the noise grew, until Maligor masked the cacophony with an enchantment of silence.

Then he rushed up the steps, the darkenbeasts first following, then overtaking him. Higher and higher the hellish creatures flew, until they reached the ground floor.

"Throw open the doors!" Maligor commanded as he reached the entry hall. But the guards couldn't hear him because of the forced silence. The wizard waved his arms to indicate what he wanted.

The guards, quaking in terror, fumbled with the latches in their attempt to comply. Maligor ran ahead of his cloud of hovering darkenbeasts to wrench the doors open himself. So elated was the Red Wizard that he neglected to punish the fearful guards.

While the wizards and the city of Amruthar watched the gnoll soldiers, the darkenbeasts flew unnoticed. No one heard or saw them, and Maligor's spirits soared on their wings.

Asp, growing accustomed to her new form, waddled to Maligor's side and gazed up into his face.

The Red Wizard grasped her pudgy hand and muttered a few words. Then the pair vanished in a wisp of smoke.

Twelve

The sun was setting on Thay in front of the heroes and their undead charges. Wynter glanced over his shoulder so he could watch the skeletons and zombies.

"Why are they here?" the centaur asked Brenna. "They're dead, aren't they?"

"It's a long story. I'll tell you later," she sighed. "I only wish you could remember." Brenna stared at the undead army. They were frightening and macabre, shuffling stiffly, some hunched over. She wondered if there was any spark of life within them. Did they realize what they were doing and whom they served? Did they know they were being denied a true death because of sorcery? It was just another form of slavery. She had thought about that a great deal during the past few hours, just as she had been thinking about a lot of other things since leaving Szass Tam's fortress.

This was wrong, she knew, Wynter's condition and this entire procession against the Red Wizard Maligor. Choosing the lesser of two evils was still an evil. And any evil in Thay was an abomination as far as the enchantress was concerned.

"They smell funny," Wynter complained, interrupting her thoughts. "They look bad, too."

"I know," she said softly, smiling at the simpleminded centaur. "Try not to think about it. Look at the sunset. Isn't it beautiful?" The orange rays spread out over the groves of trees to their right and left and the verdant plain before them. The breeze that blew over the grass teased their faces.

"Pretty," the centaur agreed. "Your name is Brenna, right?"

The enchantress nodded sadly and tilted her head so she could see Galvin. The druid was several yards behind them and was apparently studying the centaur.

"Where are we going?" the centaur persisted.

"A city called Amruthar," Brenna replied.

"Tell me when we get there. I'm going to look at the dead men," Wynter decided, falling back to march between the first two rows of the undead. Balancing his enchanted bardiche under one arm, the centaur waved happily at Galvin.

Feeling morose about his witless friend, the druid didn't acknowledge the gesture. Galvin was angry at himself for not being with Wynter when the plant trapped him. Strangely, he was even angrier that the plant hadn't killed his friend. The druid knew that, in the wilderness, only the strong survived, and Wynter could no longer survive on his own. He hated seeing his friend this way—an adult with a child's mind.

The druid scowled, frustrated and disappointed that he should wish for his friend's demise. Civilized people wouldn't be so cruel, he decided. He rode up to Brenna, hoping she could take his mind off his morbid thoughts.

Brenna smiled weakly. "We can't win, Galvin. It's only you and me now. Wynter is . . ." She was at an uncharacteristic loss for words.

The councilwoman looked over her shoulder at the hulking centaur. Her emotions had been turned inside out the past several days, and the things she considered important—laws, government, control—seemed insignificant. She had grown to care for the centaur and the druid more deeply than she cared to admit. The pair of Harpers, who embraced the wilderness and the loose structure of their organization, were opposites of almost everything and everyone she knew. She found herself thinking more about their welfare than that of Aglarond, and she wondered how she could have changed so much since she entered Thay.

The druid cocked his head, noting her troubled expression. "We can't quit," the druid stated, glancing back at the army and seeing Wynter playfully pass his bardiche to a large skeleton. Galvin grimaced. "If we quit, Szass Tam will kill us, and we can't help Wynter if we're dead."

"I just wish we had never come here. Wynter chose to leave Thay years ago. He never should have come back. We should have stayed out of this evil land, too."

The druid realized that the enchantress blamed herself for their dilemma. If the Aglarond council, of which she was a member, hadn't asked the Harpers to investigate activities in Thay, things would have turned out differently. But Galvin also recognized that sooner or later the Harpers would have poked their noses into the country anyway. The lich was right. The Harpers were meddlers.

"It's not your fault," Galvin said.

The enchantress didn't reply. She stared ahead into the sunset.

The druid picked up the pace, and Brenna followed his lead. After they had covered several hundred yards, the druid glanced over his shoulder to make sure Wynter was all right. The centaur was tugging at the cloak of a skeleton. When it tugged back, Wynter giggled and left it alone.

The sun set as the army reached an area dotted with farms. The barns and houses looked like black splotches beneath the growing grayness of the sky. Here and there lights came on in buildings as lanterns were lit and families settled in for the evening.

The night heralded the arrival of more troops for Galvin's

and Brenna's army—two dozen shadows, like the creatures that had attacked them when they camped outside of Amruthar, and twice that many of something the pair could not identify. The latter initially appeared no different than the shadows, until they took a position behind Brenna and Galvin and made the pair's horses skittish and difficult to control. The air turned cold in the presence of the creatures, and the sorceress couldn't help shivering.

These new undead first appeared as amorphous blobs, then as man-shaped clouds of darkness insubstantial enough that they could manipulate the shape of their arms, legs, and heads. Those closest to Brenna adopted her form to mock her.

"What in the name of the gods *are* those things?" Galvin asked the councilwoman. He appeared to keep his eyes focused on hers, but he was actually peering nervously behind her at the undead. The druid was finding it increasingly difficult to see in the growing darkness.

Then he spied something ahead, a small row of flickering lights. They had to be torches along Amruthar's wall, so far away they looked like fireflies. He wished that Szass Tam had allowed them to bring lanterns so he could check on Wynter and the undead army behind him. He was uncomfortable not knowing his army's precise numbers and location.

"I only wish I knew what they were," Brenna replied nervously. "They're not like anything I've ever heard about. They're certainly not shadows."

Before she could say another word, one of the creatures laughed hollowly, startling the sorceress and the druid. None of the other undead in the patrol had seemed capable of speech other than an occasional moan, which Galvin at first thought might have been the wind.

"Death," said a shape that had assumed Brenna's form. The thing's haunting tones seemed at once to come from behind and in front of her. "We are death shrouded in darkness. Sweet, sweet darkness." The thing laughed again, the sound echoing in the night until it finally receded like a tide.

"Sweet death," another of the strange creatures echoed. Then another and another took up the phrase until the words blended together and sounded like a swarm of insects.

The sorceress wondered how the things could speak. The creatures had no mouths, nor indeed any other visible facial features. Gathering her courage, she turned and was startled to find herself mere inches from one of the creatures.

"How—" Her voice cracked and she shivered. "How do you talk?"

More haunting laughter followed, then a raspy voice filtered through the terrifying cacophony. "The death master makes it so. The death master makes the grave only the beginning. The death master makes us strong."

"What are you?" Brenna persisted, surprised she found the courage to speak with the undead.

"Wraiths," the word sounded like a rush of wind and came from the figure closest to Brenna. "Mankind's lover. We embrace men with the soothing kiss of death."

"Soothing death," the others echoed.

"We are the takers of souls, the shapers of destinies, the dark powers mortals fear. We are wraiths. And we hate humans because they are the possessors of life."

"Human life," the wraiths echoed eerily over and over.

"But we will help you humans," intoned a deep-voiced speaker. "The master bade us leave the caressing recesses of our graves to help you."

"Brenna! Galvin! I'm scared!" Wynter's voice cut through the haunting banter.

Galvin whirled his horse about and dug his heels in its sides to urge it through the crowd of wraiths. The stallion protested, feeling the cold touch of the creatures, but obeyed nevertheless. Galvin felt an unearthly chill as his mount passed near the bodies of several wraiths and finally found Wynter surrounded by a ring of the dark undead.

"Galvin?" Wynter whimpered.

The wraiths mocked the centaur, hovering around and

above him, taunting him.

Galvin nudged his mount closer until he reached Wynter's side. His once-strong, confident friend was trembling and broken. Once again Galvin found himself wishing the plant had killed the centaur.

The druid growled defiantly at the disgusting undead creatures, thrusting out an arm in an attempt to push one aside. But Galvin's hand passed straight through the inky body. It felt as if he had submerged his fingers in an icy spring.

He growled again, this time his voice sounding more like a wild animal than a human, and the undead finally backed away.

"Take my hand, Wyn," the druid said gently, his emerald green eyes locked onto the closest undead. "Come with me." The centaur whimpered in fright, then followed Galvin timidly toward the front of the procession.

"You said you were here to help us!" the druid cursed at the undead. "Then help us. Leave Wynter alone!" He noticed the centaur relax a little as the forms dropped back several yards.

"They did as you said," Brenna whispered in surprise.

"For now, at least," Galvin observed. "Stay close to Wynter and keep moving toward the city." The druid slowed his stallion until the first few wraiths were even with him.

He glared at them and marshaled his fear of the strange creatures. "Maligor's army will be strong," the druid began. "How can you help us against the gnolls?"

"We drink life," one moaned. "We drink the essence of man, leaving behind only decayed husks. Husks to wither and crumble and blow away on the hot breeze. Husks to fertilize our graves. "The creature held up its black hands, which appeared to have long talons. "We rake life, clawing, tearing, spilling life's blood on the ground, on us."

"Humans first," another added in a raspy whisper. "Always humans first because their life is so short and sweet."

"Sweet death," the assembled wraiths murmured.

Shivering from the cold air that surrounded the wraiths, Galvin left the undead to rejoin Brenna and Wynter.

The enchantress and the druid kept an uneasy silence for the remainder of the journey to Amruthar. The wraiths continued their frightening banter, making the pair wish Szass Tam hadn't sent these creatures along. However, some of their dialogue proved interesting and valuable. Galvin and Brenna learned that the wraiths, in life, were powerful, evil men and women who coveted wealth and authority and now were forever damned to be under the influence of Szass Tam. Most had died from the touch of other wraiths. Galvin was curious to find out if the lich had ordered these formerly living people to be killed because they had become an annoyance to the lich or because the lich desired more creatures. However, he decided against questioning the foul creatures. He didn't trust them, and he hoped to be rid of them soon.

The druid glanced at Brenna and saw her shivering. Reaching into his mount's saddlebag, he withdrew a blanket and passed it over to her. She wrapped it about herself gratefully.

Smiling her thanks, she dug her heels into her horse's side. They were beyond most of the farm land now and almost to Amruthar's walls.

The light from dozens of torches, spaced almost evenly in heavy iron sconces about the walls, played eerily over the stonework and softly illuminated the tent town full of peasants and merchants that stood beyond the city's gates. The people had spotted the army coming and were huddled near the massive gate.

Above, on the barbicon, scores of guards readied longbows and kept careful watch on the parade of undead. Also on the barbicon were a trio of scarlet-robed men—Red Wizards, no doubt, waiting to see if their enchantments would be needed to keep the undead at bay.

Despite the number of merchants, peasants, and guards, Amruthar was quiet. Only the occasional bark of a sergeant's orders cut the air.

Galvin and Brenna directed the army to march parallel to
the city's wall in full view of the guards, as Szass Tam had
directed. It was a show of force designed to keep the city's
guards from interfering. The guards stood motionless as
the dead soldiers passed by slowly, the clinking of skeletal
bones against skeletal horses echoing hollowly off the wall.

Just outside the city stood Maligor's tower. Its top half
was visible over the northwest barbicon of the wall. Galvin
motioned the army quickly forward and urged his own
horse into a gallop, knowing the tower's occupants must
have been able to see them coming for miles and would be
ready. He worried that they might be riding into a trap.
Brenna urged her mare ahead, following on the heels of
Galvin's mount and spraying dirt at the hurrying wraiths.
The enchantress was trying to ride with minimal use of her
hands, in order to keep them free to cast a spell if necessary.

The druid drew his longsword, which emanated a soft
blue glow, revealing its magical nature, and he cried like a
hawk as he charged across the main road that led to the
western gate of Amruthar. The undead moved as quickly
as they were able to behind him, but only the shadows and
wraiths could keep pace. Brenna called for the skeletons to
ready their weapons.

The tower stood back from the road. Only a few lights
burned in the windows, and no more than a dozen gnolls
stood at attention on the lawn. Behind him, Galvin heard
the scornful laughter of the wraiths.

"Sweet death. We will give the gnolls sweet death!" one
wraith cried. "We will open their throats and let the dog-
men's blood pour over us. We will turn them to dust." The
thunderous laughter of the undead rippled like a wave, unnerving the guards standing on Amruthar's western wall
and frightening the gnolls, who were trying hard to stand
their ground.

"Such a big army," mocked a wraith.

Galvin pulled back hard on the reins of the big black stallion in an effort to stop its charge. Dirt sprayed up all

around him as the animal complied. Brenna tried to stop her horse as well, but she shot past the druid, finally halting only a few yards from the closest gnoll. It glared at her, waved its barbed spear, and shouted something in a language she couldn't understand.

The druid dismounted and rushed to Brenna's side, brandishing his longsword in front of him. The gnoll backed away reluctantly, baring its yellowed teeth like a cornered mongrel dog, and looked for support from its peers. Help wasn't forthcoming. At sight of the undead army, they, too, were slowly backing toward the tower. Galvin could smell the stench of the gnolls' fear, and he sensed their uncertainty. Gnolls were stupid creatures, but they possessed enough sense to know they couldn't stand up to hundreds of undead.

"Where are all of your brothers?" Galvin shouted to the gnolls, hoping one could understand him. There was no answer as the gnolls continued to back toward the tower. The druid couldn't tell if they comprehended his words, but he knew they understood the threat of Szass Tam's army. Galvin heard his soldiers move forward, their bones tinkling.

"That's enough!" he shouted, whirling to stand inches from a wraith. The patch of blackness wavered before his eyes, then formed legs and arms and took the shape of the druid. A chill filled the air, emanating outward from the undead creature's body. Then eyes appeared, yellow-white pinpoints of light that looked like stars against the darkness of the wraith's form. The wraith floated upward, hovering about two feet above the ground and forcing Galvin to look up to speak to it.

"I need some answers!" the druid yelled. "And if you frighten the gnolls or kill them, we won't be able to learn anything. That's not going to make Szass Tam happy."

"We are to wrest life," the floating wraith sighed. "We are to wrest life from Maligor's forces. We will tug the breath away from their withering lungs."

"Look around!" Galvin bellowed. "Maligor's forces

aren't here. These are only a few gnolls he left behind to guard the castle. We need to find out where the rest of them went. And these gnolls can tell us."

The wraith floated back to the ground and pulled its black arms back inside its body. "The master of death can learn all their feeble brains contain," it uttered hollowly. "The master of death speaks to the dead. Let us devour their organs. Then the master will devour their minds. Then we'll learn."

"That's not the way I want it," the druid returned evenly. "You're under my command for the moment. The master ordered you to obey me. What would Szass Tam do if you didn't follow his orders? Now get back up to the road. Take the skeletons and zombies with you—all of them. Do it now!" Then he glanced over his shoulder at Brenna. "Please get Wynter. I want him safe here with us."

Amid grotesque snickers, the wraith called for its brothers and slowly heeded the druid's directions.

Satisfied, Galvin pivoted sharply to see the gnolls cowering. They continued to act nervous even when the undead had retreated back to the road. The druid noticed that the air around him was growing warmer in the absence of the wraiths. He stood still, staring at the gnolls, until Brenna and Wynter joined him.

"Where is Maligor's army?" the druid demanded.

The gnolls glowered at him, but they remained silent.

"Maybe they can't understand you," Brenna interrupted. "Not all gnolls can speak human languages."

The druid growled and remembered that the gnoll spy he met in Aglarond had had difficulty with human words.

Brenna touched his shoulder softly. "If you want to talk to them, I can cast a spell. They'll be able to understand you, and you them."

"Fine," Galvin said. "Do it quickly. I don't know how long I can keep the undead away."

Brenna hurried back to her horse and tugged a small velvet sack loose from the saddlebags. She untied the drawstring and returned to the druid.

"Luckily Szass Tam left me all my spell components. This will only take a moment," she said, reaching inside the sack with three slender fingers and pulling out several grains of coarse powder. "But do you think we should take the time to bother with this? Don't you think Maligor will retaliate?"

"He's not here," the druid stated matter-of-factly. "If he was, his whole army of gnolls would be here, too. These dog-soldiers aren't the main force. I want to find out where Maligor is and where the rest of the gnolls went. Can you make it so those damned wraiths can't hear this?"

"Not exactly. The wraiths seem to understand you, and the spell won't prevent that. However, unless they're well versed in gnoll speech, they won't be able to understand that part of the conversation."

Galvin seemed reassured, so the sorceress swiftly weaved her fingers about in the air as if she was knitting something. After several minutes, she nodded to Galvin to let him know he could begin.

"Where are your gnoll brothers?" he asked again. This time he could tell by the gnolls' eyes that they understood him. "Where is the main army?"

"There is no army," a muscular guard answered, looking sullen despite its quavering voice. It was evident that this gnoll was in charge and had no intention of giving up information easily. "There only us. We guard the Red Wizard Maligor's tower."

"You are not guards. You are fools." Galvin spat for emphasis, remembering the gestures of the gnoll he had interrogated before. "You will die at the claws of the dead men behind me. Perhaps I'll let you live if you tell me what I want to know."

"I'll tell you nothing, human," the gnoll returned, making a gesture Galvin couldn't comprehend. He assumed it was something offensive.

The druid gazed over his shoulder at the mass of undead and raised his arm. He intended it as only a threat. And it worked.

Instantly three of the gnoll guards hurried forward from where they had been cowering beneath the tower's walls and extended their hands.

"Wait!" one cried. He ignored the threatening scowl from his commander. "They left at sunset. All of them. They're marching east, I think. Against a young Red Wizard. We wanted to go, too, but Maligor said someone must guard the tower."

"You'll die, scum!" the head gnoll yelled at the traitor. The druid sprang forward and cuffed the muscular gnoll, then leveled his sword at its chest.

"Let your man speak," the druid snarled, then nodded at the other guard. "Go on. Why are they marching after a wizard? How far away is it? Is Maligor with them?"

"Hurry, Galvin," Brenna whispered. "The spell won't last much longer."

"Talk to me!" he shouted at the gnoll, then jabbed the sword point at its chest for emphasis, drawing a small trickle of blood.

"I don't know the Red Wizard's name," the traitor snapped. "It won't matter, because he will die. Nothing can stand up to our gnoll army. I only know the place is three or four days' march from here, maybe more, depending on how fast the army travels. It must be important land."

"What's so important about it?" Galvin pressed.

"Maligor wants it. That makes it important."

The druid scowled. "Is Maligor with the army?"

The gnoll looked at him stupidly, the spell exhausted.

"Damn!" the druid shouted. "Can you cast it again?"

Brenna shook her head and frowned. "Sorry. What do we do now? Do we go inside? Maligor's pretty powerful. If he's waiting for us in there, it could be tough." She eyed the tower. "Do you think Szass Tam knew there wouldn't be an army here?"

"No," Galvin answered, sheathing his sword. "The army was here very recently. Look at the ground. You can tell by the tracks, the depressions in the earth, and the smell. The gnoll was telling the truth. There was an army here until just a few hours ago. That could also be why there are so many guards on the walls of the city—as a precaution against Maligor's army." Galvin glared at the undead behind him; the tinkle of bones indicated they were advancing again.

"I said stay back!" The druid was tired of trying to control the creatures. He turned to face Brenna, and his expression softened. "I think we should wait for Szass Tam to contact us. Our instructions were to deal with Maligor and his forces. Well, Maligor's forces aren't here anymore."

"Then, lowly human, you will deal with his forces elsewhere," the voice of a wraith interrupted. A shadow of blackness hovered above the druid and sorceress, having moved up silently, keeping its distance until now so the cold wouldn't give it away. "Szass Tam talked to us, too. The death master wants Maligor stopped, and the master shall not be denied. You will lead us to Maligor's army, humans."

"Unlike you, we have to sleep sometime," Galvin said.

"Sleep later, human," another wraith called softly. "If Maligor is not stopped, you will not need to worry about sleep."

Galvin sighed and cocked his head forward, rolling his helmet off. He ran his right hand over his head.

"I don't want to die," Wynter said softly.

"Don't worry," the druid replied. Galvin knew he could stay awake for another day if he had to, but he wanted an excuse to abandon the wraiths, even if only temporarily.

"Well, I guess we don't have much choice, Brenna. The army that takes its orders from us is demanding action. There were so many gnolls here, it'll be easy to track them."

"Point us in the right direction," Brenna chirped, trying hard to sound cheerful. "We'll catch up to the gnolls, finish them off, then get out of this country and see about getting Wynter back to normal."

Galvin knelt to examine the tracks more closely in the

dim light from the torches along the city walls and the scant light spilling from the tower's windows. He ran his fingertips along a particularly deep imprint of a boot, then glanced at the guards along the city wall. From their numbers, he guessed that many of them must have shifted position from the north and south walls to crowd the west wall nearest Maligor's tower.

Maybe someone should tell them the undead aren't going to attack the city, he thought. It would be nice if at least someone could get some rest.

He rose, brushed the dirt off his knees, and smiled at Brenna. "We'll eventually catch up with the gnolls because they're traveling with full arms and packs. Besides, they'll have to stop to sleep." He glanced down at the outline of a few of the footprints.

"When we do catch up with them, we're in for a fight." He knelt and drew Brenna down beside him. Taking her hand, he guided her fingers inside one of the footprints. "Feel how deep this track is? Feel here, the ridges in the track, and here and here. Feel the rounded heel and toe. This track was made by a plate boot. That means the gnolls are heavily armed and armored."

Galvin considered approaching an Amruthar guard to get an estimate of the number of gnolls. However, he worried that he would be peppered with arrows as soon as he neared the wall. The information would do him little good anyway, he realized in the end. It really didn't matter how many gnolls were involved. Galvin, Brenna, and the undead were supposed to defeat Maligor's forces whatever the odds.

Resigned, the druid rose, turned his back on the tower, and strode toward his stallion. "Let's move," he told Brenna and hoisted himself into the saddle.

"Not just yet." Brenna stood unmoving, her hands planted on her hips, and stared long and hard at the head gnoll. "Let's see if we can find out why Maligor's going after another Red Wizard." She pointed at the tower. "Maybe we can learn something in there."

Galvin weighed Brenna's idea. The more he thought about it, the more he liked it. Any information was better than none. He leapt off the black stallion, grabbed the reins, and began to lead the animal toward the tower. Two gnolls moved to block the front door.

"Out of our way!" Galvin shouted, knowing the stupid creatures couldn't understand the words but hoping they would comprehend his intent.

Brenna was at his side in a few steps. Drawing a long knife, she anticipated trouble when the gnolls refused to part and the others began to move closer.

Galvin unsheathed his longsword and advanced. The gnolls paused, eyeing the glowing blade, then screamed as a black cloud descended upon them. The wraiths, appearing as a fog with ghostly arms and legs, laughed eerily and slashed at the gnolls' faces.

Deep, black gashes appeared, and blood flowed freely down the bodies of the terrified gnolls. The dog-men thrust at the blackness with their spears, but the crude weapons passed through the undead harmlessly.

"Stop!" Galvin demanded, running up toward the gnolls and disappearing in the cloud of undead.

Brenna screamed, fearing the druid was doomed. Tears welled in her eyes and her hands shook. Although she could hear Galvin's commanding voice through the undead, she feared for his safety.

"Back away!" the druid yelled as he slashed upward with his enchanted blade, slicing a black limb from a hovering wraith. The undead being emitted a piercing shriek and fell backward behind its undead brethren.

"I said stop!" Galvin shouted once more. "Back off, or you'll have to fight me, too!"

"We could steal your lowly life, human," growled a wraith that moved to hover inches from Galvin's face. Its hot white eyes bore into the druid. "We could bring you death with one touch."

"Then try it!" Galvin shouted, thrusting upward and driving his blade between the wraith's glowing eyes. The creature screamed and dissipated like thinning fog, but several others quickly moved to take its place, chilling the air about the druid. "Szass Tam gave me this sword. You know it can kill you."

"Mortal fool!" another wraith howled, its haunting tone drifted toward Brenna and Wynter. "You could never kill all of us. We would suck the marrow from your brittle bones. Then you would be one of us."

"Never!" The druid refused to cower before Szass Tam's minions. He realized that backing down meant giving in to the undead, inviting them to overwhelm him, Brenna, and Wynter. "Now get back to the road, all of you. This is my fight."

The wraiths laughed mockingly, their hollow voices reverberating off the tower wall, but they retreated nevertheless.

Brenna rushed to Galvin's side, threw her arms around him in relief, then quickly composed herself and stood facing the gnolls.

Galvin pointed the tip of his longsword at the dog-men, then swept it to the side, pointing west, toward the escarpment. "Move!" he barked. "Move or I'll kill you!"

The gnolls didn't comprehend the words, but they understood the druid's meaning. They fled the tower, running hard without glancing back.

The druid took a deep breath, sheathed his sword, and watched their retreating forms to make sure the wraiths didn't give chase. Galvin hadn't wanted to kill the gnolls, and he wanted to keep the undead from doing so even more. No being deserved to be turned into a wraith.

With half a dozen long steps, he reached the large tower doors and yanked on the handles. The iron-bound wood remained unyielding, even after he rammed his shoulder against it several times. Frustrated, Galvin shoved the enchanted blade between the two doors and pushed.

"That won't work either," Brenna observed, laying a soft hand on his mailed shoulder. "I'm pretty sure it's magically held. If Maligor's as powerful as we're led to believe, he'd certainly have magic in the walls and doors to keep intruders out."

"Wonderful." The druid slumped against the door.

Brenna smiled, and her eyes twinkled in the moonlight. "I think I can get in," she said. "I told you a sorceress would come in handy. Now aren't you glad you brought me along?" She gestured, and Galvin moved away from the door, watching intently as she cast a simple spell that ended in a thumping sound, like a small door knocker being rapped against wood.

"Success!" she said, beaming. The doors swung slowly inward, moving silently on ancient hinges. In front of them lay a hallway bathed in the light of dozens of thick candles. Suddenly guards, both humans and gnolls, began to pour from rooms off the hall and moved to attack. All were armored, and their plates of metal clanged noisily as they swarmed forward in a wave.

Galvin leapt in front of the sorceress and deftly parried the swing of one burly guard. The massive man wielded a claymoor, a great sword that took two hands to heft. When the guard lifted the sword above his head for another attack, the druid quickly thrust his own enchanted sword forward. The blade sliced through the man's abdomen, sinking in up to the hilt.

Galvin brought his right leg up and lodged it against the dying man's waist, then pushed, sliding the man off his sword and into the advancing second rank of guards, knocking several down. The druid pressed his attack, cleaving his blade into the neck of a fallen gnoll who was starting to rise.

Shards of electric blue shot past Galvin and imbedded themselves in the chest of another guard. Brenna shouted a half-dozen arcane syllables, and more of the magical shards flew from her fingertips and into the face of a gnoll.

"Surrender!" she heard Galvin call, but the guards ignored the command. Then the enchantress felt instantly cold as a wave of wraiths passed over her, casting a dark shadow in the entranceway.

The undead enveloped the guards farthest from Galvin and Brenna, their black bodies smothering their victims' screams. Galvin futilely ordered the wraiths to retreat as he battled a pair of gnolls. Four more swings, and the druid had killed the dog-men.

Brenna and Galvin were the only living people in the hall-way. The druid stared at his bloody longsword for several moments, then glanced at the polished marble floor, now coated with blood and entrails. Farther down the hallway, where the wraiths had attacked, the dead bodies appeared twisted, their skin dried, almost mummified. The shadowy wraiths hovered over the husks.

"Leave us!" the druid ordered, glaring at the wraiths that had positioned themselves along the walls equidistant from the candles, where the light was the softest. The torches showed the wraiths to be vaguely human shapes, filled with shifting patterns of gray, black, and brown.

"No!" they hissed as one.

"Outside!" Galvin continued his commanding tone.

"When will you leave the castle?" one posed as the cloud of wraiths floated over the heads of Brenna and Galvin and out the door.

"After we have the information we need," the druid replied. "It could take a few hours."

A throaty laughed drifted through the tower's entrance-way. "If you do not return, humans, we will come get you."

Galvin turned to Brenna, relieved that the wraiths were gone, if only for a short while. She offered a weak smile, and he drew her into his arms. The action pleasantly startled the sorceress, and she ignored the uncomfortable links of his shirt that rubbed against her. She laid her head against his chest. The metal felt cool on her cheek.

Galvin kissed the top of her bald head. "We'll get out of this somehow, Brenna."

"What makes you so sure?" she asked, raising her head to meet his gaze.

"We have to," he stated. He bent to kiss her lips but stopped when he heard the clip-clop of hooves over the marble.

"I guess this isn't the right time or place," Brenna sighed, turning to look at Wynter.

The centaur stood amid the dead bodies, tears streaming down his angular face. "I want to go home, Galvin," he sobbed. "But I don't know where home is."

"We'll take you home soon," Galvin said softly, releasing Brenna and beckoning to Wynter. The centaur carefully picked his way around the bodies.

"Let's see what we can find—a diary or a map, anything to indicate where the gnolls are going and who they're attacking," the druid said, his voice businesslike. "If we're lucky, maybe we can find a servant willing to talk. There has to be someone alive here."

For the next hour, Brenna and Galvin moved from one room to the next searching the first three floors of the wizard's tower, coaxing the centaur up each flight of stairs. Galvin didn't want to leave Wynter close to the undead.

The trio searched through empty slave quarters, where crude furnishings dominated the rooms. The bunk beds were stacked four high and indicated the wizard kept nearly two hundred slaves in his tower. A barracks for the gnolls, furnished only marginally better, was filled with withered corpses, victims of the wraiths.

Galvin carefully inspected each body, looking for written orders or some other indication of Maligor's plans. All he was able to find were a few handfuls of silver and gold coins, the guards' meager pay. He scattered the coins over the bodies and continued on.

The kitchen offered some hint there might be living occupants still about. Embers glowed in the hearth, and dirty plates were stacked near a tub of water that contained traces of soapsuds. Brenna noted that the pantry was well stocked. Shelves of dried fruits, vegetables, and grains covered one entire wall. Recently skinned and gutted chickens hung from metal hooks.

They searched through storage rooms filled with discarded furniture, and they rummaged through richly appointed sitting rooms. During their foraging, Galvin lit candles, torches, and lanterns, hoping the light would keep the wraiths from coming near them.

Eventually the trio came to a series of connected sleeping rooms where scantily-clad pleasure slaves cowered behind the curtains. Their bodies were pale from lack of exposure to the sun, and their long hair hung loose about their shoulders. They trembled, and Brenna stepped closer, motioning for Galvin and Wynter to stay back.

"Don't be afraid. We won't hurt you," she said softly. She noticed that one of the slaves was an elf, and behind her cowered a human girl of about nine or ten. "We'll help you."

"But you're Thayvians," the elf said.

"No. No, we're not. I'm from Aglarond."

"Aglarond?" the girl behind the elf spoke up. "I used to live there."

After several minutes, it was obvious that Brenna was accepted by the slaves. Although they still regarded Galvin and Wynter with suspicion, they answered the druid's questions about Maligor. The slaves proved to have little useful information, other than providing a detailed description of the Red Wizard—that of an elderly, stooped bald man who wore the symbol of Myrkul on his head. The druid guessed Maligor was careful not to talk about anything significant in front of them. Galvin wondered out loud how he might go about freeing the slaves.

Surprisingly, Brenna discouraged him.

"If we don't defeat Maligor and he comes back here to find his slaves missing, he could well go looking for them—and punish them or kill them. But if we defeat him, he won't be coming back to the tower, and they'll be free anyway."

"Good point," Galvin replied. "But I think we should lock them in their chambers. If they're loyal to Maligor, I don't want any of them sneaking up behind us while we're searching this place. Bring the girl along as a guide." Galvin glanced at Wynter, standing in the doorway. "We'll need you to guard them, Wynter. Yell out if anything tries to get into this room. Okay?"

The centaur smiled, pleased to be given the task. "Okay, Galvin."

Brenna led the girl into the hallway, questioning her about her parents. The girl explained that her parents were farmers. She and a number of other children from farm families had been abducted and taken over the escarpment by their captors.

Galvin fumbled with the locks of the room for a few moments. Finally he moved a heavy wooden cabinet against the door to make certain the slaves couldn't escape. He reminded the centaur to watch them carefully.

"We'll open it again when we're ready to leave the castle," he said to Brenna, noticing the worried look on her face. Then the druid turned to the young slave. "Don't worry. We won't let them starve in there. We don't want to hurt anyone. Now, are there others in the tower? More slaves? Guards?"

The girl shrugged and quickly explained that the tower had bustled with activity early in the day. She had heard their movements from the slave chamber. But since then, the corridors had remained quiet until Galvin, Brenna, and their undead army arrived.

"Can you lead us to Maligor's private rooms . . . the places where he might keep papers or other important things?"

The girl trembled and stared wide-eyed at him, thinking of the things rumored to transpire in some of her master's chambers. Galvin had to promise that she would be safe before she agreed to guide them up a circular marble staircase.

On the fourth floor, about halfway up the tower, Galvin stopped and pushed the girl behind him. Squatting on the landing was a misshapen blob of warty flesh about twice the size of the druid's stallion. The creature had a caldron-shaped stomach, with webbed, taloned toes barely showing beneath it. Its head seemed to sit directly on its stomach, hiding any neck there may have been. Saucer-shaped, round eyes that appeared to have no pupils stared out from each side of its head over a thin mouth that stretched from one side of its face to the other. The creature had no ears, or rather none that could be discerned on its smooth, green-and-brown-mottled skin.

The froglike monstrosity spied the druid, and it snaked out a long, forked tongue that stretched nearly to Galvin's face.

"Look out, Galvin!" Brenna cried. The slave girl screamed in terror and backed halfway down the staircase behind the sorceress.

The druid vaulted forward and to his right. Drawing his longsword, he sliced at the tongue, cleaving it in two. Black ichor spilled out from the flailing appendage and hissed over the stones. Brenna and the slave girl backed farther down the stairs.

"It looks like acid," Brenna called. "Shall I get the wraiths?"

"No," he barked, taking aim at the froglike creature. "They're worse than this thing."

Again the creature attacked, this time stretching out its half-tongue, spattering the druid's chain and tabard with the acidic slime.

Galvin heard the cloth sizzle and felt the heat against his chest. Using all his strength, he jabbed the sword at the frog's leathery side, pushing it in up to the hilt. The creature responded with a pitiful cry that sounded like a baby and thrashed about, trying to dislodge the weapon. Dark, thick blood began to well from the wound. The frog's bulk worked against it, however. The druid had managed to maneuver himself around to its side, where what remained of the creature's tongue couldn't reach him.

"Can I do anything?" he heard Brenna cry.

"No. Stay back!" he shouted, as he pulled the sword out and thrust it in again. "Protect the girl and save your magic! We may encounter worse creatures than this before we're through!"

More of the black blood oozed out the frog's side as
Galvin leapt to the creature's back, but his foot slipped in
the acidic mixture and he went sprawling between the giant
frog and the wall. Although apparently dying from its
wounds, the creature struggled to the end, attempting to
pin the druid between itself and the wall.

Galvin pushed with his feet and hands against the frog's
body, trying to regain his weapon. Finally he grasped its hilt
with both hands, tugged it loose from the creature's side,
then struggled to his feet. The black blood had etched
holes in his tabard and burned patches of skin on his hands
and face, but it hadn't burned all the way through the chain
links of his shirt.

The frog moved slowly, attempting to turn itself around
on the landing so it could face Galvin. It opened its maw and
tried to snap at its attacker, but the druid was too quick for
it. He jumped behind the creature and plunged his sword
into the center of its back. The frog made a sickly gurgling
noise, and the black substance poured from its mouth and
began to flow down the stairs. Brenna and the slave girl
pressed themselves up against the wall to avoid the trail of
acidic slime. Finally the creature grew still.

On the landing, Galvin drew in several deep breaths,
then motioned for Brenna and the girl to join him. As the
sorceress reached for his hand, she stopped, staring wide-
eyed at the creature. Its skin began to bubble like a pool of
lava, and spurts of black blood shot out from its body. The
frog's skin gradually changed from green to brown to orange, then flaming red, as it melted from the thing's bones
and flowed down the stairway.

Galvin, Brenna, and the slave girl stared at the monstrous skeleton, which appeared as white as if it had been
picked clean.

Galvin was angry. "Animals shouldn't be turned into
something vile and corrupt. I want the man who did this."

"He's not here, but I'm sure you already know that.
We'll just have to do." The voice came from the darkness at
the end of the hallway beyond the landing. Three men

emerged from the shadows wearing the red rob
wizards of Thay.

The man in the center was the tallest and had large hands
and long, slender fingers. The nails glowed orange as he
extended his hands out toward the druid.

Galvin went for his sword, but the wizard was faster.
Beams of orange light shot from his fingers into Galvin's
breast, slamming him against the wall. He grabbed for his
chest, trying to make the pain stop. His sword clanked
against the marble floor.

The hands of the other two wizards began to glow as
they stared at Galvin, but Brenna was quicker. The sorceress mumbled five arcane words, and instantly the hallway
was filled with thick, black webs. They clung to the walls,
the floor, and the men in the red robes.

Recovering from the orange bolts, Galvin gasped for air
and peered into the webs, searching for the wizards.

"If they're lucky they might be able to break free, but by
then, we'll be a long way from here," Brenna said calmly.

Galvin looked about the dark hallway until he spotted
several torches along the wall. He lit them with a torch
from the landing and coaxed the slave girl to climb the
stairs. She was reluctant, but she had few other options.

Taking her hand, Galvin joined Brenna. Holding the torch
up and peering carefully into the magical web, they spotted
the three wizards, struggling futilely to break free of its
grasp.

"These wizards probably aren't very powerful," she observed. "Otherwise Maligor would have taken them with
him. They're probably apprentices, left behind to defend
the castle."

Galvin glowered at the men in the webbing, then held the
torch even closer to its fringe. "Cooperate with us," he
warned, "and we'll let you live. If you don't, you'll fry in
there." He had no intention of setting the webs on fire, but
he hoped they believed his threat.

"We'll cooperate," a muffled voice replied.

Brenna released her web spell, then chanted the phrase

Galvin remembered hearing in the orchard when she mesmerized the leader of the orc patrol. It had a similar effect on the wizards, who meekly allowed themselves to be tied up with cords from the hallway tapestries.

A group of long-haired slaves appeared in the hallway as the last of the wizards was being trussed up. "Stay back!" Brenna yelled. The slaves did as they were told. The girl at the sorceress's side rushed past the wizards and threw herself at a lanky young man in the middle of the group; Brenna guessed that he was her brother from his close resemblance to her. He held her tightly.

Galvin pulled one of the apprentice wizards to his feet. He looked at the group of slaves and the young girl. "Did Maligor have any drawings or maps? Did he keep them on this floor?"

She shook her head no.

"What's on this level?" the druid snapped at his hostage.

"The chambers for Maligor's apprentice wizards," he said reluctantly.

The druid dragged the wizard down the hallway and pushed him hard against the first door they came to, using the wizard's weight to force the door open. Inside, he saw that the wizard had apparently told the truth. It was a large, ornate room with expensive beds, plush furniture, and mahogany wardrobes. Galvin stuck his head back out into the hall.

"Bring the slaves in here!"

Brenna herded the slaves past the apprentices and down the hallway to the large room. She went back to check the room the slaves had come from to make sure it was empty, then returned and looked for the druid. He was directing the slaves into a corner of the large room. Apparently believing Maligor had been overthrown, the slaves asked Galvin which Red Wizard was in charge of the tower.

"No one at the moment," the druid replied. "We're not Thayvians. I'm a Harper. And you'll have to stay here. It isn't safe outside." He paused, glancing at their worried faces. "You'll be safe together. Just be sure to keep several candles and lanterns lit in this room and keep them going all night. We'll be back after we deal with Maligor."

"He's not here," one of the older slaves said stepping forward. The man had a yellow tinge to his skin and long, thin black hair, indicating he was from Kara-Tur, but his accent was Thayvian. "He left after the army departed, and we don't expect him back for days. You've captured the only apprentices he left behind. He took the rest with him—wherever he was going."

"We're looking for his personal effects . . . anything that might provide a clue about his destination," Galvin continued. "We need to find out what he's up to. If any of you can help, speak up."

The slaves murmured amongst themselves, but no one had any suggestions.

"The dealings of a Red Wizard aren't shared with the likes of us," the older slave said finally. "But if you're looking for information, try the top floor. Several slaves that Maligor took there were never seen again."

Galvin thanked the slave and left hurriedly, pulling the apprentice wizard out the door with him. Brenna closed the door and edged in front of the druid.

"This time I'm leading the way. I've got a few spells left in case we need them."

When they reached the top floor, they were confronted by an ornate door. Brenna told Galvin to stay behind on the landing with the apprentice, then she moved slowly toward the door. She took several minutes to study the chipped marble floor, then the inlaid bronze and silver symbols on the door itself.

"Maligor has some kind of a ward here, a type of spell that takes effect when the door is opened. I'm not sure if I can do much about it." Brenna continued to study the designs until she heard Galvin's footsteps approaching.

The door glowed a soft blue and the air began to turn intensely hot about her, blistering her lips.

"Stay back!" she yelled. "Step only on the green and black tiles. The others are enchanted."

About to step on a gray tile, Galvin whirled.

"Brenna, get to the stairwell! We'll let our wizard friend open the door. If he likes magic so much, we'll let him find out what happens."

"No, please!" the man gasped as Galvin began to push him forward. "If I touch the door, I'll burn to a crisp."

"Then tell us what's behind the door. Maybe I'll change my mind," Galvin growled.

"I—I don't know," the wizard answered, "but I'm telling you the truth. No one but Maligor and maybe Asp, has been in there."

"Asp? Who is Asp?" Galvin persisted.

"The wizard's woman," the apprentice replied, realizing that Maligor would kill him for revealing such information. He paled. Thinking his only chance for survival lay in killing the Harper, he reached into the folds of his robe and produced a curved-edged dagger. The apprentice Red Wizard thrust it at the druid, but Galvin dodged to the side, pushed the apprentice toward the door, and quickly retreated to the landing.

There was a blinding flash of white light, and the stench of charred flesh filled the air. When the smoke cleared, Brenna and Galvin saw nothing but a pile of ashes in front of the door.

Brenna pushed past the druid and stepped from green tile to black tile until she reached the door. Extending her palm and running it over the surface of the inlaid symbols, she satisfied herself that the magic was gone—at least for a while.

Cautiously Brenna opened the door. It was dark inside, but enough light filtered in from the landing to reveal part of the contents.

Galvin moved up behind her and peered inside.

"Gods, no!" he cried.

Thirteen

A heavy scent of death emanated from the tower room as the druid opened the door. The smell was almost overpowering, and although the shadows were too thick to make out all of the room's features, the druid knew there were bodies inside.

Galvin clenched and relaxed his fists, drew in a deep breath, then strode into the heart of the room, despite Brenna's protests that there may be more magical guards and wards about. He halted in front of a large, low table covered with cages—the obvious source of the odor—and lit the lantern that hung above it.

At first glance, Galvin thought each cage contained a balled-up pelt of some kind. Then, as the lantern glowed brighter, he noticed tiny, fixed black eyes, and curled paws. The ribs of most animals showed through their fur, indicating they had likely died from starvation.

Galvin's hands worked furiously with the latch on the largest cage, tearing the mechanism off when it wouldn't open fast enough. Inside were rabbits, several of them coated with dried blood. Because they had huddled together and looked like one mass of fur, it was difficult to tell how many there were. Their stiffened paws stuck outward from the pile at odd angles. The druid gently ran his hands over the soft fur, feeling the protruding ribs underneath, imagining how horribly they must have died. Quickly he searched through the cage, trying to find anything alive. His efforts yielded only one survivor.

He pulled a small, frightened brown hare from the middle of the dead mass and cradled it in his arms like a mother would a baby, then passed it gently to Brenna. The hare put up no resistance, seeming to lack the energy even to move.

With fevered urgency, Galvin wrenched the remaining cages open, prodding through the dead animals, searching to find any that gave off body heat. The lizards and snakes had been dead a long time. The birds were almost skeletal. In a small cage, where the wire mesh was bent from the occupants' futile attempts to escape, three gray rats huddled. They appeared healthy, and the druid determined they must have survived by eating the dead caged with them. Galvin released the rats, and they scurried away to find a home elsewhere in the tower.

Only one other cage evidenced life, a mole and a hedgehog that quivered beneath a pile of their dead brothers. Galvin removed them from the cage and cradled both in the crook of his left arm.

"The monster!" Galvin vented, staring into the cages. "These animals were pawns for Maligor's experiments. Up till now, I considered going after Maligor for Szass Tam as the lesser of two evils. But one less monster in Faerun—no matter how he's eliminated—is a goal worth accomplishing. I want Maligor to rot forever in the Nine Hells! He deserves nothing better."

Brenna fought to keep from retching at the grisly tableau. She wanted to run, but she didn't want to abandon Galvin.

"There's no water or food in here." The druid was talking to himself now, or maybe to the animals. "Nothing but vials of magic and poison to turn you into monsters. What makes someone think he has the right to defile nature? Why would a man play god with defenseless animals?"

Brenna glanced at Galvin, and saw tears spilling from his eyes. Here was a man who could fight his way into Thay, confront gnolls, battle the undead, and live through a meeting with Szass Tam, yet he was crushed by the sad fate of the helpless animals.

"I love you," she said simply, knowing the words were out of place but wanting to say them anyway.

Galvin ignored her and continued to look over the table. "How can any man live with himself and do this?" The druid soothed the animals, rubbing them. "How?"

"Remember, Maligor is the Zulkir of Alteration," Brenna said softly, turning her attention to the hare she held. "Maligor apparently specializes in transmuting one living thing into another. I've studied a little alteration magic myself, but nothing like this."

Brenna continued her explanation, but Galvin appeared not to hear her. He was making odd chittering and clicking sounds that were being answered by the hedgehog.

The enchantress began to pace about the room, stroking the hare and absorbing the rest of her surroundings. Occasionally she glanced back at the druid to note he was still continuing his conversation with the hedgehog. The floor was coated with dust except for a path between the door and the table. Spiderwebs were as thick as cloth in the corners. She wondered why Maligor had this simple laboratory so far from the rest of his rooms and why he guarded it with magic strong enough to turn a man to ashes. Perhaps his own malign reasoning wanted this particular torture chamber kept separate, secret, his own private sickness, she decided.

She continued to stroke the hare while she turned her attention to a rack of vials. As she bent to take a closer look, out of the corner of her eye, she saw Galvin wince as if in pain.

Galvin's mind had merged with the malnourished hedgehog's. For an instant, the druid saw through its tiny eyes,
saw Brenna pacing about the room. Then Galvin was again
assailed by the smell of the room, for the hedgehog's senses were far more acute than his own; the pungent smell
made the druid wince.

The druid concentrated through the hedgehog, going
past the animal's current surroundings to a time, a few
days ago, when more of the animals had been alive—to a
time when the Red Wizard was puttering about the table,
pouring liquids and powders into a small ceramic bowl.
Galvin stared at the wizard through the hedgehog's eyes.
He had expected to see an elderly man, but this man was
clearly middle-aged. A wild tangle of black hair hung about
his shoulders, and his penetrating black eyes held the
touch of madness. On the top of his head, just above his
brow, was the tattoo of a grinning white skull on a midnight
field. Merged with the hedgehog's senses, the druid trembled in fear.

Whatever the Red Wizard was mixing in the small bowl
made Galvin's eyes water as he peered out through the
wire mesh cage. He watched Maligor finish stirring the
noxious brew, then saw the wizard place it in the cage with
the lizards and snakes. For a moment, Galvin felt relieved,
for he and the animals watching from their crowded cage
had worried that the concoction was meant for them.

Then their relief turned to terror, as the wizard turned
his gaze toward the cage filled with hedgehogs and moles.
The wizard drummed his slender fingers across the front of
the cage, then reached up to lace his fingers about a wire
handle on top. Galvin felt himself being lifted, and his small
hedgehog feet scrabbled against the wire mesh bottom to
stay upright.

Across the room the cage was toted, then down, down.
They passed doors and long-haired humans bowing low to
Maligor. Then the wizard stopped before a wall, which
parted to reveal more stairs. A new stench wafted up from
the bowels of the tower as Maligor and his furry charges

descended still farther. The druid could smell the fear of the other animals in the cage. It mingled with the unknown scent of something living below.

Several moments later, Maligor emerged with the cage into the darkenbeast chamber, and the moles and hedge-hogs chittered amongst themselves in dread. Galvin felt himself huddling at the back of the cage, trying to hide. He closed his tiny eyes, hearing the squeals of his brothers as they were pulled from the cage by the wizard's bony hands. More and more animals were hauled out of the cage, and the druid wrapped his tiny, trembling claws about the back mesh.

Then he heard the cage door latch shut, and he relaxed enough to notice that he and four companions had been spared. Skittering to the front of the cage, he pushed his face against the mesh to see what was transpiring. The druid watched in horror as Maligor mumbled something incomprehensible, and the group of small animals on the stone at his feet began to bubble, stretch, and transform grotesquely into enormous bat creatures that screamed and flapped their leathery wings.

The druid watched as his one-time brothers took to flight in the chamber to join hundreds of other creatures just like them. The things skimmed below the ceiling, clung to the walls, and voiced their hideous screams.

Galvin felt himself being lifted again, beginning the long ascent to the laboratory.

Trembling, the druid severed his mental link with the hedgehog to see Brenna staring at him. Clutching the animal to his chest, he whirled from the table and started toward the door.

"Come on!" the druid urged. "I've got a few things to do before we start after Maligor. And we've left Wynter alone far too long."

"Do you know where Maligor's going?" Brenna asked, hurrying to catch up with him and stepping over the pile of ashes beyond the doorway, the remnants of the Red Wizard's apprentice.

"Not yet. But I know what he's up to." The druid took the steps two at a time and quickly found himself back with the slaves he had left in the apprentices' chambers.

Rushing inside, Galvin found the slaves going through the apprentices' belongings, taking objects that might be valuable. He disregarded their looting and strode to the nearest man.

"Take care of these animals. Get them food, water," Galvin ordered. "Keep them under close watch for a while. They're not healthy enough to be turned loose." Gently he handed the mole and hedgehog to the man. Brenna gave the hare to the slave girl from Aglarond.

"Somehow we have to get below the tower," Galvin said. "Maligor's got creatures there like the one that attacked us at our camp."

"What are you talking about?" Brenna was perplexed and a little worried about the druid's agitated state.

"I don't have time to explain now. We've got to hurry."

"But we've been all over the ground floor," she sputtered. "There was nothing below that tower."

"He's got some kind of a secret door," Galvin said quickly. Then he pounded down the stairs, pulling Brenna along with him, until he stopped on the third floor. He released her hand and strode to the chamber where they had left the pleasure slaves. The chest was still secure against the doors, but Wynter was nowhere to be seen.

"Damn!" he exclaimed. "I should never have asked him to stay here. He's like a child." The druid pushed the chest aside and threw open the doors. The scantily clad pleasure slaves stared at him nervously.

"Get out of here!" Galvin shouted. "Maligor won't be back. Run! Get as far away from this evil place as you can. You're free." He spun back toward the hall, not waiting to watch their response. He charged off to find the centaur.

"Why are you so certain the Red Wizard won't be back?" Brenna asked as she hurried to keep up with him.

"Because I'm going to find him, Brenna, and when I do, I'm going to kill him."

They ran down one corridor after another, throwing open doors to rooms and calling for Wynter.

The color drained from Galvin's face as he searched, fearing for the safety of his confused friend. Galvin cursed himself for not keeping Wynter with him, but the druid had feared the centaur would slow them down. His equine legs weren't meant for the spiral staircases.

With Brenna close behind him, the druid bolted into the kitchen to find Wynter staring at his reflection in the glass of the china cabinet. The centaur slowly turned, a puzzled expression etched on his tanned face.

"We're in Thay, aren't we?" Wynter stated simply. "I remember now." He scratched at a circular scab on his temple. "I remember that I used to live in Thay, but I can't remember why I'm here now."

Brenna rushed to him and threw her arms about his waist. "We'll help you remember, Wynter," she said quickly.

"My head hurts, Brenna," the centaur said, scratching at the scab again.

"Come on, both of you," Galvin coaxed. The druid was relieved to find his friend, and he was encouraged that the centaur seemed to have recovered at least a little. But the druid was in a hurry to get below the castle. He was too close to discovering Maligor's secret to slow down now.

In the hallway beyond the kitchen, Galvin began to pull tapestries and paintings from the wall, searching for some sign of a door that would lead to the chamber he had seen while he was linked to the hedgehog.

"He's probably using magic to hide the door you're looking for, altering its appearance to blend in with the walls. There are certain spells designed to mask such things." Brenna's voice was tinged with concern. "We don't have much more time, Galvin. We've been here several hours already. The undead outside . . ."

"Are no doubt getting anxious—at least the ones that can think. I know, we've got to hurry and find some answers or they'll turn on us or force us to march after the gnolls right away. I'm not even sure we should be going after the gnoll army—not if we want to catch Maligor." He stroked his chin, then began to examine the walls carefully. "I think I know how to get us underground, although not without a lot of effort. I should have done this to begin with."

The druid dropped to his knees before the smooth stone wall. Spreading his fingers wide along the base of the stone, he placed his forehead against the wall, almost as if he were pushing against it. Then he began to hum a low, simple tune Brenna had never heard. As a child, the sorceress had been told stories that powerful druids were able to talk to the very earth, get stones to speak, dirt to sing, and the ground to reveal its secrets. She hadn't dreamed that Galvin possessed such abilities.

The young councilwoman always assumed that the arcane energies of magic were the most powerful forces in the realm. Yet without any of that, using merely simple gesture and tune, the druid was performing a type of magic she thought was only legend.

Suddenly the stone began to hum back, a low, deep, vibrating sound.

She watched Galvin tremble and begin to perspire, as if the effort of talking to the stone was taking everything out of him. The druid continued the process for nearly half an hour, then collapsed, gasping, against the wall. Much to her amazement, Brenna noticed that the wall was also sweating. Brenna rushed to him and used her robe to dab his face.

"Galvin, are you all right? Please tell me you're all right. Did you actually speak to the wall? Did you?"

"I'll . . . be okay," he said weakly. "It's magic I don't call upon often because it takes so much out of me—and out of the rock. Stone always seems to think it has all the time in the world to say what it has to say." He steadied himself against the wall with both hands, drawing in as much air as his lungs could hold.

"We're going to have to convince the undead to wait

awhile longer. I'm not going to be able to go anywhere for several hours now. You'd better let the wraiths inside the tower and I'll tell them."

"What did you find out?" Brenna's curiosity couldn't be contained.

"Let the wraiths in first. I only want to go through this once."

Brenna shivered. The last thing she wanted was to deal with the undead again, but she accepted the fact that Galvin was right—the dead would have to be told what was going on, or they weren't likely to continue to cooperate.

Within moments, the dark shapes were swirling about the druid, begging him to extinguish some of the candles so they could move about more comfortably.

"Weak you are," the closest one whispered to the druid in haunting tones. The wraith tried to hover where the light was softest. "Perhaps you will be with us soon, wrapped in the sweet embrace of death."

"Noooo," another groaned, its raspy voice unnerving Wynter and Brenna. Galvin was too exhausted to be bothered by its unnatural speech. "The human cannot yet kiss the rich, dark earth of the grave, the welcoming taste of unlife. Szass Tam, the death master, thinks we need a living man to lead us." The wraith floated to the floor, bringing its amorphous black face mere inches from the druid's chin. "We can suck the last breath from your weak, mortal lungs later, bestowing upon you a precious demise. You can live forever in death. But you must be well now."

"I'm not dying. I'm just tired." Galvin grimaced. "Remember when you were alive? You used to get tired, too. Or is that too far beyond your memories?"

The wraiths ignored Galvin's jibe and continued to pester him.

"We must go," the wraiths began to chant, repeating the phrase until their voices sounded like a swarm of insects.

The one nearest Galvin rose several feet into the air. "The sun will rise soon, and then we must flee to the embrace of darkness. We must pursue the gnolls—now."

"We wouldn't get far before the sun rises," Galvin said evenly. "Listen to me. I've found out something, something most perplexing. I'm not certain that Maligor is with the gnoll army. I think he is with another army, one with numbers and power to truly concern Szass Tam.

"This is an army of malevolent, flying beasts, all under Maligor's control. There are hundreds, perhaps thousands of the things. Maligor calls them darkenbeasts. This army flew out of the tower shortly after the gnolls left, when this place was surrounded by a thick, quick-settling fog." The druid paused to take a deep breath. "It's doubtful anyone in Amruthar saw the army of darkenbeasts. The gnolls could be just a ruse, a trick."

Outwardly, the wraiths appeared no different, though their hollow voices carried a hint of surprise. "All those gnolls—a mere distraction?"

"A diversion," Galvin agreed. He eased himself to his feet, leaning against the wall for support. He was still weak, and he hoped the wraiths would cooperate, because he didn't have the strength to oppose them now. "Everyone is paying attention to Maligor's gnolls—even the mighty Szass Tam. With everyone preoccupied, Maligor's darkenbeasts are free to strike elsewhere."

"What are his real plans?" the largest wraith howled, as he hovered just beyond the druid. "Where did Maligor go? Szass Tam must know. Tell us."

"I don't know any more. But we're going to find out. I'm going to need your help, though, and at the same time, I'm going to help you. There are several levels below this tower. They should be a good place for you to stay when the daylight comes."

The wraiths protested waiting any longer, but Brenna convinced them that Galvin wasn't able to travel now. In the end, they followed the druid to a section of wall the stones had told the druid about. He pushed against it, and it slid wide, revealing a curving staircase that descended into darkness.

Galvin told the wraiths to seek out the bottommost

levels, where the staircase seemed to disappear and an overpowering stench pervaded the air. The creatures could move quickly, could see without light, and didn't seem likely to mind the rotting smell. They seemed to take a perverse glee in the task.

"The first underground level is ours," Galvin told Brenna, steadying himself against the wall. "The stone spoke of great horrors there. Wynter, come with us."

Brenna helped support the weakened druid as they made their way down the series of smooth stone steps. The centaur followed awkwardly. Wynter had difficulty negotiating the stairwell and had to bend his human torso forward to avoid scraping his head on the ceiling. He was comforted when Brenna and Galvin finally left the staircase and entered a wide, high corridor. Here the odor of death and decay wasn't too overpowering. The trio discovered lanterns placed along the walls and lit them to reveal a series of barred cells. The iron bars were thickly encrusted with filth and rust, and the straw that poked between the bars was moldy and crawling with insects.

A ring of keys hung in the center of the corridor, obviously beyond the reach of the cells' inhabitants, but within sight of most of them.

Brenna left Galvin's side and rose to her tiptoes to pull the ring loose. She hurried to the closest cell, then fumbled with the keys until she found the correct one. Throwing the door open, she stepped inside and glanced about. Twisted, tortured bodies hung from manacles. The wounds in their flesh looked deep, but the pain wasn't what had killed them. Their swollen, cracked lips and protruding ribs attested to the fact that they had starved to death. Brenna gasped and proceeded to investigate the cells.

Wynter tried to help her, but he found the cell doors were too small to accommodate his equine frame. Instead, he stood out in the hall and strained to listen.

"All the cells are like this," Brenna announced when she was through, her disgust apparent in her voice. "All the occupants are dead. It's as if Maligor forgot about them and simply let them starve."

"Maybe," Galvin said. The druid was leaning against the door to the farthest cell and peering inside. "Bring the keys over here Brenna."

The enchantress hurried over and quickly unlatched the door. Galvin entered first, then turned and held out his hand to her. Taking it, Brenna climbed down the few steps to the cell floor. This cell was cleaner than the others, but splotches of dried blood covered most of the surface and partially obliterated a map that lay spread out on the floor.

Brenna bent to tug the parchment loose from the floor and study it. It was crude map, drawn with a shaky hand. The map depicted tunnels and traps and bore a few markings she couldn't decipher. She showed it to the druid, then blanched as he leaned against the wall to brace himself.

"You're weak. You need to rest," she admonished.

The druid nodded, too exhausted to argue.

They carried their find upstairs, noticing that the candles they had lit had all burned out. The trio had been below ground more than an hour, and the first rays of the dawning sun were spilling in through the windows and reflecting off the marble floor.

Galvin padded through the main hallway until he reached the doors through which they had entered the tower. He still moved unsteadily in his weakened state, and he tottered when he threw open the doors. Wynter trotted after him, the clip-clop of the centaur's hooves reverberating off the polished marble floor.

Brenna remained inside, studying the map and wondering what Galvin was doing. The clink of bones and swish of old, tattered cloth told her. He was ushering all of the undead inside to keep them from worrying Amruthar's citizens and from wandering away. The sorceress went several feet up the staircase and sat down to avoid rubbing up against the ambling corpses that flooded the hallway. The druid directed the skeletons and zombies down to the chambers below and called out to the wraiths to take charge of the other undead.

"I'll summon you when we're ready to leave," Galvin called, his tone halting, as if he were out of breath.

"Heal thyself, human," came the haunting reply. "We will leave at sunset."

It took a long time for the hundreds of sluggish corpses to file into the chambers below. When the last was gone, Wynter pushed the hidden door closed behind them.

Brenna spread the crude map out on some nearby steps, then hunched over to scrutinize it again. Galvin sat beside her.

"The map might not mean anything," he said, leaning back on his elbows and fighting to keep his eyes open.

"Maybe," she replied quickly, "But then again, maybe it's important."

The clip-clopping of Wynter's hooves caused the enchantress to glance up from the parchment. The centaur stood at the bottom of the short staircase and held out his hand. Brenna shrugged and passed him the map.

The centaur's dark eyes puzzled over the rough lines, then grew wide. "There are some hills marked here," Wynter said thoughtfully. "They've got to be Thay's gold mines, its lifeblood. People here will tell you the citrus and other crops support the country. But it's really the gold. If you have enough gold you don't need crops. You can buy anything you want. I'm starting to remember things, Brenna."

The enchantress grabbed the bannister and pulled herself up. Galvin stayed rooted to the stairs.

"Show me," Brenna encouraged, and she hurried to Wynter's side.

The centaur pointed to various features on the map. Then he scratched his head. "I don't know what Maligor wants with the gold mines. There's a tharchion who supervises the mines. He's appointed by all the zulkirs jointly. The tharchion isn't going to throw in with Maligor, or with Szass Tam, for that matter," Wynter added. "Besides, the mines are north of here. Galvin said Maligor's army moved east."

"Could a large bird fly to the mines in an evening?" Galvin asked. "Are the mines close enough?"

The centaur knit his brows, puzzled at the question. "I suppose it could," he answered, "if the bird could fly fast. It really isn't all that far, but it would take a man several days, perhaps, to walk there."

Galvin sighed, then grinned at his Harper friend. Wynter certainly seemed to be recovering. The druid wanted the centaur fit and at his side when the confrontation with Maligor came.

"I don't know for sure what Maligor is up to, but I'll wager he's going after the mines," the druid suggested.

"Are we going to the mines?" Brenna asked. "After we rest?" she added hopefully.

"I need to rest." Galvin stood shakily. "There are beds in the apprentices' chambers, where we put the slaves. I'd like to sleep there. I'd feel more comfortable—for a change—with plenty of company around."

"I'll join you later," the centaur said, eyeing the long, circular staircase. "I've got some thinking to do first."

Brenna and Galvin slowly climbed the stairs. Above, in the chamber, they saw that many of the slaves were sleeping. A few groups remained awake, talking in low voices among themselves and examining some of the baubles they had collected.

The hare, mole, and hedgehog rested on a large silk pillow beneath the window.

The druid approached one of the older slaves. "We need to sleep awhile. Wake us in the early afternoon. I have to go into Amruthar to buy horses before the market closes."

"Horses?" Brenna asked incredulously. "There's nothing wrong with the ones we have. They'll certainly be rested enough."

"We can't ride dead ones." Galvin's tone was terse. "It seems that some of the zombies got hungry last night while we explored the tower."

The druid selected an unoccupied bed against the far wall, far from the windows, where it was darker. Removing his sword belt, tabard, and chain shirt, he pushed them under the bed, lay down, and made room for Brenna.

The enchantress paused, uncertain of what to do.

The druid stretched and raised his head off the satin-covered pillow. His green eyes gazed up at her. "Brenna . . . ?"

The young councilwoman eased off her boots and climbed in beside him. He curled about her protectively and held her close about her waist.

"I thought you preferred to sleep on the ground," she said.

"Shhh," he replied, nuzzling the back of her neck.

She enjoyed the sensation, but it stopped much too quickly. Already the druid was sound asleep.

Fourteen

The dense fog lay across the land like a heavy gray blanket, its wispy tendrils wrapping themselves tightly around the dead trees, concealing them. Galvin picked his way through the cloaked terrain, one hand extended in front of him. The fog was so thick he could barely see six inches in front of his face. His other hand was firmly wrapped around Brenna's wrist.

Slowly he inched forward with one foot, discovering a fallen limb and gingerly stepping over it. He knew he couldn't afford stepping on a branch that would crack and give them away.

The druid was uncertain how long they had been moving away from Maligor's tower, but he knew they hadn't covered enough ground to satisfy him. He tried to increase the pace.

His hand met a branch, spooking a horned owl that had been perching on it. The bird hooted loudly as it flew high into the fog, and Galvin's heart raced.

Behind him, quite nearby, he heard the rustle of bushes and the snap of twigs. It was the sound of their pursuers. The druid considered standing still like a statue and pulling Brenna close to him; those following might pass by harmlessly in the fog. But then he heard their voices. Panicking, he ran, pulling Brenna along behind him.

"Death we will bring you," hissed a hollow voice. "We will tear the muscles from your bones and wash our bodies in your blood. You will taste sweet death."

Faster and faster Galvin and Brenna ran, scraping their skin against the coarse bark of fog-concealed trees, nearly stumbling over unseen rocks and fallen branches. The air felt chill, signaling the nearness of the advancing wraiths, but still the druid and enchantress ran on.

"Hurry, Brenna," Galvin whispered. "We've got to make it. We're almost to the escarpment."

The fog seemed thinner here as their feet continued to pound over the Thayvian soil. The druid could begin to make out the shapes of trees and bushes and a horse and rider—no, it was Wynter—ahead. He pulled Brenna toward the centaur.

"Galvin!" Wynter shouted at the sight of his friend. "I've been looking for you. I've been wanting to tear out your weak, mortal heart."

The druid halted, open-mouthed, in front of his Harper ally. From a distance, the fog had masked the centaur's undead state. Wynter's angular face was now skeletal and covered with bits of rotting flesh. Ribs protruded from his equine rear portion, and he reeked of the grave.

Galvin screamed, then immediately awoke to find himself curled about Brenna in a soft bed in Maligor's tower. The enchantress slept soundly, oblivious to the druid's nightmare.

The druid withdrew his arm from about Brenna's waist and rubbed his eyes. He guessed he must have slept eight or more hours, and he was surprised one of the slaves hadn't awakened him earlier. Reluctantly he left the soft bed, gently moving away from Brenna. He wanted to let her sleep a little while longer.

The slaves—and most of the furnishings—were gone. Galvin surmised that the slaves had looted Maligor's tower and fled while he slumbered. He pulled his chain armor from under the bed, dressed, and strapped on his sword. Then, carrying his boots in the crook of his right arm, he shoved Szass Tam's black tabard back under the bed with his bare feet.

Galvin strode to the far side of the room, where he had spied a basin full of water. The bowl was porcelain, and the slaves likely would have taken it, he thought, had it not been so large. The druid bent forward and splashed water on his face and arms, then padded out into the hallway and put on his boots.

Galvin knew he needed to get to the Amruthar market quickly, to purchase the horses for himself and Brenna. Running down the circular stairs, he found Wynter at the bottom.

"I was just coming in to wake you," the centaur said, grinning broadly. "I'm glad I didn't have to. I didn't want to climb all those stairs."

The druid scrutinized his friend. "How are you feeling?"

Wynter frowned. "I feel terrible. I'm in Thay." The centaur paused and reached up to scratch the spot on his head where the plant had attacked him. "But at least I'm remembering things. We came to this country on purpose."

The druid exhaled slowly, relieved that his friend seemed to be returning to normal. "I'm in a hurry, Wyn. I've got to get some horses and some food. We've got to get going. We can talk later."

"I've already bought horses," the centaur replied smugly. "I went to the market an hour ago." The centaur pointed at the large double doors. "They're outside. And you'd better get out there, too, so the undead don't eat this pair as they did the others. Oh," he said, nodding toward the concealed door that lead to the bowels of Maligor's tower, "I let the skeletons and zombies out. They're waiting outside. The wraiths might still be down there, though."

"They'll find a way to join us after it's dark." Galvin turned and sprinted up the stairs to get Brenna.

Several minutes later, the entourage, with Galvin, Wynter, and Brenna at its lead, was gathered outside Maligor's tower. The horses Wynter purchased were a pair of sorrel mares, healthy, but not of the quality that Szass Tam had provided. The enchantress chose the smaller of the two horses and mounted while Galvin kept an eye on the guards who remained in force along the walls of Amruthar. The druid estimated he saw two hundred perched on the western wall alone, and all seemed armed with longbows.

The druid leapt into the saddle and urged his mount forward. The clinking of bones behind him signaled that the undead were following. He cast a last glance at the city, then faced north toward the verdant Thayvian landscape and the distant hills where the mines were nestled.

When they had put a few miles between themselves and Amruthar, Galvin pulled out the crude map of the mines they had found in Maligor's tower and rested it against his horse's neck. Studying it, he guessed it would take at least three days for the slow-moving undead to reach the mines. Replacing the map, he wondered what Maligor would do in those three days.

The army wound its way along the dirt roads that cut through the citrus groves. North of Amruthar, the groves were vast, well established, and had many crews of slaves. As the undead marched by, guards and slaves hid behind the largest trees and watched nervously.

The sun had begun to set as Galvin, Wynter, and Brenna passed a row of tall birches, which marked the end of one grove and the beginning of another. The precise rows of citrus trees, all carefully pruned, had begun to look monotonous.

When the sun edged below the distant tree line, the shadows and wraiths joined the assembly, the latter beginning their incessant, haunting banter. As the miles went by, Galvin studied Brenna. The enchantress had pulled about her a woolen cloak that Wynter had purchased in the market. The druid was uncertain what to do about her. If they lived through whatever awaited them and were able to leave Thay, she would likely return to Aglarond. He knew he would miss her, but he realized she wouldn't want to stay in the wilderness with him and Wynter. He also knew he could never stay in a city. Although he had proved to himself he could function within their confining walls, he had no desire to live in one. Her nearness was making all of it considerably more difficult to figure out.

"I'm going to scout ahead for a while," he told her. "It looks like there are a few lights up there."

"No, human," a wraith protested, floating to Galvin's side. "You will stay with us. The master wishes it."

"I'll be back soon," the druid said firmly.

"If you leave, we will go with you. Death will travel at your side."

"Only if 'death' can keep up," the druid said, scowling. He glanced at the distant lights on the horizon. The druid knew it would take the undead quite a while to reach them. Dropping the big mare's reins, he handed Brenna his close helm and pulled off his chain shirt. Laying it across the front of his saddle, he held his arms out to his sides and closed his eyes.

"Human! What are you doing?" the wraith demanded.

Galvin ignored the undead creature and willed himself to transform. Feathers quickly sprouted on his chest and spread like fire to cover his body. His mare became skittish as wings formed underneath the druid's arms, but Galvin, still retaining his human visage, made neighing and whinnying sounds until the horse answered and calmed down. Then the druid's body shriveled, his legs becoming muscular hawk legs, and his feet yellow claws with curved talons. His head shortened, and his nose grew into a curved beak. The green-eyed hawk cried and leapt from the mare's back, flying toward the lights.

The druid relished the sensation of flight, the wind ruffling the feathers about his face and the cool air flowing beneath his wings. His hawk form was sleek and made for speed, and the miles sped away beneath his wings. In this form, the druid knew he could have reached the mines in a day, but he also knew that going there alone might not accomplish anything. Nor would he find any comfort in leaving Wynter and Brenna behind with the undead.

The lights grew larger as he neared them. Ahead was a hamlet, a collection of wood and stone buildings, likely the homes of some of the citrus workers or nearby farmhands. Lanterns were set on tables in kitchens or hanging from front porches. Swooping low, the hawk skimmed through the town and saw a few families gathered inside the buildings. The hamlet's residents were apparently oblivious to the presence of Szass Tam's undead army. No one seemed armed or nervous.

The hawk made another pass through the area, then soared back to rejoin the undead. Hovering above the saddle of the big mare, Galvin transformed once again. His claws lengthened, the yellowed skin turning to boots that fit neatly into the stirrups, the feathers melting away to reveal skin and his chain shirt. The horse began to bolt, but the hawk-man's wings receded, and human hands shot forward to grasp the reins and calm the skittish beast.

"There's a small hamlet ahead," Galvin said as he put on his chain shirt. He turned to Brenna and extended his hand for his close helm. The enchantress ignored his gesture and leaned over to place the helmet on his head herself. "Everything appears normal."

"Are we going to stop there and rest?" Wynter asked, overhearing the druid.

"No. We're going around it. No use upsetting the villagers. And no use alerting people who might be sympathetic to Maligor. It's bad enough to be by guards when we pass the orchards."

Galvin directed the undead in a broad arc around the settlement. It was nearly midnight by the time the army had circumvented the hamlet and was again on the road to the hills. For several more hours, the force continued to plod onward, the clip-clopping of the horses' hooves mingling with the tinkling of skeletal bones.

Shortly before dawn, the army reached the edge of a lime grove. The druid decided to camp here, since he,

Wynter, Brenna, and the horses needed to rest. As the first rays of the sun peeked through the trees, the trio watched incredulously as the wraiths huddled near the ground, then appeared to seep into the very cracks in the earth. The druid wondered if the undead would stay there until dark or could travel underground.

Shortly before noon, the army started north again. The breeze had picked up and was coming from the direction of the far hills, carrying with it billowy clouds and the fragrant scent of lime blossoms. The druid sniffed the air.

"It's going to rain today, maybe in a few hours—sooner if the wizards decide to tamper with the weather," Galvin announced.

"What do you think we'll find at the mines?" Brenna posed. "Maligor may have been there for a day already."

"Maybe he's dead," Wynter speculated. "The mines are well guarded. The tharchion in charge is a man to be reckoned with."

"Maligor's alive," Galvin said finally. "I think Szass Tam would know if his rival was dead."

The centaur glanced back at the columns of zombies and skeletons. "In any event," Wynter said, "we'll know in another two or three days."

The Harpers and Brenna passed most of the day in silence, tolerating the midafternoon downpour and staring at the lush countryside, where apple orchards and groves of citrus trees dominated. In the distance, to the east and west, and in between the rows of fruit-laden trees, they saw farmland.

By sunset, the orchards were behind them, and they found themselves on a prairie dotted with waist-high wild flowers. Far to the east, Galvin saw a complex of buildings, which had to be immense considering they could be seen from so far away. Wynter explained that it was a slave plantation and most of the buildings were barracks for the slaves.

The army marched until dusk, when the buildings were lost from sight. After resting for several hours, they resumed the trek shortly before midnight, and by morning they were in the foothills.

"We've been making good time. Do you think we'll reach the mines by nightfall?" Brenna asked Galvin.

The druid was eager to find Maligor and finish Szass Tam's task. He pulled out the crude map, then glanced at it and the hills.

"I doubt it," Wynter interposed before Galvin could speak. The centaur had also been eyeing the hills. "We probably won't even make it by tomorrow morning—and that's provided the map is reliable. These hills, if I remember correctly, are riddled with caves. Finding the mine might not be easy. Then we have the undead to consider."

The enchantress looked at Wynter quizzically.

The centaur laughed and waved his arm, indicating the skeletons and zombies. "As difficult a time as I have dealing with obstacles and hills, they'll have a worse time. Their bony feet might have trouble finding purchase."

Brenna scowled. "It shouldn't be a problem in the low hills," she decided, pointing at the foothills, "but when we get farther up, maybe we'll have to leave some of them behind. Or maybe we can find a path with better footing. There's got to be a path or road leading to the mine."

Galvin was only vaguely paying attention to his friends' conversation. He had been scrutinizing the ground around the foothills, looking for tracks, anything to indicate that others had been this way within the past few days. However, he found only signs of small animals. The druid dismounted and led his big mare toward a dead tree at the beginning of a rise. Wrapping the reins loosely about a branch, he neighed and whinnied at the animal, instructing it to stay in the area until he returned.

"Time's wasting," Galvin said, starting up the low rise and motioning for Wynter, Brenna, and the undead to follow him.

The sorceress left her horse near his and sprinted to catch up. Wynter ambled behind them.

The low portion of the hills was much like a savanna, covered with grasses that stretched nearly three feet high. Trees were scattered over the hillsides, their trunks swollen with water and their leafy tops flat. Traveling was difficult because of the incline, and the heat was oppressive, causing Galvin and Wynter to shed their armor. They toted it behind them, bundled inside their cloaks. Bare-chested, they found the warmth easier to handle, especially when an occasional breeze whipped over the savannah, cooling them as it evaporated the sweat from their bodies.

Wynter explained as they traveled that the wizards had no need to make it rain near the mines, since the hills were devoid of crops. Still, the natural rains seemed enough to support the trees and grasses.

By nightfall, their course steepened even more, and Galvin located a wide, well-worn path with deep wagon ruts. Although the Harpers and Brenna were nearly exhausted because they had been pushing themselves so hard, they forced themselves to continue, climbing the steep slope, slowing only when Wynter had difficulty negotiating the sharper grades.

The vegetation had changed once again to resemble a montane forest, and the air was cooler at this elevation. The army pressed on until shortly before dawn, when the trees began to thin.

Brenna was pale from exertion, and even Wynter and Galvin were glad to stop and rest. The druid directed the undead to spread themselves out among the trees, hoping the cover would lessen their chances of being spotted by any patrols or by wizards magically scrying the area.

Lying down on the ground, under the shade of a thick-leafed tree he couldn't identify, the druid again studied the map. "These marks in the tunnel indicate something— maybe traps, maybe veins of gold, maybe guards. There are two large *X*s right outside the mine entrance. I wonder what they indicate."

"Worrying about it won't get you an answer," Wynter said, stretching himself out on a large patch of soft grass and folding his hoofed legs beneath him. "Wake me in a few hours and I'll stand watch."

The enchantress settled herself next to the druid and eyed the map. Galvin rubbed her head. "You get some sleep, too."

As the sun set, painting the mountain peaks vermilion, Galvin moved the undead forward once more. He noticed fewer and fewer animal tracks as they ascended. With the decline in vegetation, there was less food to support wild-life. Bamboo grew in small clumps to either side of the path; the druid suspected a band of bamboo grew at this altitude all the way around the mountain.

In another few hours the bamboo thinned, too, then dis-appeared, to be replaced by short, coarse grass. The druid noted the caves that dotted the mountainside, but he avoided them. No paths led to them, nor was the ground smooth enough around them to indicate the presence of miners who had tramped the earth flat. As the army contin-ued its climb, the druid began quizzing the few birds he spotted, chirping to them in their own language and learn-ing that a congregation of men could be found on the north-ern exposure of the mountain.

Within a few hours more, shortly before dawn, the druid found a wide, winding road capped by torches that led to a large black opening in the rocks. It was obviously the en-trance to the Thayvian mines.

"Should I go ahead and see what's going on?" the cen-taur suggested.

The druid shook his head. "They must know we're com-ing. Their sentries have probably spotted us in the dis-tance. The night hides our numbers, but it doesn't hide the fact that there's an army on the mountain."

Galvin took several deep breaths and mentally ran through the possibilities. If Maligor had control of the mines, he would have been there for three or four days. The druid's force would be fighting the wizard's darkenbeasts and any other defenses he might have added. If Maligor's forces were defeated, but the Red Wizard still lived, their task might take them elsewhere in the pursuit of him.

He glanced at Brenna. She appeared worried, her lips pursed in concern.

"Let's see the mine up close," the enchantress said, placing a hand around the pouch that held her spell components and returning Galvin's stare evenly.

The macabre army wound its way up the mountain to the edge of a plateau ringed with torches. A quintet of miners, armed with picks, stood at the entrance to the shaft, a massive black maw between two large oval-shaped rocks. Galvin padded forward, and the eldest miner, a squat, middle-aged, hairless man with a barrel of a chest, stepped forward to meet him.

"Halt!" boomed the man, who sported a tattoo on his brow, barely visible in the torchlight. The tattoo was of a taloned hand, the symbol of Malar The Beastlord.

Galvin stopped and scrutinized the ground, looking for traces of blood and other signs of a struggle. He saw only footprints, likely belonging to the miners.

"I'm the tharchion here, and you are trespassing," the man stated, showing no fear at the throng of skeletons behind the druid. "Turn your creatures around. We have no place for dead men at the mines."

"We're looking for the one who controls the mines," Galvin returned.

"I control the mines," the man replied. "Who is your master? Which Red Wizard do you serve?"

Wynter moved between Galvin and the human. "Tharchion," he said, "our force is not here to attack the mines. Szass Tam, who directs the undead behind us, is fully aware that the mines belong to all the Red Wizards."

"Then leave!" the tharchion sputtered. "My men must get back to work. Leave now, or I warn you, I will summon my guards to fight your corpses! I'll call the magic of the mines down on you! You'll all perish!"

Wynter was persistent. "We want some information, that's all."

"Be quick about it, then," snapped the tharchion.

"Just answer a few questions and we'll leave. We came

here to learn about Zulkir Maligor."

"Maligor isn't here," the tharchion sputtered. The stout man reddened in anger, puffed out his considerable chest, and pointed down the mountain. "Leave while you can."

Galvin moved to Wynter's side. The enchantress stayed in the background, digging in her pouch for precious components. She began a simple spell, wanting to know if the tharchion was telling them the truth.

"Was he here?" Wynter continued.

"No!" the tharchion hissed.

The centaur eyed the tharchion, annoyed by his manners. "Maligor moved a large force north recently. Have you seen it? Have you heard rumors of it?"

"Maligor's force might not have been human," the druid added.

"I've seen nothing unusual," the tharchion replied, appearing more calm. "The slaves and guards would have reported anything out of the ordinary." The tharchion squinted his eyes, then they flew open, as if he had just thought of something.

"But I have heard rumors about trouble to the south. Something about an army of Maligor's gnolls. If your master, Szass Tam, is having difficulties with Maligor, you should investigate to the south. Now leave! Get those stinking undead out of here!"

"We're sorry to have inconvenienced you, tharchion. Our apologies." Wynter turned, being careful not to lose his footing, and headed down the mountain. The undead did not move until Galvin started after him.

Brenna grasped the druid's arm as he passed by. "He's lying," she whispered. "Trust me. He's lying about something—about Maligor's forces, about not seeing anything, perhaps. I think he knows a lot more than he's telling you."

"What are you saying?" the tharchion bellowed, striding toward the enchantress.

"I was telling my friend you should be concerned about Maligor," Brenna replied, meeting the squat man's gaze.

"The mines might be his target. He could be after them!"

"I told you to leave—you, your stinking undead, all of you. You're breaking Thayvian law by disrupting the operation of the mines. I could have you eviscerated—or worse!" the tharchion bellowed. "I know nothing of Maligor's plans, so crawl back to Szass Tam."

"Liar!" Brenna cried, watching for a reaction. "I bet you're in league with Maligor. I bet you know where he is."

"I'll see you dead!" the tharchion hissed. "The Council of Zulkirs will be told about this—in full." He waved one thick arm, and the quartet of miners rushed forward, raising their picks above their heads threateningly.

Brenna stepped behind Galvin, her fingers twirling. Feigning fear, she began to mumble softly so the tharchion couldn't tell she was casting a spell.

The tharchion's eyes narrowed to slits so thin they appeared to be closed. He moved until he could see the sorceress, then began to twitch his fingers and mouth his own arcane words.

Wynter had whirled around when he heard the confrontation and headed back to the plateau. The skeletons and zombies shuffled behind him, struggling to keep their balance on the steep incline.

"Kill them!" the tharchion screamed as he continued to manipulate his fingers. The quartet of miners moved forward, and Wynter reared back and charged the closest one. Galvin leapt at another one, willing his body to change as he dove at the tallest miner. The druid's body sprouted short yellow-orange fur that flowed like water over his arms, legs, and clothing. His chest thickened, his legs became feline and muscular, and his facial features melted away to reveal the snarling visage of a jaguar. The big cat extended its claws as it closed the distance to its quarry.

At the same time, the undead began to swarm forward on the plateau, their bony feet clicking over the rocks.

Brenna completed her spell, a force that dispelled magic and that would eliminate the sorcerous hold she believed Maligor held over the tharchion. The force, which only

Brenna could see, shot from her fingers in ribbons, avoiding the skeletons and wrapping about her target.

But Brenna's magic enchantment wasn't what she had expected. As the spell took effect, the tharchion grew taller and more slender, his form continuing to change as the bands of magic writhed about him. The magic Brenna had dispersed was not Maligor's but Asp's own ability, which enabled the naga to look like the tharchion. The spirit naga's tail undulated as it grew to its full length, and her human torso sprouted from the stocky man's dissolving chest. Finally, fully formed, Asp threw back her head and cried, "You'll die!"

Asp's appearance startled Wynter, giving one of the miners an opening. Sinking his pick into the back of the centaur's leg, the miner continued his assault, trying to throw Wynter off balance. The centaur groaned and fought to keep his balance. Then he swung his fist into the miner's face. The man rolled down the side of the mountain and into the waiting arms of the juju zombies.

While Galvin in his jaguar form slashed at a miner, Brenna rushed the spirit naga, hurling herself on the creature and attempting to pin the snake-woman's arms. Too late, the enchantress realized her mistake, as the naga's tail whipped about her legs and restrained her. A dozen skeletons ringed the two women, thrusting forward with their bony arms in an attempt to grab the spirit naga.

Meanwhile, the centaur pulled the pick from his right leg and swung it wildly at another miner, who stood rooted in fear at the sight of the approaching skeletons. Embedding the point of the pick solidly in the man's neck, the centaur followed through by rearing on his hind legs and pounding his front hooves against the man's chest. The miner went down in agony as a wave of skeletons stormed by him toward the remaining miner.

The miner ran, but in his panic, his feet tripped him up, and he was quickly lost from sight amid a sea of bones.

The great cat finished with its victim and tried to leap to Brenna's side. The enchantress was thrashing about on the plateau with the naga. The thick ring of skeletons and zombies that were forming about them kept Galvin from getting through. The druid growled, but still the undead did not open a path.

"Foolish creature," said a wraith that had floated over the edge of the plateau and was hovering above him. "We smell sweet, sweet death."

"Get back!" Wynter barked, brushing by the wraith and pushing several skeletons aside so he and Galvin could get closer to Brenna. The druid snarled for emphasis and darted between a pair of bony legs to get inside the circle.

Asp was attempting to strangle Brenna. At the same time, she flailed her tail back and forth like a whip to keep her enemies at bay. But Galvin was desperate, and he sprang forward, pouncing on the naga's tail and sinking his sharp cat's teeth into her scales. The naga screamed in pain and released her grip on Brenna's throat. The enchantress rolled free, leaving the naga open to attack from Galvin and the onrushing skeletons.

"I'll see you in hell!" the naga cried as the druid, in his great cat form, closed in. Then Asp screamed a single word, and the mountain rumbled in response.

The mine shaft yawned as a large boulder on each side of it trembled and seemed to pull away from the mountainside. The plateau shook, and the twin rocks vibrated and began to crack. The cracks spread quickly and uniformly as stony arms extended from the sides of the boulders and squat legs pushed outward from the bases of the great stones. The face of the boulders cracked still more, chips of rocks flying away from them, leaving behind the chiseled visages of two huge bald-headed men. The rocks' eyes stared at the undead.

"Trespassers!" the one on the south side of the shaft boomed as its lips cracked open. Its deep voice reverberated loudly over the plateau, bringing a shower of small pebbles down from the mountain that stretched above the mine.

"Tres-pass-ers die!" the other grumbled in rough, slow

tones so thunderous the entire mountain seemed to shake. A stumpy rock arm gestured threateningly. The mountain groaned, and fist-size rocks began to roll toward the heroes and their undead charges.

The boulder gestured again, and more rocks shook loose, all rolling down the mountainside and bypassing the mouth of the mine, all under the direction of the rock creatures. The rocks cascading down now were larger, the size of full-grown melons. They picked up speed and crashed into a wave of skeletons, splintering their bones and bowling them over the side of the plateau.

Wynter summoned his strength and galloped at full speed toward the rockslide, angling his body toward the mine entrance, which the rocks somehow avoided. Stones pummeled his body, but he pressed forward, his hooves pounding over the plateau.

Meanwhile, the druid dodged the rockslide agilely, his cat reflexes signaling him when to leap out of the way, but when the slide increased in intensity, he leapt into the air and willed another transformation. The great cat seemed to fold in upon itself, its fur turning to feathers, its front legs to wings and its rear claws to talons. The hawk let out a cry and rose upward, above the mass of tumbling rocks.

At the same time, Brenna and Asp were about to be pushed over the edge of the plateau by the rocks and fallen skeletons. The naga wrapped her tail about a stone outcropping as the rocks pelted her. The dying naga reached toward Brenna, who had begun to slide slowly down the mountain, attempting to claw the enchantress's face.

Brenna rolled to the side to avoid the naga's grasp. Her action only sped her descent down the slope, and she gritted her teeth in pain as her ribs bore the brunt of the ride. She heard the naga scream, then, glancing quickly upward, she saw a sizable rock crash into the naga's side, knocking her loose from the outcropping and sending her careening down the mountain slope.

Brenna closed her eyes, ignored the pain, and concentrated on casting a spell. The enchantress's words were nearly lost in the slide as rocks of all sizes pounded over the side of the plateau toward her. Then she felt herself being lifted gently; in moments, she was floating above the rocks and tumbling zombies and skeletons, whose bony bodies were being split apart by the slide.

Gasping for breath, the enchantress levitated toward the plateau, praying to find Galvin and Wynter alive.

The hawk flew toward the mine shaft, willing his human form to return when he was safely within the mouth of the cave. The hawk's wings melted away and grew, becoming arms, and his claws lengthened into legs. Struggling to stay on his feet as the mountain continued to tremble, Galvin reached his hand out to touch a stone face.

"Stop!" Galvin shouted, hoping to be heard above the pounding rocks. "You'll kill everyone!"

"Tres-pass-ers die," the rock rumbled.

"We're not trespassers!" the druid retorted, gasping for air as a shower of dirt fell from above the mine opening into his face.

"Tres-pass-ers die," the rock repeated, reaching a rocky arm out from its body and grabbing the druid about the waist. The rock lifted Galvin off the ground, and its great stone eyes bore into his.

The druid stared back, calling on his own magic, trying to speak to the rock as he had to the wall in Maligor's tower. "Stop this!" he croaked, straining to clear his lungs.

The rock pulled him closer, until Galvin's face was only inches from its right eye. It studied the druid for several long moments, then closed its stony eyelids and the rumbling ceased.

"We're not trespassers," Galvin repeated, extricating himself from the rock's grasp. "We're Harpers, and we're here to help." Taking a step backward from the living boulder, the druid looked frantically about the plateau, searching for some sign of Brenna. His heart hammered in his chest, fearing she had been killed.

"Wynter!" Galvin cried. "Where's Brenna?"

"I saw her go over the side," the centaur said. "I

couldn't reach her."

The druid bolted from the living rock, coming to a stop when he reached the edge of the plateau and saw the enchantress float into view. "Brenna!" he called, embracing her when she glided to the ground in front of him. He held her for only a moment, then tugged her toward the mine opening.

The living boulders were watching them.

"What are you?" Wynter gasped as he faced the boulders. The pounding rocks had injured his human chest and horse underbelly, and it hurt him to breathe and talk. He gently prodded his horse side, checking for broken ribs.

"Galeb duhr," one said slowly. Then he went on to explain in his deep voice that he was one of a race of rock creatures whose lifespans dwarfed those of Faerun's humans and demihumans.

"Guard-i-ans," the other stated. "We watch the mine."

"We're not after the mine," Wynter offered, gesturing at the mountain and the land below. "In fact, we're here to protect it."

The galeb duhr on the north side of the mine entrance wrinkled its craggy nose and stared past the Harpers and Brenna toward the remaining undead who were clawing their way onto the edge of the plateau. Only a handful of skeletons had survived the pummeling, and the zombies' numbers were halved. The wraiths and shadows seemed unaffected.

"The dead men will help the mine, too?" the rock's booming voice was tinged with sarcasm.

"Yes," Brenna said, explaining their ordeal with Szass Tam and their promise to stop Maligor and his forces, who threatened the mine.

"But we can't help unless you help us. We need some information," she continued.

The rocks stared at her quizzically.

"Has a Red Wizard been here recently?" she asked, brushing the dirt from her clothes.

"No," came the deep reply in unison.

She inhaled sharply and pursed her lips. "Have you seen any strange creatures? Horrid, batlike things?"

The rock on the north side of the mine opening nodded, and the ground shook again. "Saw bat crea-tures. Hun-dreds, may-be more. Dark, like a cloud. Flew in-side. Can-not re-mem-ber why we did not stop them."

Brenna positioned herself in front of the living boulder, directly between its eyes. "Maligor could have ensorceled you. Maybe that's why you don't remember. Something's wrong here, that's certain. The tharchion I fought wasn't human."

"Doubt-ful some-thing is wrong," the other galeb duhr answered. "We no-ticed noth-ing odd in the mines."

"We've got to go inside and find out for sure," Galvin tried. "Please trust us."

"Trust un-dead?"

"We'll control them," Galvin continued, staring past the living boulders and into the mine.

"If you lie," the other galeb duhr interjected, "we will know. We could bring mountain down on top of you, then hollow it out again as if nothing happened."

"You can trust us," Galvin emphasized again.

"We trust you. But only because you know language of the earth," the boulder answered.

Relieved that he seemed to have the approval of the rock creatures, Galvin started into the mine. Wynter and Brenna followed him cautiously. The enchantress cast a last glance at the plateau; the zombies and skeletons that had survived the rockslide were shuffling toward the shaft.

Fifteen

Szass Tam nudged Maligor's mind. The lich had been unable to find his rival Red Wizard, and the legion of undead headed by his Harper pawns had uncovered nothing substantial, nothing other than hints of Maligor's whereabouts.

Annoyed and intensely curious, the lich concentrated, probing outward with his thoughts. Szass Tam had spent the past several hours linked to his favorite crystal ball, uncharacteristically tired of waiting for word of Maligor. The ball had yielded nothing, so he had focused his efforts at communication only.

Finally the lich met with success.

"What do you want, Szass Tam?" Maligor's thoughts haughtily projected. "I am very busy today."

The lich strained to get inside Maligor's mind, but the wards were too strong. "You are not with your gnolls," Szass Tam began. "You are not in Amruthar."

"So you seek to know where I am?" Maligor said, feigning mild surprise. "Beyond your grasp, lich."

Angered, Szass Tam furrowed his brow and funneled his energies on Maligor, attempting to look through the rival wizard's eyes into his mind. But the lich saw only blackness, and he heard only Maligor's hollow, echoing laughter.

"I will live up to my part of our arrangement," Maligor said with a chuckle. "You will get half the lands my gnolls take. But you will not be included in future endeavors if you press me."

The lich ran his bony hand over the smooth surface of the crystal ball, the hot pinpoints of light staring out of his sockets reflected on the crystal's surface.

"You will not best me, Maligor," Szass Tam said simply.

"And you will not interfere with my dealings," Maligor replied. "However, you may watch my gnolls if you desire. And we can speak again when I return to Amruthar in a few days."

"As we agreed," the lich added, "I will not lift a hand to stop you—or your gnolls." But, he thought to himself, my Harper puppets are a different matter, and they will be your undoing.

The lich closed the link and settled back into the large chair in his study.

*   *   *   *   *

"Who was that snake-woman?" Brenna whispered as she and Galvin trod into the black maw of the mine. Although she could see the faint flicker of torches ahead, the darkness in the tunnel seemed to swallow them, and she had difficulty seeing. She grasped the druid's arm. "She wasn't human."

"A creation of a Red Wizard, maybe. Perhaps some poor animal Maligor corrupted." Galvin kept his voice low, not wanting to alert others in the mine to their presence. However, he realized such caution was probably useless. He heard the steady clip-clop of Wynter's hooves behind him, and the clinking of the undeads' bones echoed through the shaft. The druid scowled as he thought of the skeletons and zombies; the army had been halved by the rockslide, and he wondered if the remaining force was strong enough to take whatever lay ahead.

"I just hope she—or it—is dead," Brenna added, still feeling sore from her ordeal with the naga. "I saw her go down the mountainside. I just hope there's no more of them in here."

The procession wound its way into the mountain, navigating the twisting main shaft. Wynter had difficulty moving through the tunnel. The top of his head brushed against the ceiling in places, and the rocky floor felt uncomfortable beneath his hooves. His human chest and his equine body ached from being pelted by the rocks in the slide, but he plodded forward, focusing on Galvin several feet ahead.

The shaft was nearly twenty feet wide, allowing the undead to spread out behind the centaur. Torches spaced at irregular intervals provided only scant light and made the complex seem like a mass of shifting gray shadows.

The druid, however, was becoming accustomed to the meager light, and he concentrated on his surroundings. From somewhere ahead, he heard the sounds of metal striking against rock—miners with picks, perhaps. Because the noise echoed through the shaft, it was impossible for Galvin to guess how far away the miners might be.

Wynter glanced about nervously, wondering why they hadn't met with any resistance since entering the mines. "There should be guards in this shaft," he whispered. "This is too easy, Galvin."

"Perhaps," the druid replied. He slowed and studied the tunnel. Galvin guessed they were about two hundred yards into the mountain. The shaft ahead straightened out and was angling downward. The tunnel was supported by massive oak beams, some reinforced where the wood had splintered. The druid eyed the construction, noting that the mine was of considerable age and this main shaft had been mined out decades ago. After traveling another hundred yards over rock worn smooth by human traffic, he raised his hand signaling the undead to stop. He wanted to listen to the sounds of the miners ahead and try to determine if anything else was in the tunnel. The druid was certain that Wynter was right—the mine had more defenses than what they had encountered on the plateau.

Scanning ahead, he spotted unnatural, thumb-sized crystals embedded in the shaft's walls at roughly waist height. They started at about the point the torches stopped. Farther down the shaft, the torches started again. Perhaps its some sort of magic, he thought, staring at the closest crystal. He started to stoop beneath the crystal when Brenna's arm shot out, grabbing him.

"It's a ward of some kind," she said.

"So we go under it. The miners go through here somehow."

"No," she stated simply. "Passing beyond a ward, a magical guard, triggers it. If you speak the right words, the ward lets you by."

"And if you don't have the right words?"

Brenna frowned. "The ward could kill you."

Galvin studied her features amid the shadows. "Is there any way we can learn the words?"

"Of course not," the enchantress replied, pursing her lips. "At least, not in the time we have. But . . ." She stared at the crystals for several long moments, then reached toward the druid and pulled his longsword from its sheath.

"What is it?" the druid started. But a motion from Brenna kept him quiet.

She extended the tip of the sword toward the crystal, then past the crystal. Nothing happened. Handing the sword back to the druid, she stretched out her hand. As it neared the ward the crystal began to glow and she heard a soft hum. Snatching her hand back, she turned to Galvin and smiled.

"It senses heat. I can get around this, but it will be uncomfortable."

The druid nodded and gestured with his hand, waiting to see what Brenna would do. The enchantress began mumbling something, the words coming so quickly the druid couldn't make them out. As her voice rose, the air grew chill. And when she extended her hands, pointing away from her and down the shaft, frost leapt from her fingertips and headed down the tunnel with a *whoosh*, coating the walls, floor, and ceiling.

"Let's hurry," she urged, sliding forward toward the torches beyond the crystals.

Shivering, the druid quickly followed, but Wynter had a difficult time navigating the ice-coated floor. By the time the centaur managed to make it to the end of the frost, it had started to melt.

"The undead!" Brenna cried. "The crystals will—"

Galvin interrupted, gently grasping her shoulders. "The undead don't give off heat, Brenna. The dead are cold."

She slumped her shoulders, feeling foolish yet relieved, and continued at Galvin's side down the shaft. They trodded downward for a hundred yards. As the torches became farther and farther apart, the shadows grew thicker, and the druid grabbed a torch from the wall so they could see better.

Ahead were a series of crosscuts, tunnels that had been dug off the main shaft. Some of those tunnels, or adits as the druid had heard miners call them, led to ventilation holes; Galvin felt a slight breeze coming from them. The moisture became more noticeable the deeper the army marched, and the clinking bones of the skeletons echoed hauntingly off the walls.

The druid noticed that the sounds of mining had stopped. Whatever or whoever was ahead had likely been alerted to their presence, probably hearing the centaur's hooves and the skeletons' bony feet. Galvin continued to inspect the mine as they moved along. The pressure of the mountain was strong, he noted. The support beams were closer together here, and some were bowed from the weight of the rock above. The mine was massive, the druid was certain, probably winding throughout the mountain like tunnels in an anthill.

He wondered if he should investigate the crosscuts, but he heard no sounds there, either. And he knew better than to speak with the stone here; it was so old and probably had so many stories to tell that he'd be totally exhausted after listening. Along the way, he spotted deposits of sand within layers of rock, a sign that precious metals were present.

Although the druid knew little about mining, he knew the earth, and his eyes told him where veins of gold had been stripped, the layers of stone robbed of their wealth. He was uncertain where all the rock and dirt that had been mined was taken. There was little evidence of discarded gravel and silt outside the shaft's main mouth. Perhaps they had a way to dissolve it magically, he thought.

"Galvin," Brenna whispered. "Listen."

The druid cursed himself for becoming so lost in his thoughts that he had dropped his guard.

He heard a whisper, or something that sounded like one. It was a soft noise, a shushing sound that slowly increased in volume.

Bats? he thought. The noise could be the flutter of wings, but the way sound was distorted in the shaft, it was difficult to be certain. If it was bats, there must be many of them, and something had disturbed them to get them aloft.

Concerned, he urged the army forward, scanning the walls to make sure no more crystals were present and indicating Brenna should do the same. Then he reached out with his mind, trying to contact the bats deeper in the shaft. Brenna cursed softly and tried to keep pace, at the same time watching the tunnel's walls for more of the dangerous crystals.

The centaur also struggled to stay ahead of the undead. As he picked up the pace, his head bumped against a support beam.

The shaft continued to descend as Galvin trotted faster. The torches were spaced even farther apart now, leaving most of the tunnel blanketed in darkness except for the small area around the torch Galvin held. Then, somewhere below in the blackness, the druid's mind reached out to another consciousness. But it was not a bat's, as he had anticipated. This mind felt twisted, alien, corrupt. But the creature thought in human terms, and as Galvin became more intimate with it, the mind took on a human quality, a human intelligence. The druid tried to close the link, but the other intelligence held on to his mind.

Death to you, Harper, the consciousness spoke inside the druid's head. Galvin grabbed at his temples, dropping the torch. Concentrating, he tried to force the presence out. Still the intelligence persisted, pulling from the druid's thoughts his name, his history, and the reason for his intrusion into the mine.

Death to you who would spoil my finely wrought plans. Galvin buckled over in agony as the mind bored into his, seeking information about his forces, his strengths, why he had come here, what magic he possessed.

Szass Tam! the intelligence screamed, and the druid cupped his hands over his ears in a futile gesture to shut out the sound. The words were coming from inside his head. *You are Szass Tam's servant!*

Galvin fought to keep the details from the intelligence, but the druid's mind wasn't strong enough. It seemed as if all of Galvin's being was flowing from him, his experiences, knowledge, emotions—all were being assimilated by the probing mind. Then he felt the mind—no, minds—coming closer. And he heard the flutter of wings even more clearly.

* * * * *

Deep in the bowels of the mine, Maligor screamed. How had Szass Tam found out about the mine? How had the lich managed to bring an accursed Harper under his control?

Maligor's mind whirled. He wouldn't be able to covertly control the mines now; the lich would see to that. Nor could he confront the lich, as Szass Tam avoided direct involvement.

"I will not be undone by a dead man!" Maligor bellowed, his voice bouncing off the walls of the deep chamber. "If I cannot have the mines, no one will!" The Red Wizard's staccato voice repeated a simple enchantment, and before the words could echo back from the chamber's shadow-cloaked walls, the wizard was gone. His form, replaced by a small cloud of white, swirling vapors, floated up a narrow shaft.

I will turn your forces to ashes, the cloud thought as it moved along the shaft's rocky ceiling. "I will destroy your army, Szass Tam. I will make you regret your treachery."

*   *   *   *   *

Brenna reached the druid's side and knelt beside him. His palms were pushed against the sides of his head, and his teeth were clenched in pain. She tugged his hands away from his face, and their eyes met.

"What—what happened?" she asked, glancing behind her at Wynter. The centaur waved the undead to a stop.

"I—I don't know," the druid gasped. "But there's something ahead. Something . . ."

Then Brenna and Wynter heard the rush of wings, too, and smelled an overpowering stench. The tunnel ahead gave way to blackness as the flying creatures buffeted the torches out and filled the shaft with their misshapen bodies. The creatures' horrid shrieks filled the shaft, echoing off the walls.

"Darkenbeasts!" Brenna cried, as she saw a myriad of burning red eyes rapidly closing on them. She jumped to her feet, pulling the druid along with her.

In one fluid motion, Galvin drew his longsword and strode forward. Swinging fiercely at the air in front of him, he connected with the lead darkenbeast, slicing halfway through its grotesque neck. Its dead body thudded at his feet, but another creature flew forward to take its place.

The beast's talons stretched toward Galvin's eyes, and

the Harper bent his arm across his face to shield them. The gesture allowed a pair of darkenbeasts to fly past him toward the sorceress and Wynter.

The enchantress flattened herself against a tunnel wall, narrowly avoiding a sharp beak. Fumbling through the small bag at her side, she drew out a pinch of coarse powder. Hoping she had found the correct components in the darkness, she began mumbling a series of incoherent-sounding words.

At the same time, Wynter charged forward. Using his bardiche, he skewered one of the darkenbeasts against the ceiling. A second creature closed on him, its beak sinking into his left shoulder. Dropping his weapon, Wynter reached out with his bare hands to capture his arcane attacker, bashing the beast's head against the mine wall. The centaur continued beating the creature until it ceased to move.

Finished with her incantation, Brenna stirred the powder in her hand, then held her palm toward the ceiling. A gout of flame whooshed from her hand and danced along a portion of the ceiling beyond Galvin, catching several darkenbeasts hovering there and lighting up the tunnel. The macabre creatures' wings caught fire, and they cried out in agony.

The Harpers and Brenna ducked, and the burning darkenbeasts flew beyond them, into the waiting grasp of the skeletons and zombies. The rotting flesh and tattered clothes of the zombies burst into flame on contact with the darkenbeasts. Impervious to pain, the zombies struggled with the winged creatures, tearing them apart and dashing their misshapen heads against the tunnel walls.

The darkenbeasts' beaks and claws were wasted on the skeletons, who latched onto the creatures and began pulling at their leathery limbs until no life remained in Maligor's constructs.

At the forefront of the struggle, Galvin continued to slice through the darkenbeasts, suffering numerous minor injuries and scratches in the process. Behind him, he saw

Wynter catch one of the loathsome creatures and hurl it to the shaft floor, trampling it beneath his hooves.

In the dark tunnel below, Galvin saw more darkenbeasts, hovering in the shaft, waiting for a chance to join in the fight. The druid realized the numbers eventually would overwhelm the three of them, although the undead could likely hold their own against the creatures.

Edging backward in the shaft, closer to the centaur, Galvin split the nearest darkenbeast nearly in two with his sword, then ducked and pulled his longsword free as another creature dove at him. The centaur reached above the druid's head, smashing his large fist into the creature's side and sending it careening wildly against the shaft wall. It crumpled and flapped feebly, trying to rise.

"Head for the crosscut!" Galvin shouted, barely able to be heard above the sounds of the darkenbeasts' wings and the skeletons' clanking bones. "Hurry!"

Brenna inched her way along the shaft wall and darted into the side tunnel. Wynter fought his way through a half-dozen of the darkenbeasts before he could join her. The centaur squinted to catch some sign of Galvin in the mass of flailing bones and leathery wings.

"How many are there?" the enchantress whispered, staring wide-eyed at the cloud of darkenbeasts.

"Hundreds," the centaur guessed. "There are more down the shaft. Galvin's somewhere out there in the middle of them."

Then suddenly the druid hurled himself through an opening in the wall of skeletons and dove into the side tunnel. Wheezing, he sheathed his longsword and moved deeper into the tunnel.

"We'll follow this passage," he said in a hushed tone. "Maybe it will lead back to the main shaft and we can come at the darkenbeasts from behind."

"And if it doesn't?" The centaur seemed skeptical.

"Then we'll try another tunnel." The druid felt his way along the crosscut, then spied the light of a torch ahead. "We don't have much chance back there," he said, pointing toward the sounds of battle. "The undead are better able to deal with those creatures, anyway. We need to find Maligor."

Ahead, the torch illuminated barrels and buckets lined against the shaft wall, filled with ore. Several picks lay on top of the largest barrel. Wynter examined them and selected the sharpest pick. The centaur, who could not move quickly in the confined tunnel, feared the darkenbeasts would find them, and he didn't want to fight them bare-handed again.

The druid discovered another opening just beyond the mined ore and started down it. This tunnel was better lit, and from the discarded picks and buckets along the wall, Galvin could tell it was in the process of being mined. Ahead, he heard the tramping of feet, and he rushed forward, leaving Brenna and Wynter to lag behind.

The tunnel opened into a small chamber. A dozen long-haired miners were loading ore into a stack of crates. They stopped and gaped at Galvin as he hurried inside the chamber. The miners' clothes were worn and soiled, and their skin was pale from working underground.

"We won't hurt you," the druid stated calmly, putting his arms to his sides, away from his weapon. Galvin assumed they were slaves.

"Are there any other miners near?" The druid feared another confrontation.

One of the slaves nodded, then stared beyond Galvin at Brenna and Wynter, who were just emerging into the chamber. "The miners are all over," he said flatly.

"And what about the creatures? The darkenbeasts?" the druid asked, lowering his hands and realizing the miners didn't fear him. "Are those winged creatures all around here, too?"

The slave miner nodded yes.

"How about Maligor? Is the Red Wizard Maligor here?" Brenna questioned.

"Maligor controls the mines now," came the slave's emotionless reply. The gaunt man explained how Maligor and his minions descended on the mine, slaughtering the guards and taking over the complex. "He controls the creatures, the things you call darkenbeasts."

"Does he control you?" she posed.

"We serve Maligor."

The enchantress turned to Galvin. "They're charmed, I think. Just like I charmed the guard in the orchard."

The druid scowled and began to pace nervously. "Has Maligor been here long?"

The slave scratched his head. "A few days," he said after a pause. "Two, three days. Maybe four, but not more than that."

"Where is he?" Galvin demanded, his voice rising.

The slaves backed against the wall.

"Where?" he persisted.

"We—we shouldn't tell you," one answered. "The master would be angry."

"I'm angry. And I'm here," the druid snapped. "Where's the Red Wizard?"

"Deep in the mines," came a slave's monotone reply.

The druid scrutinized the miners. The slaves appeared tired, and they were thin from lack of food. He realized telling them to leave the mines would be pointless. Maligor's servants wouldn't leave, unless, perhaps, Maligor was dead, the druid thought.

The slaves continued to stare at the Harpers and Brenna, then after several minutes, they resumed loading ore into the barrels.

"Damn!" the centaur cursed. "They're not like real people. They've no free will. We've got to get them out of here, Galvin."

The druid looked up into his friend's pained face. "After we deal with Maligor," he said simply, then turned to a slave. "We need to find our way back to the main shaft. Tell us how."

The slave gestured back the way they had come.

"Not that way. Is there another tunnel that links up?"

The slaves looked at each other and shrugged. "Hundreds of tunnels," one croaked. "The widest ones lead to chambers below. Others lead to the main shaft."

Galvin whirled and trotted back down the tunnel. Brenna stayed even with him, but the centaur was having an increasingly difficult time maneuvering in the sloping shafts. The next two crosscuts led to dead ends and more slave miners, who also seemed to lack any will of their own. But the third tunnel twisted down into the depths of the mountain and angled back toward the main shaft. The tunnel ceiling was lower here, forcing the centaur to stoop.

Ahead and off to the right, they heard a series of clinking and thudding sounds, mixed with the cries of the darkenbeasts. The druid began to run through the shaft, intent on discovering the nature of the confrontation ahead.

He rounded a sharp corner and gasped as he spotted a wispy cloud bearing down on him. The cloud hovered, its tendrils becoming arms and legs, and a mass of white forming a fleshy face with a wild tangle of black hair. Maligor willed himself to solidify into his human form as the druid stood, unmoving. The wizard's red robes looked like dying embers in the light of a distant torch.

The Red Wizard's dark eyes held the druid, and with a gesture, Maligor drew the air away from Galvin's face, leaving the druid breathless.

"You'll die, meddlesome Harper!" Maligor spat, weaving his hand in the air, then pointing his fingers at the druid's chest. Red shards of energy shot from the wizard's hand and sunk themselves in Galvin's abdomen.

The druid doubled over in shock, just as Brenna reached his side. She stood transfixed, staring at the symbol of Myrkul on the wizard's forehead and realizing it was Maligor they faced. As the wizard glanced past the druid, straight at her, she quickly composed herself and began a spell.

"You!" Maligor roared, remembering the face of the woman in the clearing, the woman who had killed his darkenbeast many days ago with a bolt of lightning. Furious, the Red Wizard directed his next spell at Brenna, hurtling her small frame backward against the tunnel wall with an unseen force that left her crumpled like a rag doll.

Galvin struggled to his feet and drew his sword, slashing at the wizard just as Wynter came upon the scene. But the wizard was too fast. With a quick gesture, his fleshly form became intangible, ghostlike, and the blade passed harmlessly through him. Maligor lolled his head back and laughed, a deep, throaty laugh that sent chills racing down the druid's spine.

The centaur charged forward, cleaving his pick through the wizard's intangible chest.

"Harper fools!" Maligor bellowed, becoming solid again and casting a magic daggerlike shard into the druid's chest. "I'll not waste my time on you! The mine and my creatures will kill you!"

Galvin fell to his knees and watched with disbelief as the Red Wizard gestured grandly with his hands, transformed again into a wispy white cloud, and floated down the corridor.

The druid forced himself to his feet and started after the wispy trail, but the centaur's hand held his shoulder. "Don't go after him, Galvin. That's what he wants. He'll lead you to the darkenbeasts—or worse."

Brenna steadied herself against the wall and felt the back of her head; she was bleeding from being slammed against the rock. The enchantress was dizzy, but she fought the sensation and made her way toward Galvin.

"We have to stay together," she stated flatly. "Otherwise he can pick us off one by one."

The druid nodded his agreement, then glared down the corridor. Dimly, the clang of metal and the cries of the darkenbeasts could still be heard. Galvin strode purposefully toward the sounds of battle.

As the distance melted away beneath their footsteps, the sounds of fighting lessened, then ceased altogether, plunging the mine into an eerie quiet. Unnerved, the trio plodded forward for an interminable time until the shaft opened into an immense, well-lit chamber. The shaft continued beyond the natural room, but the passage was of no concern to the Harpers. Hugging the shaft of the tunnel, they stared at the floor of the chamber.

The broken bodies of skeletons and zombies lay strewn about. Their slayers—a mass of darkenbeasts—floated like a thick, black cloud above the hellish battlefield.

Judging from the numbers on the cavern floor, the druid assumed Szass Tam's army had been eliminated at the claws of Maligor's creatures, and the darkenbeasts were stationed here to prevent Brenna, Wynter, and him from going farther. He was certain other darkenbeasts were searching the tunnels for them.

Galvin clenched his fists, and for the first time in many long years—since he was a child of seven watching his parents hang—he truly feared death. Alone, Wynter, Brenna, and he couldn't take on Maligor and his darkenbeasts. Nor could they run; Szass Tam would find them.

The druid feared he would die deep in the bowels of the gold mines. If only he could save Wynter and Brenna, he thought, if somehow he could buy time for them to leave. . . .

Beyond the sea of darkenbeasts, which stretched from one end of the chamber to the other, the walls glistened. Thick streaks of gold flashed in the pale light of crystals whose blue gleam illuminated the room.

Brenna cringed behind the druid, horrified by the gruesome scene. Galvin turned to her, placing his hands on her shoulders.

"You and Wynter need to get out of the mines. I'm going to find Maligor and end this," the druid stated softly.

"No!" Brenna gasped. Quickly Galvin moved a finger to her lips to quiet her.

"I can get past the darkenbeasts. You and Wynter can't. If you stay here, sooner or later the darkenbeasts will see you. You have to find a way out."

"We won't leave you," she said in hushed tones.

"You have to." The druid glanced up at the centaur. "Wynter, get out of Thay. Take Brenna with you. Let the

Harpers know what happened."

The centaur nodded reluctantly.

The druid moved a few steps forward, clinging to the shadows of the tunnel for a moment more, not wanting to be discovered by Maligor's creatures in the cavern beyond. Galvin closed his eyes and focused his mind on the mass of darkenbeasts.

The druid fell to all fours, his head twitching and his hands and feet quivering.

The enchantress glanced at Galvin, then at Wynter, uncertain of what to do. The centaur held her arm to keep her back, and in an instant, she saw Galvin's face contort.

The bones in Galvin's face cracked and popped as they pushed outward into a funnel-shaped beak filled with sharp, jagged teeth. His eyes shrunk into his sockets and became red pinpoints beneath a bony brow.

The druid groaned again; this transformation was particularly painful and unnatural. His sides heaved as thin membranes found their way through the chain shirt on each side of his chest and attached themselves to arms that were becoming covered with a yellowish-brown hide. Galvin's legs shriveled and jerked while his body took on a vaguely reptilian appearance and his clothes and skin vanished beneath the leathery exterior. A barbed tail sprouted from his rump and quivered. His batlike wings flapped against the shaft floor, and the darkenbeast-druid lifted its head on a thin, bony neck bearing a white crescent moon. The wings flapped again, and the creature propelled itself out of the tunnel and into the chamber beyond.

The stench of the cloud of darkenbeasts assailed the druid as he glided over the bodies of skeletons and zombies and joined with the malign creatures hovering overhead. The darkenbeasts were so numerous that the druid couldn't count them. Hundreds of animals perverted by the Red Wizard, he thought. Galvin fought back a wave of nausea and kept his mind occupied by thinking of Brenna and Wynter.

Several minutes passed . . . then a half-hour. The druid

hoped Wynter was leading the sorceress out of the mine. An hour drifted by, the druid estimated. Then finally part of the cloud separated, and a few dozen of the beasts peeled off and headed down a tunnel. Galvin followed them.

Through a darkened maze of twisting tunnels, the darkenbeasts and the druid flew. In places, they virtually hovered as they navigated sharp turns. The tunnels angled sharply downward, and at one point, it appeared the tunnel ahead had collapsed. The darkenbeasts veered off into a natural chamber to the north, from which the sounds of picks hitting rocks drifted. The druid hovered behind his sorcerous brethren to scrutinize the battered support beams. It appeared they had been hacked through with some kind of weapon. Perhaps that part of the mine was no longer valuable, the druid surmised.

Flying into the natural chamber to catch up with the darkenbeasts, the druid's beak flew open in surprise. The walls of this cavern looked as if they had been painted with gold. The veins were so thick and so close together that little of the rock showed between them. A crew of slave miners was hard at work mining the area.

Beating his wings faster, Galvin caught up with the grotesque flock. The darkenbeasts wound through a series of small chambers, all circled by thick veins of ore. The last chamber they entered was huge—larger even than the one in which the skeletons and zombies had died. Magical orbs of light spaced about the room caused the thick veins to shine and made them look like gold ribbons circling and dancing about the cavern.

All the men working here had long, tangled hair, pale white skin, and bony frames, evidence they had been slaving here for years. They struck at the veins with their picks almost in unison, as if their movements were orchestrated. All but one man, that is. At the far edge of the cavern, standing on a rise of rocks several feet above the chamber floor, was a red-robed man with a mass of black hair and a well-nourished frame. A white skull on a black field gleamed in the magical light. Maligor.

The druid's heart raced.

Galvin hid amidst the group of darkenbeasts, which had begun to circle the chamber. Concentrating, he focused on a nob of rock against the wall behind the Red Wizard. It quivered as the druid mentally shaped it, willing it to come forward. For an instant, the rock trembled, then it shot forward like a fist, striking Maligor solidly in the back.

The Red Wizard fell face forward from his stone pedestal to the floor of the cavern below. The slaves dropped their picks and looked blankly about the chamber. With Maligor unconscious, or perhaps dead, the wizard's control on the slaves was over. Still flying with the darkenbeasts, Galvin watched as the slave miners glanced at the chamber walls, then at Maligor, who appeared to be still breathing. A handful of the slaves grabbed their picks, and for a moment, the druid thought they would begin working on the mines again. But instead the men began to advance toward Maligor, the picks raised above their heads.

Galvin decided he would do nothing to prevent the miners from finishing off the wizard. The druid had intended to kill him anyway.

The nearest slave raised his pick higher, and in a quick, fluid motion brought it down upon the prone body of the Red Wizard. But the pick stopped with a loud *thunk* inches from the wizard's back, as if it had hit something hard yet unseen.

Galvin watched the miner's mouth drop open in shock as Maligor quickly rolled away from him. In one movement, the Red Wizard leapt to his feet and cast out his hand, sending a bolt of energy into the slave's chest. The slave was hurled backward, a gaping hole burned in the center of his body.

Then the wizard turned his attention to the other slaves. "Fools!" he shouted. "You all will die for this!" Maligor began twirling his fingers about in the air, and the slaves dropped their picks and whirled to run from the room.

Galvin's path with the darkenbeasts had taken him behind the Red Wizard, who was oblivious to any threat from that direction. Separating from the mass of darkenbeasts, he dove toward the wizard. He slammed his extended claws into Maligor's back, and the Red Wizard fell forward again. The druid continued his flight, rejoining the rest of the darkenbeats.

The maneuver had bought the slaves time to flee from the chamber, which further infuriated the wizard.

This time when Maligor rose, his black eyes seemed to burn, and a trickle of blood flowed from a broken nose. Galvin decided to press his attack.

Through his pain, Maligor spotted a single darkenbeast heading his way, claws outstretched. The Red Wizard sensed the creature was not one of his own, and he marshaled his powers and pointed a finger at the beast that dared to assault him.

"Die!" the Red Wizard shouted.

Simultaneously Galvin felt a tearing in his gut, an intense torment that rivaled anything he had previously suffered. His darkenbeast form shrieked in response, and he fought to stay conscious and on course. Part of him rebelled and begged him to flee, but the human in him forced himself to concentrate on the Red Wizard and on all the pain the madman had inflicted upon the animals in the tower back in Amruthar.

Maligor's eyes bore into the darkenbeast's, and he raised his hands again, chanting words the druid could not discern. Red darts flashed from his fingers and found their mark in the darkenbeast's breast.

The darkenbeast floundered, struggling to stay aloft under the new wave of misery that shot through his body. Then he dove away from the wizard, losing himself in the cloud of darkenbeasts and hoping the wizard's magic could not reach him there.

Galvin realized he couldn't physically best Maligor; the Red Wizard was far too powerful. A bolt of lightning from the wizard's hand punctuated that sentiment and nearly bisected the druid, missing him by inches and sending a shower of rocks onto the floor below. However, it gave

Galvin an idea.

The druid concentrated, focusing on the rocks about the Red Wizard and draining himself to the point of exhaustion. The elder druids who had schooled him a decade ago had taught Galvin how to manipulate the earth in various ways, ways Galvin was loath to use. This was a necessary act, however, and might be the only way to defeat Maligor, he thought.

Galvin's mind sang to the rocks, to the mine, in the words of the first druids. The music poured from him, echoing off the veins and filling the chamber, rising above the beating of the darkenbeasts' wings into a whining, deafening pitch. The dazzling, shrill strain swelled until it became overpowering.

The music continued to pour from the druid, the stone, the very earth. Maligor thrust his hands over his ears, trying to shut out the sound so he could concentrate. But the music was too strong.

As the druid's song became louder still, the cavern wavered and began to groan. The ground quaked under the pressure of the mountain above, which had begun to tremble menacingly.

Maligor screamed as rocks began to fall from the ceiling, smashing into his darkenbeasts and narrowly missing him. The Red Wizard concentrated on his creatures, determined that they should slay the imposter darkenbeast. He touched their sorcerous minds, then recoiled as the song increased in volume again.

*   *   *   *   *

What began as a soft humming sound that Brenna and Wynter had difficulty discerning had risen to a deafening cacophony as it was joined by the rumbling of the mountain itself. They stood where Galvin had left them, fighting to stand as the very floor shook beneath their feet and small pieces of the ceiling began to break away.

Wynter placed a hand on Brenna's shoulder and nodded down the tunnel, in the direction from which they had come.

"But what about Galvin?" she shouted, trying to be heard above the tumult in the cavern.

"He told us to get out. We should have listened!" Wynter shouted. "Besides, he can fly out of here! I can't!"

The centaur turned and trotted as fast as he could down the narrow shaft. Brenna cast a worried glance behind her, then bolted after Wynter.

* * * * *

Inside the deep chamber, the darkenbeasts screamed as chunks of the ceiling continued to pelt them, killing many and injuring others so they could no longer fly.

The druid had so far managed somehow to avoid the stones. Now he sang once more through his darkenbeast mouth, and the rumbling grew in intensity.

Maligor fell to his knees, unable to stand in the wildly trembling cavern. The Red Wizard screamed as the rocks continued to pummel him, crushing his bones, burying him and making his body a permanent inhabitant of the mine he so wanted to control.

Yet Galvin's magic had been more effective than he had planned. Although he had ceased his song, the rumbling continued. The weight of the mountain had pushed down on the weakening chambers and was causing them to collapse.

Still in pain from the red shards Maligor had hurled at his chest, Galvin began flapping his wings madly, flying from the chamber and swerving crazily to avoid the falling chunks of ceiling.

Faster and faster the druid flew, through one shaking, twisting shaft after another, until he feared he was hopelessly lost. Soaring into a small chamber filled with buckets of ore, the druid spotted picks lying at odd angles and hoped the miners who had been here had fled when the quake began. Three tunnels led from this chamber. The druid chose the center one, praying it led toward the outside.

The mountain groaned again, and the tunnels began to collapse. Behind the druid, massive chunks of rock crashed from the ceiling as the timbers buckled. His darkenbeast chest felt tight and his breathing quickened, fear overwhelming him. Still his wings beat furiously, carrying him just ahead of the destruction.

At last Galvin shot into a large chamber filled with blue light. The floor was littered with the bodies of Szass Tam's undead. Continuing his panicked flight, he entered the tunnel where he had left Wynter and Brenna, but he saw no trace of them.

A deafening crash sounded behind him, and he didn't have to look back to know it signaled the collapse of the large chamber. He continued his course for what seemed an eternity. He spotted miners and guards running ahead of him.

Galvin's wings beat faster, spurred on by the crashing sounds of rock behind and below him. He watched the shaft shudder and saw torches fall from their sconces along the rock wall. Support beams buckled, and he felt himself being pelted by chunks of rock that dropped from the ceiling.

Faster he flew, staying just behind the slave miners as he heard the beams and rock groan behind him under the weight of the mountain. A rush of stale air passed him, evidence that the tunnel was collapsing behind him, and he heard the thunderous roar of crashing rocks as he spied light ahead—the entrance to the mine!

Flapping his wings still harder, the druid propelled himself from the main shaft and out onto the plateau beyond. Galvin collapsed on the rumbling plateau, gasping for air and willing his darkenbeast form to vanish. The leathery skin burned horribly under the sun's light as the hide receded, revealing scratched and bruised human skin. Brenna scrambled over to him, fighting her way through the mass of slaves and tearing her knees on the rock. Throwing her arms around his neck, she called to Wynter.

"It's Galvin! He made it!" She began to sob uncontrollably with the release of pent-up emotions.

The centaur moved through the crowd and bent forward, extending his hand. Galvin took it and let himself be helped to his feet.

"Let's get out of here," the druid said, putting his arm about Brenna's shoulders. Starting down the still-trembling mountain, they threaded their way through the confused miners. "Let's get out of here before Szass Tam notices that we finished his army, too, and decides to use us to start a new one."

Epilogue

Three days later, the heroes eased themselves down the steep bank of the First Escarpment, a task that seemed surprisingly simple now, even for Wynter, after their ordeals in Thay.

Although Aglarond was not as verdant as Thay, the trio thought they had never seen anything more beautiful than the untainted land that spread out before them. They threaded their way along the River Umber, stopping only to bathe in the cool water and wash away the grime and memories of the struggle in the mine.

Galvin knew Thay's economy would suffer because of the mine's collapse, and that the Red Wizards would be furious. But he also knew the mines would eventually reopen. The wizards had more than enough magic to repair them.

"What will you do now?" Brenna asked as they moved deeper into Aglarond, toward the capital city.

The centaur shrugged and ran a callused hand across the top of his head. "I'm not sure. Rest for a few days, certainly, then report to the Harper council about what went on. After that, I don't know."

Brenna glanced hopefully up at Galvin. "And you?"

The druid stared ahead, watching a doe drink deeply from the river. The animal tilted its head in their direction, then bounded away. "Go home," he said simply.

"You could make a home for yourself back in Glarondar where I live," she said, smiling up at him.

Galvin returned her smile, then shook his head.

The trio broke through the line of willows and birches and emerged into a plain of wild wheat—the same plain Brenna had had so much difficulty traversing not so many days ago.

"You've proved you can handle the wilderness," the druid said, glancing at Brenna. "You could come home with me instead." He gestured north, toward the forest.

"The water and food are free, Brenna. No one takes advantage of you." Galvin looked wistfully toward the forest.

The enchantress followed his gaze, then stared toward the west, toward Glarondar, the tallest buildings of which she could just make out in the distance.

"I—I can't," she stammered.

"I know."

The druid realized that each of them had grown to accept the other's lifestyle and respect it. But living in that lifestyle would be too drastic a change.

"Wynter will take you home," he said simply.

"I'll miss you," she said softly, her eyes moist.

Galvin pulled her gently to him, wrapping his arms about her. "I won't be so far away. I'll come when you need the Harpers' help again." He kissed her and she returned his embrace, then rested her chin on his shoulder and gazed toward the First Escarpment, tears running down her cheeks. They were too far away to see the cliffs, but for a moment, she imagined she saw the faint image of Szass Tam hanging above the cliffs, his angry eyes hot, glowing pinpoints of light. She blinked and the image vanished.

In the distance, she spied a rain cloud, heralding another storm over Thay.

FORGOTTEN REALMS

FANTASY ADVENTURE

■ THE HARPERS ■

A Force for Good in the Realms!

Elfshadow
Elaine Cunningham
Harpers are being murdered, and the trail leads to Arilyn Moonblade. Arilyn must uncover the ancient secret of her sword's power in order to find and face the assassin before he finds her.

The Parched Sea   Troy Denning
The Zhentarim have sent an army to enslave the fierce nomads of the Great Desert. Only one woman, the outcast witch Ruha, sees the danger--and only one Harper can counter the evil plot.

The Night Parade   Scott Ciencin
Myrmeen Lhal, the seductive ruler of Arabel, enlists the aid of the Harpers to rescue her long-lost daughter from the Night Parade, a shadowy group of creatures that feeds off human misery and fear. Available May 1992.

The Ring of Winter   James Lowder
Harper Artus Cimber travels to the jungles of Chult to find the fabled Ring of Winter, but the Cult of Frost also seeks the ring, which contains the power to bring a second Ice Age to the Realms. Available October 1992.